PENGUIN CL/

HOW MUCH LAND DOES A MAN NEED?

COUNT LEO NIKOLAYEVICH TOLSTOY was born in 1828 on the family estate of Yasnaya Polyana, in the Tula province, where he spent most of his early years, together with his several brothers. In 1844 he entered the University of Kazan to read Oriental Languages and later Law, but left before completing a degree. The following years were spent largely in the pursuit of life's pleasures: wine, women and cards, until weary of his idle existence he joined an artillery regiment in the Caucasus in 1852. In the autumn of that year his first story, *Childhood*, was published, bringing instant literary success. *Sebastopol Sketches* (1855–6) secured his position in the literary world. After leaving the army in 1856 Tolstoy spent some time mixing with the literati in St Petersburg before travelling abroad and then settling at Yasnaya Polyana, where he involved himself in the running of peasant schools and the emancipation of the serfs. His marriage to Sophie Andreyevna Behrs in 1862 marked the beginning of a period of seeming contentment, centred around family life. Tolstoy managed his vast estates, continued his work with the peasants, fathered thirteen children and wrote both his great novels, *War and Peace* (1869) and *Anna Karenina* (1877). During the seventies he underwent a spiritual crisis, the moral and religious ideas that had always dogged him coming to the fore. *A Confession*, written in 1879–82, pointed to a watershed in both his personal and literary life. He became an extreme rationalist and moralist, and in a series of pamphlets written after 1880 he expressed theories such as rejection of the institutions of Church and State, indictment of the demands of the flesh, denunciation of private property and pacifism. His teaching earned him numerous followers at home and abroad as well as much opposition. In an attempt to silence him and discredit his revolutionary ideas, the Russian Holy Synod excommunicated him in 1901. He died in 1910 in the course of a dramatic flight from home, at the small railway station of Astapovo.

RONALD WILKS studied Russian language and literature at Trinity College, Cambridge, after training as a Naval interpreter, and later Russian literature at London University, where he received his Ph.D. in 1972. Among his translations for Penguin Classics are *My Childhood*, *My Apprenticeship* and *My Universities* by Gorky, *Diary of a Madman* by Gogol, filmed for Irish

Television, *The Golovlyov Family* by Saltykov-Shchedrin, *Tales of Belkin and Other Prose Writings* by Pushkin, and four volumes of stories by Chekhov: *The Party and Other Stories, The Kiss and Other Stories, The Fiancée and Other Stories* and *The Duel and Other Stories.* He has also translated *The Little Demon* by Sologub for Penguin.

A. N. WILSON is a novelist and writer who lives in London. His novels include *The Sweets of Pimlico* (1978 John Llewellyn Rhys Memorial Prize), *The Healing Art* (1981 Somerset Maugham Award), *Who Was Oswald Fish?, Wise Virgin* (1983 W. H. Smith Literary Award), *Scandal, Gentleman in England, Love Unknown, Incline Our Hearts, A Bottle in the Smoke, Daughters of Albion* and *The Vicar of Sorrows.* He has written biographies of Walter Scott, Milton, Hilaire Belloc, Tolstoy (1988 Whitbread Biography Award) and C. S. Lewis. Other books include *Penfriends from Porlock* and *Eminent Victorians.* Many of his books are published by Penguin.

LEO TOLSTOY

HOW MUCH LAND DOES A MAN NEED?

AND OTHER STORIES

TRANSLATED BY
RONALD WILKS
WITH AN INTRODUCTION BY
A. N. WILSON

PENGUIN BOOKS

PENGUIN BOOKS

Published by the Penguin Group
Penguin Books Ltd, 80 Strand, London WC2R 0RL, England
Penguin Putnam Inc., 375 Hudson Street, New York, New York 10014, USA
Penguin Books Australia Ltd, 250 Camberwell Road, Camberwell, Victoria 3124, Australia
Penguin Books Canada Ltd, 10 Alcorn Avenue, Toronto, Ontario, Canada M4V 3B2
Penguin Books India (P) Ltd, 11 Community Centre, Panchsheel Park, New Delhi – 110 017, India
Penguin Books (NZ) Ltd, Cnr Rosedale and Airborne Roads, Albany, Auckland, New Zealand
Penguin Books (South Africa) (Pty) Ltd, 24 Sturdee Avenue, Rosebank 2196, South Africa

Penguin Books Ltd, Registered Offices: 80 Strand, London WC2R 0RL, England

www.penguin.com

Published in Penguin Books 1993

038

Copyright © Ronald Wilks, 1993
Introduction copyright © A. N. Wilson, 1993
All rights reserved

The moral right of the translator has been asserted

Typeset by Datix International Limited, Bungay, Suffolk

Printed and bound in Great Britain by Clays Ltd, Elcograf S.p.A.

ISBN 978-0-14-044506-0

www.greenpenguin.co.uk

CONTENTS

INTRODUCTION

The story known as 'The Raid' is one of the earliest Tolstoy wrote. It dates from 1853, when he was barely twenty-four. He had spent the previous year in the Caucasus, following his military brother, and eventually joining up himself. Writing in French to an aunt at the beginning of that year, he said, 'I rather fancy that the really frivolous idea I had of making a journey to the Caucasus is an idea which I was inspired with from above. It's the hand of God that has guided me . . .' This conviction sprang from a Romantic belief that he was more capable of virtue in the stupendous mountain scenery of the Caucasus than in the gambling saloons of St Petersburg or the bordellos of Moscow. He was also in the company of his family – his brothers – and Tolstoy's emotional dependency on his family was always intensely strong. In that same letter to his aunt, he imagines his elder brother Nikolay, old and bald, still living with his brothers. 'I imagine how, as in the old days, he will tell the children fairy stories of his own invention; how the children will kiss his greasy (but deserving) hands; how he will play with them . . .' etc.

For whatever reasons, it was during this period that Tolstoy himself had started to write – the vivid (almost stream-of-consciousness) *A History of Yesterday*, which he never finished, a translation of Laurence Sterne's *A Sentimental Journey* and a first draft of his novella, *Childhood* (begun while recovering from a bout of venereal disease in the Georgian capital of Tiflis). In the event, Nikolay died young, and it was he, Lev Nikolayevich, who lived to tell the children and grandchildren stories.

'The Raid' is of different, and I should say of higher, quality than any of his earlier attempts. Rereading it here in an excellent new translation, I am struck by how much of Tolstoy there is in it, how archetypically Tolstoyan it is. So many of the qualities which we associate with the masterpieces of his maturity are to be found here. So, too, are the simple-minded moralistic concerns which were to haunt him all his life, and which were to find their finest expression in the fables and short stories, some of which ('How Much Land

Does a Man Need?', 'Where Love is, God is') are to be found in this book. In fact, I now think that if I wanted to introduce a new reader to Tolstoy, and to give them some small taste of what he is like, I should probably recommend that they start with 'The Raid'. It is a story full of Tolstoyan simplicities and ironies. The Caucasus is the scene of many Romantic stories and poems of the previous generation. Lermontov had immortalized it in his brilliantly cynical novel *A Hero of our Time*. Pushkin and others had exploited the full Byronic potential of these mountain landscapes, populated by exotically clad Caucasian Muslims. Rosenkrantz, one of the soldiers in Tolstoy's story, is living, imaginatively speaking, in these tales from the past ('He was one of those young, daredevil officers who model themselves on Marlinsky's or Lermontov's heroes.') with his ostentatious uniform and his show-off manners. Tolstoy's story is in self-conscious contrast to Marlinsky's popular adventure story, *Mullah Nur*. It has the quality of *cinéma vérité*. Tolstoy is at his most effective as a moralist – and as an artist – when he is listening in, editing reality for us, no doubt, but doing it so skilfully that, as in a good film, we take what is offered as a slice of reality itself.

We feel this most strongly when the narrator is confronted with Captain Khlopov, the 'good soldier', whose experience of war has left him diffident about heroics. His mother, a neighbour of the narrator's in Russia, had asked him to deliver a small icon to her son, convinced that the Mother of God had protected him from being wounded throughout his military career. In fact, of course, Captain Khlopov has been wounded four times, but always concealed the fact from his mother!

There is a scene which could be in *War and Peace* (in fact it seems to anticipate Nikolay Rostov's naïve views of battle) when the young ensign in this story (destined to be fatally wounded in the raid) is over-excited in anticipation of action:

'Where does he think he's dashing off to?' the captain muttered with a dissatisfied look, his pipe still in his mouth.

'Who is he?' I asked.

'Ensign Alanin, a subaltern from my company. He arrived from the Cadet Corps only last month.'

'So this is the first time he's seen action, is it?'

'Yes – that's why he's so pleased!' the captain replied, thoughtfully shaking his head. 'Youth!'

'But why shouldn't he be pleased? I can imagine how interesting it must be for a young officer.'

For a couple of minutes the captain did not reply.

It was with this story that Tolstoy had his first serious brush with the official Government censors. When it was sent to the periodical *The Contemporary* (*Sovremennik*), the censor removed all those passages which appeared to question the justifiability of Russian soldiers gunning down Muslim tribesmen in their native mountain villages. More fundamentally than that, the story contains the seeds of Tolstoy's later pacifism. As the detachment approaches the village by night, it does so in such silence that

> I could distinctly hear all the mingling sounds of night, so full of enchanting mystery: the mournful howling of distant jackals, now like a despairing lament, now like laughter; the sonorous, monotonous song of crickets, frogs, quails; a rumbling noise whose cause baffled me and which seemed to be coming ever nearer; and all of Nature's barely audible nocturnal sounds that defy explanation or definition and merge into one rich, beautiful harmony that we call the stillness of night. And now that stillness was broken by – or rather, blended with – the dull thud of hoofs and the rustle of the tall grass as the detachment slowly advanced.
>
> Only occasionally did I hear the clang of a heavy gun, the clatter of clashing bayonets, hushed voices, or a horse snorting. Nature seemed to breathe with pacifying beauty and power.
>
> Can it be that there is not enough space for man in this beautiful world, under those immeasurable, starry heavens? Is it possible that man's heart can harbour, amid such ravishing natural beauty, feelings of hatred, vengeance, or the desire to destroy his fellows?

An absolutely typical Tolstoyan passage! David Cecil used to say that only second-rate minds are afraid of the obvious. Tolstoy, who belonged so self-confidently to the 'first rate' in the literary league-table of the world – with Homer and Shakespeare – was never afraid of the obvious, was never worried by the fear of simplicity. He can move into a mountain pass at night, and, as it were, *film* it for us, and he can allow his characters to have the big, important, (yes, obvious) thoughts about the strange disparities between Nature (or, what's natural) and the complicated desires, yearnings, hatreds in the heart of man.

To this extent, the narrator of 'The Raid' anticipates the feelings of a long line of Tolstoyan heroes – the main character in 'A Landowner's Morning' has such thoughts. Prince Andrew has them, lying wounded on the battle field of Borodino and looking up at the stars; Pierre, of course, has them in the same novel; Levin, the hero of *Anna Karenina*, is obsessed by them; and so is Nekhlyudov, the agonized hero of *Resurrection*, a novel which has had many hostile critics but is always worth rereading for its unshakeable sense, from first paragraph to last, that Nature is *stronger* than man.

If the peaceful Caucasian night – moments before the raid itself – makes us think of the futility of war, the wide open spaces of Samara (where Tolstoy himself had bought estates with the money he made from *War and Peace* in 1867) might fill our minds with the futility of 'ownership' – particularly of land-ownership. As a landowner of the *ancien régime* who felt guilty about his position, Tolstoy was one of those (he was not unique) who wished to dispossess himself and hand the estates over to the peasants who farmed them. But, as in so many areas of life, he was not consistent in this aim, and his wife and family, whose livelihood depended on their estates, took an understandably dim view of his philanthropism.

His story 'How Much Land Does a Man Need?' was written thirty-three years after 'The Raid', in 1886. By then, his major literary masterpieces were behind him, and his children were nearly all grown up. His marriage, which had been happy for the first twenty years or so, had become an ideological and psychological battleground, with Tolstoy's wife and most of his sons representing what they regarded as common sense, and Tolstoy with disciples and daughters on the other side representing what they regarded as Truth. A total distrust of systems, governments, ideologies, and of human 'culture' itself had come upon Tolstoy, who was by now a sort of holy anarchist, believing himself to be inspired by Jesus but hostile to Russian Orthodoxy, to Capitalism, to Socialism and, of course, to the Government. Distrusting art, despising his own earlier *oeuvres*, he gave himself over to the production of propaganda such as *What then Must we Do?* He affected to believe (and perhaps almost persuaded himself, in spite of a natural musicality and a considerable gift as a pianist) that Beethoven was no good – peasant folk-songs were better; Shakespeare was a non-starter – folk-tales were the best form of literature.

So, he set himself to work in this 'simple' genre. Many of the simple stories he wrote were meant for children. (His ABC first reading primer is still used in some Russian schools to help children learn to read.) Others were meant to be, like the parables of Jesus, so direct and uncomplicated that anyone, from the Tsar to the humblest peasant, could understand them. Of such is 'How Much Land Does a Man Need?', a cruel, brilliant parable about human greed (but also about the nature of land itself – and therefore, by implication, the whole mysterious concept of how people persuade themselves that they 'own' pieces of Nature.) The Bashkir tribesmen tell Pakhom that he can have as much of their land as he can circumambulate in a day. He is greedy. He traces too wide a circuit. In order to complete his circle, he has to break into a run, and by the time he reaches the Bashkirs, at the end of a long day's journey, the question of the title has been answered for him. A man needs six feet of land: just enough to be buried in. Again, typical Tolstoy, in its elemental simplicity. The dream which Pakhom has on the night before his death is also typically Tolstoyan. All the figures who have done bargains with him – who have been stepping-stones towards greater and greater prosperity for him – appear, until he sees the Devil himself, laughing. And before the Devil, there lay 'a barefoot man wearing only shirt and trousers. When Pakhom took a closer look he saw that the man was dead and that it was himself.' That recalls Tolstoyan masterpieces such as 'The Death of Ivan Ilyich' (*the* great short masterpiece).

Tolstoy is at his best as an artist when he portrays life so faithfully that the reader loses the sense that what he is reading is literature. The illusion seems complete. Even Tolstoy himself felt this about his own work, in his rare moments of unselfconsciousness. Writing a fan letter to his English translator (and future biographer) Aylmer Maude, he said how much he had been enjoying 'Two Hussars', 'and read it straight through as though it were something new, written in English' (23 December 1901, *Letters* p. 607).

Maude himself makes the point that 'Two Hussars' was one of the first stories Tolstoy wrote (1856) which was not based on personal experience:

> The description of the elder Turbin (like that of Eroshka in *The Cossacks* and later on of Hadji Murad) shows how attracted he was by a strong, fearless, intense personality made all in one piece – *tselni* as the Russians call it – who regardless of scruples goes direct to his goal unlike Tolstoy himself who often felt drawn in different directions.

This is surely only true of the Tolstoy of 'real life' – the man who lost his mother at the age of two, who longed to remember her face, who could never reconcile within himself the warring factions of sexual impulse and self-loathing, Voltairean scepticism and peasant faith, love for his family and loathing of them, hope and despair. Beneath this mixed-up character, or somewhere deep down inside him, there was an artist of supreme self-confidence, who knew exactly what he was doing every time he picked up a pen (even when he did so to denounce literature!) and who was, in his own way, every bit as self-confident as Turbin in 'Two Hussars'. There is more melodrama in this novella than in his greatest works, but even here, on page after page, one notes the unmistakable Tolstoyan eye at work. Lukhnov has cheated at cards. Ilin, who has lost everything and is in despair, is lying in an adjoining room chewing a horsehair sofa and contemplating suicide. Turbin barges next door and insists on Lukhnov paying the money back. Swashbuckling stuff, which could be told by Alexandre Dumas or Anthony Hope. But then, the true Tolstoyan touch. As he tosses the money to the unhappy young man on the sofa, Turbin *pretends not to notice* the expression of joy and gratitude which passes over the cornet's face.

One of the things which Tolstoy hated about art, particularly his own, was that it was so much more vivid than *life*. There is a scene in *Anna Karenina* where the heroine is reading an English novel – in a train – and feels reproached by the *life*, the vigour of the characters on the page. It is an odd thought to have given to Anna. We feel it belongs more appropriately in the mind of Tolstoy. It was given to him (as he said as a young man in the Caucasus, by 'the hand of God') to convey, and to sense, the multifarious facets of consciousness itself in a wide range of human beings – what it is like to *be them*. We feel this in all his early stories, particularly in the tales of army life which are to be found in this book — 'The Prisoner of the Caucasus', 'The Woodfelling', 'The Raid'.

At the same time, no one writes with more self-confidence than Tolstoy about the moral life. He was never really a Christian, because he never truly believed that Nature was at war with Grace, or that it needed to be redeemed. The wise, in his stories, like the Bashkirs who watch poor Pakhom toiling round the field, live in tune with Nature, they are elemental. The same is true of the peasants in his parables, who act wisely and virtuously *by instinct*. This is a quality which Tolstoy admired and coveted more than any other.

The simplicity of such a story as 'Where Love is, God is' works — as the religious passages in the novels *work* — because this is actually what it is like to read the Gospels, and to feel, as old Martin the shoemaker felt, that we should be able to put these teachings into practice by welcoming the old soldier and the young mother with her baby *as if they were Christ*. With his scornful sense of the gulf between Jesus's teachings and the practices of the Orthodox Church, Tolstoy may be said to have rescued Jesus, not just for the Russians, but for the nineteenth century, and for the modern world.

His own life and career were tempestuous and painful, as was the history of nineteenth-century Russia. But, like his allegorical tale 'What Men Live by', it was also emblematic, representative, important as the lives of few artists have been important. His great contemporary came to feel that Holy Russia could never be sane unless and until she came to kneel at the feet of Jesus. Dostoyevsky's Christ is more orthodox than Tolstoy's anarchic Jesus — but it is remarkable to note the extent to which Dostoyevsky's prophecy was fulfilled in Tolstoy's later writings, and in his parables in particular. Tolstoy's Christ is not to be found in the obscure doctrines of the Orthodox faith nor in its theatrical rituals; he is found in the goodness of men and women. The angel in the story learns that 'men live, not by selfishness, but by love'.

No wonder that men and women in Tolstoy's lifetime approximated to the view that he was the oracle of God. No wonder either that Lenin and the Bolsheviks despised Tolstoy so absolutely. His anarchic individualism, his distrust of theories, his belief in the absolute value of every person, however poor or insignificant they might seem, could not appeal to Marxist theory. Now Lenin's experiment has failed, and across the vast expanses of Russia, Georgia, Samara and beyond, these old questions remain. The Muslims in their Caucasian fastnesses are at last independent of the Russians, as they wanted to be in 'The Raid'. Surveying the huge, inefficient collective farms, wise old agriculturalists must be smiling ruefully, like the Bashkir peasants, at the question of how much land a man requires. And all over Europe, where the futility of war and nationalism, and Capitalism and Socialism and greed and violence, is never more in evidence, men and women are continuing to ask themselves what men live by. If we can give Tolstoy's answer – Love – then we shall survive. Otherwise, we shall simply continue to destroy ourselves with all the very efficient means at our disposal. This is a good time to have retranslated Tolstoy's stories: they all seem as fresh and strong and relevant to our condition as they must have done to his contemporaries.

A. N. WILSON

THE WOODFELLING

A CADET'S STORY

I

In the midwinter of 185–, a section of our battery was stationed with an advance detachment in the Great Chechnya District.* On the evening of February 14th, when I learnt that the platoon I was commanding in the absence of a regular officer had been detailed to fell wood the following day, I retired earlier than usual to my tent after I had received and transmitted all necessary orders. Since I did not have the bad habit of heating my tent with charcoal, I lay down without undressing on my bed, which stood on small pegs above the ground, pulled my fur cap over my eyes, wrapped myself in my fur coat and fell into that mysterious, deep and heavy sleep that usually comes over one in the anxious, nerve-racking hours before imminent danger. Anticipation of tomorrow's action had put me in this state of mind.

At three o'clock in the morning, when it was still pitch-dark, someone pulled away my warm sheepskin coat and a candle's crimson flame glared unpleasantly in my sleepy eyes.

'Please get up, sir,' a voice said.

I closed my eyes again, half-consciously pulled up my sheepskin coat again and fell asleep. '*Please* get up, sir!' Dmitry repeated, cruelly shaking my shoulder. 'The infantry's leaving.'

I suddenly came to my senses, shuddered and leapt to my feet. After a hurried glass of tea and a wash in icy water I crept out of my tent and went to the artillery-park. It was dark, misty and cold. The faint crimson light of the bonfires, glowing here and there in the camp and illuminating the figures of drowsy soldiers sitting around

---

* Part of the North Caucasus, with a mainly Muslim population. During the 1830s and 1840s the Russian army was engaged in numerous campaigns, leading to the eventual subjugation and colonization of the region.

All notes are the translator's, unless specified otherwise.

them only seemed to intensify the darkness. Nearby I could hear a regular, gentle snoring and from further off came the voices and clatter of the bustling infantrymen's rifles as they prepared to move. There was a smell of smoke, dung, fuses and mist; the early morning cold sent shivers down my spine and my teeth chattered involuntarily.

Only from the snorting and occasional stamping of hoofs was it possible to tell the position of the limbers to which the horses were harnessed and the ammunition-boxes in the impenetrable darkness, and only from the shining points of linstocks where the guns were. To the words 'God be with us' the first gun moved off with a clang, an ammunition-wagon rumbled after it and the platoon followed. We all doffed our caps and crossed ourselves. After taking up a position between the ranks of infantry, the platoon halted and waited a quarter of an hour for the whole column to assemble and for the commanding officer to ride out.

'One man's missing, Nikolay Petrovich,' said a black figure coming up to me and whom I recognized as Artillery-Sergeant Maximov only from the voice.

'Who?'

'Velenchuk, sir. He was there all right when they were harnessing – saw him with my own eyes, I did. Now he's disappeared.'

Since the column was not likely to move off immediately, we decided to send Lance-Corporal Antonov to look for him. Shortly after, a few officers trotted past in the dark – the commander and his suite. Then the head of the column stirred and moved off, until finally it was our turn. But still there was no Antonov or Velenchuk. However, we had hardly gone a hundred paces when both of them caught up with us.

'Where was he?' I asked Antonov.

'Sleeping in the artillery-park.'

'Oh – had he been drinking?'

'No, sir.'

'Then why did he fall asleep?'

'Don't know, sir.'

For about three hours we slowly advanced, in silence and darkness, over unploughed, snowless fields and through clumps of low bushes that crackled under the gun-carriage wheels. Finally, after crossing a shallow but extremely fast-flowing stream, we were ordered to halt and bursts of rifle fire came from the vanguard. As always, these sounds had a most stimulating effect on everyone. The whole detachment seemed to wake up; the ranks were full of voices, movement, laughter. Two soldiers wrestled with each other; another hopped from foot to foot; others chewed dry biscuits or shouldered and grounded arms to while away the time. Meanwhile, the mist was growing noticeably whiter in the west. One could feel the damp more now and surrounding objects gradually began to emerge from the gloom. I could already distinguish the green gun-carriages and ammunition-boxes, the brass of guns wet with mist, the familiar figures of my men whom I could not help studying down to the last detail, bay horses and ranks of infantrymen with gleaming bayonets, kitbags, ramrods and mess-tins on their backs.

We were soon moved on again and were led to a spot a few hundred yards off the road. To the right we could see the steep bank of a meandering stream and the tall wooden posts of a Tartar cemetery; to the left and in front a black strip showed through the mist. The platoon unlimbered. The Eighth Company, which was covering us, stacked arms, and a battalion with rifles and axes marched into the forest.

Within five minutes fires were crackling and smoking all around. The soldiers spread out to bring up branches and logs and then fanned the fires with their hands and feet. The forest echoed incessantly to the sound of hundreds of axes and falling trees.

The artillerymen, with a certain feeling of rivalry towards the infantry, made their fire, and although it was already blazing so fiercely that it was impossible to come within two paces of it, and dense black smoke was pouring through the frozen branches which hissed as they were piled on to the fire by the soldiers, and although the wood underneath was turning to charcoal and the deathly pale grass was thawing all around, this still did not satisfy them. They dragged great logs up, pushed weeds under them and fanned the flames even higher.

When I went to the fire to light a cigarette, Velenchuk, who was the bustling type and who now, having a guilty conscience, was busying himself more than the others around the fire, pulled a burning coal from the heart of the fire in a fit of zeal, with his bare hand, tossed it a couple of times from one hand to the other and then let it fall to the ground.

'Light one of them twigs for him,' said one of the soldiers.

'Get him a linstock, lads!' said another.

I finally managed to light my cigarette without the assistance of Velenchuk, who was again attempting to pick out a live coal. He rubbed his burnt fingers on the flaps of his sheepskin coat and, most probably for want of something to do, lifted a huge piece of plane-tree wood and with a mighty swing hurled it on to the fire. When at last he felt that he was entitled to a rest, he went right up to the fire, flung open his coat, which he wore like a cloak, parted his legs, thrust out his big black hands, twisted his mouth slightly and frowned. 'Damn! I've forgotten my pipe. What a nuisance, lads!' he said after a brief silence, not addressing anyone in particular.

2

There are three main types of soldier in Russia according to which men from all the armed forces can be classified, whether they serve in the line, in the Caucasus, the Guards, infantry, cavalry, artillery and so on.

These three main types (with many subdivisions and permutations) are:

(1) the submissive
(2) the domineering
(3) the reckless

The submissive can be further subdivided into:

(a) the coolly submissive
(b) the fussily submissive

The domineering can be subdivided into:

(a) the sternly domineering
(b) the diplomatically domineering

The reckless can be subdivided into:

(a) reckless humorists
(b) reckless libertines

The commonest type in the army – the most likeable and, for the most part, endowed with the noblest Christian virtues, meekness, piety, patience and devotion to God's will – is, broadly speaking, the submissive. The distinctive trait of the coolly submissive type is imperturbable calmness and contempt for all the reverses of fortune that might befall him. The distinctive trait of the submissive drunkard is his gentle romantic nature and sensibility; that of the fussily submissive is his limited mental capacity, combined with undirected zeal and industry.

The domineering type is most commonly found in the higher ranks of ordinary soldiers – lance-corporals, non-commissioned officers and so forth. In the first subdivision of the sternly domineering we find exceptionally high-minded, energetic, pre-eminently military types who, nevertheless, are not lacking in lofty romantic impulses (Lance-Corporal Antonov, with whom I intend acquainting the reader, was this type). The second subdivision comprises the diplomatically domineering, whose numbers have been increasing considerably of late. The diplomatically domineering type is invariably highly articulate, literate, wears pink shirts, does not eat from the common bowl, occasionally smokes expensive Musatov tobacco, considers himself immeasurably superior to the rank and file and is rarely such a good soldier as the sternly domineering type of the first subdivision.

The reckless, like the domineering types, are good soldiers if they belong to the first subdivision – the humorists, characterized by unshakeable cheerfulness, tremendous versatility, rich personality and daring – but in the second subdivision (the libertines) tend to be thoroughly disreputable. However, to the glory of the Russian army, they are very rare and where they do appear are usually ostracized by the soldiers themselves. The main characteristics of this section are godlessness and a certain bravado in their debauchery.

Velenchuk was the fussily submissive type. He was Ukrainian, had already served for fifteen years and although he was a rather insignificant-looking, blundering soldier, he was simple-hearted, kind, extremely zealous (although this zeal tended at times to be misdirected) and extraordinarily honest. I say extraordinarily honest, because something happened the previous year where he showed this characteristic very clearly. Here I must point out that almost every soldier knows a trade, the most common being tailoring and bootmaking. Velenchuk had learnt the first of these and, judging by the fact that none other than Sergeant-Major Mikhail Dorofeich ordered clothes from him, had attained a certain degree of skill. The previous year, in camp, Velenchuk had undertaken to make a fine coat for Mikhail Dorofeich but, on the very night he cut the cloth, measured the trimmings and hid everything under his pillow in his tent, disaster struck: the cloth, which had cost *seven roubles*, vanished during the night. With tears in his eyes and pale, trembling lips, suppressing his sobs, Velenchuk reported the theft to the sergeant-major. Mikhail Dorofeich was furious. In the first moments of anger he issued the tailor with dire threats. But then, as he was well off and a reasonable man, he forgot all about it and did not ask Velenchuk to pay for the material. No matter how much fuss that busy Velenchuk made, no matter how many tears he shed as he told of his woes, the thief was not found. Although a certain Chernov (one of the reckless libertines) who slept in the same tent was strongly suspected, there was no conclusive evidence. As Mikhail Dorofeich (the diplomatically domineering type) was well off, being engaged in various business activities with the quartermaster and mess caterer – the aristocrats of the battery – he soon completely forgot the loss of his civilian coat. Velenchuk, however, could not forget his misfortune. The soldiers said at the time that they feared he might do away with himself or run off into the mountains, so shattering was the effect of the disaster on him. He would not drink or eat, could not even work and was always crying. Three days later he went to see Mikhail Dorofeich. White as a sheet and with trembling hands he took a gold rouble from under his cuff and handed it to him. 'I swear that's all I have, Mikhail Dorofeich, and I even had to borrow that from Zhdanov,' he sobbed. 'But I promise to pay back the other two roubles as soon as I've earned them, I swear by God I will! *He* (who "he" was even Velenchuk did not know) made me a crook in your eyes. *He*, the rotten bastard, has squeezed the last breath out of his own comrade . . . and I've been fifteen years in the army . . .' But it should be said, to Mikhail Dorofeich's credit, that he would not accept the two roubles, although Velenchuk brought them two months later.

3

Besides Velenchuk, five other soldiers from my platoon were warming themselves by the fire.

Maximov, the platoon gun-sergeant, was sitting on a wooden
bucket in the best place, protected from the wind, smoking his pipe.
His posture, his whole bearing and expression – not to mention the
wooden bucket on which he was sitting, an emblem of authority at
stopping-places, and his nankeen-covered coat – clearly showed that
he was used to giving orders and highly conscious of his own dignity.

When I went up to him he turned his head, but his eyes remained
fixed on the fire and only followed his head movement much later.
Maximov came from a family of small landowners, had money and
had been given a rating at military training school where he had
acquired a great deal of knowledge. He was awfully well off and
awfully learned, in the words of the soldiers. I remember how once,
as we were practising plunging fire with a quadrant, he explained to
a group of soldiers around him that a spirit-level is 'nothing other as
it occurs, than atmospheric mercury possessing its own motion'. In
actual fact, Maximov was far from stupid and really knew his job.
But he had the unfortunate habit of sometimes deliberately speaking
in such a way that it was impossible to understand him. I am
convinced that he himself did not understand what he was saying
either. He had a particular passion for the words 'occurs' and 'continuing' and whenever he said either of them I knew in advance that I
would be unable to understand anything of what followed. On the
other hand, the soldiers, as far as I could make out, loved to hear
those 'occurs' and were convinced that this word had some profound
significance although, like me, they did not understand a word he
said. However, they ascribed their lack of comprehension to their
own stupidity and respected Fyodor Maximov all the more. In brief,
Maximov was the diplomatically domineering type.

The second soldier by the fire, who was putting his sinewy red feet
into a pair of boots, was Antonov – that same Bombardier Antonov
who, in 1837, when he was one of three left to man an exposed gun,
had fired back at a powerful enemy and had continued to stand by
his gun and reload it – with two bullets in his thigh. 'He would have
been made a sergeant long ago if it weren't for that temper of his,'
the soldiers used to say. And he really did have a strange character.
When he was sober there was no one more docile, quiet and well
behaved, but after a few drinks he became a completely different
person. He would defy all authority, fight and brawl and become a

useless soldier. Only a week before, on Shrove Tuesday, he had got drunk and, despite all manner of threats and warnings – even being tied to a gun – he had persisted in his drunken brawling until the following Monday. Throughout Lent, although the entire detachment was under orders to eat meat as normal, he ate nothing but dry rusks and in the first week even refused the regulation cup of vodka. However, one just had to see his short, steely, bandy-legged figure, his shiny, whiskered face when, under the influence, he would take a balalaika in his sinewy hands, casually glance round and strike up 'The Young Maiden'; or when he strolled down the street, his coat thrown over his shoulders, his medals dangling, his hands in the pockets of his blue nankeen trousers; one only had to see that expression of soldierly pride and contempt for all things non-soldierly to realize how impossible it was for him to resist a fight with any batman, Cossack, infantryman, settler – with anyone, in fact, who was not an artilleryman, who had been rude to him or had just happened to cross his path. He fought and brawled not so much for personal satisfaction as for the morale of all the soldiers, whose representative he considered himself to be.

The third soldier squatting by the fire, with one earring, bristly whiskers, a bird-like face and a clay pipe between his teeth was Chikin, a driver. 'Old Chikin', as the soldiers called him, was a humorist. Wherever he was – in a biting frost, up to his knees in mud and having gone two days without food, marching, on parade or at drill, that dear man would always pull funny faces, twist his legs comically or crack jokes that had the whole platoon rolling with laughter. The young soldiers would always crowd round Chikin at stopping-places or in the camp, and he would play filka* with them, tell them stories about the crafty soldier and the English lord, mimic Tartars and Germans, or simply say funny things which had them splitting their sides. In fact, his reputation as the battery humorist was so firmly established that he had only to open his mouth or wink to produce guffaws from everyone. But that man really had a flair for the unexpected. He was able to discover something unusual in everything, that others would never dream of. But, most of all, this

* A soldier's card game. [*Tolstoy*]

ability to see the funny side of everything was never affected by any kind of ordeal or misfortune.

The fourth soldier was an unattractive young lad, recruited the previous year and on active service for the first time. He was standing in the middle of the smoke, so close to the fire it seemed his shabby sheepskin coat would burst into flames at any moment, but, judging from the way his coat was flung open, his calm, complacent pose with thighs out-thrust, he was obviously deriving a great deal of pleasure from it.

The fifth and last soldier, who was sitting some way from the fire, whittling away at a stick, was 'Grandpa' Zhdanov. He had served longer than any other soldier in the battery and had known all the others as young recruits, all of whom called him 'Grandpa' out of force of habit. It was said that he never drank or smoked, never played cards or used foul language. He spent all his free time making boots, went to church on holidays, whenever he could, or would light a cheap candle before his icon and open his psalm-book – the only book he could read. He rarely mixed with the other soldiers and to those who were his senior in rank but junior in years he was icily polite. As he never drank, he had little chance of keeping company with his equals. But he had a particular liking for recruits and young soldiers, always taking them under his wing, admonishing them when necessary and frequently helping them. The whole battery considered him a capitalist, as he had about twenty-five roubles which he would willingly lend to anyone in real need. That same Maximov who was now a gun-sergeant told me that when he first arrived as a recruit ten years before and had drunk away all his money with the old, hardened drinkers, Zhdanov saw the dreadful mess he was in, called him over, severely reprimanded him for his behaviour, even beat him, lectured him on the good soldier's life and sent him away with a shirt on his back (Maximov had none left by then) and a half-rouble. 'He made a man of me,' Maximov always said of him with respect and gratitude. He also helped Velenchuk, whom he had protected ever since he was a recruit, at the time of the stolen cloth disaster. And there were so many others whom he had helped during his twenty-five years in the army.

One could not have wished for a soldier who knew his job better, who was braver or more conscientious. But he was too meek and self-effacing to be promoted to gun-sergeant, although he had been a bombardier for fifteen years. Zhdanov's sole joy, his passion even, was singing, although he himself didn't sing. There were a few songs he particularly loved and he was always collecting a choir from the young soldiers. He would stand with them, stuff his hands in his coat pockets, screw up his eyes and show how deeply affected he was. I cannot explain why, but for me there was something extraordinarily expressive about that regular movement of his jaw-bones just beneath the ears which seemed uniquely his. His snow-white hair, blackened moustache and wrinkled, bronzed face gave him at first sight a stern, forbidding look. But if one inspected his big eyes more closely, especially when they smiled (he never smiled with his lips), one was immediately struck by something exceptionally meek and almost childlike.

4

'Blow, I've forgotten my pipe. What a nuisance, lads!' Velenchuk repeated.

'Then you should smoke siggars, old chap,' Chikin said, twisting his mouth and winking. 'When I'm at home I always smoke siggars – they're sweeter!'

Naturally, everyone burst out laughing.

'So you forgot your pipe, did you?' Maximov chimed in, ignoring the general mirth and imperiously knocking his pipe against the palm of his left hand. 'Where did you get to this morning, Velenchuk? Tell me.'

Velenchuk half-turned towards him and was about to raise his hand to his cap but let it drop.

'It seems like you had a lot to sleep off if you couldn't keep awake standing up! Your comrades won't thank you for that.'

'You can strike me down dead, Fyodor Maximovich, if one drop passed my lips. I just don't know what came over me,' Velenchuk replied. 'What do you think *I* could have had to celebrate?'

'That may well be, but one of us has to carry the can for you and it's a real disgrace the way you go on,' remarked the eloquent Maximov, in a calmer voice.

'It was a miracle, lads,' Velenchuk continued after a moment's pause, scratching the back of his neck and addressing no one in particular. 'It was like a miracle. I've been sixteen years in the army and nothing like this has ever happened to me. When we were ordered to form up, I formed up and felt fine. But when I was in the artillery-park *it* suddenly grabbed me and threw me to the ground, and that was that! I didn't even know what was happening. I just dropped off, lads! Must have been the sleeping-sickness,' he concluded.

'I had a terrible job waking you up, I can tell you!' Antonov said, pulling on his boot. 'I had to shake you, push you, but you were sleeping like a log.'

'Yes', observed Velenchuk, 'but it would have been different if I'd been drunk . . .'

'Reminds me of an old woman back home,' Chikin joined in. 'She didn't budge from over the stove for two years. One day they tried to wake her, thinking she was just asleep. But she was dead! She was always dropping off – just like you, old chap!'

'Come on, Chikin, tell us about the time you started cutting a dash when you were on leave,' Maximov said, smiling and glancing at me as if to say, 'Would *you* like to hear what this clown has to say?'

'What d'ye mean, cutting a dash?' Chikin replied, giving me a fleeting, sidelong glance. 'Well, I naturally told them exactly what the Corkersuss is like.'

'Come on, don't be so modest . . . tell us how you *instructed* them.'

'You know very well how I instructed them. They asked me what life's like here,' Chikin replied in a rapid patter, like a man who has told the same story many times. 'I told them we live well here. Loads of grub – a cup of chockolad morning and night for every soldier and barley broth fit for a lord at midday. And instead of vodka a glass of Modeera – to cheer us all up!'

'That's a good one, Modeera!' Velenchuk exclaimed, roaring with laughter louder than anyone else. 'I'll give you Modeera!'

'What did you tell them about the Hazians?' Maximov asked when the general laughter had somewhat subsided.

Chikin leant over the fire, fished out a small piece of charcoal with his stick, put it to his pipe and for a long time silently puffed at his cheap shag, as if completely unaware of the mute curiosity he had aroused in his audience. When at last he had worked up enough smoke he threw the charcoal away, pushed his cap even further back and after a slight twitch and a faint smile continued. 'They also asked what the Circassians and Turks were like down here in the Corkersuss, if they were fierce warriors. So I told 'em there's different sorts of Circassians, that they come in all shapes and sizes. There's the Daghestanians who live up in the mountains and eat stones instead of bread. They're as big, I told 'em, as tree-trunks, with one eye in their forehead and they wear red caps – flaming red like yours, me lad!' he added, turning to the young recruit who was in fact wearing an extremely comical cap with a red top.

At this unexpected remark the recruit suddenly squatted, slapped his knees and laughed and coughed so violently he was barely able to gasp, 'So that's what the Daghestanians are really like!'

'And there's the Gapers,' Chikin went on, shaking his cap on to his forehead with a toss of the head. 'They're different – they're little people, always going around in pairs, hand in hand, and they run so fast you couldn't even catch 'em up on a horse.' Then, in a deep throaty voice, attempting to imitate a country yokel, he continued, 'So they ask me, "Is those Gapers born loike that, hand in hand?" Why yes, I say, they go round like that from the day they were born. And if you try and cut 'em apart the blood just gushes out, same as a Chinaman – if you take his hat off he'll start bleeding. And then they ask, "Are they fierce fighters?" Well, I say, when they catch you they slit yer belly open and twist yer guts round yer arm. There they are, twisting away and you can't stop laughing – yes, you laugh yourself to death you do!'

'Did they really believe all that, Chikin?' Maximov said with a faint smile, while the others were splitting their sides.

'That strange lot'd believe anything, Fyodor Maximov. Oh yes! But when I told 'em that the snow doesn't melt all summer on Mount Kizbeck* they laughed their heads off! "What's so special about that?" they say. "It's a high mountain, so of course the snow never melts! When there's a thaw here the snow on any little hillock melts first, but it lingers on in the hollows." Now, who would have thought there were such folk!' Chikin winked in conclusion.

* Mount Kazbek, one of the highest mountains in the Caucasus.

5

The bright orb of the sun shining through the milky-white mist was now quite high. The violet-grey horizon was gradually widening and although now much further away, was marked just as sharply by a deceptive white wall of mist.

Beyond the felled trees quite a large clearing opened up before us. Smoke from the fires – black, milky-white or violet – spread over the clearing from all sides and white layers of mist drifted past in the weirdest shapes. In the far distance groups of Tartars on horseback appeared now and then, and the occasional sound of fire from our rifles and guns could be heard.

'That wasn't what you call action, only a bit of fun!' as good Captain Khlopov would say.

The commander of the Ninth Company of Chasseurs, which had been escorting us, came up to our guns and pointed to three Tartar horsemen riding along the edge of the forest about a mile away, and with that love of artillery fire so typical of infantry officers he asked me to fire a ball or shell at them.

'Can you see that?' he asked with a kind, persuasive smile as he stretched his arm over my shoulder. 'There's one of them in front of those two large trees on a white horse and in a black cloak. The other two are behind. Can you see them? Couldn't you? . . . please . . .'

'And there's another three skirting the forest,' added Antonov, who was renowned for his astonishingly keen eyesight, as he came up to us and hid the pipe he had been smoking behind his back. 'The one in front has drawn his rifle – you can see them clear as daylight, sir!'

'Look – he's fired, lads! There's the white smoke,' remarked Velenchuk, who was standing in a group of soldiers just behind us.

'He must have been firing at our line, the devil!' another observed.

'Just look at all that lot pouring out of the forest. They must be looking for somewhere to put a gun,' added a third.

'If we dropped a shell in the middle they wouldn't like it!'

'Yes, we could just about reach them from here, couldn't we?' Chikin asked.

'It's only about twelve or thirteen hundred yards,' Maximov

replied coolly, as though talking to himself although, like the others, he was obviously dying to open fire. 'At an angle of forty-five degrees our Unicorn★ could hit them plumb in the middle!'

'Well you really couldn't miss if you sent a shell into that crowd! Yes, now's the moment, while they're all bunched. Please give the order to fire at once,' the company commander kept begging me.

'Shall we take aim?' Antonov suddenly asked in a jerky bass voice and with a rather sullen, spiteful look.

I must confess I was longing to fire, so I gave orders for them to aim number two gun.

Hardly had I given the order when the shell was ready charged and loaded into the gun, while Antonov, clinging to the side-plate of the gun-carriage and holding his chubby fingers to the back-plate, was already aligning the trail.

'A trifle to the left ... a fraction to the right ... a bit more ... that's it!' he said, proudly walking away from the gun.

One by one, the infantry officer, Maximov and I peered through the sights and each of us gave our different opinions.

'I'm positive it will overshoot!' Velenchuk said, clicking his tongue, although he had only just looked over Antonov's shoulder and therefore did not have the slightest grounds for this assumption. 'God, I bet you'll overshoot, lads, and hit that tree!'

'Fire number two!' I ordered.

The crew moved away to the guns. Antonov ran to one side to watch the flight of the shell. There was a flash and the sound of ringing brass. At that moment we were enveloped in gunpowder smoke and the resounding boom was followed by the metallic hum of the shell receding at the speed of lightning and dying away in the distance.

Just behind the group of riders a puff of white smoke appeared and the Tartars galloped away in all directions. Then the sound of the explosion reached us.

'Great! That made 'em gallop all right. Those devils don't like it!' Chuckles and murmurs of approval came from the ranks of artillery and infantry.

'If only we'd aimed a fraction lower we'd have hit them,' Velen-

★ Field-gun with a unicorn engraved on it.

chuk remarked. 'I told you we'd hit a tree and that's what we've
done – it carried too far to the right.'

6

After I had left the soldiers to discuss how the Tartars had galloped
away when they saw the shell, what they were doing there in the
first place and whether there were many still left in the forest, I took
a few steps with the company commander and sat down under a tree
waiting while the meatballs he had offered me were warmed up.
Company Commander Bolkhov was one of the officers nicknamed
'Bonjour' in the regiment. He was well off, had served in the Guards
and spoke French. Despite this, his comrades were fond of him. He
was quite intelligent and had sufficient tact to wear a St Petersburg-
style frock-coat, to dine well and to speak French without causing
too much offence to his fellow officers. After we had chatted about
the weather, military operations and mutual officer friends and had
satisfied ourselves, by means of question and answer, that each other's
ideas were acceptable, we involuntarily turned to more intimate
topics. When people from the same social circle meet in the Caucasus
the question, 'Why are you here?' even if unspoken, invariably arises,
and I had the feeling that my companion wanted to reply to this
unasked question.

'When will this action ever finish?' he said lazily. 'I find it so
boring.'

'I don't,' I replied. 'After all, it's even worse at headquarters.'

'Oh yes, it's ten thousand times worse at headquarters,' he said
irritably. 'No, I mean, when will all *this* be over for good?'

'What do you want to be over?' I asked.

'Everything. And for good! ... Well now, are those meatballs
ready, Nikolayev!?' he asked.

'Then why did you come here in the first place if you dislike the
Caucasus so much?' I asked.

'I'll tell you why,' he replied with uncompromising candour. 'It's
all because of some tradition. In Russia they really do believe that the
Caucasus is some kind of Promised Land for all sorts of unfortunate
people.'

'I'd say that's true, roughly. Most of us . . .'

'Yes, but the main thing is, all of us who follow tradition and come to the Caucasus are terribly mistaken in our calculations. For the life of me I cannot see why, because of some unhappy love affair or financial trouble one should opt for the Caucasus rather than Kazan or Kaluga. In Russia, you know, people visualize the Caucasus as such a magnificent place, with eternal virgin ice, raging torrents, daggers, felt cloaks, Circassian maidens, but basically there's nothing very cheerful about it. If only these people at least knew that we never go anywhere near virgin ice, and if we did we wouldn't be very amused by it, and that the Caucasus is divided into many different provinces – Stavropol, Tiflis and so on.'

'Yes,' I laughed. 'Living in Russia we view the Caucasus quite differently. Have *you* ever felt that? It's really like reading poetry in a language you don't know very well – you imagine it's much better than it really is – '

'I don't know, to tell you the truth,' he interrupted, 'but I detest the Caucasus.'

'Well, I like it here now, but in a different way . . .'

'Oh, perhaps it's all right,' he continued rather irritably, 'but all I know is, I don't like it.'

'Why is that?' I asked, for the sake of saying something.

'Firstly, because it's deceived me. All that I came to the Caucasus (following tradition) to be cured of has followed me here and the only difference is that previously it was all on the grand scale and here it is on a small and pretty sordid one. Wherever I go I'm besieged with millions of trivial worries, dirty tricks and insults at every step. Secondly, because I feel myself declining morally every day. But the main reason is that I don't consider myself fit to serve here: I cannot endure danger . . . to put it in a nutshell, I'm not brave . . .' He stopped to look at me. 'I'm not joking.'

Although I was startled by this unsolicited confession I did not contradict my companion, as that was what he apparently wanted. Instead, I waited for him to retract his words, as always happens in such cases.

'Do you know,' he continued, 'this is my first taste of action and you just cannot imagine how I felt yesterday. When the sergeant-major came with the order that my company was to join the main column I went as white as a sheet and was too nervous to speak. And what a night I had – if you only knew! If it's true that people go grey from fear then my hair should be completely white now, since no condemned prisoner can have suffered as much as I did in one night. Even now, although I'm rather more relaxed than during the night, this is what happens inside me,' he added, twisting his fist in front of his chest. 'And the funny thing is,' he continued, 'that the most awful tragedy is being enacted while here we sit scoffing meatballs and onions, persuading ourselves that it's all very jolly. Is there any wine, Nikolayev?' he said, yawning.

Just then we heard a soldier cry out in alarm, 'They're there, lads!' whereupon all eyes turned to the edge of the distant forest.

Far off a bluish cloud of smoke was growing ever larger, drifting upwards as the wind carried it. When I realized that the enemy was firing at us, everything before me suddenly took on a new and majestic character. The stacks of rifles, the bonfire smoke, the blue sky, the green gun-carriages, Nikolayev's sunburnt, whiskered face – all this seemed to be telling me that the ball which had now left the muzzle and was flying through space at that very moment could well be aimed straight at my chest.

'Where did you get that wine?' I lazily asked Bolkhov, while deep down inside me two equally distinct voices were speaking: one was saying, 'Lord receive my soul in peace,' and the other, 'I hope I won't duck and will keep smiling when that ball comes flying over.' And that instant something terribly nasty whistled over my head and a cannonball fell with a thud about two paces from where we were standing.

'Now, if I had been Napoleon or Frederick the Great,' Bolkhov said, turning to me with the greatest composure, 'I would doubtless have paid you a compliment.'

'But you just have,' I replied, finding it difficult to conceal the panic that the danger (now past) had stirred in me.

'Well, so what? No one will write it down.'

'*I* will, though.'

'But if you write it down it will only be to criticize, as Mishchenkov says,' he added, smiling.

'Damn and blast you!' Antonov called out behind us, angrily spitting. 'Within a whisker of grazing my leg!'

After this ingenuous remark all my efforts to appear calm and collected, all our smart talk, struck me as impossibly stupid.

7

The enemy had in fact positioned two guns just where the Tartars had been riding around and every twenty or thirty minutes fired at our woodfellers. My platoon was moved forward into the clearing and ordered to return their fire. A puff of smoke appeared at the edge of the forest, then we would hear a report and a whistling sound and then a cannon-ball would fall behind or in front of us. The enemy's shots were very much off target and no losses were sustained.

As always, our artillerymen were splendid, swiftly loading and diligently aiming whenever they saw puffs of smoke and calmly joking among themselves. Nearby, awaiting its turn in silent inactivity, was our infantry escort. The woodfellers carried on with their work and the forest was filled more and more with the sound of axes. Only when a cannon-ball whistled overhead did everything go quiet and in the deathly silence rather anxious voices would ring out, 'Watch it, lads!' and all eyes would be fixed on the ball ricocheting among the fires and lopped branches.

By now the mist had completely cleared and was turning into clouds that gradually disappeared in the dark blue sky. The sun came out and shone brightly, gleaming cheerfully on the steel bayonets, the brass guns and the thawing earth spangled with hoar-frost. In the air one could feel both the freshness of the morning frost and the warmth of the spring sun. Thousands of different shades and colours mingled in the dry forest leaves and the tracks of wagon wheels and horseshoe nails could be seen quite distinctly on the even, shiny path.

The exchanges between the two forces were growing fiercer and louder on all sides. Puffs of bluish smoke appeared more often now. The dragoons rode on, the pennants on their lances streaming; songs came from the infantry companies and a train of carts laden with firewood was drawn up in the rear. A general rode over to our platoon and ordered us to withdraw. The enemy had positioned himself in the bushes opposite our left flank and was harassing us with heavy rifle fire. A bullet came humming out of the forest to the left and struck a gun-carriage, followed by another, and a third . . . The infantry who were nearby covering us noisily got up, took their rifles and formed a line. The firing intensified and more and more bullets began to fly. The withdrawal began, which meant (as is always the case in the Caucasus) that the real action had begun.

It was obvious that the artillerymen disliked bullets just as much as the infantry disliked cannon-balls. Antonov frowned. Chikin mimicked the bullets and cracked jokes about them – but he clearly did not like them. 'That one's in a hurry!' he said of one, calling another 'little bee'. A third, which screeched slowly and plaintively over our heads, he called 'poor little orphan', which made everyone laugh.

Unused to bullets, the young recruit leant his head to one side and bent his neck every time a bullet flew past, which also made the soldiers laugh. 'Bowing because they're friends of yours?' they asked. Velenchuk, usually so indifferent to danger, was now quite agitated. Evidently he was annoyed that we weren't firing case-shot in the direction of the bullets. Several times he remarked in a disgruntled voice, 'Why do we let them fire and get away with it? If we turned a gun on them and peppered them with case-shot that would soon quieten them down!'

It was in fact high time we did this, so I ordered the men to fire a last shell and then load the gun with case-shot.

'Case-shot!' Antonov shouted, jauntily walking through the smoke to his gun with his linstock as soon as the shell had been fired.

Just then, not far behind me, I heard the rapid hum of a bullet suddenly end in a dull thud. My heart sank. 'One of ours has been hit,' I thought, too afraid to look around, from a feeling of grim foreboding. And in fact the thud was followed by the sound of a body falling heavily and the heart-rending 'O-oh!' of a wounded soldier. 'They've got me, lads!' a familiar voice just managed to say. It was Velenchuk. He was lying on his back between limber and gun. The bag he had been carrying was thrown to one side. His forehead was covered with blood and over his right eye and his nose flowed a thick, red stream. He had been wounded in the stomach, but there was hardly any blood there – he had smashed his forehead against a tree-stump in falling.

I only discovered all this much later and at first I could only make out some vague heap and what appeared to be a dreadful amount of blood.

None of the soldiers who had loaded the gun said a word, except for the young recruit who kept muttering something that sounded like 'God, just look at all that blood!' while Antonov frowned and grunted angrily. But it was clear that the thought of death had run through everyone's mind. Everyone got on with their work with renewed energy. The gun was charged in a moment and the gunner, who brought up some case-shot, walked about two feet away from the spot where the wounded Velenchuk lay, still moaning.

8

Anyone who has seen action must surely have experienced that strange, illogical but nonetheless powerful feeling of revulsion for the place where a soldier has been killed or wounded. The soldiers under my command evidently yielded to this feeling when they should have lifted Velenchuk and carried him to a cart which had come up. Zhdanov angrily went over to the wounded man and, although it made him scream all the more, lifted him by the armpits.

'What are you standing there for? Get hold of him?' he shouted. Velenchuk was immediately surrounded by about ten helpers – more than was needed. But the moment he was moved, Velenchuk started struggling and screaming horribly.

'Why are you screaming like a hare?' Antonov said gruffly as he held his leg. 'If you don't stop we'll leave you here.'

And the wounded soldier in fact quietened down, only muttering occasionally, 'Oh, I'm dying! I'm dying, lads!'

When he was placed in the cart he even stopped groaning and I could hear him telling one of his comrades something in a soft, but audible voice: no doubt words of farewell . . .

No soldier likes to see a wounded comrade and as I instinctively hurried to escape that sight I gave orders for him to be immediately rushed to the dressing-station and then returned to the guns. But a few minutes later I was told that Velenchuk was calling for me, so I went back to the cart.

The wounded man was lying at the bottom of the cart, gripping the sides with both hands. Within a few minutes his broad, healthy face had completely changed: he seemed to have grown thinner and to have aged several years. His pale, thin lips were pressed together with obvious strain. A bright, serene glow had replaced the dull restless look of his eyes and the stamp of death already lay on his bloody forehead and nose.

Although the slightest movement caused him the most appalling pain, he asked for the small purse that was tied like a garter around his left leg to be removed. The sight of that bare, white and healthy leg when they took off his boot and untied the purse aroused the most oppressive feeling in me.

'There's three and a half roubles in it,' he told me as I took the purse. 'Look after them.'

The cart was about to move off when he told them to stop.

'I was making an overcoat for Lieutenant Sulimovsky. He . . . he gave me two roubles. I spent one and a half on buttons and there's another half-rouble with the buttons in my kitbag. Give them to him.'

'Of course, of course,' I said. 'Now you get better, old man.' He did not answer, the cart moved off and he started groaning and moaning in the most dreadful heart-rending way. It was as though, having tidied up his earthly affairs, he could find no more reason to exercise any self-control and considered it quite permissible to let himself go now.

9

'Where do you think you're going? Come back!' I shouted at the young recruit who, as calmly as could be, with his spare linstock under one arm and some sort of stick in his hands, set off after the cart bearing the wounded soldier. But the recruit merely glanced back lazily, muttered something and carried on, so that I had to send someone after him.

He doffed his red cap and smiled stupidly at me.

'Where were you going?'

'Back to camp.'

'Why?'

'Because Velenchuk's been wounded, of course,' he said, smiling again.

'And what's that got to do with you? You must stay here.'

He looked at me in amazement, then nonchalantly turned round, put on his cap and went back to his post.

On the whole the operation was successful. We heard that the Cossacks had carried out a glorious attack and returned with three dead Tartars; that the infantry had stocked up with firewood and had only six wounded; that in the artillery only Velenchuk and two horses had been put out of action. But then about two square miles of forest had been felled and the area cleared beyond recognition: in place of the dense row of trees of before, a vast clearing had now opened up along the forest edge, covered with smoking fires, and cavalry and infantry returning to camp. Although the enemy continued pursuing us with artillery and rifle fire right up to the graveyard and the stream we had crossed in the morning, the withdrawal was successfully carried out. I was already beginning to dream of the cabbage stew and side of mutton with buckwheat porridge that were waiting for me in the camp when news came that the general had ordered a redoubt to be built by the side of the stream and that the third battalion of K– Regiment and a platoon from the Fourth Battery were to stay there until morning. Carts laden with firewood and wounded, Cossacks, artillery, infantry bearing rifles and with firewood on their backs, all passed us with a great deal of noise and singing. Everyone's face expressed animation and contentment, stimulated by the thought that the danger was past and by the prospect of a rest. Only we and the Third Battalion would have to wait until morning before we could entertain such pleasant thoughts.

10

While we artillerymen were busy with the guns, parking the limbers and ammunition-wagons and tethering the horses, the infantry had already stacked their rifles, made fires, built small shelters from branches and maize straw and were now cooking their buckwheat porridge.

It was getting dark. Bluish rain clouds drifted across the sky. The mist had turned into a fine drizzle, soaking the earth and the soldiers' coats. The horizon seemed to contract and the whole area took on a sombre hue. The damp, which I could feel through my boots and on my neck, the incessant motion and conversations in which I took no part, the sticky mud over which my feet slid and my empty stomach all put me in a thoroughly miserable mood after a day of physical and moral exhaustion. I could not get Velenchuk out of my mind. The whole simple story of his soldier's life kept haunting my imagination.

His last moments had been as bright and calm as his whole life. He had lived too honestly, too simply, for his unquestioning faith in the heavenly life to come to falter at the moment of truth.

'Your Honour,' Nikolayev said, coming up. 'The captain would like you to have tea with him.'

Somehow I managed to pick my way through stacks of rifles and bonfires and followed Nikolayev to Bolkhov's quarters, relishing the prospect of a glass of hot tea and some cheerful conversation to dispel my gloomy thoughts.

'Well, did you find him?' came Bolkhov's voice from a straw hut where a small light was burning.

'Yes, I've brought him, Your Honour,' Nikolayev replied in his deep voice.

Bolkhov was sitting on his dry felt cloak, his coat unbuttoned, and without his fur cap. By his side a samovar was on the boil and there was a drum with food on it. A bayonet with a candle on the end was stuck into the ground. 'Well, what do you think?' he proudly asked, casting his eye over his comfortable quarters. In fact it was so pleasant in the hut that as we drank our tea I completely forgot the damp, the darkness and Velenchuk's wound. We talked about Moscow and things that had nothing at all to do with the war and the Caucasus.

After one of those silent moments which occasionally punctuate even the most lively conversations, Bolkhov smiled at me.

'I think our talk this morning must have seemed very odd to you,' he said.

'No, why should it? Only I felt that you were rather too frank – there are things all of us know but which we should never divulge.'

'Why not? No! If I had the slightest chance of exchanging this life for the poorest, most wretched existence – as long as there was no danger of military service – I wouldn't hesitate for one moment.'

'Then why don't you return to Russia?' I asked.

'Why?' he asked. 'Oh, I've been thinking about it for a long time now, but I can't go to Russia until I receive the Anna or Vladimir medals – an Anna round my neck and a major's rank were precisely why I came here in the first place.'

'But why don't you go back if, as you say, you feel unfit for service here?'

'I feel even more incapable of returning to Russia the same as when I left it. It's just one more of those legends in Russia, confirmed by Passek,* Sleptsov† and others, that one only has to come to the Caucasus to be showered with decorations. Everyone expects it of us, demands it of us. But I've been here two years, taken part in two expeditions and received nothing. For all that, I've so much pride that I won't leave this place until I'm a major, with an Anna or a Vladimir round my neck. I've reached the point where it really rankles when some Gnilokishkin is decorated and I'm not. What's more, how could I look my elder in the face again, or merchant Kotel'nikov to whom I sell grain, or my aunt in Moscow and all those fine gentlemen in Russia, if I return after two years in the Caucasus with nothing to show for it? No, I don't want to know those gentlemen and I'm sure that they couldn't care less about me. But such is man's nature that although I couldn't give a damn about them they're the reason why I'm ruining the best years of my life, my happiness and whole future.'

I I

At that moment the battalion commander called from outside, 'Who's that you're talking to, Nikolai Fyodorych?'

Bolkhov told him my name, whereupon three officers came into the hut: Major Kirsanov, a battalion adjutant and Company Commander Trosenko.

Kirsanov was a shortish, stout man with black moustache, red cheeks and sensuous little eyes. These eyes were his outstanding feature and when he laughed all that remained of them was two moist little stars. These, together with his tight lips and arched neck, sometimes made him look extraordinarily stupid. Kirsanov behaved and bore himself better than anyone else in the regiment: his subordinates never said a bad word about him and his superiors respected

---

* Major-General D.V. Passek, who served with distinction in the Caucasus.

† General N.P. Sleptsov, a hero of the war in the Caucasus and an extremely popular commander.

him, although he was generally thought to be very dense. He knew the army, was industrious, diligent, always had money, kept a carriage and cook and was good at pretending to be proud with great naturalness.

'What are you discussing, Nikolai?' he asked as he entered.

'Oh, only the pleasures of army life here.'

Just then Kirsanov spotted me, a mere cadet, and to make me aware of his importance he stared at the drum and asked, 'What's wrong, Nikolai? Tired?' as if he hadn't heard Bolkhov's reply.

'No, we were just – ' Bolkhov began.

But again it was probably the sense of self-importance of a battalion commander that made him interrupt and ask another question: 'A splendid engagement today, wasn't it?'

The battalion adjutant was a young ensign, recently promoted from the cadets. He was a modest, quiet lad with a shy, good-natured expression. I had seen him at Bolkhov's before and he often dropped in on him. He would bow, sit in one corner without saying a word for several hours, roll cigarettes and smoke them, after which he would get up, bow and leave. He was a typical poor Russian gentleman's son who had chosen a military career as the only possible one for someone with his education and who considered an officer's rank the most precious thing in the world. He was the simple-hearted and likeable type, despite those comical accessories invariably associated with it – the tobacco-pouch, the dressing-gown, the guitar, the toothbrush moustache. In the regiment he was said to have boasted that he was fair but strict with his batman. 'I rarely punish him,' he had claimed, 'but when I'm driven to it, then God help him!' Once, when his batman was drunk and had robbed him, even sworn at him, he had taken him to the guardhouse and ordered him to be flogged, but when he saw the necessary preparations he was so upset that he could only murmur, 'Well, you see, I can if I want to . . .' and then he lost his head, ran back to his quarters and ever since was afraid to look Batman Chernov in the eye. His fellow officers did not give him a moment's peace, teased him unmercifully and more than once I heard that simple-hearted youth make excuses, blushing furiously as he assured them that what they had heard was not true, but in fact quite the contrary.

The third officer, Captain Trosenko, was an old Caucasian in every sense of the word: that is, he was a man for whom the company he commanded had become his family, the fortress where the headquarters were his home and the songs sung by the soldiers his only pleasure. He was a man for whom everything that was not the Caucasus was beneath contempt and almost inconceivable. He really thought that everything that was the Caucasus was divided into halves – 'ours' and 'theirs'. He loved the first and hated the second with all his heart. Above all, he was a coolly courageous, battle-hardened soldier, exceptionally kind to his comrades and inferiors, but dreadfully brusque and even downright rude towards adjutants and 'Bonjours', whom he detested for some reason. As he entered the straw hut he nearly put his head through the roof, suddenly sank down and sat on the ground.

'Well, what's new?' he asked, suddenly stopping when he saw my unfamiliar face and fixing his dull, staring eyes on me.

'What were you talking about?' the major asked, taking out his watch and looking at it, although I was quite sure there was no need to do this.

'Well, this gentleman's been asking why I'm serving here.'

'Nikolai obviously wants to distinguish himself and then make tracks for home.'

'Come on, Abram Ilich, you tell us why you want to serve in the Caucasus.'

'Firstly, you know, because each of us must do his duty . . . *What?*' he added, although no one had said anything. 'Yesterday I had a letter from Russia, Nikolai Fyodorych,' he continued, obviously wanting to change the subject. 'They write that . . . well, they ask such peculiar questions.'

'What kind of questions?' asked Bolkhov.

He burst out laughing.

'Very strange questions . . . They ask if there can be jealousy without love . . . *What?*' he asked, looking at all of us.

'You don't say!' Bolkhov laughed.

'Yes, you know life is good in Russia,' he went on, as if everything he said followed quite logically from the previous remark. 'In 1852, when I was in Tambov, everyone received me as if I was the Tsar's aide-de-camp. Would you believe it – at the governor's ball – I was given a very warm reception when I went in. The governor's wife

herself, you know, talked to me and asked about the Caucasus, and
they were all so . . . I don't know what . . . They looked at my gold
sabre as if it were some rarity and asked why I had been awarded it –
and the Order of Anna and the Vladimir, and I told them . . . *What*?
That's what the Caucasus is good for, Nikolai Fyodorych!' he continued, without waiting for a reply. 'In Russia they have a high opinion
of us Caucasians. A young man, you know, a staff officer with the
Orders of Anna and Vladimir – it all carries a lot of weight in Russia
. . . *What*?'

'I really think you did a little bit of boasting there, Abram Ilich!'
Bolkhov said.

'Hee-hee!' Kirsanov laughed his stupid laugh. 'It was necessary,
you know! How superbly I dined for those two months!'

'So, life is good up north in Russia, is it?' Trosenko asked, as if he
were talking about China or Japan.

'I should say so! When I think of the champagne we drank in those
two months – gallons of the stuff!'

'Come off it! It was probably lemonade,' Trosenko said. 'Now I'd
have shown them how we can knock it back here and made myself
famous! I'd have showed them – eh, Bolkhov?'

'But *you've* been in the Caucasus more than ten years, old man,'
Bolkhov said. 'And you remember what Yermolov* said. Abram
Ilich has been here only six – . . .'

'I'll give you ten – it will soon be sixteen!'

'Bolkhov, let's have some sage-vodka. Brrr! It's damp in here!' he
added, smiling. 'Let's have a drink, Major!'

But the major, already unhappy with the way the old captain had
first addressed him, now winced visibly and sought refuge in his own
grandeur. He hummed something as he again looked at his watch.

'So, I'll never go back there,' Trosenko continued, ignoring the
frowning major. 'What's more, I've lost the habit of walking and
speaking as they do in Russia. They'd ask, "What kind of freak is
this? Something that blew in from Asia!" Isn't that so, Nikolai
Fyodorych? And what is there for me in Russia? Anyway, some day
I'll be shot here and then they'll ask, "Where's old Trosenko?" "Shot,"

---

* A.P. Yermolov – Russian general, commander-in-chief in Georgia and
before that in command of a corps in the Caucasus.

will be the answer. And what would you do with the Eighth Company then, eh?' he added, addressing all these remarks to the major.

'Send the battalion officer on duty!' Kirsanov shouted, without replying to the captain, although once again I was convinced that there was no need for any orders.

'As for you, young man, I bet you're pleased to be on double pay now,' the major told the adjutant after a few minutes' silence.

'Yes, sir. Very pleased.'

'I think the pay's very good these days, Nikolai Fyodorych,' he continued. 'A young man can live quite decently on it and even permit himself a few small luxuries.'

'No, Abram Ilich!' the adjutant replied timidly. 'Although it's double I can only just make ends meet . . . One has to keep a horse . . .'

'What's this you're telling me, young man? I was an ensign once myself and *I* know. Believe me, you can live very well on it. Go on, add it up,' he said, crooking the little finger of his left hand.

'We're always paid in advance, so that's all you need to count,' Trosenko commented, emptying a glass of vodka.

'That may well be . . . but . . . *What?*'

Just then a head with white hair and a flat nose poked through an opening in the hut and a shrill voice said in a German accent, 'Are you there, Abram Ilich? The duty officer's looking for you.'

'Come in, Kraft,' Bolkhov said.

A tall figure wearing a general staff officer's coat squeezed through the door and shook everyone's hand with the utmost fervour. 'Ah, my dear Captain, so you're here too,' he said, turning to Trosenko.

In spite of the gloom the new guest managed to find his way over to him and, to the captain's extreme amazement and displeasure (or so it seemed to me), kissed him on the lips.

'Just a German trying to be a really good chap,' I thought.

12

My assumption was immediately confirmed. Captain Kraft asked for vodka and gave a dreadful grunt as he tossed back his head and emptied the glass.

'Well, gentlemen, we had a very pleasant outing today, cavorting over the plains of Chechnya,' he began, but when he spotted the duty officer he immediately stopped so that the major could give his orders.

'Did you go round the lines?'

'Yes, sir.'

'Have the listening-posts been set up?'

'Yes, sir.'

'Then go and order the company commanders to be on the alert.'

'Yes, sir.'

The major screwed up his eyes and thought deeply.

'And tell the men they can make their porridge now.'

'They already are.'

'Good. You may go.'

Turning to us with a condescending smile, the major continued, 'Well, now, we were trying to work out how much an officer needs. Let's see. There's your uniform and a pair of trousers – right?'

'Yes, sir.'

'Let's say that comes to fifty roubles over two years, which makes twenty-five per annum on clothes. Then about fifty copecks a day for food – right?'

'Perhaps not as much as that.'

'Well, let's just suppose, for the moment. You need thirty roubles for a horse, there's saddle repairs – that's all. So, that makes twenty-five, plus one hundred and twenty, plus thirty – one hundred and seventy-five. So you're left with about twenty for luxuries such as tea, sugar, tobacco. There – do you see? Aren't I right, Nikolai Fyodorych?'

'I'm afraid not, Abram Ilich!' the adjutant timidly replied. 'You wouldn't have enough for tea or sugar. You can reckon a uniform will last you two years, but with all these campaigns you'll never have enough trousers to see you through. And what about boots? I wear out a pair almost every month. Then there's underclothes, shirts, towels, leggings – all that has to be paid for, sir. Add it up and you'll find you won't have a copeck left. It's true, Abram Ilich!'

'Yes, it's lovely wearing leggings,' Kraft suddenly remarked after a minute's silence, pronouncing 'leggings' with particular affection. 'All this is so very Russian!'

'Let me tell you,' Trosenko said, 'however you add it up you'll find that we should all really be starving. But in actual fact we manage to survive, smoke our tobacco and drink our vodka. If you've been serving in the army as long as I have,' he continued, turning to the ensign, 'then you'll learn how to get by. Do you know how this officer treats his batman, gentlemen?'

Trosenko almost died with laughter as he told us the whole story of the ensign and his batman, although we had heard it a thousand times.

'And why are you sitting there looking like a rose-bud, old chap?' he continued, still addressing his remarks to the ensign who could not stop blushing, sweating and smiling – so much so, one felt really sorry for him. 'Don't worry, lad, I was like you once, but you can see for yourself what a fine fellow I am now! When those young hotheads first come here from Russia – we know their sort all right – they get spasms and rheumatism. But here am I, snug as a bug. This place is my house, my bed – *everything*! You see . . .'

He downed another glass of vodka.

'*What*?' he said, staring right into Kraft's eyes.

'Now there's a man I respect! A real Caucasian! Allow me to shake your hand.' Kraft pushed us all aside as he made his way over to Trosenko, grasped his hand and shook it with deep feeling.

'Yes, we can rightly say we've gone through everything here,' he continued. 'In '45 – yes, you were there, Captain, weren't you? Do you remember the night of the twelfth, when we were knee-deep in mud and then attacked the enemy next morning? In those days I was attached to the commander-in-chief and we captured twenty enemy positions in one day. Do you remember, Captain?'

Trosenko nodded, stuck out his lower lip and screwed up his eyes.

'You see,' Kraft went on, extremely excited and making quite inappropriate gestures as he turned to the major. But the major, who must have heard the story many times, suddenly gave the other such a dull, glazed look that Kraft turned away and addressed Bolkhov and me, looking at each of us in turn. He did not look at Trosenko once during the whole narrative.

'So you see, when we came out that morning the commander-in-chief told me, "Kraft! Capture those barricades!" Well, you know how it is in the army – no arguing. You salute and get on with it. "Yes, Your Excellency!" I said – and off I went. The moment we reached the first defences I turned round and told my men, "Now lads, no retreating. Keep your eyes open. If anyone lags behind I'll chop him to pieces myself!" Well, you can't mince words with Russian soldiers. And then, suddenly, a shell landed . . . and I could see one soldier, a second, a third . . . then bullets . . . Eeee-eeee-eeee! I called out, "Come on lads, follow me!" But the moment we got there I saw a . . . you know what it's called . . .?' At this point the narrator waved his arms as he tried to find the right word.

'A ditch?' Bolkhov ventured.

'No . . . Ach, what on earth is it called? Why yes . . . a ditch!' he said quickly. 'So, rifles at the ready . . . Hoorah! Ta-ra-ta-ta! But there wasn't a soul to be seen. We were all surprised, you know. So far so good! On we went towards the second position. Now, that was quite a different proposition. All of us were burning for action! We moved closer, you know, and I took a good look at the second position and saw it was impossible to go on – there was a . . . what do you call it? Ach, what's it called?'

'Another ditch?' I suggested.

'No, nothing like it,' he continued irritably. 'No, not a ditch . . . oh, what do you call it?' And he made an inane gesture with his hand. 'Ach, what on earth is it called?'

He was obviously suffering so much that one could not help prompting him.

'A river, perhaps?' Bolkhov said.

'No, just a ditch. We were about to go over when, would you believe it, they opened up with such intense fire it was sheer hell!'

At that moment someone outside the hut asked for me. It was Maximov. As I had heard the eventful story before and knew that there were still thirteen barricades to go, I eagerly seized the opportunity of returning to my platoon. Trosenko came out with me.

'What a load of rot,' he said when we were a few yards from the hut. 'He was never anywhere near any barricades,' he added, laughing so heartily that I too had to laugh.

13

The dark night had closed in and only dim bonfires lit the camp when I finished my duties and went off to join my men. A large stump was smouldering on the coals and only three soldiers were sitting around it: Antonov, who was turning a tin of riabko* on the fire; Zhdanov, who was pensively raking the embers with a long dry branch; and Chikin with his pipe that was always out. The others had already lain down to sleep, some under the ammunition-wagons, some in the hay, some by the fires. In the feeble light of the coals I could distinguish familiar backs, legs, heads. Among those around the fire was the young recruit who lay very close and seemed asleep already. The all-pervading smell of mist and the smoke from the damp firewood made my eyes smart and the same fine drizzle fell from the dreary sky.

Near by could be heard the regular sound of snoring, the crackle of twigs in the fire, soft voices and the occasional rattle of infantry rifles. All around fires were burning, lighting up the dark shapes of the soldiers within a small radius. Just by the nearest fires, where the light was strongest, I could make out the bare figures of soldiers waving their shirts right over the flames. Many soldiers were still awake, moving around and talking within an area of about sixty square yards. But that melancholy, deathly night lent a peculiar, mysterious air to every movement, as if the men were affected by the dismal silence and were afraid to disturb its peace and harmony. Whenever I spoke I felt that my voice sounded different and I could read the same mood on the face of every soldier sitting by the fire. Before I arrived I thought that they had been discussing their wounded comrade. Not a bit of it: Chikin was telling everyone about receiving goods in Tiflis and about the schoolboys there.

Everywhere I have been, and especially the Caucasus, I have always noted the peculiar tact shown by the Russian soldier who, in times of danger, passes over in silence anything that could have a bad effect on his comrades' morale. The spirit of the Russian soldier, unlike that of southern nations, is not based on easily inflammable but rapidly waning enthusiasm: it is as difficult to rouse him to action as to demoralize him. He needs no special effects – speeches, war-cries, songs or drums. On the contrary: he needs order, and calm, and a complete lack of pressure. In the Russian – the *true* Russian – soldier, one will never encounter boasting, any kind of bravado or

* Soldier's food of soaked rusks and lard. [*Tolstoy*]

the desire to stupefy or excite himself in times of danger. On the contrary: humility, modesty and the ability to see in danger something quite different from danger are the distinctive features of his character. I once saw a soldier with a leg wound, whose first thoughts were of the hole in his sheepskin coat, and a cavalryman who crawled out from under his horse that had just been killed and unbuckled the girths to save the saddle. Who can ever forget that incident during the siege of Gergebil, when the fuse of a live bomb caught fire in a laboratory and the gun-sergeant ordered two soldiers to run and throw it into a ravine. But they did not get rid of it at the nearest point, which was just by the colonel's tent, on the edge of the ravine, but ran further away with it lest they wake the gentlemen asleep in the tent and as a result were both blown to bits. I can still remember the time when, during the campaign of 1852 a young soldier happened to comment, during some action, that the platoon didn't have a hope in hell of getting out alive, whereupon the entire platoon furiously attacked him for such a cowardly remark, which they could not even bring themselves to repeat. And now, when everyone's thoughts must have been of Velenchuk, when Tartars might creep up on us and fire a volley any moment, everyone listened to Chikin's lively tale and no one mentioned either the day's action, or the impending danger, or the wounded comrade, just as if it had all happened God knows how long ago, or not at all. But it did strike me that their faces were somewhat gloomier than usual: they did not pay much attention to Chikin's story and even Chikin felt that they were not listening. All the same, he carried on.

Maximov came over to the fire and sat beside me. Chikin made room for him, stopped talking and started sucking his pipe again.

'The infantry have sent to the camp for some vodka,' Maximov said after a rather long silence. 'The sergeant said that he saw our Velenchuk there.'

'Well, is he alive?' Antonov asked, turning his mess-tin.

'No, he died.'

The young recruit suddenly raised his small head with its red cap above the fire, stared at Maximov and me for a minute or so and then quickly lowered it again and wrapped himself tighter in his greatcoat.

'So, you see, death didn't call on him for nothing this morning

33

when I had to wake him up in the artillery-park,' Antonov remarked.

'Rubbish!' Zhdanov retorted, turning a smouldering log; everyone fell silent.

Amidst the general silence a shot rang out behind us in the camp. Our drummers replied by beating the tattoo. When the last drum rolls had died away, Zhdanov was first to get to his feet and take off his cap.

We all followed his example.

A harmonious chorus of manly voices echoed in the deep silence of the night.

'Our father, which art in heaven, hallowed be Thy name. Thy kingdom come. Thy will be done on earth, as it is in heaven. Give us this day our daily bread and forgive us our debts as we forgive our debtors. Lead us not into temptation, but deliver us from evil . . .'

'In '45 a soldier was struck by a shell just here,' Antonov said after we had put our caps on and sat down again by the fire. 'We carted him around for two days on a gun-carriage – do you remember Shevchenko, Zhdanov? . . . and then we had to leave him under that tree over there.'

Just then an infantryman with enormous side-whiskers and a moustache, carrying a rifle and cartridges pouch, came over to our fire.

'Give us a light for my pipe, lads,' he asked.

'Help yourself, there's plenty of fire!' Chikin said.

'I suppose it's Dargo* you're talking about?' the infantryman asked Antonov.

'Yes, Dargo in '45,' Antonov replied.

The infantryman shook his head, screwed up his eyes and squatted beside us.

'Yes, we had a rough time of it there,' he remarked.

'Why did you leave him?' I asked Antonov.

'He was suffering terribly from a stomach wound. Whenever we stopped he was all right, but he screamed his head off the moment we moved. He begged us to leave him, but we didn't have the heart.

---

* A mountain stronghold captured by Count Vorontsov, Viceroy of the Caucasus, in 1845. It was the scene of fierce fighting.

Well, then *they* started letting us have it. Three of our gun crew were killed and one of the officers, and somehow we got cut off from our battery. We were in a right mess and didn't think we'd ever get our guns out, what with all that mud.'

'It was muddiest of all by the Indian Mountain,' a soldier said.

'Yes, that's where he got worse. Anoshenko – the old gun-sergeant – and me thought about it and decided he didn't have a dog's chance of getting out of it alive and he kept begging us in God's name to leave him there. So that's what we did. There was a tree, a kind of willow. We put some soaked rusks down in front of him – Zhdanov had a few – propped him up against that tree there, put a clean shirt on him, said a proper goodbye and left him.'

'Was he much of a soldier?'

'He was all right,' Zhdanov said.

'God only knows what became of him,' Antonov continued. 'We lost a lot of our lads there.'

'At Dargo?' the infantryman asked, rising to his feet, scraping his pipe and again screwing up his eyes and shaking his head. 'It was really tough.' And he walked away.

'Were there many from our battery at Dargo?' I asked.

'Oh yes, Zhdanov was there, myself, Patsan, who's on leave just now, and about another six – no more.'

'Has old Patsan gone on a spree? He's been away for so long now,' Chikin said, stretching his legs and laying his head on a log. 'I reckon he's been gone nearly a year now.'

'And what about you – have you had your year's leave yet?' I asked Zhdanov.

'No, not yet,' he replied reluctantly.

'But it's good to go, you know,' Antonov said. 'If you're from a rich family, or if you're able to work, it's good to go. Everyone at home's usually so pleased to see you.'

'But what if you have two brothers, like me?' Zhdanov continued. 'They have to worry about finding enough food for themselves without having to feed a soldier as well. You can't be much good after twenty-five years in the army. And who knows if they're still alive?'

'Didn't you write to them?' I asked.

'Of course I did. I sent two letters but didn't get a reply. Either

35

they're dead or they don't write because they're living from hand to mouth themselves. So what can I do?'

'Was it long ago that you wrote?'

'The last time was when I came back from Dargo. Come on, sing us "The Little Birch Tree,"' Zhdanov asked Antonov who was sitting with his elbows on his knees, humming some tune. Antonov started singing.

'It's Grandpa Zhdanov's favourite song,' Chikin whispered to me, tugging at my coat. 'Sometimes, when Filip Antonych sings it, he fair cries his heart out.'

At first Zhdanov sat quite still, his eyes fixed on the smouldering coals and his face extremely gloomy in the reddish glow. Then his jaws started moving faster and faster beneath the ears and finally he got up, spread his coat out and lay down in the shadows behind the fire. It was either his tossing and groaning as he settled down to sleep, or it may have been the effect of Velenchuk's death and the miserable weather on me, but I really had the impression he was crying.

The bottom of the stump that had now turned to charcoal occasionally flared up, illuminating Antonov's figure with his grey whiskers, red face and medals on the coat slung over his shoulders, or someone's boots, head or back. The same mournful drizzle was falling and that same smell of damp and smoke was in the air. All around I could see the bright dots of dying camp-fires and the plaintive sounds of Antonov's song broke the general silence. Whenever he stopped for a moment the faint, nocturnal noises of the camp – the snoring, the clash of sentries' rifles and those soft voices – seemed to take up the tune.

'Second watch! Makatyuk and Zhdanov!' shouted Maximov.

Antonov stopped singing, Zhdanov got up, sighed, stepped across a log and slowly made his way to the guns.

[15 June 1855]

TWO HUSSARS

A TALE DEDICATED TO COUNTESS M.N. TOLSTOY

... for ever Jominy, Jominy,
But never a mention of vodka ...
– Denis Davydov*

In the early nineteenth century, when there were no railways or metalled roads, no gaslight or stearin candles, no low, spring-cushioned couches or unvarnished furniture, no disenchanted young men with monocles or liberal-minded women philosophers, no sweet *dames aux camélias* who have become so plentiful of late – in those naïve times, when anyone making the journey from Moscow to St Petersburg by carriage or coach would take a whole kitchenful of home-cooked provisions and travel for eight days and nights along soft, dusty or muddy roads and put his trust in fried cutlets, hard rolls and sleigh-bells; when, during long autumn evenings, tallow candles that provided light for family groups of twenty or thirty burned low and had to be snuffed; when ballrooms were lit by candelabra with fine wax or spermaceti candles; when furniture was arranged symmetrically; when our fathers were still young and proved it not only by the absence of grey hairs or wrinkles but by the duels they fought over ladies and the speed with which they rushed from one end of a room to the other to pick up a tiny handkerchief dropped accidentally or on purpose; when our mothers wore short-waisted gowns with enormous sleeves and decided all family disputes by drawing lots; when charming *dames aux camélias* shunned the light of day – in those naïve times of masonic lodges, Martinists,† the

---

* H. Jomini (1779–1869), French general, writer on theory of military tactics. The lines are from Denis Davydov's 'Song of an Old Hussar'. Davydov was a very popular soldier in the Napoleonic wars, well known for his spirited verses in praise of reckless valour, both on the battlefield and off it. He was highly regarded by Pushkin.

† A sect of mystics, founded in the eighteenth century.

Tugendbund,* Miloradovich,† Davydov and Pushkin, a group of landowners gathered in the provincial town of K— and the election of representatives of the nobility was almost completed.

I

'All right, the public lounge will do,' said a young officer in fur coat and hussar cap who had just stepped out of a post-sledge and entered the best hotel the town of K— had to offer.

'It's a large gathering this year, Your Excellency,' said the hotel boots who had already managed to find out from the batman that it was Count Turbin, which was why he called him 'Your Excellency'. 'The lady who owns the Afremovo estate has promised to leave with her daughters this evening, so I can let you have number eleven as soon as it's free, sir,' he added, walking softly down the corridor in front of the count and continually glancing back.

In the lounge, around a small table beneath a time-blackened, full-length portrait of Alexander I, several men – most probably local gentry – were sitting drinking champagne; on the other side of the room were some travelling merchants in their dark blue, fur-lined coats.

After entering the lounge and summoning Blücher, the huge grey mastiff he had brought with him, the count threw off his coat (the collar of which was still white with hoar-frost), ordered vodka, sat down at the table in his blue satin tunic and got into conversation with the gentlemen. They were instantly impressed by his handsome, open face and offered him a glass of champagne. The count first downed his vodka and then ordered another bottle of champagne for his new acquaintances. At this point in came the sleigh-driver for his tip.

'Sashka!' the count shouted. 'Give him something!'

The driver went out with Sashka and soon returned with some money in his hand.

'What's this, Yer Excellency? You know how I bent over backwards to please Yer Honour! You promised me a half-rouble and all he gives me is a measly quarter!'

---

* 'Union of Virtue' – an anti-Napoleonic Prussian political society founded in 1808.

† M.A. Miloradovich (1771–1825) – Russian general who took part in the Napoleonic wars.

'Give him a rouble then, Sashka!'

Sashka scowled at the driver's boots. 'He's had enough,' he grumbled in a deep voice. 'Besides, I don't have any more.'

The count took two five-rouble notes from his wallet, which was all it contained, and handed one to the driver, who kissed his hand and left.

'A fine thing! Now I'm down to my last five roubles!'

'Done like a true hussar, Count!' one of the gentlemen said with a smile. From his moustache, his voice and a certain energy about his leg movements he was obviously a retired cavalry officer. 'Do you intend staying long, Count?' he asked.

'If I didn't need money I wouldn't be staying at all. And they don't even have a room ready, blast them, in this damned pot-house!'

'Please, Count. Will you do me the honour of sharing with me?' asked the cavalry officer. 'I'm in number seven. I mean to say, if you can put up with me for one night. But you should really stay three days. The Marshal of the Nobility is giving a ball tonight. He'd be absolutely delighted to see you.'

'Yes, Count, please do stay,' joined in another of the company, a handsome young man. 'What's the hurry? After all, it's only once every three years – the elections, I mean. You might at least cast your eye over our young ladies, Count.'

'Sashka! Get me some clean linen, I'm going to have a bath,' the count said, getting up. 'And then we'll see. Perhaps I will drop in on the marshal.'

Then he called the waiter over and told him something that made him grin and reply, 'All that can be arranged, sir', and left.

'So, my dear young sir, I'll have my trunk taken up to your room,' the count shouted from the corridor.

'Please! It would make me so happy!' the cavalry officer replied, running to the door. 'Number seven – don't forget!'

When the count's footsteps died away, the cavalry officer returned to the table, drew his chair closer to the civil servant who was sitting next to him, smiled right into his face and said, 'Yes, that's the man himself!'

'You don't say!'

'I'm telling you it is! It's Count Turbin, the famous duelling hussar. I bet you anything you like he recognized me. I'm sure of it. When I was down in Lebedyan for remounts, the two of us went on a spree that lasted three weeks – and without a break! But something he and I got up to there explains why he's pretending not to recognize me. A fine fellow, eh?'

'Oh yes, a very fine fellow. And he has such a pleasant manner,' the handsome young man replied. 'You'd never guess he was the type to . . . But how quickly we hit it off – did you see? He can't be more than twenty-five, can he?'

'No, he doesn't look it, but in fact he's older. But let me tell you more about him. Who ran off with Mrs Migunov? Why, he did. *He* killed Sablin, dropped Matnyov out of the window by his legs, won three hundred thousand roubles off Prince Nesterov. You've no idea what a wild character he is! Gambler, duellist, seducer. He has the soul of a true hussar – he's a perfect jewel of a man! I know that we in the cavalry have a bad reputation, but if only people knew what hussars are really like. Oh, those were the days!'

And the cavalry officer launched into an account of such wild drinking bouts in Lebedyan with the count that not only never happened, but which could not possibly have happened. They could not have happened firstly, because the officer had never set eyes on the count before and had retired from the army two years before the count had joined it; and secondly, because the cavalry officer had never in fact served in the cavalry, but for four years had been the humblest of cadets with the Belevsky Regiment and had resigned the moment he was promoted to ensign. Ten years before, however, he had come into some money and really did make the trip to Lebedyan, where he squandered seven hundred roubles with some officers who were there for remounts. Intending to join the uhlans,* he had even had a uniform made, complete with orange facings. The three weeks spent with the remount officers at Lebedyan (together with his passionate desire to join the uhlans) were the happiest, brightest time of his life and consequently he transformed what was merely a longing into something real, then into a fond memory, so that eventually he became firmly convinced of a past career in the cavalry. None of this, however, prevented him from being, in honesty and gentleness, the most worthy of men.

'Yes, only those who have served in the cavalry will ever

* Uhlan – a cavalryman armed with a lance.

understand us,' he continued, straddling his chair and thrusting out his lower jaw. 'I'd be riding at the head of my squadron on a steed more like the Devil incarnate than a horse – how it used to try and throw me off! And I'd ride it like the devil too. Over would come the squadron commander to take the review. "Lieutenant," he'd say, "we can't manage without you, please lead the squadron on parade." "Certainly, sir," I'd reply – and no sooner said than done. I'd wheel round and shout the order to my mustachioed troopers. Oh God, those were the days!'

The count returned from the bath-house, red-faced and with wet hair. He went straight to room seven, where the cavalry officer was already sitting in his dressing-gown, smoking his pipe and contemplating his good luck in being able to share a room with the famous Turbin with mixed feelings of delight and apprehension. 'What if he suddenly decides to strip me, drive me out of town and dump me naked in the snow . . . or smear me with tar . . . or simply . . .? No, he wouldn't treat a fellow officer like that,' he reassured himself.

'Sashka, feed Blücher!' shouted the count.

Sashka, who had drunk a large glass of vodka to warm himself after the journey and was decidedly tipsy, came in.

'So, you couldn't wait, you drunken pig! . . . Now, feed Blücher!'

'He won't starve, just look how sleek he is,' Sashka replied, stroking the dog.

'Don't answer back! Now, go and feed him.'

'All you care about is feeding your dog, but when a man has his glass of vodka you start shouting at him.'

'Mind, or I'll smash your face in!' shouted the count in a voice that made the window-panes rattle and even scared the cavalry officer a bit.

'You might at least ask if your Sashka's had anything to eat today. Go on, smash my face in if you think more of your dog than your batman,' Sashka muttered. But just then the count struck him such a fierce blow in the face with his fist that he fell and hit his head against the wall. Then, clutching his nose, he leapt to his feet, rushed out and collapsed on to a trunk outside in the corridor.

'He's gone and knocked my teeth out!' Sashka groaned, wiping his bloody nose with one hand and at the same time scratching the back of Blücher (who was licking himself) with the other. 'He's knocked my teeth out, Blücher old pal. But he's still *my* count and I'd go through fire and water for him. Oh yes I would! Because he's *my* count. Do you understand, Blücher? Now, do you want your supper?'

After lying still for a few minutes he got up and fed the dog. Then, having sobered up somewhat, he went off to wait on his count and offer him some tea.

'I should be most offended,' the cavalry officer was saying rather sheepishly as he stood before the count, who was lying on the other's bed with his legs up on the partition. 'After all, I'm an old campaigner and fellow officer myself, if I may say so. Why should you borrow from someone else when I'd be only too pleased to lend you two hundred roubles? I don't have all that much at the moment – only a hundred – but I'll get hold of the rest later on. I'd be most offended, Count.'

'Thanks, old man,' the count said, immediately divining the kind of relationship that was to be established between them and slapping him on the back. 'Thanks. Well now, let's go to the ball if that's all there is. What shall we do in the meantime? Tell me what this town has to offer. Pretty girls? Rakes? Card players?'

The cavalry officer explained that there would be scores of pretty girls at the ball; that the most inveterate rake was Kolkov, the newly elected police chief – although he did not have the reckless daring of a true hussar he was still a very good chap; that the Ilyushkin Gypsy Chorus had been performing in town since the elections started, with Steshka as leading singer and that simply *everyone* was planning to go and hear them after the ball.

'And you can get quite a decent game of cards here too,' he said. 'There's that rich Lukhnov who's just passing through and who never stops playing, and in number eight there's Ilin, an uhlan cornet who's been losing heavily. They've already started and they play every evening. What a wonderful person that Ilin is, Count! He's so generous he'd give you the shirt off his back.'

'Let's go to his room then and see what kind of crowd they are,' the count said.

'Yes, let's go. They'll be awfully pleased!'

2

Ilin, the uhlan cornet, had not long been awake. The evening before he had sat down at the card-table at eight o'clock and played for fifteen hours non-stop, until eleven the next morning. He had lost heavily, but had no idea exactly how much, since he had three thousand roubles of his own, plus fifteen thousand in regimental funds which had long since got mixed up with his own and which he was afraid to count in case his fears that he might have lost some of the latter were realized. It was almost noon when he had fallen into that deep, dreamless sleep which comes only to the very young, and after a heavy loss. When he woke at six in the evening – the exact time of the count's arrival – and saw the cards and bits of chalk scattered over the floor, and those soiled tables in the middle of the room, he remembered with horror last night's game – and the last card in particular, a knave, on which he had lost five hundred roubles. However, still unwilling to accept the grim reality of the situation, he took the money from under the pillow and started counting it. He recognized several notes that had passed from hand to hand in 'corners' and 'transports' several times, and this reminded him of the whole course of the game.* His own three thousand roubles were gone, together with two and a half thousand of the regimental funds.

This uhlan had been playing for four nights running. He was on his way from Moscow, where he had been entrusted with the regimental funds, but had been delayed in the town of K— by the posting-stage keeper on the pretext that there were no fresh horses, whereas in fact the keeper had a long-standing secret arrangement with the hotel proprietor that all travellers were to be delayed for one day. The uhlan, a cheerful young lad who had just been given three thousand roubles by his parents in Moscow to equip himself for his new regiment, was only too pleased of the chance of spending a few days in K— during the elections and was looking forward to a thoroughly good time there. One of the local landowners, a family man, was a friend of his and he was about to drive out to his place so

---

* The game is *shtos*. If a player turned down a corner of a card he increased his stake two or three times.

that he could flirt with his daughters when the cavalry officer turned up and introduced himself. That same evening, with no ill intention, the officer had introduced him to his friend Lukhnov and some of the other card players in the public lounge. From then on the uhlan was constantly at the card-table. As a result he not only forgot all about visiting his friend, but did not even inquire about the horses. In fact, he had not left his room for four days.

As soon as he was dressed and had some tea he went over to the window. A little stroll, he felt, might help him forget those persistent memories of the card-table, so he put on his greatcoat and went out into the street. The sun was already hidden behind the red-roofed, white houses; twilight was drawing in. It was mild for the time of year and large wet snowflakes were softly falling on the muddy streets. Suddenly the thought that he had slept through practically the whole of that day, which was now ending, depressed him deeply. 'This day which is now past can never be recovered,' he reflected.

And then he told himself, 'I've wasted my youth' – not because he thought for one moment that this was so – the question had never entered his mind – but because the phrase suddenly crossed his mind for no particular reason.

'What am I going to do now?' he wondered. 'Borrow from someone and then go away?' A lady passed him on the pavement. 'What a stupid-looking woman!' he thought. 'There's no one to borrow from. I've wasted my youth.' He approached a row of shops where a shopkeeper was standing at his door in his fox-fur coat trying to attract customers. 'If I hadn't withdrawn that eight I'd have recouped my losses.' An old beggar-woman followed him, whimpering. 'There's no one to borrow from,' he thought once more. A gentleman in a bearskin coat drove past, then he saw a watchman standing at his post. 'How could I create a sensation here? Fire at them? No, that's too boring! I've wasted my youth. Oh, just look at those superb horse trappings over there! What wouldn't I give for a troika ride! Gee up, my beauties! Well, I think I'll go back to the hotel now, Lukhnov will be coming soon and then we can start playing.'

So he returned to the hotel and counted his money again. No, he had made no mistake the first time: two and a half thousand roubles in regimental funds were missing. 'I'll stake twenty-five on the first card, then make a "corner" on the second . . . then seven times the stake, then fifteen, thirty, sixty times . . . up to three thousand. Then I'll buy those horse-collars and leave. But that devil won't let me win! I've wasted my youth . . .'

These thoughts were passing through the uhlan's mind when Lukhnov came into his room.

'Have you been up long, Mikhailo?' asked Lukhnov, slowly removing his gold spectacles from his bony nose and studiously wiping them on his red silk handkerchief.

'No, I've only just got up. I slept beautifully.'

'Some hussar or other's arrived. He's staying with Zavalshevsky . . . haven't you heard?'

'No, I haven't . . . so where are the others?'

'I think they've gone to Pryakhin's. They won't be long.'

And sure enough the others soon arrived: the garrison officer, Lukhnov's perpetual companion; a Greek merchant with an enormous brown hooked nose and deep-set black eyes; a fat, puffy landowner who owned a distillery and who played all night long, always for half-rouble points. Everyone was eager to start, but nothing was said on the subject by the principal players, particularly Lukhnov, who very casually started discussing street crime in Moscow.

'Just think of it,' he said. 'In a city like Moscow ruffians dressed up as devils go around at night with hooks in their hands terrifying the stupid rabble and robbing passers-by. Nothing is done about it. What are the police supposed to be doing? – that's what puzzles me.'

The uhlan listened attentively to the account of lawlessness in Moscow, but the moment it was finished he stood up and quietly ordered the cards. The fat landowner was first to put his wishes into words. 'Well, gentlemen, we're wasting precious time. Let's get down to business,' he said.

'Yes, after all that lot you won last night I'm not surprised you're so eager,' the Greek said.

'Really, it's time we started,' the garrison officer said.

Ilin glanced at Lukhnov, who looked him in the eye and calmly continued his account of those ruffians dressed up as devils with claws.

'Will you be banker?' the uhlan asked.

'Isn't it too early?'

'Belov!' shouted the uhlan, blushing for some reason. 'Bring me some supper . . . I haven't had anything to eat, gentlemen . . . and a bottle of champagne and the cards.'

Just then the count entered with Zavalshevsky. It turned out that Turbin and Ilin were from the same division. They immediately hit it off, clinked glasses and within five minutes were chatting away like old friends. The count had taken a great liking to Ilin and he smiled as he watched him, teasing him for being so young.

'There's a fine dashing young uhlan for you!' he said. 'And what whiskers! So fierce!'

The down on Ilin's upper lip was perfectly white.

'So, you're about to start, are you?' the count asked. 'Well, I hope you win, Ilin. I should think you're an expert,' he added, smiling.

'Yes, they're ready now,' Lukhnov replied, tearing open a pack of cards. 'Wouldn't you care to join us, Count?'

'Not for the moment. I'd thrash the lot of you! I can make any bank crack wide open, the way I play! But I've no money just now, I lost all I had at the posting-stage near Volochok, where I was cleaned out by some damned infantryman with rings on his fingers. He must have been a sharper.'

'So you had to wait there a long time?' Ilin asked.

'Twenty-two hours. I shan't forget that damned place in a hurry! But the keeper won't forget me either!'

'How's that?'

'Well, I drive up and out rushes the keeper with his crafty thieving mug. "We've no horses," he tells me. Now, I have a golden rule: if I'm told there's no horses I never take my coat off, but go straight to the keeper's parlour – not the public room but the keeper's own parlour – and I order all the doors and windows to be opened wide, as if the room was full of stove fumes. Well, that's what I did on this occasion. And was it cold! You remember the frosts we had last month, about twenty below? Well, the keeper starts arguing, so I give him one on the nose. Then along comes some old crone, and some other women and young girls, and they start yelling their heads off, grab their pots and pans and want to run off to the village . . . But I stand right in the doorway and tell them, "If you give me some horses I'll leave you in peace. If not, I'll keep you in here and let you all freeze to death!"'

'Brilliant – that's the way to deal with their sort!' the fat landowner said, roaring with laughter. 'That's how they freeze cockroaches out.'

'But I wasn't careful enough – I only went out for a moment and the keeper and the women gave me the slip. So my only hostage was the old crone lying over the stove. And she started sneezing her head off and saying her prayers. Then we started negotiations. Up comes the keeper and tries to persuade me – keeping his distance – to let the old girl go. But I set Blücher on him – he makes short work of station-keepers does Blücher! But for all that, the swine still didn't give me any horses until the morning. In the meantime that lousy infantry officer turned up and I went into the other room and started playing. Have you seen Blücher anywhere . . .? Blücher . . . here, boy.' Blücher came rushing in. The card players paid him token attention, but it was obvious that their minds were on something quite different.

'Why don't you start, gentlemen?' Turbin asked. 'Don't mind me . . . I'm an old windbag! Cards are cards, there's no getting away from it.'

3

Lukhnov drew two candles nearer himself and took out a huge brown wallet stuffed with banknotes. Then, very slowly, as if performing some sacred rite, he opened it, pulled out two one-hundred rouble notes and placed them under the cards. 'Two hundred for the bank, same as yesterday,' he said, adjusting his spectacles and unsealing a fresh pack.

'Good,' Ilin said without looking at him and continuing his conversation with Turbin.

The game started. Lukhnov dealt with machine-like precision, occasionally stopping unhurriedly to record a point, or peering sternly over his spectacles and saying in a weak voice, 'You lead!'

The fat landowner spoke louder than anyone, audibly conferring with himself and wetting his podgy fingers when he turned down the corner of a card. The garrison officer silently noted the points in his neat hand and slightly turned down the corners of his cards under the table. The Greek sat beside the banker, attentively following the game with his deep-set black eyes and apparently waiting for something. Zavalshevsky, who was standing by the table, suddenly twitched all over as he took a red or blue banknote from his trouser pocket, laid a card over it, clapped his palm over it and muttered, 'Come on the seven, save me!' Then he bit his moustache, nervously shifted from foot to foot, blushed and continued twitching until his card was dealt. Ilin sat on the horsehair sofa eating some veal and pickled cucumber from a plate beside him and hurriedly wiped his hands on his jacket as he threw down one card after the other. Turbin, who from the very start had been sitting on the sofa, immediately realized what was going on. Lukhnov did not even deign to look at the uhlan or speak to him – all he did was peer through his spectacles every now and then at the uhlan's hands. Most of Ilin's cards lost.

'I'd like to beat that one,' Lukhnov remarked about one card played by the fat landowner who was staking half-roubles.

'Well, you go ahead and beat Ilin's, don't worry about mine,' the fat landowner observed.

In fact, Ilin's cards lost more often than anyone else's. He would nervously tear up the losing card under the table and choose another with trembling hands. Turbin got up from the sofa and asked the Greek to let him sit next to the banker. The Greek changed places and the count took his chair and stared intently at Lukhnov's hands.

'Ilin!' he suddenly said in his normal voice which was still loud enough to drown all the others. 'Why do you keep thinking that one's your lucky card? You've no idea how to play.'

'It seems to make no difference whatever I do.'

'But you're bound to lose if that's your attitude. Come on, give me your cards.'

'Oh no, if you don't mind. I never let others play for me. But you go ahead and play yourself if you want.'

'I told you I don't want to. I want to play for you. It really does annoy me, seeing you lose like that.'

'Well, it's obviously my fate!'

The count did not reply, leaned on his elbows and then fixed his eyes on the banker's hands as intently as before.

'That's bad!' he suddenly said in a loud, drawling voice.

Lukhnov glanced at him.

'Really bad!' he said, even louder, looking Lukhnov right in the eye.

The game continued.

'That's disgraceful!' Turbin said when Lukhnov beat one of Ilin's cards on which a great deal of money was staked.

'What's troubling you, Count?' Lukhnov asked in a tone of polite indifference.

'The way you let Ilin win the small cards and then beat him on the big ones. That's a dirty trick.'

Lukhnov made a slight movement with his shoulders and eyebrows, which seemed to suggest one should always bow to destiny, and carried on playing.

'Blücher! Here, boy!' the count shouted, getting up. 'At him!' he quickly added.

Bumping his back and almost knocking the garrison officer over as he leapt out from under the sofa, Blücher ran to his master, growled, looked round at everyone and wagged his tail as if to ask, 'Who's misbehaving, eh?'

Lukhnov laid down his cards and moved his chair back.

'I can't play like this,' he said. 'I simply detest dogs. How can anyone play with a pack of hounds running loose?'

'And especially that breed, I think they're called "leeches",' agreed the garrison officer.

'Well? Are we carrying on or not, Mikhailo?' Lukhnov asked the host.

'Please don't interfere, Count!' Ilin told Turbin.

'Come here a moment,' Turbin said, taking Ilin's arm and disappearing behind the partition with him.

From there the others could make out every word the count said, for he was talking in his normal voice, which could invariably be heard three rooms away.

'Have you gone mad, or what? Can't you see that the gentleman in spectacles is a sharper of the first order?'

'Come off it! What are you saying?'

'No, I won't come off it. I'm telling you to stop. But it's no skin off my nose, another time I'd be pleased to take your money myself. I can't bear to see you cheated like that. Are you sure you're not playing with the regiment's money?'

'Yes . . . well . . . What are you driving at?'

'My dear chap, I've seen it all and I know the tricks these sharpers get up to only too well. I'm telling you that the one in the spectacles is a cheat. Now, please stop playing!'

'Just one more hand and then I'll stop.'

'I know these "just one more hands"! Well, we'll see.'

They returned to the table. Ilin staked as many cards as before and so many were beaten that he lost a small fortune.

Turbin planted his hands right in the middle of the table. 'Enough! Let's go.'

'No, I can't. Please leave me alone,' Ilin said irritably, shuffling the bent cards and ignoring Turbin.

'All right, go to hell! Carry on losing if that's what you want, I'm going. Zavalshevsky, let's go to the marshal's.'

The two men left. No one said a word and Lukhnov did not start dealing again until the sound of their footsteps and the scratching of Blücher's paws had died away in the passage.

'What a crazy fellow!' the landowner laughed.

'Well, he won't interfere now,' the garrison officer hurriedly whispered.

And the game continued.

4

The musicians (the marshal's servants) stood at the buffet end of the room which had been specially cleared for the occasion, their coat-sleeves already turned up, and at a given signal struck up the old-fashioned polonaise 'Alexander-Elizabeth'. In the soft bright light of the wax candles the couples had just begun to glide over the parquet floor of the great ballroom – a governor-general from Catherine the Great's time with a star on his breast, arm-in-arm with the marshal's skinny wife, then the marshal himself holding the arm of the governor's wife, then local dignitaries in various combinations and groupings – when Zavalshevsky, wearing a blue frock-coat with an enormous collar and puffs on the shoulders, stockings and dancing-shoes, and reeking of jasmine which had been liberally sprinkled on his moustache, lapels and handkerchief, entered the ballroom together with the handsome hussar in tight blue riding-breeches and a gold-embroidered red jacket on which were pinned a Vladimir Cross and an 1812 medal. The count was not tall, but extremely well-built. His clear blue, exceptionally bright eyes and his thick curly chestnut hair lent a unique character to his handsome appearance. His arrival at the ball had been expected, since the handsome young man who had seen him at the hotel had already informed the marshal. The news met with a mixed response, for the most part not very favourable. 'That whippersnapper will make fools of us,' was the opinion of the gentlemen and elderly ladies. 'What if he runs off with me?' was the opinion (more or less) of the younger married women and girls.

As soon as the polonaise was over and the partners had bowed to each other and separated, the ladies rejoining the ladies, and the men the men, Zavalshevsky, proud and happy, led the count to the hostess. The marshal's wife, slightly apprehensive that the count might make her an object of ridicule in front of her guests, turned away haughtily and contemptuously with the words, 'I'm so delighted. I do hope you will dance,' after which she gave him a distrustful look which seemed to say, 'If you dare insult a lady you would be a scoundrel indeed!' But the count soon overcame her misgivings by his charm, attentiveness and handsome, cheerful appearance, so that within five minutes her face was telling everyone around her, 'I know how to manage his type. He understood from the start to whom he was talking. Now he'll be charming to me for the rest of the evening.'

At this point the governor, who had known the count's father, most amiably drew him aside for a chat, which calmed the provincial gentry even more and raised the count in their estimation. Shortly afterwards Zavalshevsky introduced him to his sister, a plump young widow who had not taken her eyes off the count from the moment he arrived. Turbin invited her to a waltz, which the orchestra had just begun, and this time the immense skill with which he danced finally removed any lingering doubts.

'He's certainly a wonderful dancer!' remarked a fat lady of the manor as she watched those legs in blue riding-breeches whirl past and counted to herself, 'One two three, one two three – splendid!'

'Just watch him trip round the room!' remarked another lady, a visitor to the town and considered rather vulgar in local society. 'How does he manage not to catch anyone with his spurs? Oh, he's *so* skilful!'

Through his expertise the count eclipsed the three best dancers in the district: the tall, fair-haired adjutant to the governor, famed for his speed in the dance and for holding his partners very close; a cavalry officer, renowned for his graceful swaying motion in the waltz and the rapid, very light tapping of his heels; and a civilian who, although he was a little on the dim side, was considered a first-rate dancer and the life and soul of every ball. Indeed, from start to finish, this gentleman never rested for one moment – except to mop his very weary but cheerful face with a wet cambric handkerchief – inviting all the ladies in the order in which they were sitting. The count outshone them all and danced with the three most important ladies at the ball: a large one, rich, pretty and stupid; a medium-sized one, not particularly pretty but beautifully dressed; and a small one, very plain but extremely intelligent. He danced with others too – with all the pretty ones, of whom there were many. But the one he liked the most was Zavalshevsky's sister, the little widow, and he danced a quadrille, écossaise and mazurka with her. In the quadrille he showered her with compliments, comparing her to Venus, to Diana, to a rose and some other flower. But the widow responded to all this flattery by bending her white neck, looking down at her white muslin dress, or shifting her fan from one hand to the other. When she said, 'Stop it, Count, you're only teasing me,' and other words to that effect, her somewhat guttural voice expressed such naïve simplicity and engaging innocence that one had the feeling this was no woman, but a flower – not a rose, but some gorgeous pink and white, odourless wild flower growing in utter solitude, in a virgin snowdrift somewhere far, far away.

This blend of *naïveté* and unconventionality, combined with such fresh beauty, made such a strange impression on the count that several times during the conversation, when he mutely gazed into her eyes or at the exquisite outline of her arms and neck, he was gripped so strongly by an overwhelming desire to take her in his arms and shower her with kisses that he had difficulty controlling himself. The little widow was delighted with the impression she was making, yet there was something about the count's behaviour that was beginning to disturb and frighten her, even though the count, in addition to his ingratiating charm, was excessively well-mannered, if judged in the light of present-day standards. He dashed off to fetch her a cold drink, picked up her handkerchief, snatched a chair away from a scrofulous young landowner who also wanted to be her willing slave so that he would be first to offer it to her, and so on.

When he realized that his gallantry (so typical of the times) was having little effect on the widow, he tried to amuse her by saying some funny things. He assured her that she had but to give the word and he would leap out of the window or jump into the water through a hole in the ice. This was a complete success and the widow brightened up considerably, breaking into peals of laughter and revealing her beautiful white teeth. Now she was perfectly happy with her cavalier. The count grew more infatuated every minute, so that by the end of the quadrille he was deeply in love.

After the quadrille the widow's long-standing admirer, the idle eighteen-year-old son of a rich landowner – that same scrofulous young man from whom Turbin had snatched the chair – came over. The widow gave him a cold reception and did not show a fraction of the confusion the count had aroused.

'You're a fine one!' she told him, looking all the time at Turbin's back and unconsciously calculating how many yards of gold braid had gone into his jacket. 'You're a fine one. You promised to come and take me for a sleigh-ride and bring me some chocolates.'

'I did call, Anna, but you had already gone. And I did leave you a box of the very best chocolates,' said the young man who, despite his height, had a very high-pitched voice.

'Always finding excuses! I don't want your chocolates now. And don't imagine . . .'

'I can see that you have changed towards me, Anna. And I know why . . . it's quite wrong of you . . .' he added, obviously unable to finish because of the deep feeling of agitation that made his lips tremble in the most rapid, peculiar manner.

Anna did not listen and kept watching Turbin.

The master of the house, the stout, toothless, majestic old marshal, went up to the count, took his arm and invited him into the study for a smoke and drink. The moment Turbin was gone Anna felt that there was absolutely no point in staying there a moment longer and so she took the hand of a thin elderly spinster with whom she was friendly and went out to the dressing-room with her.

'Well, is he nice?' asked the spinster.

'Yes, but terribly persistent,' Anna replied, going over to look at herself in the mirror.

Her face brightened, her eyes laughed, she even blushed, and suddenly, imitating the ballerinas she had seen during the elections, she pirouetted on one foot, laughed that guttural but charming laugh of hers, bent her knees and leapt into the air.

'What do you think of this? – he asked me for a keepsake,' she told her friend. 'Only he'll get no-th-ing!' she added, singing the last word and lifting one finger in a kid glove that reached to her elbow.

In the study, where the marshal had taken Turbin, there were various brands of vodka, liqueurs, champagne and assorted hors d'oeuvres. Some local gentlemen were walking about or sitting in clouds of tobacco smoke, discussing the elections.

'Since the gentry in this district honoured him by their choice,' the newly elected and already quite tipsy police chief was saying, 'he has no right to neglect his duties, no right at all to –'

This speech was interrupted by the count's entrance. Everyone wanted to be introduced to him and the police chief kept pressing the count's hand in his for some time, and begged him repeatedly to accompany him to a new tavern where he intended treating the gentlemen after the ball and where there would be gypsy singing. The count promised to go without fail and drank several glasses of champagne with him.

'But why aren't you dancing, gentlemen?' the count asked as he was about to leave the study.

'We're not much good at that kind of thing,' the police chief said, laughing. 'We're better at knocking back the bubbly, Count ... Besides, I've seen all those young ladies grow up! ... But now and then I can stroll my way through an écossaise! Oh yes, Count, I can still do it ...'

'Well, come and stroll now!' Turbin said. 'Let's have a little more fun here before we go off to the gypsies.'

'Why not, gentlemen? It will please our host.'

And three or four red-faced gentlemen put on their gloves, black kid or silk knitted, and were just about to enter the ballroom with the count when they were stopped by the scrofulous young man who looked as white as a sheet and was barely able to hold back his tears. He went up to Turbin and said, 'Just because you're a count you think you can push people around as if this was a market-place,' he said, having difficulty with his breathing. 'Now I consider that very rude . . .'

Once more his trembling lips stemmed the flow of words.

'What?' Turbin shouted, suddenly frowning. 'What did you say, you little brat?' he roared, seizing him by the arms and squeezing them so hard the blood rushed to the young man's head, not so much from a sense of injury as from fright. 'Do you want a duel? I'm at your service.'

The moment Turbin released the arms he had been squeezing so hard two gentlemen seized them and hauled the young man towards the back entrance.

'What's the matter with you – have you taken leave of your senses? You've obviously had too much to drink. We'll tell your father about this. What on earth's got into you?' they asked.

'No, I'm not drunk, but he thinks he can push people around without apologizing. He's a swine, that's what!' the young man whined, bursting into tears.

But they turned a deaf ear and took him home.

'I wouldn't worry about him, Count,' the police chief and Zaval-shevsky said, anxious to pacify Turbin. 'He's only a child – he still gets thrashed. But we really don't understand what's got into him. He must be out of his mind. And his father is such a respectable man, our candidate . . .'

'Well, to hell with him if he doesn't want satisfaction . . .'

And the count returned to the ballroom, danced an écossaise as gaily as before with the pretty little widow, laughing heartily at the gentlemen who had come from the study with him as they performed their steps and filling the whole room with roars of laughter when the police chief slipped and went sprawling in the middle of the dancing couples.

5

While the count was in the study Anna had gone up to her brother. Feeling that she should feign almost complete indifference towards the count she asked, 'Who is that hussar who was dancing with me?'

The cavalry officer did his best to explain what a great man the hussar was, stressing that he was staying in town only because his money had been stolen on the road, that he himself had lent him one hundred roubles and since that was not enough, could his dear sister please oblige with another two hundred? He begged her not to breathe a word to a soul, especially the count. Anna promised to send the money over the same evening and to keep the whole affair a strict secret, but during the écossaise she felt an irresistible urge to offer the count whatever he needed. She took a long time to pluck up courage but after a great effort and much blushing she finally broached the subject.

'My brother's told me that you had some bad luck on the road and that you've no money now, Count. If you need any, perhaps you will accept some from me – it would make me extremely happy.'

No sooner had she said this than Anna suddenly felt frightened and blushed. All the gaiety instantly went out of the count's face.

'Your brother's a fool,' he said brusquely. 'You know that when one man insults another they usually fight a duel. But what happens when a woman insults a man?'

Poor Anna's neck and ears burnt with embarrassment. She lowered her eyes and did not say a word.

'The man kisses the woman in front of everyone,' the count whispered, leaning towards her ear. 'Allow me at least to kiss your hand,' he added softly after a long pause, pitying his lady for the embarrassment she was suffering.

'But not now!' Anna exclaimed with a deep sigh.

'When? I'm leaving early tomorrow morning . . . you owe it me, you know.'

'Well, if that's so, I cannot pay what I owe you,' Anna said, smiling.

'Just give me the chance to see you tonight so I can kiss your hand. Anyway, I'll find one.'

'But how?'

'That's no concern of yours. I'd go to any lengths to see you . . . It's agreed then?'

'Agreed.'

The écossaise ended. Then they danced another mazurka in which the count performed such wonders, catching handkerchiefs, dropping on to one knee and clicking his spurs in the special Warsaw style, that all the old men left their game of bridge for the ballroom. The cavalry officer, reputedly the best dancer there, acknowledged defeat. Supper was served and after a final *'Grossvater'** the guests began to leave. All this time the count had not taken his eyes off the widow and he had not been making idle boasts when he declared that he would dive into a hole in the ice for her. Whether it was a passing whim, love or sheer obstinacy, all his faculties were concentrated on only one desire that evening: to see her and make love to her. The moment he saw Anna take leave of the hostess he ran to the footmen's room and from there (without his coat) to the place outside where all the carriages were waiting.

'Mrs Zaitsev's carriage!' he shouted. A high four-seater with lanterns moved towards the entrance. 'Stop!' he shouted to the coachman, running knee-deep in snow.

'What d'ye want?' the coachman shouted back.

'I want to get in,' the count replied, opening the door and trying to climb up as the carriage was moving. 'Stop, damn you! You idiot!'

'Stop, Vaska!' the coachman shouted to his postilion, pulling up the horses. 'What d'ye think you're up to, climbing into someone else's carriage? It belongs to my mistress, Mrs Zaitsev – not to you, Yer Honour!'

'Shut up, blockhead! Take this rouble. Now, get down and close the door,' the count said. But as the coachman would not budge he pulled up the steps himself, opened the window and somehow managed to slam the door. Like most old carriages, especially those with gold braid on the upholstery, it had a musty odour and smelt of burnt bristles. The count's legs, wet with snow up to the knees, and with only those thin boots and riding-breeches over them, felt frozen and in fact his whole body was chilled to the bone. The coachman was grumbling up on his box and seemed about to climb down. But the count neither heard nor felt a thing. His face was burning, his heart was pounding. With tensed hand he seized the yellow strap and thrust his head out of the side window: his whole being was concentrated in one moment of anticipation. But this sensation was short-lived. Someone called from the entrance, 'Mrs Zaitsev's carriage!' The coachman shook the reins, the carriage rocked on its high springs

---

* *'Grossvater'* or 'Grandfather', a German dance very popular in Russia.

and the illuminated windows of the house sped past the carriage windows.

'Now watch out, you old devil!' the count warned the coachman. 'If you tell the footman I'm here,' he continued, poking his head out of the front window, 'I'll thrash you. But if you keep quiet there'll be another ten roubles for you.'

He hardly had time to lower the window when the carriage lurched to a halt. He huddled into one corner, held his breath, even closed his eyes, he was so terrified that his passionate hopes might be dashed. The door opened, one by one the carriage steps clattered down, a woman's gown rustled and the scent of jasmine floated into the musty carriage. Tiny feet swiftly pattered up the steps and Anna sank silently and breathlessly on to the seat beside the count, brushing his leg with the skirt of her cloak.

Whether she saw him or not no one could have said, not even Anna herself. But when he took her arm and told her, 'Well, now I'm going to kiss your hand,' she wasn't in the least alarmed and mutely surrendered her arm which he covered much higher than the top of her glove with kisses. The carriage moved off.

'Please say something! You're not angry, are you?' he asked.

She silently shrank into the corner, but then, for some reason, suddenly burst into tears and her head dropped of its own accord on to his breast.

6

The newly elected police chief and his party, the cavalry officer and some other gentlemen had been drinking and listening to the gypsies in the new tavern for some time when the count, wearing a blue cloth cloak lined with bearskin that had belonged to Anna's late husband, joined them.

'At last, Your Excellency! We'd almost given up hope,' said a dark, cross-eyed gypsy, flashing his white teeth as he rushed to the entrance to greet the count and help him off with his cloak. 'We haven't seen you since Lebedyan . . . Stesha's been pining for you . . .'

Stesha, a shapely young gypsy girl with a brick-red glow to her brown skin and deep-set, sparkling black eyes edged by long lashes, came running out to meet him too.

'Ah, my dear sweet Count! My darling! Oh, what joy it is to see you!' she murmured, happily smiling.

Ilyushka himself ran to welcome the count, pretending to be very pleased to see him. Old women, middle-aged women, young girls jumped up and surrounded the new guest. Some claimed that they were related to him, as he had been godfather to their children, or because he had exchanged crosses with them.

Turbin kissed all the young gypsy girls on the lips; the old women and the men kissed his shoulders and hand. The gentlemen, too, were delighted that the count had come, especially as the high spirits and revelry, having reached their peak, were now losing their zest. Everyone was beginning to feel surfeited. The wine no longer exhilarated and lay heavily on the stomach. Each of them had exhausted his stock of bravado and was now tired of the others. All songs had been sung and remained a confused medley in everyone's head, leaving only a sensation of noise and dissipation. No matter what original or daring tricks anyone attempted, no one found anything either amusing or agreeable about them. The police chief, who was lying in a shocking state on the floor at an old woman's feet, kicked his legs out and shouted, 'Champagne . . . the count's here! Champagne! He's here . . . on with the champagne. I shall fill a tub and have a bath in it. Gentlemen of the nobility! I simply love being in such distinguished, aristocratic company . . . Stesha, sing "The Country Lane" for us.'

The cavalry officer was also drunk, but it showed differently. He sat on a couch in one corner, very close to a tall handsome gypsy girl called Lyubasha. The drink blurred his eyes, which made him blink and toss his head. Again and again he whispered the same words in an attempt to persuade the girl to run away with him. Lyubasha, smiling and listening as if what he was telling her was both extremely amusing and rather pathetic, kept glancing at her husband, cross-eyed Sashka, who was standing behind a chair opposite her. In reply to the cavalryman's declaration of love she leant down and whispered in his ear, asking him to buy her some ribbons and perfume, provided no one got to hear about it.

'Hurrah!' shouted the cavalry officer when the count entered. The handsome young man, with an anxious look and with an unnaturally heavy step, paced the room, humming a tune from *Il Seraglio*.

An elderly paterfamilias, who had been lured to the gypsies by the persistent requests of the other gentlemen and who maintained that if the count refused to join them everything would be spoilt and that there would be no point in going, was lying on the couch on to which he had sunk the moment he had arrived and no one was taking the slightest notice of him. A government official had taken off his frock-coat and perched himself on the table, his feet right up, and was ruffling his hair to show them all what a roué he was. The moment the count entered he unbuttoned his shirt collar and perched even higher on the table. Things livened up altogether with the count's arrival. The gypsy girls, who had been idly wandering around the room, sat down in a circle again. The count set Stesha the solo singer on his knee and ordered more champagne.

Ilyushka came and stood with his guitar in front of Stesha and the 'dancing' began, i.e., the singing of gypsy songs such as 'When I Walk down the Street', 'Oh, You Hussars!', 'Listen and Understand' and so on, in set order. Stesha sang beautifully. The rich, flexible contralto that flowed from deep down, the way she smiled as she sang, her passionate laughing eyes, that tiny foot which involuntarily tapped in time to the music, her wild cries at the beginning of each chorus – all this touched some resonant but seldom-plucked chord. Clearly she lived only for the song she was singing. Ilyushka accompanied her on his guitar and expressed his feeling for the song in his smile, in the movements of his back and legs, in his whole being, nodding as he kept time and watching her closely and anxiously, as though he had never heard it before. Then, as the last melodious notes died away, he suddenly drew himself up and, as if feeling superior to the whole world, proudly and determinedly sent his guitar spinning with a jerk of the knee, twirled it round as he tapped his heels, tossed his hair back and surveyed the choir with a sweeping frown. His body, from neck to heel, started dancing in every muscle – and twenty powerful and energetic voices rang out, each vying with the other to give the most original and unusual rendering. The old women bobbed up and down on their chairs, waving their handkerchiefs and showing their teeth as each tried to shout louder than the other, but in tune and in time with the music. Their heads tilted and neck-muscles straining, the men sang in their deep bass voices as they stood behind the chairs.

Whenever Stesha took a high note, Ilyushka would bring his guitar closer to her as if he wanted to help, while the handsome young man cried out in ecstasy, now that they were reaching the highest and most difficult notes.

When they struck up a dance tune and Dunyasha paraded herself before the count, her shoulders and breasts quivering, and then sailed on, Turbin leapt from his chair, threw off his jacket and jauntily walked up and down with her in his red shirt, keeping perfect time and performing such amazing tricks with his legs that the gypsies looked at one another and smiled their approval.

The police chief squatted like a Turk, beating his chest with one fist and shouting, 'Bravo! Bravo!' Then he grabbed the count's legs and told him that he had come with ten thousand roubles but now had only five hundred left and he would do anything, as long as the count allowed it. The old paterfamilias woke up and wanted to leave, but they would not let him. The handsome young man persuaded one of the gypsy girls to waltz with him. The cavalry officer left his corner and embraced Turbin, obviously wanting to show everyone how friendly he was with the count.

'My dear fellow!' he said. 'Why on earth did you leave us?' The count did not reply, his mind evidently on other matters. 'Where did you get to? Oh, you old rogue, Count! I know where you've been!'

For some reason the count did not take kindly to this show of familiarity. Without smiling or saying a word he stared into the cavalry officer's face. Then suddenly he let loose such a terrible flood of abuse that the officer was quite taken aback and for some time could not decide whether it was meant as a joke or not. Finally he concluded that the count must have been joking, smiled and rejoined his gypsy girl, assuring her that he would marry her after Easter, come what may. They sang another song and another, danced again, sang songs in each other's honour and everyone felt he was having a very jolly time. The champagne kept flowing. The count drank a great deal: his eyes seemed to grow moist, but he remained steady on his feet and danced better than ever. His speech did not falter for one moment and he even harmonized superbly with the choir when he joined Stesha in 'Love's Gentle Thrill'.

In the middle of one of the songs the tavern owner came in and requested the guests to leave, as it was nearly three in the morning.

The count seized him by the scruff of his neck and ordered him to dance squatting, Cossack-style. When he refused, he grabbed a bottle of champagne, stood him on his head and made the others hold him while he slowly emptied it over him amidst general laughter.

It was already growing light. Everyone looked pale and weary – except the count.

'Well, it's time to leave for Moscow,' he said suddenly, getting up. 'I want you all to come back to the hotel with me and see me off . . . we'll have some tea.'

Everyone agreed, except the paterfamilias, who was fast asleep. They piled into the three sledges waiting at the door and drove off to the hotel.

7

'Harness the horses!' shouted the count as he entered the public lounge with all his guests and the gypsies. 'Sashka! – not the gypsy but my own Sashka – tell the posting-stage keeper that I'll beat him black and blue if he gives me bad horses. And bring us some tea! Zavalshevsky – you see to it, I just want to see how Ilin's getting on,' he added, going out into the corridor and heading for the uhlan's room.

Ilin had just finished playing. He had lost his last copeck and was lying face-down on the torn horsehair sofa, pulling out the hairs one by one, putting them in his mouth, biting them through and spitting them out. Two tallow candles, one of which had burnt right down to the paper, stood on a table littered with cards and their light struggled feebly against the morning light which now streamed through the windows. The uhlan's mind was a complete blank, as his mania for gambling had stifled all capacity for thought, like a thick blanket of fog. And he did not even have any regrets. He *had* tried to consider what he should do next – how he could leave without a copeck, how to repay the fifteen thousand roubles that belonged to the regiment, what the commanding officer would have to say about it, what his mother would say and what his fellow officers would say – and he had become so terrified and disgusted with himself that, to banish all these thoughts, he had got up and started pacing the room, trying to step only on the cracks between the floorboards. Once again he went over every detail of that last game. He remembered quite clearly that he had started winning again, cutting a nine and staking two thousand roubles on the king of spades. But the queen was on the right, an ace to the left, the king of diamonds to the right, and so all was lost. If the six had been on the right and the king of diamonds on the left, he would have recouped all his losses, staked everything and won another fifteen thousand clear. And then he would have bought himself an ambler from his regimental commander, another pair of horses – and a phaeton! And what else? Well, everything would have been wonderful, just wonderful!

He lay on the sofa again and chewed hairs.

'Why are they all singing in number seven?' he wondered. 'Turbin must be giving a party. Shall I join them and get well and truly plastered?' Just then the count entered.

'Well, old man, have they cleaned you out?' he asked in his loud voice.

'I'll pretend I'm asleep,' Ilin decided. 'Otherwise I'll have to talk and I really must get some sleep now.'

But Turbin went over and stroked his head.

'Tell me, old man, have you been cleaned out? Lost everything? Well?' Ilin did not reply. The count tugged his sleeve.

'Yes, I've lost. And what's that to you?' Ilin muttered in a sleepy, indifferent, peevish voice, without changing his position on the bed.

'Everything?'

'Yes. And what of it? *Everything*. Why should *you* worry?'

'Now listen to me and tell me the truth, as a fellow officer,' the count said, in an affectionate, sentimental mood after all the wine he had drunk, still stroking the uhlan's hair. 'Honestly, I've really taken a liking to you. Now, tell me the truth: if it's the regiment's money you've lost I'll come to your rescue. Tell me before it's too late . . . was it the regiment's money?'

Ilin leapt from the sofa.

'Well, if you want me to tell you . . . don't talk to me . . . because . . . well, please don't talk . . . a bullet in the brains – that's all that's left!' he added in genuine despair, letting his head fall on his hands and bursting into tears, although only a few moments before he had been calmly contemplating the purchase of an ambler.

'Stop behaving like a little girl! We've all been in trouble at some time or other. It's not as bad as you think, and I'm sure we can sort it out. Wait for me here.' And the count left the room.

'Where's Squire Lukhnov's room?' he asked the hotel boy.

The boy offered to take the count there. Despite the valet's protests that his master had only just returned and was undressing, the count went in. Lukhnov was sitting at a table in his dressing-gown, counting several piles of banknotes that lay in front of him. A bottle of hock, to which he was very partial, stood on the table – after winning so much he had permitted himself this little self-indulgence. Lukhnov eyed the count coldly and sternly through his spectacles, as if he did not recognize his visitor.

'It seems you don't know me,' the count said, determinedly striding over to the table. Lukhnov then appeared to recognize him and asked, 'What can I do for you?'

'I want to play cards with you,' Turbin said, sitting down on the sofa.

'Now?'

'Yes.'

'Any other time I'd be only too pleased, but I'm tired now and about to go to bed. Would you care for a glass of wine? It's excellent.'

'I want to play *now*.'

'I really don't feel like playing any more tonight, Count. Perhaps one of the others will oblige, but I won't, Count. You must excuse me.'

'So you won't play?'

Lukhnov shrugged his shoulders to express regret at his inability to comply with the count's wishes.

'So, is that final?'

Another shrug of the shoulders.

'I'm begging you . . . will you play?'

Another silence and a swift glance over the top of his spectacles at the count's frowning face.

'*Will* you play?' the count roared, banging the table so hard that the bottle fell over and all the wine spilled out. 'You cheated, didn't you? Now, will you play? I'm asking you for the third time.'

'I told you, no! This is all rather odd, Count. And it's really not quite the thing to come bursting in like this and holding a knife to a man's throat,' Lukhnov remarked without looking up.

A brief silence followed, during which the count's face turned paler and paler. Suddenly Lukhnov was stunned by a terrible blow on the head. He fell on to the couch and as he tried to grab the money he gave a piercing, desperate cry that one would never have expected from someone who always gave an impression of such unruffled calm and dignity. Turbin collected the money that was left on the table, brushed aside the valet who had rushed to his master's aid and swiftly strode from the room.

'If you want satisfaction, I'm at your service. I shall be in my room for another half hour,' the count added, returning to Lukhnov's door.

'Scoundrel! Thief!' came from the room. 'I'll see you in court!'

Ilin, who had completely ignored the count's promise to rescue him, was still lying on the sofa, choking with tears of despair. Awareness of the predicament he was in, which the count's sympathy and concern had aroused, despite the odd mixture of feelings, thoughts and memories which flooded his mind, had not deserted him. His youth, so rich in hope, his honour, the respect of society, his dreams of love and friendship – all were lost for ever. The fount of his tears had begun to run dry and an all too apathetic feeling of hopelessness was strengthening its hold on him. The thought of suicide, which no longer inspired either repugnance or horror, increasingly crossed his mind. But just then he heard the count's firm footsteps.

Turbin's face still bore traces of anger, his hands shook slightly, but his eyes shone with kindly good humour and satisfaction.

'There you are, I've won it back for you!' he said, tossing several bundles of banknotes on to the table. 'As soon as you've checked it, come to the public lounge – I'm leaving,' he added, pretending not to notice the unbounded joy and gratitude on the uhlan's face. Whistling a gypsy tune, he left the room.

8

Sashka tightened his belt and announced that the horses were ready. But he insisted that they first go and recover the count's greatcoat which, with the fur collar, was worth three hundred roubles, and return the shabby blue cloak to the scoundrel who had exchanged it for the greatcoat at the ball. But Turbin told him there was no need and went to his room to change.

The cavalry officer hiccuped incessantly as he sat silently by his gypsy girl. The police chief ordered vodka and invited all the gentlemen to come and have breakfast with him at his house, promising that his wife would make an appearance and dance with the gypsies. The handsome young man was earnestly explaining to Ilyushka that there was more soul in a piano and that it was impossible to play A flats on a guitar. The civil servant sat in one corner drinking his tea and seemed ashamed of his debauchery in the cold light of day. The gypsies quarrelled among themselves in their own language and insisted on honouring the gentlemen with one more song, but Stesha objected, maintaining that the baroray (meaning 'count' or 'prince' or, more accurately, 'great nobleman' in gypsy language) would be angry. In short, the last sparks of revelry were dying now in everyone.

'All right, one farewell song and then we all go home!' the count said, entering the lounge in his travelling clothes and looking fresher, more cheerful and more handsome than ever.

Once more the gypsies formed a circle and were about to sing when Ilin came in with a bundle of banknotes in his hand and called the count to one side.

'I had only fifteen thousand in regiment money and you've given me sixteen thousand three hundred!' he said. 'So this must be yours.'

'Splendid! Hand it over.'

Ilin looked timidly at the count as he handed him the money, then opened his mouth to speak, but instead he blushed until the tears came to his eyes. Then he seized the count's hand and squeezed it hard.

'Now, be off with you . . . Ilyushka!' the count said. 'Listen to me. Here's some money, but you must accompany us with songs up to the town gates.' And he threw the thirteen hundred roubles that Ilin had given him on to Ilyushka's guitar. But he forgot to pay back the cavalry officer the hundred roubles he had borrowed the previous night.

It was already ten o'clock in the morning. The sun was high over the roofs, the streets were busy, shopkeepers had long opened their doors, gentlefolk and civil servants were driving past and young ladies were strolling from shop to shop in the arcade when the gypsy band, the cavalry officer, the handsome young man, Ilin and the count in the blue bearskin-lined cloak appeared on the front steps of the hotel. It was a sunny day and the snow was melting. Three post-sledges, each drawn by three horses with their tails tied up short, splashed through the slush up to the hotel entrance and the whole lively company got in. The count, Stesha, Ilyushka and the count's batman Sashka sat in the first sledge. Blücher was beside himself with excitement, wagging his tail and barking at the shaft-horse. The rest of the gentlemen climbed into the other two sledges, together with the gypsy men and women. As soon as they left the hotel, the three sledges drew abreast and the gypsies sang in chorus.

And so, with songs ringing out and bells jingling, they drove right across town until they reached the gates, forcing every vehicle they met up on to the pavement. Shopkeepers, strangers and particularly those who knew them well were absolutely startled at the sight of those gentlemen riding along the streets in broad daylight, accompanied by songs, gypsy girls and drunken gypsy men. When they had passed the town gates the post-sledges stopped and everyone began to take their leave of the count.

Ilin, who had drunk a great deal at the farewell party and had driven the horses himself, suddenly became sad and tried to persuade the count to stay just one more day. But when he was finally convinced that this was impossible, he unexpectedly threw himself on his new friend with tearful eyes, embraced him and vowed that he would apply for a transfer to the same hussar regiment as Turbin's the moment he got back. The count was in particularly high spirits. He pushed the cavalry officer who had been over-familiar with him that morning into a snowdrift, set Blücher on the police chief, took Stesha in his arms and wanted to take her with him to Moscow. Finally he leapt into his sledge and made Blücher sit beside him, although his dog would have preferred to sit in the middle. Sashka, having once again urged the cavalry officer to recover the count's greatcoat and send it on, leapt on to the driver's seat. The count shouted, 'Let's go!', took off his cap, waved it over his head, whistled at the horses like a sleigh-driver, and the three sledges moved off in their respective directions.

A monotonous snowy waste with a dirty yellow ribbon of road winding over it stretched far into the distance. The bright sun sparkled playfully on the transparent icy crust over the thawing snow, pleasantly warming one's face and back. Clouds of steam rose from the sweating horses. Sleigh-bells jingled. A peasant with an overloaded sledge that kept swerving away from him hastily made way, tugging at the ropes that served as reins, his wet bast* shoes plashing as he ran through the slush. A fat, red-faced peasant woman with a child wrapped in the breast of her sheepskin coat was sitting on another laden sledge, urging on her white, thin-tailed nag with the ends of the reins. The count suddenly remembered Anna.

'Turn back!' he shouted.

The driver did not understand at first.

'Turn back. Back to town! And hurry up!'

The sleigh passed through the gates again and briskly drove up to the wooden steps of Mrs Zaitsev's house. The count dashed up and raced through the entrance-hall and drawing-room. Finding the little widow still in bed, he took her in his arms, lifted her out of bed, kissed her sleepy eyes and quickly retraced his steps. Anna was so drowsy that she could only lick her lips and ask, 'What happened?' The count leapt into his sleigh, shouted to the driver and, with no further delay, without even a thought for Lukhnov, for the little widow, for Stesha, but only for what was in store for him in Moscow, left the town of K— for ever.

9

Twenty years had passed. Much water had flowed under the bridge, many had died, many had been born, many had grown up or become old; even more ideas than people had been born and had died. Much of what was good, much of what was bad in the old days, had perished; much that was new and beautiful had come to maturity; and even more that was immature and monstrous had come into the world.

Count Fyodor Turbin had been killed long ago in a duel by some foreigner he had horsewhipped in the street. His son, an exact replica of his father, was a charming young man of twenty-three and was serving in the Horse Guards. In temperament, young Turbin was completely different from his father. There was no trace in him of

---

* The inner bark of a lime-tree, commonly used for peasant shoes.

those wild, passionate and, frankly speaking, dissipated urges so typical of the older generation. Besides intelligence, education and inherited talent, his outstanding qualities were a love of respectability and comfort, a practical way of judging people and circumstances, prudence and good sense. The young count had made rapid progress in the army and at twenty-three was already a lieutenant. When military operations began he decided his best chance of promotion was to enlist for active service, so he obtained a transfer to a hussar regiment, where he served as captain, and before long was given a squadron to command.

In May 1848 the S— hussar regiment was passing through the province of K— and the squadron under young Count Turbin's command was to stay the night in the village of Morozovka – Mrs Zaitsev's estate. Anna was still alive, but now she was so far from young that she no longer looked upon herself as such, which of course is highly significant for a woman. She had grown very plump (which is supposed to make a woman look younger), but deep wrinkles now lined that soft white corpulence. She never rode into town and in fact found it quite an effort to climb into her carriage. But she was as good-hearted as ever and just as silly: the truth may now be told, as she no longer possessed the captivating beauty to seduce us into thinking otherwise. Living with her were her daughter, Liza, a Russian country beauty of twenty-three and her brother – that same cavalry officer with whom we are already acquainted. Having squandered his inheritance through his generosity, he had finally found refuge in his old age at Anna's. His hair was quite grey now and his upper lip drooped, although the moustache over it was still carefully dyed black. Not only his forehead and cheeks, but even his nose and neck were covered with wrinkles; his back was bent. For all that, there was still something of the old cavalry officer in his feeble, crooked legs.

That same evening Anna, with all her family and the servants, was sitting in the small drawing-room of the old house whose veranda door and windows opened on to an old-fashioned, star-shaped garden full of lime-trees. Grey-haired, in her lilac quilted jacket, she was sitting on the sofa by a round mahogany table laying out cards for patience. Her old brother, in clean white trousers and blue jacket, had settled himself by a window and was crocheting something with white cotton thread, a hobby his niece had taught him and of which he had become extremely fond, as he could really do nothing else and his eyes were now too weak to allow him to read the newspaper, his favourite pastime.

Pimochka, a little girl adopted by Anna, was sitting nearby doing her lessons under the supervision of Liza, who at the same time was knitting her uncle a pair of goat's wool stockings with wooden needles. As always at this time of day the last rays of the setting sun shone obliquely through the avenue of lime-trees, illuminating the furthest window and the *étagère* standing just by it. It was so quiet in the garden and the room that one could hear the rapid flutter of a swallow's wings outside the window, Anna's soft sighs inside the room, or the old man's grunts as he crossed his legs.

'Where should I put this card? Please show me, Liza, I keep forgetting,' Anna said, stopping for a moment.

Without interrupting her work, Liza went over to her mother and glanced at the cards.

'Oh, you've mixed them all up, dear Mamma!' she said, rearranging the cards. 'Now, that's how it should go. But it will still come out – you guessed correctly,' she added, taking away one card without her mother noticing.

'You're always deceiving me, telling me it will come out!'

'But it will – look, it has!'

'All right, all right, you crafty girl. Now, isn't it time for tea?'

'I've already told them to heat the samovar. I'll go and see to it right away . . . Would you like your tea in here? Come on Pimochka, if you finish your lesson we can go for a run in the garden.'

And Liza went towards the door.

'Liza, dear Lizanka!' her uncle exclaimed, looking intently at his crocheting hook. 'I seem to have dropped a stitch again. Pick it up for me, there's a dear.'

'In a minute. Just let me give the maids this lump of sugar to break up.'

And sure enough, three minutes later, she ran back into the room, went over to her uncle and pulled his ear.

'That's for dropping your stitches.' She laughed. 'Why, you haven't even finished today's lesson!'

'Oh, never mind. Please see to it, there's a little knot or something.'

Liza took the hook, pulled a pin out of her kerchief, which gently billowed in the breeze from the window, somehow managed to pick up the stitch with it, looped it through twice and handed the hook back to her uncle.

'Now, I'd like a kiss for helping you,' she said, offering her rosy cheek and pinning back her kerchief. 'You may have some rum in your tea today, it's Friday, you know.'

Again she went to the tea-room.

'Uncle, come and look! The hussars are coming!' she called out in her rich voice.

Anna went with her brother to the tea-room, whose windows faced the village, to watch the hussars. But all they could see from the window in that thick cloud of dust was a moving mass of men.

'What a shame, sister,' Liza's uncle remarked to Anna, 'that the house is so small and that the new wing's not finished yet. We could have invited some officers to stay. Hussar officers are such fine, cheerful young men. I'd have loved to see them.'

'Well, I'd have been only too pleased, but you know we've no room. There's just my bedroom, Liza's room, the drawing-room and your own. So where could we have put them? Mikhailo has cleaned the elder's hut, he says it's spotless now.'

'Liza, shouldn't we go and find a husband for you, a nice dashing hussar!' her uncle said.

'No, I don't want a hussar. I want an uhlan. Weren't you in the uhlans, Uncle? . . . I don't want anything to do with hussars. People say they're a terribly wild lot.'

Liza blushed faintly, but again she laughed her sonorous laugh. 'Look, there's Ustyushka running back. We must ask her what she's seen,' she said.

Anna sent for Ustyushka. 'I suppose you don't have enough work to do,' Anna said. 'I ask you, running off like that to look at some soldiers! Well, tell me where the officers are being put up for the night.'

'In Yeremkin's hut, madam. There's two of them, and so handsome! They say one's a count!'

'What's his name?'

'Kazarov, or Turbinov, or something like that. Sorry, I've forgotten.'

'You stupid girl, can't you tell us anything! You might at least have found out his name.'

'I'll run off and ask if you like.'

'That's what you're good at, isn't it, running off! No, let Danilo go. You tell him, brother, and ask if the officers need anything. We must be as polite to them as we possibly can. Let Mikhailo say his mistress sent him.'

The old couple sat down in the tea-room again, while Liza went to the maids' room to put the sugar back in the box. Ustyushka was there, telling the others all about the hussars.

'Yes, Miss, that count is so handsome!' she said. 'Just like a cherub, with black eyebrows. Now, if you found a husband like that what a lovely couple you'd make!'

The other maids smiled approvingly. The old nurse who was sitting by the window darning a stocking sighed and drew a deep breath as she murmured a prayer to herself.

'So those hussars really took your fancy?' Liza said. 'Yes, you like nothing better than gossiping about these things! Now, bring us a fruit drink, Ustyushka. Something sharpish that the hussars will like.'

Laughing to herself, Liza left the room with the sugar-bowl.

'I'd love to have a look at that hussar,' she thought. 'Is he dark or fair? I've no doubt he'd be delighted to meet us. But then he might pass by without even knowing I existed, without ever knowing that I was here thinking about him. And how many like him have already passed me by! No one ever sees me, except Uncle and Ustyushka. However nicely I do my hair, whatever sleeves I wear, there's no one here to admire me,' she reflected, sighing as she looked at her plump white arm. 'I suppose he is tall, with large eyes and possibly a small black moustache. Oh dear, I'm already twenty-two and the only person ever to have fallen for me was that pock-faced Ivan Ipatych. Four years ago I was even prettier. But now my girlhood has passed without bringing joy to anyone. Oh, I'm so unlucky! I'm just a poor country girl!'

The country girl was roused from her brief reverie by her mother calling her to pour out the tea. She tossed her head back and went into the tea-room.

The best things in life always happen by chance: the more one tries, the worse things turn out. Country dwellers rarely do very much about their children's education, so for the most part the education turns out excellent. This was so in Liza's case. With her limited intellect and easy-going nature, Anna herself had not given Liza any education at all. She had taught her neither music, nor French, which is so very useful. Purely by chance she had presented her husband with a healthy, pretty child – a daughter – whom she entrusted to a wet-nurse and nanny. She had fed her, dressed her in cotton frocks and goatskin shoes, sent her out to play and gather mushrooms and berries and engaged a young student to teach her reading, writing and arithmetic. Sixteen years later she came to realize (purely by chance) that in Liza she had a good friend and a perpetually cheerful, kind-hearted and hard-working housekeeper. As she herself was so kind-hearted, Anna was always looking after little girls, either serf children or foundlings.

Ever since she was ten, Liza had helped to look after these children. She taught them, dressed them, took them to church and scolded them when they were particularly naughty. And then along came her senile, good-hearted uncle, who needed to be tended like a baby. Then there were the house servants and the peasants, who came to the young mistress with all their aches and pains, which she treated with elderflower water, mint and camphorated spirits. Then there was the housekeeping which – purely by chance – had fallen on her shoulders. And then there was an unsatisfied longing for love which awoke in her and for which she found an outlet in love of nature and in religion. And so, purely by chance, Liza grew into a busy, good-natured, cheerful, independent, chaste and deeply religious young woman. True, her pride suffered somewhat when she saw neighbours in church wearing fashionable hats brought from the town of K—; and her irritable old mother's whims sometimes drove her to tears. And there were those dreams of love which took the most absurd and sometimes crude forms, but which were banished by her useful work, which had grown into a necessity. Consequently, at twenty-two, not one blemish, not one regret marred the pure, serene soul of this mature young woman, so rich in moral and physical beauty.

Liza was of medium height, with a full rather than slight figure. Her eyes were small, brown and faintly shadowed on the lower lids; her hair was long and fair. She would walk with long strides and with a gentle swaying motion. When she was busy and had no particular worries on her mind, her expression seemed to say to all who looked at it: life is wonderful, life is a joy for those whose consciences are clear and who have someone to love. Even in moments of annoyance, indignation, alarm or sadness, when tears came to her eyes, when her lips became tightly pressed and her left eyebrow frowned – even then, as if against her will, the light of her kind, honest heart, untainted by sophistication, would shine in the dimples of her cheeks, the corners of her mouth and in those sparkling eyes that were always smiling with the joy of living.

10

It was still hot, although the sun was setting, when the squadron entered Morozovka. A spotted cow that had strayed from the herd ran ahead of it along the dusty village road. Unable to understand that it only had to move to one side, it kept anxiously looking round, stopping to low every now and then. Both sides of the road were crowded with old peasants, their wives and children, and with servants from the manor-house eagerly watching the hussars ride along in a thick cloud of dust, curbing their black, bridled, snorting horses. To the right of the squadron rode two officers, loosely seated on their handsome black horses. One of them was Turbin, the commanding officer, and the other was Polozov, extremely young and recently commissioned.

Out of the best hut in the village emerged a hussar in a white tunic.

Raising his cap, he went up to the two officers.

'Where are our quarters?' asked the count.

'For Your Excellency?' the quartermaster replied, stiffening up. 'We've cleaned this hut out – it belongs to the village elder. I did ask if they had anything at the manor-house, but they said they've no room. The lady there seems very bad-tempered.'

'All right,' the count said, dismounting and stretching his legs as he went over to the hut. 'Has my carriage arrived?'

'That it has, Your excellency!' the quartermaster replied, pointing with his cap at the leather body of the carriage that could be seen through the gates and dashing forward to the entrance of the hut where a whole peasant family had gathered to look at the officers. He even pushed one old woman over as he flung open the door of the freshly cleaned hut to let the count pass.

The hut was quite large and roomy, but not very clean. The German valet, dressed like a gentleman, had put up an iron bedstead and was taking linen out of a travelling-bag.

'Ugh, what a dump!' the count said, extremely annoyed. 'Dyadenko! Did they really have nothing at the manor-house?'

'If Your Excellency so wishes I'll send someone over again,' Dyadenko replied. 'But it's not much of a place either – not much better than this hut.'

'Don't bother, it's too late now. Go away!'

And the count lay down on the bed with his hands under his head.

'Johann!' he shouted to his valet. 'You've made a lump in the middle again! Why can't you make a bed properly?'

Johann started smoothing it out.

'No, leave it. Where's my dressing-gown?' he continued in a petulant voice. The valet gave him his dressing-gown.

Before putting it on, the count inspected the front.

'Just as I thought, you haven't got rid of that stain. I don't think anyone can have a worse valet than you!' he added, snatching the dressing-gown from him and putting it on. 'Tell me, do you do this on purpose? Is tea ready?'

'I haven't had time . . .' Johann replied.

'Idiot!'

The count picked up a French novel that lay open and read for some time in silence. Johann went out to heat the samovar. The count was clearly in a very bad mood, doubtless due to tiredness, a dusty face, tight clothing and an empty stomach.

'Johann!' he shouted again. 'Account for those ten roubles I gave you. What did you buy in town?'

The count inspected the list and grumbled about the high prices.

'I'd like some rum in my tea.'

'I didn't buy any,' Johann replied.

'That's splendid! How many times have I told you that we should always keep some rum?'

'I didn't have enough money.'

'Then why didn't Polozov buy some? You could have got some from his man.'

'Cornet Polozov? I don't know . . . I think he only bought tea and sugar . . .'

'You swine! Now get out! There's no one who tries my patience like you . . . You know I always have rum in my tea when we're on the move.'

'Here's two letters from headquarters for you,' the valet said.

Without getting up, the count opened the letters and started reading.

The cornet, who had just seen to his men's quarters, entered with a cheery face. 'Well, what do you think, Turbin? Not bad. I must confess, I'm damned tired. It was very hot today.'

'Not bad? A filthy stinking hut, and no rum, thanks to you. That blockhead of yours didn't buy any, nor did this one. You could at least have told your man to buy some.'

And he carried on reading. When he finished the first letter, he crumpled it up and threw it on the floor.

Meanwhile, out in the hall, the cornet whispered to his orderly, 'Why didn't you buy any rum? You had enough money, didn't you?'

'But why do *we* always have to fork out? As it is, I pay for everything. That German of his does nothing but smoke his pipe!'

The second letter was evidently not disagreeable, since the count smiled as he read it.

'Who is it from?' asked Polozov, who had returned to the room and was making up a bed on some boards by the stove.

'It's from Mina,' the count replied gaily, handing him the letter. 'Care to read it? What a delightful woman . . . really, so much better than our local girls . . . Just see how much feeling and wit there is in that letter! But there's one thing I don't like – she's asking for money.'

'Yes, that's bad,' the cornet agreed.

'To be honest, I did promise her some, but then we all went marching off and besides . . . Anyway, if I'm in command of this squadron for another three months I'll be able to send her some. I certainly wouldn't begrudge her . . . Charming, eh?' he asked with a smile, watching Polozov's face as he read the letter.

'Awfully ungrammatical, but rather charming. It seems as if she really loves you,' the cornet replied.

'Hm! Of course she does. It's only women like her who truly love – when they do happen to love!'

'And who's the other one from?' the cornet asked, handing back the letter he had just finished reading.

'Oh, that? It's from some rotter to whom I lost at cards and this is the third time he's reminded me of the fact . . . I can't pay him just now . . . A stupid letter!' the count added, clearly annoyed by the reminder.

After this the two officers said nothing for a while. The cornet, evidently influenced by the count's mood, did not feel like talking and drank his tea in silence, glancing every now and then at the handsome but clouded face of Turbin, who stood and stared out of the window.

'Oh well, it might turn out all right,' the count suddenly said, turning to Polozov with a cheerful shake of the head. 'If there are promotions this year by seniority and we manage to get some active service in as well, I might be able to steal a march on some of my friends who are captains in the Guards.'

They were still discussing the same topic over a second glass of tea when old Danilo came in with Mrs Zaitsev's message.

'And I was also to ask if Your Honour happens to be Count Turbin's son,' Danilo added of his own accord, recognizing the name and remembering the count's stay in the town of K—. 'Mrs Zaitsev, my mistress, knew him very well.'

'He was my father. Go and tell your mistress that I'm deeply grateful, but there's nothing we need. But you might ask her if she could find us a cleaner room – at the manor-house perhaps, or somewhere else.'

'Why did you say that?' Polozov asked when Danilo had gone. 'What does it matter? – we're only here for one night. Now they'll go and put themselves to a lot of trouble.'

'What are you talking about? I think we've both had our fair share of dossing down in smoky huts. Obviously you're not the practical type. Why shouldn't we take advantage of living like human beings again, if only for one night? They'll be only too pleased. But there's one thing I don't like . . . if she really did know my father,' the count continued, displaying his white, sparkling teeth in a broad smile. 'At times I feel ashamed of dear departed Papa, I'm always hearing about some scandal, some debt. That's why I simply hate running into his old friends. Well, that's how they lived in those days!' he added solemnly.

'I forgot to tell you,' Polozov said, 'that I happened to bump into an uhlan brigade commander by the name of Ilin. He was very keen to meet you, simply doted on your father.'

'From what I hear, that Ilin's absolute trash. The worst of it is that these fine gentlemen who claim to have known my father in order to get into my good books like to tell stories about him as if they were pleasing to the ear. But it makes me really ashamed to listen to them. It's all true and, as you know, I always try to look at things coolly and objectively. I don't deny that he was too hot-tempered and sometimes did things that were nothing to be proud of, but we can blame the times for that. Nowadays he might have been a great success and, to give him his due, he was extremely talented.'

A quarter of an hour later Danilo returned with an invitation from his mistress: would the gentlemen be so good as to spend the night at the manor-house.

II

When she discovered that the hussar officer was the son of Count Turbin, Anna bustled about the house with a vengeance.

'Good heavens! The dear boy! Danilo! Run and tell them your mistress is inviting them to stay . . .' she had said, leaping to her feet and dashing off to the maids' room. 'Lizanka, Ustyushka! Liza – we must prepare your room – you can move into Uncle's. As for you, dear brother, you won't mind spending the night in the drawing-room, will you? It won't hurt you, for one night.'

'Of course I don't mind, dear sister! I can bed down on the floor.'

'He must be handsome if he's anything like the father. Oh, just to have one look at the dear boy! You'll see, Liza. The father was so handsome! . . . Where are you taking that table? Leave it here,' Anna said, rushing about. 'And bring two beds – you can fetch one from the estate steward's place. And take that crystal candlestick, the one my brother gave me for my birthday, and put a stearin candle in it.'

Finally all was ready. Despite her mother's interference, Liza arranged her room for the officers the way she wanted. She brought fresh bed-linen scented with mignonette, made the beds herself and had a carafe of water and some candles placed on the small bedside tables. Then she burned some perfumed paper in the maids' room and made up a bed for herself in her uncle's room. Anna felt more relaxed now that all the preparations had been made and she sat down in her usual place and even picked up her cards again. But instead of laying them out she leaned her puffy elbows on the table and became lost in thought. 'How time flies!' she whispered to herself. 'Can it be so long ago? I can see him now. Oh, he was so daring!' And tears came to her eyes. 'Now it's Liza's turn . . . but she's not the same as I was at her age . . . She's pretty, but not how I used to be . . .'

'Liza, you should wear your mousseline-de-laine dress this evening.'

'You're not going to entertain them this evening, are you, Mother? I don't think you should,' Liza said, unable to suppress her excitement at the thought of meeting the two officers. But in actual fact fear of some deeply disturbing happiness that possibly awaited her out-weighed any desire to see them.

'Perhaps they themselves will want to meet us, Liza dear,' Anna said, stroking her daughter's hair and thinking, 'No, her hair isn't like mine was at her age. No, Liza, how I would wish . . .'

And there really was something she earnestly desired for her daughter. But she would not even think of her marrying the count, nor did she want her to have the kind of relationship she had had with the father. Yet there was something she fervently desired for her daughter. Perhaps it was just that she wanted to relive, through her, what she had felt for the late count?

The old cavalry officer was also excited at the count's arrival. He went to his room, locked himself in and emerged a quarter of an hour later in military tunic and light blue trousers. With that same look of self-conscious pleasure assumed by young girls when they don a ball gown for the first time, he entered the room that had been prepared for the officers.

'Now I'll be able to look at this new breed of hussars, dear sister! The late count was a true hussar, in every sense of the word. Well, we shall see!'

The officers went to the room that had been prepared for them by the back door.

'There – what did I tell you?' the count said, lying down on the freshly made bed as he was, in his dusty boots. 'Isn't this better than that cockroach-infested hut?'

'Yes it is, but we've put ourselves under an obligation to our hosts . . .'

'Rubbish! You must always be practical. Rest assured that they'll be delighted . . . Boy!' he shouted. 'Ask them to hang something over that window or there'll be a terrible draught in here tonight.'

Just then the old man came in to introduce himself. Although it brought a faint blush to his cheeks, he did not omit to tell them of course that he and the late count had been bosom friends, that the count had shown him many favours and that more than once the count had been indebted to him for certain services rendered. Whether by 'services' he meant the count's non-payment of the hundred roubles he had borrowed, or the time when he was shoved into a snowdrift, or sworn at, the old man did not say. The young count was extremely polite to the old officer and thanked him for putting them up for the night.

'You must forgive us, Count, if it's not very luxurious (he almost said 'Your Excellency,' so unused had he become to addressing people of high rank). My sister's house is so small. Yes, we'll hang something up over that window right away to stop the draught,' the old man added, using the curtain as an excuse to go and tell the others all about the officers without delay and shuffling away.

Pretty Ustyushka came in to drape her mistress's shawl over the window. Her mistress had also told her to ask the gentlemen if they would care for some tea.

The civilized surroundings had evidently raised the count's spirits. He smiled gaily and joked with Ustyushka so cheerfully that she called him naughty and when she asked them if they would like some tea he told her that she could by all means bring it, but most important, since their batman had not prepared supper yet, could they have some vodka, something to eat, and some sherry, if there was any in the house?

Uncle was enraptured by the young count's manners and praised the younger generation of officers to the skies, saying that the young men of today were far superior to their predecessors.

Anna disagreed – no one could ever outshine Count Fyodor

Turbin – and in the end became quite angry, drily remarking, 'For you, dear brother, the last person to be kind to you is always the best. Of course, everyone knows that people have become more clever these days, but Count Turbin danced the écossaise so superbly and was so charming that everyone simply lost their heads – although he only had eyes for me. So you see, there were fine men in the old days too.'

Just then the maid came in to tell them of the officers' request for vodka, food and sherry.

'Honestly! You never do the right thing, dear brother! You should have ordered some supper for them,' Anna said. 'Liza, please see to it, dear.'

Liza ran to the larder for pickled mushrooms and fresh butter, and told cook to make some rissoles.

'Do you have any sherry left, brother?'

'No, I never had any.'

'How's that? What is it you're always pouring in your tea?'

'Rum, my dear Anna.'

'Well, it doesn't make any difference, does it? Give them some of that . . . rum. But shouldn't we invite them in here? You know about these things, brother. I don't think they would take offence.'

The cavalry officer said he would vouch for the fact that the count would be much too good-natured to refuse and that he would bring them without fail. Anna went to put on her silk dress and a new bonnet, but Liza was too busy to change her wide-sleeved pink linen dress. She was terribly nervous: she sensed that something momentous was about to happen and it was as if some dark, menacing storm-cloud were hanging over her. She imagined this hussar, this handsome count, to be some perfectly new kind of being, incomprehensible but beautiful. His manners, his habits, his conversation – everything about him must be unusual, so unlike anything she had ever encountered before. All that he said or thought must be true and clever; all that he did must be honourable; and his whole appearance must be beautiful in every detail. If he had requested a perfumed bath, besides the food and sherry, she would not have been surprised, nor would she have blamed him: on the contrary, she would have been firmly convinced that it was only right and proper.

The count agreed at once when the cavalry officer extended his sister's invitation. He combed his hair, put on his coat and took out his cigar-case.

'Let's go,' he told Polozov.

'I really don't think we should,' the cornet replied. *'Ils feront des frais pour nous recevoir.'*

'Nonsense. They'll be only too delighted. Besides, I've already made some inquiries – it seems there's a pretty daughter ... Come on,' the count replied in French.

'Je vous en prie, messieurs!' the cavalry officer said, to let them know that he too knew French and understood what they had said.

12

Too shy to look at the officers when they entered the room, Liza blushed and looked down, pretending to be busy filling the teapot. But Anna quickly got up, curtseyed and, without taking her eyes off his face, she talked to the count, commenting on his remarkable likeness to his father, introduced her daughter and then offered him tea, jam and fruit compote. The cornet was so modest in his appearance that everyone ignored him: this pleased him immensely, as it gave him the opportunity of studying (within the bounds of propriety) Liza's beauty, which had evidently taken him quite by surprise. Uncle sat and listened to his sister talking to the count, eagerly awaiting his chance to narrate his reminiscences as a cavalry officer. During tea the count lit such a strong cigar that Liza found it difficult not to cough. He was very talkative and charming, at first filling the intervals in Anna's incessant chatter with a few little anecdotes and then holding the stage himself. One thing, however, struck his audience as rather odd and this was his use of certain words which, although they would not have been considered at all risqué in his own circle, were a little daring in the present company. Anna was somewhat alarmed, while Liza blushed furiously. But the count did not notice and he remained as charming and composed as ever.

Liza silently filled the glasses and instead of putting them in her guests' hands, set them down within easy reach. She still had not got over her initial excitement and eagerly listened to every word the count said. The triteness of his stories and rather hesitant delivery gradually made her feel more relaxed. She heard none of the brilliant witticisms that she had been expecting, nor could she detect a trace of that general refinement she had been vaguely hoping for. Over the third glass of tea, when her timid eyes happened to meet his and he had continued to stare at her – rather too calmly for her liking – smiling the faintest of smiles, she felt a certain hostility welling up inside her and soon came to realize that not only was he very ordinary, but that he was no different from anyone else she knew and that she had no reason to feel afraid of him. True, he did have long, well-manicured finger-nails, but he was not particularly handsome. And Liza suddenly abandoned her cherished dream (not without a certain regret) and regained her composure. All that disturbed her now was the taciturn cornet's gaze, permanently fixed on her. 'Perhaps it's not to be the count, but this one!' she thought.

13

After tea the old lady invited her guests into the other room and settled into her usual place.

'Don't you feel like a rest, Count?' she asked. 'Well, how can we amuse you, my dear guests?' she continued, after a negative answer. 'Do you play cards, Count? Come on, dear brother, you should be looking after them! Why don't you arrange a hand of something? . . .'

'You play preference,* don't you?' replied the cavalry officer. 'Why don't we all play? Would you like to, Count? And you?'

The officers expressed their willingness to do anything their charming hosts suggested.

Liza brought the old pack of cards she used for telling the future – whether Anna's toothache would soon be better, whether Uncle would return from town the same day as he went, whether a neighbouring lady would visit them that morning, and so on. Although these cards had been used for about two months, they were cleaner than those used by Anna for telling fortunes.

'Perhaps you don't care to play for small stakes?' Uncle asked. 'Anna and I usually play for half a copeck a point. Even so, she usually wins all our money.'

* Preference – A type of whist.

'I'd be delighted to play for whatever you wish,' the count replied.

'Splendid! So, let it be one copeck a time in paper money* – in honour of such distinguished guests! Let them make a beggar out of an old woman!' Anna said, settling into her armchair and arranging her mantilla. 'Who knows, perhaps I'll win a rouble off them,' Anna wondered. In her old age she had conceived a mild passion for cards, it seemed.

'If you like, I'll show you how to play with *tables* and *misères*'† the count suggested. 'It's great fun.'

Everyone was delighted with the new St Petersburg style of playing. Uncle even claimed that he was familiar with it, that it was in fact the same as boston, only he was a little rusty. Anna understood nothing, however, and she understood nothing for so long that she finally felt compelled to smile and nod approvingly that she did understand it and that all was perfectly clear. There was a loud outburst of laughter in the middle of the game when Anna, holding the ace and king, declared '*misère*' and was left with six tricks. She became quite flustered, smiled weakly and hastened to assure the others that she was not really used to the new style yet. All the same, the others scored against her, and scored heavily, particularly as the count, accustomed to playing for high stakes, played very cautiously, keeping an exact tally of the points and failing to understand the reason either for the cornet's kicks under the table or the latter's glaring blunders when calling tricks.

Liza fetched some more compote, three kinds of jam and some specially soaked apples. She stood behind her mother, watching the game and occasionally glancing at the officers, particularly at the count's white hands and pink manicured nails as he threw down his cards and took tricks with such skill, assurance and style.

Anna rashly tried to outbid the others, declaring seven tricks and making only four, for which she was fined and had to pay a forfeit. After scribbling some indecipherable figures at her brother's request, she became dreadfully confused and completely lost her head.

* The word used is *assignats*, a form of paper money that officially went out of use in 1840.

† A player who declared '*misère*' undertook to make no tricks and was fined for any trick taken.

'Don't worry, Mamma, you can still win it back!' Liza said, smiling, anxious to rescue her mother from her ridiculous situation. 'Let Uncle make a forfeit, then *he'll* be in trouble!'

'I wish you'd help me, Liza!' Anna exclaimed, giving her daughter a frightened look. 'I don't know how to play . . .'

'I don't know either,' Liza replied, mentally adding up her mother's losses. 'But I do know that you'll lose everything if you go on like that, Mamma. We won't even have enough for Pimochka's new dress,' she added in jest.

'Yes, that way you can very easily lose ten silver roubles,' said the cornet, looking at Liza and longing to talk to her.

'Oh – I thought we were playing with paper money?' Anna asked, glancing at everyone.

'I don't know what we're playing with, but I can't calculate in paper money,' the count said. 'What is it? I mean, what *is* paper money?'

'Well, nowadays nobody counts in paper money any more,' chimed in Uncle, who had played very steadily and was winning.

The old lady ordered some sparkling fruit drinks, drank two glasses herself, became very flushed and appeared to have abandoned herself to her fate. She did not even bother to tuck in a lock of her grey hair that had strayed from under her bonnet. No doubt she thought that she had lost millions and was completely ruined. The cornet kicked the count under the table even more. As for the count, he made a careful note of all the old lady's losses. Finally the game finished. Despite all Anna's dishonest attempts to increase her score, pretending to have made a mistake in her arithmetic, at which she had never been very good, and despite her horror at the extent of her losses, it finally turned out that she had lost nine hundred and twenty points.

'Is that nine roubles in paper money?' she asked several times. She was quite unable to understand the magnitude of her losses until her brother explained to her great dismay that she had lost thirty-two and a half roubles in paper money, which must be paid without fail. The count did not even bother to add up his winnings, but as soon as the game was over went to the window at which Liza was laying out refreshments and emptying some pickled mushrooms from a jar on to a plate for supper. Quite coolly and calmly he did what the cornet had been dying to do the whole evening but had not succeeded – he began a conversation with Liza about the weather.

Now the cornet was in a most disagreeable situation. In the absence of the count, and especially of Liza, who had managed to keep her mother cheerful, Anna gave full vent to her feelings.

'It's too bad, winning all that money from you,' Polozov remarked for the sake of saying something. 'It's quite disgraceful!'

'I should say so, with all those "*tables*" and "*misères*" you thought up! I've no idea how to play them. Well then, what did you say it comes to in paper money?'

'Thirty-two roubles, thirty-two and a half,' said the old cavalry officer, whose winnings had put him in a jolly mood. 'Now, give me the money, dear sister! Give it to me!'

'I'll pay up, but you won't catch me again, oh no! I'd never win all that money back as long as I live!'

And Anna hurried off to her room, hurriedly swaying from side to side and returned with nine paper roubles. It was only at the old man's insistence that she paid up in full.

Polozov was rather apprehensive that Anna would give him a taste of her tongue if he ventured a conversation with her, so he quietly slipped away and joined the count and Liza, who were talking at the open window.

On the table laid for supper stood two tallow candles. Now and then their flames flickered in the fresh, warm breath of the May night. It was light at the window opening on to the garden, but it was quite different from the light in the room. An almost full moon, which was losing its golden tinge, was sailing over the tall lime-trees, shedding ever more light on the delicate white clouds that ran across it from time to time. A full-throated chorus of frogs croaked down by the pond and part of its surface, silvered by the moon, could be glimpsed through the trees in the avenue. Some little birds lightly hopped from branch to branch and ruffled their feathers in the fragrant lilac bush whose dewy blossoms occasionally gently swayed beneath the window.

'What marvellous weather!' said the count, going over to Liza and sitting on the window-sill. 'I suppose you go for lots of walks?'

'Yes,' replied Liza, who for some reason did not feel at all embarrassed talking to the count. 'At seven o'clock in the morning I see to things in the house and then take a short stroll with Pimochka, the little girl Mamma adopted.'

'It must be so pleasant living in the country,' the count said, screwing his monocle into his eye and looking at the garden and Liza in turn. 'Do you ever walk at night, when there's a moon?'

'Not any more. But about two years ago Uncle and I used to go out every night there was a moon. But then he began suffering from a strange complaint – insomnia. Whenever the moon was full he couldn't sleep. His room – that one over there – opens directly on to the garden. The window's very low and the moon shone straight on to him.'

'Strange,' remarked the count. 'I thought that it was your room.'

'No, I'm sleeping there only tonight. The one you have is mine.'

'Really? . . . Good heavens, I'll never forgive myself for putting you out,' the count said, letting his monocle drop from his eye as a sign of his sincerity. 'Had I known that I was inconveniencing you . . .'

'It's no inconvenience! On the contrary, I'm only too pleased. Uncle's room is so charming, so light and cheerful, with that low window. I think I'll sit there until I fall asleep, or perhaps I'll climb out into the garden and walk a little before I go to bed.'

'What a splendid girl!' the count thought, replacing his monocle to get a better look at her and trying to touch her foot with his as he pretended to be making himself comfortable on the window-sill. 'And how artfully she let me know that I can see her at the window if I so wish.' So easy did a conquest appear now that Liza even lost most of her attraction.

'How delightful it must be,' he observed, looking thoughtfully at the dark avenue of trees, 'to spend a night such as this in a garden, with someone you love.'

This remark, and a further seemingly chance touch of his leg, embarrassed Liza. Without thinking and in her anxiety to hide her confusion she said, 'Yes, it's lovely walking in the moonlight.' A rather unpleasant feeling came over her, so she put away the mushroom-jar and was about to walk from the window when the cornet joined them. Now she had a sudden impulse to discover what kind of man he was.

'What a beautiful night!' he said.

'All they can talk about is the weather,' Liza thought.

87

'And what a marvellous view!' the cornet continued. 'But I should imagine you're tired of it by now,' he added, from his strange habit of saying something disagreeable to those he liked very much.

'What makes you think that? One grows tired of the same food or wearing the same dress, but never of a beautiful garden if one likes walking, especially when the moon is even higher. From Uncle's room you can see the whole pond – I shall look at it tonight.'

'You don't have any nightingales, do you?' the count asked, furious at Polozov for joining them, thus preventing him from finding out what precisely she had in mind regarding a rendezvous.

'No, we used to have them, but only last year some sportsman caught one and this year – last week in fact – I heard one singing beautifully. But then the police officer drove up and his carriage bells frightened it away. Two years ago Uncle and I used to sit under the trees in the avenue listening to them for two hours at a time.'

'What's that little chatterbox telling you now?' Uncle asked, coming up. 'Would you care for something to eat, gentlemen?'

After supper, during which the count, by praising the food and eating with great appetite, somehow managed to put his hostess in a better humour, the two officers said goodnight and went to their room. The count shook Uncle's hand and, to Anna's amazement, shook hers without kissing it and even shook Liza's hand, looking at her straight in the eye and giving her one of his faint but pleasant smiles. Once again she was troubled by that stare.

'He's very good-looking,' she thought, 'but he thinks too much of himself.'

14

'Well, aren't you ashamed?' Polozov asked when the officers had returned to their room. 'I was trying to make us lose – that's why I kept kicking you under the table. Aren't you ashamed? The old lady was most upset.'

The count roared with laughter. 'That woman's killingly funny – she took it really badly!'

Once again he roared with laughter – so heartily that even Johann, who was standing in front of him, looked down at the floor and gave a weak, furtive smile.

'Now, there's the son of an old family friend for you! Ha, ha, ha . . .'

'Really, it wasn't very nice. I felt quite sorry for her,' the cornet said.

'Rubbish! You're still so young! Did you want me to lose? Why should I? I used to lose often enough before I learned how to play. Ten roubles, old man, will come in very handy. You must look at life practically, or people will walk all over you.'

Polozov said nothing. He wanted to be left alone to think about Liza, who struck him as a remarkably pure, beautiful creature. He undressed and lay down on the soft clean bed that had been made for him. 'All that talk about the honour and prestige of a soldier's life is sheer nonsense!' he reflected as he looked at the window draped with the shawl and through which pale moonbeams were stealing. 'Yes, true happiness is life in some quiet, small retreat with a dear, clever, unspoilt wife. *That* is true, lasting happiness!'

But for some reason he did not communicate these thoughts to his friend, nor did he even mention the country girl, although he was convinced that the count was thinking of her too.

'Why don't you get undressed?' he asked the count, who was pacing the room.

'Somehow I don't feel like sleeping. Put the candle out if you want, I don't need it.'

And he carried on pacing the room.

'I don't feel like sleeping,' Polozov repeated to himself. The events of that evening had made him deplore even more the influence the count had over him and put him in a rebellious mood. 'I can just imagine,' he said to himself, mentally addressing Turbin, 'what's going on in that well-groomed head of yours. I saw how you took to her! But you are incapable of understanding such a simple, honest creature. What *you* really need is your Mina and a colonel's epaulettes. Now, why don't I ask what he thought of her?'

But just as Polozov was about to turn over and speak to the count he changed his mind. He felt that not only would he be unable to stand up to him if there was an argument (and if the count's feelings for Liza were as he supposed), but also that he would be forced to agree, so accustomed was he to bowing to that influence which seemed to be growing more unbearable and unjust with every passing day.

'Where are you going?' he asked as the count put on his cap and went towards the door.

'To check if everything's all right in the stables.'

'Strange!' thought the cornet, but he snuffed the candle, turned over and tried to banish those absurdly jealous and hostile thoughts that his former friend had aroused in him.

Meanwhile Anna had tenderly kissed and made the sign of the cross over her brother, daughter and ward, as was her custom, and retired to her room. It was long since the old lady had experienced so many powerful sensations in one day and as a result she could not pray calmly, she was so distressed by those sad and vivid memories of the late count and the thought of that young fop who had so shamelessly taken her money. She climbed into bed after undressing and drinking her usual half glass of kvass* which was always left on the little bedside table for her. Her favourite cat softly crept into the room. Anna called it over and started stroking it, listened to its purr, but could not fall asleep.

'It's the cat that's keeping me awake,' she thought and she pushed it away. The cat softly dropped on to the floor, slowly curled its fluffy tail and jumped up on to the bench over the stove. Just then the maid who slept on the floor in Anna's room brought her felt mat, spread it out, snuffed the candle and lit the icon lamp. Before long she was snoring away, but sleep still would not come to calm Anna's excited imagination. Whenever she closed her eyes the hussar's face appeared and whenever she opened them in the dim lamplight to look at the chest of drawers, the table, her white dress, she imagined she could see the count there, in many strange and varied guises. One moment she felt terribly hot in her feather bed and the next she was irritated by the clock striking or the maid snoring. She woke the girl and told her to stop. Once again thoughts of her daughter, of the old count, and the young one, of the game of preference mingled curiously in her mind. Now she pictured herself waltzing with the old count, saw her own plump white shoulders, felt someone's lips on them; then she saw her daughter in the arms of the young count. Ustyushka started snoring again . . .

'No, people have changed. The other count was ready to go

* A home-brewed beer made from rye bread and malt.

through fire and water for me – and there was good reason! But this one, so pleased with his winnings, is sleeping like the idiot he is without a thought of making love . . . How his father went down on his knees and declared, "What would you have me do? I'll kill myself here and now, I'll do anything you command!" And he would have killed himself had I told him to.'

Suddenly she heard the patter of bare feet out in the passage and Liza, pale and trembling, with only a shawl over her dressing-gown, ran into the room and almost fell on to her mother's bed . . .

After bidding her mother goodnight Liza had gone alone to her uncle's room. Then she had put on her white dressing-jacket, covered her long, thick plait with a kerchief, put out the candle, opened the window and sat on a chair with her legs tucked under her, pensively gazing at the pond whose whole surface was shimmering in the silvery light. All her usual occupations and interests suddenly appeared to her in a completely new light: her capricious old mother, unquestioning love for whom had become part of her very existence; her senile but amiable old uncle; the servants and villagers who idolized their young mistress; the milch-cows and calves; the natural life around her, dying and renewing itself with the changing seasons and in the midst of which, loving and loved herself, she had grown up – everything that had brought such joy and contentment to her soul now struck her as nothing, as wearisome and unnecessary. It was as if someone had told her, 'Little fool! Little fool! For twenty years you've been wasting your time waiting on others, without knowing what life and happiness really are.' Now, as she gazed into the depths of that bright, still garden, she thought about these things far more deeply than ever before. What had prompted these thoughts? Definitely no sudden love for the count, as one might have supposed: on the contrary, she did not like him. She could have been interested in the cornet, but he was so plain and quiet, poor man. She had so easily forgotten him and it was with annoyance and anger that she kept visualizing the count. 'No, he's not the one,' she told herself. Her ideal was someone beautiful, someone who could be loved on such a night as this, in such a setting, without disturbing its beauty – an ideal that had never been debased to fit crude reality.

At first, solitude and the absence of anyone to interest her had ensured that the power of love, which Providence has implanted in the heart of each and every one of us, remained whole and undisturbed in her heart. But she had lived too long with the sad joy of sensing within herself the presence of this *something* (although she did occasionally examine the secret coffer of her heart to delight in its riches), too long recklessly to lavish them on the first person who came along. God grant that she might enjoy that meagre joy until the day she died! Who knew whether this joy was the best and greatest, whether it alone was the only true and possible joy?

'God!' she thought. 'Have I really let youth and happiness pass me by . . . shall I never know them? Can this be the truth?' And she looked up into the depths of the bright sky where fleecy white clouds were veiling the tiny stars as they moved towards the moon. 'If that highest cloud touches the moon, it is the truth,' she reflected. A misty, smoky strip ran across the lower half of that bright disc and gradually the light that was shining on the grass, on the crowns of the lime-trees, on the pond, began to fade and the black shadows of the trees grew less distinct. And, as if following close upon those gloomy shadows darkening nature, a gentle breeze passed over the leaves, bringing the dewy scent of leaves, moist earth and blossoming lilac to the window.

'No, it's not the truth,' she consoled herself. 'And if the nightingale sings tonight, then what I am thinking now is nonsense and I mustn't despair.' And for a long time she sat there in silence, waiting for someone. Suddenly everything brightened up – but then those tiny clouds ran across the moon and all was dark again. She was beginning to fall asleep as she sat there at the window when the nightingale woke her with its warbling from across the pond. The country girl opened her eyes. Once more her soul was revived and filled with new joy by that mysterious union with nature, which lay so bright and serene all around her. She leaned on both elbows. A sweet and languid sadness lay heavily on her heart and tears of pure, unbounded love that yearned for fulfilment – fine, comforting tears – filled her eyes. She folded her arms on the window-sill and laid her head on them. Her favourite prayer entered her heart of itself and she fell asleep, just as she was, her eyes moist with tears.

The touch of a hand awoke her: it was so light and pleasant. Then it clasped her arm tighter and she suddenly realized what was happening. She gave a little cry, leapt to her feet and fled from the room, trying to convince herself that it was not the count standing there by the window, bathed in moonlight . . .

15

But it *was* the count. When he had heard the girl's cry and the night-watchman coughing on the other side of the fence as he came to see what was wrong, he had rushed headlong over the dewy grass into the depths of the garden, feeling like a thief caught in the act. 'Oh, what an idiot I am!' he told himself. 'I've frightened her. I should have been more gentle and woken her by speaking to her. Oh, I'm such a clumsy fool!' He stopped and listened: the watchman had come into the garden through the gate, dragging his stick along the sandy path. He had to hide, so he ran down to the pond. The frogs made him shudder as they hurriedly plopped into the water from under his feet. Although his boots were wet through, he squatted and recalled everything he had done: how he had climbed the fence, looked for her window and finally saw her pale shadow; how, listening for the slightest rustle, he had approached the window several times, only to retreat; how, at one moment he had been sure she was waiting, annoyed that he was taking so long, and at the next he had felt that she could not possibly have so readily consented to a rendezvous; and how, finally, on the assumption that only the bashfulness of a simple country girl had led her to pretend to be sleeping, he had gone up to her and seen quite clearly that she *was* asleep. Then, for some reason, he had immediately run away, but had felt deeply ashamed of his cowardice and had come back and boldly touched her arm. The watchman had coughed again and the gate creaked as he left the garden. The windows in the girl's room had slammed to and the shutters were fastened inside. It was all so annoying. What would he have given just to start again! No, he would never have behaved so idiotically a second time. 'What a lovely girl, so fresh, absolutely charming! And I let her slip through my fingers . . . what a silly ass I am!' By now he had no desire to sleep and with the determined step of a frustrated man he went down the covered lime-tree avenue.

But, even to him, the night brought its consoling gifts of soothing sadness and a longing for love. The clay path, with sprouting blades of grass and dry stalks sticking out here and there, was mottled by the pale moonbeams which fell directly through the thick foliage of the lime-trees. Occasionally a twisted branch would be lit up on one side so that it seemed overgrown with white moss. Now and then silvery leaves whispered to each other. All the lights in the house were extinguished, all sounds died away: only the song of the nightingale filled that boundless, silent, bright expanse. 'What a night! What a wonderful night!' thought the count as he filled his lungs with the fresh garden scents. 'But something is wrong. I seem to be dissatisfied with myself and others, dissatisfied with life in general. What a sweet, lovely girl! Perhaps she was deeply hurt . . .' And here his day-dreams became confused: now he imagined himself in the garden with that country girl, in the most weird and varied situations, then her role was taken by his darling Mina. 'What a fool I was. I should have put my arms around her waist and kissed her.' And with these regrets the count returned to his room.

The cornet was still awake. Immediately he turned in bed and faced the count.

'Not asleep yet?' the count asked.

'No.'

'Shall I tell you what happened?'

'Well?'

'No, I'd better not . . . all right, I will. Move your legs over.' Dismissing all thoughts of the bungled opportunity from his mind, the count sat down on his friend's bed with a lively smile on his face. 'Would you believe it, the young lady agreed to a rendezvous!'

'What did you say?' Polozov cried, leaping up.

'Listen . . .'

'But how? When? It can't be true!'

'Well, while you were totting up your winnings after preference, she told me that she would be waiting at her window tonight and that I could get into her room through it. There's a practical man for you! So, while you were doing your sums with the old lady, I was arranging it. But you must have heard her say that she would sit at the window tonight and look at the pond.'

'She couldn't have been serious.'

'That's just what I can't understand, whether it was something that happened to slip out. Perhaps she didn't want to agree to it right away, but that's how it looked. It all turned out so strangely! I acted like a perfect idiot!' he added, smiling in self-contempt.

'But what happened? Where were you?'

The count told him everything, omitting only his repeated indecision in going up to the window.

'I ruined it. I should have been bolder. She cried out and ran away from the window.'

'So, she cried out and ran away,' the cornet said, smiling awkwardly in response to the count's smile which for so long had exerted such a powerful influence over him.

'Yes . . . well, it's time we got some sleep.'

The cornet turned his back to the door again and lay silently for about ten minutes. Heaven knows what he was feeling deep down, but when he turned again, his face expressed both anguish and determination.

'Count Turbin!' he said abruptly.

'What is it? Talking in your sleep?' the count calmly asked.

'Count Turbin, you're a cad!' Polozov shouted as he jumped out of bed.

16

Next day the squadron left. The two officers did not see their hosts and did not say goodbye. Nor did they speak to each other: they had agreed to a duel at the first halting place, but Captain Schultz, a good comrade and excellent horseman, who was held in great esteem by the whole regiment and was chosen by the count as his second, managed to patch things up so well that not only was a duel averted, but not a soul in the regiment knew anything about it. And Turbin and Polozov, although no longer the friends of before, still remained on familiar terms and occasionally met at dinners and parties.

[*11 April 1856*]

HOW MUCH LAND
DOES A MAN NEED?

I

An elder sister came from the town to visit her younger sister in the country. This elder sister was married to a merchant and the younger to a peasant in the village. The two sisters sat down for a talk over a cup of tea and the elder started boasting about the superiority of town life, with all its comforts, the fine clothes her children wore, the exquisite food and drink, the skating, parties and visits to the theatre.

The younger sister resented this and in turn scoffed at the life of a merchant's wife and sang the praises of her own life as a peasant.

'I wouldn't care to change my life for yours,' she said. 'I admit mine is dull, but at least we have no worries. You live in grander style, but you must do a great deal of business or you'll be ruined. You know the proverb, "Loss is Gain's elder brother." One day you are rich and the next you might find yourself out in the street. Here in the country we don't have those ups and downs. A peasant's life may be poor, but it's long. Although we may never be rich, we'll always have enough to eat.'

Then the elder sister said her piece.

'Enough to eat indeed with nothing but those filthy pigs and calves! What do you know about nice clothes and good manners! However hard your good husband slaves away you'll spend your lives in the muck and that's where you'll die. And the same goes for your children.'

'Well, what of it?' the younger sister retorted. 'That's how it is here. But at least we know where we are. We don't have to crawl to anyone and we're afraid of no one. But you in the town are surrounded by temptations. All may be well one day, the next the Devil comes along and tempts your husband with cards, women and drink. And then you're ruined. It does happen, doesn't it?'

Pakhom, the younger sister's husband, was lying over the stove listening to the women's chatter.

'It's true what you say,' he said. 'Take me. Ever since I was a youngster I've been too busy tilling the soil to let that kind of nonsense enter my head. My only grievance is that I don't have enough land. Give me enough of that and I'd fear no one – not even the Devil himself!'

The sisters finished their tea, talked a little longer about dresses, cleared away the tea things and went to bed.

But the Devil had been sitting behind the stove and had heard everything. He was delighted that a peasant's wife had led her husband to boast that if he had enough land he would fear no one, not even the Devil. 'Good!' he thought. 'I'll have a little game with you. I shall see that you have plenty of land and that way I'll get you in my clutches!'

2

Not far from the village lived a lady with a small estate of about three hundred acres. She had always been on good terms with the peasants and had never ill-treated them. But then she had taken on an old soldier to manage her estate and he proceeded to harass the peasants by constantly imposing fines. No matter how careful Pakhom was, one of his horses might stray into the lady's oats, or a cow might sometimes wander into her garden, or some calves might venture out on to her meadows. Every time this happened he would have to pay a fine.

Pakhom would pay up and then he would go and swear at his family and beat them. All that summer Pakhom had to put up with a great deal from that manager, so he welcomed winter when it came and his cattle had to be kept in the shed: although he begrudged the fodder, at least he wouldn't have to worry about them straying.

That winter word got round that the lady wanted to sell some of her land and that the innkeeper on the highway was trying to agree on a price with her. The peasants took this news very badly. 'If that innkeeper gets his hands on that land he'll start slapping even more fines on us than that manager. But we can't survive without it, we all depend on it for our living.'

So a few peasants, in the name of the village commune, begged the lady not to sell any of her land to the innkeeper and to let them buy it, offering her a better price. The lady agreed. Then the members of the commune thought of buying the whole estate. They met once, they met twice, but no progress was made: the Devil had set them at loggerheads and there was nothing they could agree upon. In the end they decided to buy the land in separate lots, each according to what he could afford. The lady agreed to this as well.

One day Pakhom learned that one of his neighbours was buying about fifty acres and that the lady had taken half payment in cash, allowing the man one year to pay the balance. This made Pakhom very envious. 'They'll buy up all the land,' he thought, 'and I'll be left with nothing.' So he conferred with his wife.

'Everyone's buying land,' he said. 'We must get hold of twenty acres, or thereabouts. If we don't we won't be able to live, what with that manager bleeding us white with fines.'

So they racked their brains as to how they could buy some of the land. They had a hundred roubles saved up, so that by selling a foal and half their bees, by sending one of their sons out to work for someone who paid wages in advance and borrowing from a brother-in-law, they managed to scrape together half the money.

Then Pakhom took the money, chose about thirty acres of partly wooded land and went off to the lady to see if he could strike a deal. He managed to get the thirty acres, they shook hands on it and Pakhom paid a deposit. Then they went into town and signed the deeds, Pakhom paying half cash down and pledging to settle the balance within two years.

And so Pakhom now had land. He borrowed money for seeds and sowed the newly bought land; the harvest was excellent. Within a year he had repaid both the lady and his brother-in-law. Now he was a landowner, in the full sense of the word: he ploughed and sowed his own fields, reaped his own hay, cut his own timber and could pasture his cattle on his own land. Whenever he rode out to plough the land which was now his for ever, or to inspect his young corn and meadows, he was filled with joy. He felt that the grass that grew and the flowers that bloomed were different from any other grass and flowers. Before, when he had ridden over that land, it had seemed the same as any other. But now it was something quite special.

3

So Pakhom lived a landowner's life and he was happy. And in fact all would have been well had other peasants not trespassed on his cornfields and meadows. He spoke to them very politely, but they took no notice. Herdsmen let their cows stray on to his meadows, then horses wandered into his corn on their way home from night pasture. Again and again Pakhom drove them out without taking further action, but in the end he lost patience and complained to the District Court. He knew very well that the peasants weren't doing it deliberately but because they were short of land. But still he thought, 'I can't let this go on. Before long they'll have destroyed all I have. I must teach them a lesson.'

So he taught them a lesson in court, then another, making several of them pay fines. Pakhom's neighbours resented this and once again began to let their cattle stray on his land, this time on purpose. One night someone managed to get into Pakhom's wood and felled about ten young lime-trees for their bark. Next day, when Pakhom was riding through his wood, he suddenly noticed something white on the ground. He went nearer and saw tree-trunks lying all around, stripped of their bark, with the stumps lying nearby. 'If he'd only just cut one or two down, but that devil's left me with one tree standing and cleared the rest.' Pakhom seethed with anger. 'Oh, if I knew who did it I'd show him a thing or two!' For a long time he racked his brains and finally concluded, 'It must be Semyon, it can't be anyone else.' So off he went to search Semyon's place, but he found nothing and all the two men did was swear at each other. Pakhom was more convinced than ever that it was Semyon's work and he lodged a complaint. The magistrates sat for ages debating the case and finally acquitted Semyon for lack of evidence. This incensed Pakhom even more and he had a stormy session with the village elder and the magistrates.

'You are hand in glove with thieves,' he protested. 'If you were honest men you wouldn't let a thief like him off the hook.'

As a result Pakhom fell out with the magistrates as well as his neighbours, who threatened to burn his cottage down.

And so, although Pakhom had plenty of leg-room now, he felt that the commune was hemming him in.

Around that time rumours were in the air that many peasants were leaving to settle in new parts of the country. Pakhom thought, 'I don't really need to go away, what with all that land of mine. But if some of the villagers were to go there'd be more room for others. I could buy their land and make my estate bigger. Life would be easier then, but as things are, it's still too cramped here for my liking.'

One day a peasant who was passing through stopped at Pakhom's cottage. They let him stay the night and gave him food. Pakhom asked where he was from and the man replied that he had come from the south, from the other side of the Volga, where he had been working. Then he told how people from his own village had settled there, joined the commune and had been allotted twenty-five acres each. 'The land is so fertile,' he said, 'that rye grows as high as a horse and it's so thick you can make a whole sheaf from only five handfuls! One peasant arrived with a copeck and only his bare hands to work with and now he has six horses and two cows.'

Pakhom was terribly excited by this news. 'Why should I have to scrape a living cooped up here,' he thought, 'when I could be leading a good life somewhere else? I could sell the land and cottage and with the money I'd be able to build myself a house there and start a whole new farm. But here there's no room to breathe and I get nothing but aggravation. I must go and find out what it's like for myself.'

When summer came he was ready and he set off. He went down the Volga to Samara by steamboat, then walked the remaining three hundred miles to the new settlement, which was just as the visitor had described. All the men had plenty of space, each having been allotted twenty-five acres without charge and welcomed into the commune. Anyone who had the money could also buy as much of the finest freehold land as he wanted, at three roubles an acre – there was no limit!

Towards autumn, after finding out all he needed to know, Pakhom went home and started selling up. He sold the land at a profit, his home and all his cattle, resigned from the commune and waited until the spring, when he left with his family for the new settlement.

4

When he arrived with his family Pakhom managed to get himself on the register of a large village commune, having duly moistened the elders' throats. All was signed and sealed and Pakhom was granted a hundred acres (twenty for each member of his family, in different fields), besides the use of the communal pasture. Then he put up some buildings and stocked his farm with cattle. The allotted land alone was three times as much as at home and it was perfect for growing corn. He was ten times better off here, for he had plenty of arable land and pasturage, and he was able to keep as many cattle as he wanted.

At first, while he was busy building and stocking up, everything seemed wonderful. But no sooner had he settled down to his new life than he began to feel cramped even here. During the first year he had sowed wheat on the allotted land and the crop had been excellent. But when he wanted to sow more wheat he found he needed more land: the other land he had been allotted was not suitable for wheat. In the south wheat is sown only on grass or on fallow land. They sow it for one or two years and then leave it fallow until the land is overgrown with feather-grass again. This type of land was in great demand and there wasn't enough to go round, so that people quarrelled over it. The richer ones sowed their own, whilst the poorer ones had to mortgage theirs to merchants to pay their taxes. Pakhom wanted to sow more wheat, so the following year he rented some fields from a dealer for one year. He sowed a great deal of wheat and had a good crop. But the fields were a long way from the village and the wheat had to be carted more than ten miles. Then Pakhom noticed that some peasant farmers with large homesteads in the neighbourhood were becoming very wealthy. 'What if I bought some freehold land and built myself a homestead like theirs?' he wondered. 'Then everything would be within easy reach.' And he tried to think how he could buy some.

Pakhom farmed the same way for three years, renting land and sowing wheat. They were good years, the crops were good and he was able to save some money. But Pakhom grew tired of having to rent land, year after year, of having to waste his time scrambling after it. Whenever good land came up for sale the peasants would immediately fall over themselves to buy it and it would all be gone before he could do anything: he was never quick enough and so he had no land for sowing his wheat. So in the third year he went halves with a merchant in buying a plot of pasture land outright from some peasants. They had already ploughed it when someone sued the peasants over it and as a result all their work was wasted. 'If it had been *my* land,' Pakhom thought, 'I wouldn't have been under an obligation to anyone and I wouldn't have got into that mess.'

So Pakhom tried to discover where to buy some freehold land. He came across a peasant who, having purchased some thirteen hundred acres, had then gone bankrupt and was selling the land off very cheaply. Pakhom bargained with him. After much haggling they finally agreed upon fifteen hundred roubles, half cash down, half to be paid at a later date. The deal was all but signed and sealed when a passing merchant called at Pakhom's to have his horses fed. They drank tea together and got into conversation. The merchant said that he was on his way back from the far-off land of the Bashkirs, where he had bought some thirteen thousand acres for a mere thousand roubles. When Pakhom questioned him further the merchant told him, 'All I had to do was give the old men there a few presents – a hundred roubles' worth of silk robes and carpets, a chest of tea, and vodka for anyone who wanted it. I managed to get the land for twenty copecks an acre.' He showed Pakhom the title deeds. 'The land is near a river and it's all beautiful grassy steppe.'

Pakhom continued to ply him with questions.

'There's so much land that you couldn't walk round it all in a year. It all belongs to the Bashkirs. Yes, the people there are as stupid as sheep and you can get land off them for practically nothing.'

'Well,' Pakhom thought, 'why should I pay a thousand roubles for thirteen hundred acres and saddle myself with debt? To think what I could buy with the same money down there!'

5

Pakhom asked him how to get there and as soon as he had said goodbye to the merchant he prepared to leave. He left his wife behind and set off, taking a workman with him. First they stopped off in town and bought a chest of tea, vodka and other presents, just as the old merchant had advised. Then they travelled for miles and miles until, on the seventh day, they reached the Bashkir settlement. Everything was as the merchant had described: the people lived on the steppe, near a river, in tents of thick felt. They neither ploughed the soil nor ate bread, and their cattle and horses wandered in herds over the steppe. The foals were tethered behind the tents and the mares brought over to them twice a day. These mares were milked and from the milk kumiss* was made. The women also made cheese from the kumiss and all the men seemed concerned with was drinking kumiss and tea, eating mutton and playing their pipes. All of them were cheerful and well-fed, and they spent the whole summer idling about. The Bashkirs were very ignorant, knew no Russian, but were kindly people.

The moment they spotted Pakhom, the Bashkirs streamed out of their tents and surrounded their visitor. An interpreter was found and Pakhom told him that he had come about some land. The Bashkirs were delighted and took Pakhom off to one of the finest tents, where they made him sit on some rugs piled with cushions, while they formed a circle and offered him tea and kumiss. Then they slaughtered a sheep and fed him with mutton. Pakhom fetched the presents from his cart, handed them round and shared the tea out. The Bashkirs were delighted. For a while they talked away amongst themselves and then told the interpreter to translate.

'They want me to tell you,' the interpreter said, 'that they've taken a great liking to you and that it's our custom to do all we can to please a guest and repay him for his gifts. You have given us presents, so please tell us if there is anything of ours that you would like so we can show our gratitude.'

'What I like most of all here,' Pakhom replied, 'is your land. Back home there isn't enough to go round and, what's more, the soil is exhausted. But here you have plenty and it looks very good. I've never seen soil like it.'

The interpreter translated and then the Bashkirs went into a lengthy conference. Although Pakhom did not understand, he could see how cheerful they were, laughing and shouting. Then they all became quiet, glanced at Pakhom and the interpreter continued, 'I'm

---

* Fermented mare's milk. In 1860 Tolstoy had travelled down the Volga to Samara and lived with the Bashkirs for more than two months, drinking large quantities of kumiss to improve his health. It was renowned for its health-giving properties.

to tell you that they would be only too pleased to let you have as much land as you like in return for your kindness. All you have to do is point it out and it will be yours.'

Then they conferred again and started arguing about something. Pakhom asked what it was and the interpreter told him, 'Some of them are saying they should first consult the elder about the land. They can't do anything without his permission, but some of the others say it's not necessary.'

6

While the Bashkirs were arguing, a man in a fox-fur cap suddenly came into the tent, whereupon they all became quiet and stood up.

'It's the elder,' the interpreter explained.

Pakhom immediately fetched his best robe and presented it with five pounds of tea to the elder, who accepted the gifts and then sat in the place of honour. The Bashkirs immediately started telling him something. After listening for a while the elder motioned with his head for them to be quiet and then spoke to Pakhom in Russian.

'Well now,' he said. 'It's all right. Choose whatever land you like, there's plenty of it.'

'How can I just go and take whatever I like?' Pakhom wondered. 'I must have it all signed and sealed somehow. Now they tell me it's mine, but who knows, they might change their minds?' So he told them, 'Thank you for your kind words. Yes, you do have a great deal of land, but I need only a little. However, I would like to be sure which will be mine, so couldn't it be measured and made over to me by some sort of contract? Our lives are in God's hands and although you good people are willing to give me the land now, it's possible your children might want it back again.'

'What you say is true,' said the elder. 'We can have a contract drawn up.'

Pakhom said, 'I've heard that you made some land over to a merchant not long ago, together with the title deeds. I would like you to do the same with me.'

The elder understood. 'That's no problem,' he said. 'We have a clerk here and we can ride into town and have the documents properly witnessed and signed.'

'But what about the price?' Pakhom asked.

'We have a set price – a thousand roubles a day.'

Pakhom did not understand.

'What kind of rate is that – a *day*? How many acres would that be?'

'We don't reckon your way. We sell by the day. However much you can walk round in one day will be yours. And the price is a thousand roubles a day.'

Pakhom was amazed. 'Well, a man can walk round a lot of land in one day,' he said.

The elder burst out laughing. 'Well, all of it will be yours,' he replied. 'But there's one condition: if you don't return to your starting-point the same day, your money will be forfeited.'

'But how can I mark where I've been?'

'We'll all go to whatever place you select and wait until you've completed your circuit. You must take a spade, dig a hole at every turning and leave the turf piled up. Afterwards, we will go from hole to hole with a plough. You may make as large a circuit as you like, only you must be back at your starting-point by sunset. All the land you can walk round will be yours.'

Pakhom was absolutely delighted. An early start was decided on and after talking for a while they drank kumiss, ate some mutton and then had tea. This went on until nightfall. Then the Bashkirs made up a feather-bed for Pakhom and left. They promised to be ready to ride out to the chosen spot before sunrise.

7

Pakhom lay down on the feather-bed, but the thought of all that land kept him awake. 'Tomorrow,' he thought, 'I shall mark out a really large stretch. In one day I can easily walk thirty-five miles. The days are long now – just think how much land I'll have from walking that distance! I'll sell the poorer bits, or let it to the peasants. I'll take the best for myself and farm it. I'll have two ox-ploughs and hire a couple of labourers to work them. Yes, I'll cultivate about a hundred and fifty acres and let the cattle graze the rest.'

Pakhom did not sleep a wink that night and dozed off only just before dawn. The moment he fell asleep he had a dream: he seemed to be lying in the same tent and could hear someone roaring with laughter outside. Wondering who was laughing like that he got up, went out and saw that same Bashkir elder sitting there, holding his sides and rolling about in fits of laughter. He went closer and asked, 'What are you laughing at?' And then he saw that it wasn't the elder at all, but the merchant who had called on him a few days before and told him about the land. And just as Pakhom asked him, 'Have you been here long?' the merchant turned into the peasant who had come up from the Volga and visited him at home. And then Pakhom saw that it wasn't the peasant, but the Devil himself, with horns and hoofs, sitting there laughing his head off, while before him lay a barefoot man wearing only shirt and trousers. When Pakhom took a closer look he saw that the man was dead and that it was himself. Pakhom woke up in a cold sweat. 'The things one dreams about!' he thought. Then he looked round and saw that it was getting light at the open door – dawn was breaking. 'I must go and wake them,' he thought, 'it's time to start.' So Pakhom got up, roused the workman, who was sleeping in the cart, ordered him to harness the horse and went off to wake the Bashkirs. 'It's time to go out on the steppe and measure the land,' he said. The Bashkirs got up, assembled, and then the elder came and joined them. They drank some more kumiss and offered Pakhom tea, but he was impatient to be off. 'If we're going,' he said, 'let's go. It's time.'

8

So the Bashkirs got ready and left, some on horses, others in carts. Pakhom went to his little cart with his workman, taking a spade with him. They came out on to the open steppe just as the sun was rising. They climbed a small hill (called a 'shikhan' in Bashkir). Then the Bashkirs got out of their carts, dismounted from their horses and gathered in one place. The elder went over to Pakhom and pointed.

'Look,' he said, 'that's all ours, as far as the eye can see. Choose any part you like.'

Pakhom's eyes lit up, for the land was all virgin soil, flat as the palm of one's hand, black as poppy-seed, with different kinds of grass growing breast-high in the hollows.

The elder took off his fox-fur cap and put it on the ground.

'Let this be the marker: this is the starting point to which you must return. All the land you can walk round will be yours.'

Pakhom took out his money, placed it on the cap, took off his outer coat, so that he was wearing only a sleeveless undercoat, tightened his belt below the waist and stuffed a small bag of bread inside his shirt. Then he tied a flask of water to the belt, pulled up his boots, took the spade from his workman and was ready to leave. He could not decide which direction to take at first as the land was so good everywhere. Then he decided, 'It's all good land, so I'll walk towards the sunrise.' He turned to the east, stretching himself as he waited for the sun to appear above the horizon. 'There's no point in wasting time,' he thought. 'And it's easier walking while it's still cool.' The moment the sun's rays came flooding over the horizon Pakhom put the spade on one shoulder and walked out on to the steppe.

Pakhom walked neither quickly nor slowly. When he had gone about three quarters of a mile he stopped, dug a hole and piled the pieces of turf high on top of each other so that they were easily visible. The stiffness had now gone from his legs and he lengthened his stride. A little further on he stopped again and dug another hole.

When Pakhom looked back he could see quite clearly the small hill in the sunlight with all the people standing on it, and the gleaming tyres of the cart-wheels. Pakhom guessed that he had covered about three miles. He was beginning to feel warmer, so he took off his undercoat, flung it over his shoulder and walked another three miles. It was hot, and a look at the sun reminded him it was time for breakfast.

'Well, that's the first stretch completed!' he thought. 'But there are four to a day and it's too early to start turning. I must take these boots off, though.'

So he sat down, took off his boots, stuck them behind his belt and moved on. The going was easy now and he thought, 'I'll do another three miles and then turn left. The land's so beautiful here, it would be a pity to miss out on any of it. The further I go, the better the land gets.' So for a while he carried straight on and when he looked back the hill was barely visible and the people on it looked like black ants; he could just glimpse something that glinted in the sun.

'Well,' thought Pakhom, 'I've walked enough in this direction, I should be turning now. Besides, I'm stewing in this heat and terribly thirsty.' So he stopped, dug a large hole, piled up the turf, untied his flask, drank and then turned sharp left. On and on he walked – the grass was higher here and it was very hot.

Pakhom began to feel tired. He glanced at the sun and saw that it was noon. 'Well,' he thought, 'I must have a little rest.' So he stopped, sat down and had some bread and water. He did not stretch out, though, thinking, 'Once I lie down I'll fall asleep.' After a few minutes he carried on. At first it was easy – the food had given him strength. But by now it was extremely hot and he began to feel sleepy. Still, he kept going and thought of the proverb, 'A moment's pain can be a lifetime's gain.'

He had walked a long way in the same direction and was just about to turn left when he spotted a lush hollow and decided it would be a pity to lose it. 'What a good place for growing flax!' he thought. So he carried straight on until he had walked right round the low-lying meadows, dug a hole the other side, and then he turned the second corner. Pakhom looked back at the hill: it was shimmering in the heat and through the haze it was difficult to see all the people there – they were at least ten miles away. 'Well,' thought Pakhom, 'I've made those sides too long, this one has to be shorter.' So he started the third side, quickening his step. He looked at the sun and saw that it was already half way to the horizon, but he had completed only about one mile of the third side. The starting-point was still ten miles away. 'No,' he thought, 'although it will make the land a bit lopsided I must take the shortest way back. It's no good trying to grab too much, I've quite enough already!'

Pakhom hastily dug another hole and headed straight for the hill.

9

On the way back Pakhom found the going tough. The heat had exhausted him, his bare feet were cut and bruised and his legs were giving way. He wanted to rest, but this was out of the question – he would never get back by sunset. The sun waits for no man and was sinking lower and lower. 'Oh,' he wondered, 'have I blundered, trying to take too much? What if I'm not back in time?' He looked towards the hill, then at the sun. The hill was far off, the sun was close to the horizon.

But Pakhom struggled on. Although it was very hard, he walked faster and faster. On and on he went – but there was still a long way to go. He started running and threw away his coat, boots, flask, cap, keeping only the spade which he used for leaning on. 'Oh dear,' he thought, 'I've been too greedy. Now I've ruined it. I'll never get back by sunset.' His fear made him only more breathless. On he ran, his shirt soaking and his trousers clinging to him; his throat was parched. His lungs were working like a blacksmith's bellows, his heart beat like a hammer and his legs did not seem to be his – he felt that they were breaking . . . Pakhom was terrified and thought, 'All this strain will be the death of me.'

Although he feared death, he could not stop. 'If I stopped now, after coming all this way – well, they'd call me an idiot!' So on he ran until he was close enough to hear the Bashkirs yelling and cheering him on. Their shouts spurred him on all the more, so he summoned his last ounce of strength and kept running. But by now the sun was almost touching the horizon: veiled in mist, it was large and blood-red. It was about to set, but although it did not have very far to sink it was no distance to the starting-point either. Pakhom could see the people on the hill now, waving their arms and urging him on. He could see the fox-fur cap on the ground with the money on it; he could see the elder sitting there with his arms pressed to his sides. And Pakhom remembered his dream. 'I've plenty of land now, but will God let me live to enjoy it? No, I'm finished . . . I'll never make it.'

Pakhom looked at the sun – it had reached the earth now: half of its great disc had dipped below the horizon. With all the strength he had left Pakhom lurched forwards with his full weight, hardly able to move his legs quickly enough to stop himself falling. He reached the hill – and everything suddenly became dark. He looked round and saw that the sun had set. Pakhom groaned. 'All that effort has been in vain,' he thought. He wanted to stop, when he heard the Bashkirs still cheering him on and he realized that from where he was at the bottom of the hill the sun had apparently set, but not for those on top. Pakhom took a deep breath and rushed up the hill which was still bathed in sunlight. When he reached the top he saw his cap with the elder sitting by it, holding his sides and laughing his head off. Then he remembered the dream and he groaned. His legs gave way, he fell forward and managed to reach the cap with his hands.

'Oh, well done!' exclaimed the elder. 'That's a lot of land you've earned yourself!'

Pakhom's workman ran up and tried to lift his master, but the blood flowed from his mouth. Pakhom was dead.

The Bashkirs clicked their tongues sympathetically.

Pakhom's workman picked up the spade, dug a grave for his master – six feet from head to heel, which was exactly the right length – and buried him.

WHERE LOVE IS, GOD IS

In a certain town there lived a shoemaker called Martin Avdeich. He had a small basement room, with one window looking out on to the street. Through it he could see people passing by and although only their feet were visible Martin could tell who they were from their shoes. Martin had lived there for a long time and so he had many friends. There were few pairs of shoes in the neighbourhood that had not passed once or even twice through his hands. Some he had re-soled, others he had fitted with new side-pieces, others he had stitched up, and some he had fitted with new toe-caps, so he could often see the fruits of his own handiwork through the window. He was always busy, since he always did an excellent job, used good materials, never overcharged and could be relied upon. If he knew that he could complete a job on time he would undertake it. If not, he would not make false promises and would tell his customers. Everyone knew Martin and he was never short of work. He had always been a good man, but as old age approached he began to think more about his soul and drawing nearer to God.

His wife had died when he was still an apprentice, leaving him with a three-year-old son. None of their other children survived infancy. At first Martin was inclined to send his little boy to his sister's in the country, but then the thought of parting with him made him decide against it. 'It would be very hard for my little Kapiton to grow up in a strange family,' he thought, 'so I'll keep him here with me.'

When Martin had left his master he went to live with his son in lodgings. But it was not God's wish that he should find happiness in his children. As soon as he had grown up and was able to help his father and bring him joy, he became ill and after being in bed for a week with a high fever he died. After Martin had buried his son he fell into despair, so deep that he blamed God for everything. He was so overwhelmed by grief that more than once he begged God to let him die and reproached Him for taking his only beloved son instead of an old man like himself. And he stopped going to church.

One day a wise old man from the same village as Martin, who had been wandering around the countryside for eight years, called in to see him on his way back from the Monastery of the Holy Trinity. Martin opened his heart to him, bemoaning his sad lot.

'Holy man,' he said, 'I've lost the will to live. All I want is to die, that's all I ask of God. There's nothing left for me now.'

And the wise man told him, 'It is wicked to talk like that, Martin. It is not for us to question the ways of God. We must bow to God's judgement and not always be guided by our own reason. If it was God's will that your son should die and that you should live, then it must be for the best. You are in such despair because you only want to live for your own happiness!'

'What else should I live for?' Martin asked.

'You must live for God, Martin,' the old man replied. 'He gave you life, so it is He you should live for. If you live for Him you will never grieve again and all your sorrows will be easy to bear.'

'But how should one live for God!'

The old man replied, 'It was Christ who showed us how to live for God. Can you read? Well, go and buy the Gospels and study them. Then you will discover how to live for God. Everything is written there.'

These words imprinted themselves on Martin's heart and that same day he bought himself a large-print copy of the New Testament and sat down to read.

At first Martin meant to read the Gospels only on church festivals, but once he had started he felt so uplifted that he read them every day. Sometimes he became so engrossed that all the oil in his lamp was used up before he could tear himself away. And Martin would sit down to read every evening and the more he read the more clearly he understood what God required of him and how he could live for Him. Consequently his heart grew lighter and lighter. Before, when he had gone to bed, he would lie moaning and sighing as he thought of his little Kapiton, but now he would simply repeat, 'Glory to Thee, O Lord! Thy will be done.'

And from then on Martin's life was completely transformed. On church holidays he had been in the habit of going to drink tea at a tavern and would never refuse a glass or two of vodka. Sometimes he liked to have a few drinks with a friend and although he was never drunk when he came out, he would be fairly tipsy – and then he would talk a lot of nonsense, shout at his friend and say nasty things. But now all that was a thing of the past and his life became peaceful and full of joy. In the morning he would sit down to work and when he had finished he would take the lamp off its hook, put it on the table, fetch the Bible from the shelf and start reading. And the more he read the more he understood, and the clearer and happier in his mind he became.

Once Martin sat over his Bible until very late. He was reading the sixth chapter of the Gospel of St Luke and came to the following verses:

And unto him that smiteth thee on the one cheek offer also the other; and him that taketh away thy cloke forbid not to take thy coat also. Give to every man that asketh of thee; and of him that taketh away thy goods ask them not again. And as ye would that men should do to you, do ye also to them likewise.

And he read further, where the Lord says,

And why call ye me, Lord, Lord, and do not the things which I say? Whosoever cometh to me and heareth my sayings, and doeth them, I will shew you to whom he is like: he is like a man which built an house, and digged deep, and laid the foundation on a rock: and when the flood arose, the stream beat vehemently upon that house, and could not shake it: for it was founded upon a rock. But he that heareth, and doeth not, is like a man that without a foundation built an house upon the earth; against which the stream did beat vehemently, and immediately it fell; and the ruin of that house was great.

When Martin read those words his heart was filled with joy. He took off his spectacles, placed them on the Bible, leant his elbows on the table and pondered for a moment. As he reviewed his own life in the light of those words he thought, 'Is my house built on rock or on sand? If it is built on rock, then all is well. It's easy enough, sitting here thinking I've done all that God has commanded. But then I might be tempted and sin again. Never mind, I shall not give up. Yes, that would be good. Help me, O Lord!'

After these reflections he wanted to go to bed, but was reluctant to tear himself away from the book. So he began the seventh chapter and read about the centurion, the widow's son and the answer to John's disciples, and he came to the passage where the rich Pharisee invited Christ into his house and where the woman who had sinned anointed His feet and washed them with her tears. Christ had forgiven her. At verse forty-four he read,

> And he turned to the woman, and said unto Simon, Seest thou this woman? I entered into thine house, thou gavest me no water for my feet: but she hath washed my feet with tears, and wiped them with the hairs of her head. Thou gavest me no kiss: but this woman since the time I came in hath not ceased to kiss my feet. My head with oil thou didst not anoint: but this woman hath anointed my feet with ointment.

After reading these verses he thought, '... thou gavest me no water for my feet ... gavest me no kiss ... didst not anoint my head ...'

And he took off his spectacles again, placed them on the Bible and thought hard.

'That Pharisee must have been like me. I've only ever worried about myself, thinking of the next cup of tea, keeping warm and cosy and I've never shown anyone hospitality. Simon only worried about himself and couldn't have cared less about his guest. And who was his guest? Why, it was Christ Himself. Now, would *I* have behaved like that if Christ had come here?'

And he laid his head on both arms and dozed off almost before he knew it.

'Martin!' he suddenly heard, as though someone were whispering into his ear.

Martin started and sleepily asked, 'Who's there?'

He turned round and glanced at the door – no one was there. He laid his head down again to sleep and then heard quite distinctly, 'Martin, Martin! Look out into the street tomorrow, for I will come.'

Martin roused himself, got up from his chair and rubbed his eyes. He did not know whether he had been dreaming or awake when he heard those words and he put the lamp out and went to bed.

Next morning Martin got up before dawn, said his prayers, and then lit the stove, warmed up some cabbage soup and porridge, lit the samovar, put his apron on and sat down to work by the window. And as he sat there he could not forget what had happened the night before. And he was in two minds about it, thinking first that he had imagined everything and then persuading himself that he *had* heard a voice.

'Well,' he decided, 'I think I really did hear one.'

Martin went and sat at his window, but he concentrated more on what was happening outside than on his work. Whenever anyone came past in unfamiliar boots he would crouch in such a way that he could clearly see that person's face as well as the feet. A house-porter went by in new felt boots, then a water-carrier. Then an old soldier from Nicholas I's time, wearing old, patched felt boots, with a shovel in his hand, appeared outside the window. Martin recognized him from the boots: the man's name was Stepanych and a neighbouring tradesman gave him food and lodging out of charity. His job was to help the house-porter and he began clearing away the snow outside Martin's window. Martin looked at him and resumed work.

'I must be going soft in the head!' Martin exclaimed, laughing at himself. 'It's only old Stepanych clearing away the snow and I immediately conclude that it's Christ who's come to visit me! Silly old fogy!'

However, after about a dozen more stitches, Martin again felt the urge to look out of the window. This time he saw that Stepanych had propped his shovel against the wall and he could not quite see whether he was warming himself or simply resting.

He was obviously only a poor, broken-down man who just did not have the strength to clear the snow away. Martin thought he might offer him a cup of tea, especially as the samovar happened to be on the boil. Martin stuck his awl in a piece of leather, put the samovar on the table, made the tea and tapped on the window. Stepanych turned round and came over. Martin beckoned to him to come inside and went to open the door.

'Come in and warm yourself,' he said. 'You must be frozen stiff.'

'God bless you! My bones are aching,' Stepanych replied.

Then he came in, shook off the snow and started tottering as he wiped his feet so as not to dirty the floor.

'Don't bother about that,' Martin said, 'I'll clean up afterwards. It's all in a day's work! Come through and sit down. Now, have some tea.'

Martin filled two glasses, offering one to his guest and emptying his own into a saucer and blowing on it.

When Stepanych had emptied his glass he turned it upside-down, put the remains of the sugar on it and thanked his host. But he obviously wanted some more.

'Drink up,' Martin said, refilling his guest's glass and his own. As he drank his tea Martin kept looking out into the street.

'Are you expecting someone?' his guest asked.

'Am I expecting someone? Well, I feel too ashamed to tell you. As it happens I'm both expecting and not expecting. The fact is, there are some words I just cannot get out of my head. Whether I imagined I heard them I can't really say. You see, my friend, last night I was reading the Gospels, about our dear Lord Christ and how He suffered and walked this earth. I'm sure you must have heard all about it.'

'Yes, I've heard about it,' Stepanych replied. 'But I'm an ignorant man, can't read or write.'

'Well, I was reading about how He walked this earth and how He went to the house of a Pharisee who did not make Him welcome. Well, as I read further I thought to myself how badly Christ the Father was treated. Supposing Christ had come to my house – or to someone like me – what wouldn't I have done to give Him a proper welcome! But that Simon would not receive Him into his house. That's what I was thinking when I fell asleep. And in my sleep I heard someone call my name. Then I lifted my head and thought I could hear someone whispering, "Expect me, for I shall come and see thee tomorrow." Twice I heard that voice whisper. Well, as you can imagine, those words affected me deeply. I know I'm being silly, but I'm expecting our heavenly Father!'

Stepanych silently shook his head, emptied his glass and laid it on its side. But Martin stood it up again and refilled it.

'Here, drink some more. And I was thinking about the time when our Lord was upon this earth, despising no one and mixing mostly with ordinary folk. Yes, He always went with the humble and chose His disciples mainly from folk like us, from ordinary sinners and working people. "Whosoever exalts himself," He said, "the same shall be abased; and whosoever shall abase himself, the same shall be exalted." "You call me Lord," He said, "but I shall wash thy feet." "He who would be first," He said, "let him be the servant of all." "Because," He said, "blessed are the poor, the humble, the meek, and the merciful." '

Stepanych completely forgot his tea. He was an old man, easily moved to tears and as he sat there listening, the tears rolled down his cheeks.

'Come on, drink your tea,' Martin said. But Stepanych crossed himself, thanked him, moved the glass away and got up.

'Thank you, Martin,' he said. 'You have welcomed me and nourished me in spirit and in body.'

'You are always welcome here. I'm only too glad to have a visitor,' Martin replied.

Stepanych left and Martin poured out what was left of the tea, drank it, cleared the glasses away, sat down again by the window and began stitching the back of a shoe. And as he stitched he kept looking out of the window, waiting for Christ and thinking only of Him and His works. And his head was full of Christ's many sayings.

Two soldiers went past – one in army boots, the other in his own; then the owner of the house next door, in shining galoshes; then a baker with a basket. They all went by and then a woman in woollen stockings and rough peasant shoes came towards the window. But then she stopped by the wall. Martin looked up at her from the window and saw that she was a stranger, poorly dressed, and that she had a child in her arms. She stood against the wall with her back to the wind and tried to wrap the baby up, although she had nothing warm to wrap it in, as she was wearing a summer dress – and a very shabby one at that. Through the window Martin could hear the baby crying. The woman was trying to soothe the child but there was no way it would be comforted. Martin got up, went to the door, climbed the steps and called out, 'My dear woman!'

She heard him and turned round.

'Why are you standing out there in the freezing cold?' he asked. 'And with a little child! Come inside, you can make him nice and warm in here. Follow me.'

The woman was surprised to see an old man in an apron, with spectacles on his nose calling out to her, but she followed him down the stairs and into the little room, where he led her to the bed.

'There, sit by the stove, dear. You can warm yourself and feed the baby.'

'But I've no milk,' she replied. 'Haven't eaten a thing this morning.' But still she tried to put the child to her breast.

Martin shook his head, went to the table for some bread and a bowl, after which he opened the stove door and poured some cabbage soup into the bowl. He also took the porridge pot out, but the porridge was not ready, so he served only the soup, putting the bread next to it, together with a napkin that he took from a hook.

'Please sit down,' he said, 'and have something to eat, dear woman, while I hold the baby. Why, I had children of my own once, so I know how to nurse them.'

The woman crossed herself, sat down and began to eat, while Martin sat on the bed with the baby. He tried to make a smacking sound with his lips to soothe the child, but since he had no teeth he made a poor job of it. The baby would not stop crying, so Martin wagged his finger at the baby's mouth and then quickly withdrew it, without letting the baby suck it as his finger was black with shoe-maker's wax. The child stopped crying when it saw the finger and then it began to laugh. Martin was delighted. As she drank her soup the woman told him who she was and where she had been.

'I'm a soldier's wife,' she said. 'They sent my husband somewhere far away about eight months ago and since then I've heard nothing of him. I was a cook until my baby was born, and then they wouldn't keep me any more. So I've been struggling along without any job for three months now. All the money I had was spent on food. I wanted to become a wet-nurse, but no one would take me – they said I was too thin. I've just been to see a tradesman's wife – a woman from our village is working for her. She had promised to take me and I thought everything would be all right, but now she's told me to come back next week. She lives such a long way from here. I'm worn out and my baby's cold and hungry, poor darling. Thank God my landlady's taken pity on us and given us free lodging, otherwise I don't know what I'd do.'

Martin sighed. 'Don't you have anything warmer to wear?'

'Yes, I should be wearing warm clothes in this weather, but only yesterday I had to pawn my last shawl for a few copecks.'

The woman went over to the bed and took the child. Martin stood up and rummaged about in some things hanging on the wall until he found an old jacket.

'Here you are,' he said, 'it's nothing very much, but you can wrap him up warm in it.'

The woman looked at the jacket, then at the old man and she burst into tears as she took it. Martin turned away, crept under the bed and brought out a small chest. He searched for a while (apparently finding nothing) and then sat down opposite the woman.

'May the Lord bless you!' she exclaimed. 'It must have been Christ Himself who sent me to your window, otherwise my baby would have perished with cold. When I set out this morning it was mild, but now it's really freezing. It must have been Christ who encouraged you to look out of your window and take pity on a poor wretch like me.'

Martin smiled and said, 'You are right, it was He who encouraged me. And I had good reason, my dear!'

And Martin told the soldier's wife about his dream, how he had heard a voice promising him that the Lord would visit him that day.

'Yes, all things are possible,' the woman said, getting up. She threw the jacket over herself, wrapped the baby, curtseyed and thanked Martin again.

'Please take this, for Christ's sake!' Martin said, handing her a twenty-copeck piece to get her shawl out of pawn. The woman crossed herself and so did Martin as he saw her out.

When she was gone Martin ate some soup, cleared the table and sat down to work. As he worked he kept watching that window and every time a shadow fell across it he would immediately look up to see who was passing. People he knew and strangers passed, but no one in particular.

And then an old market woman stopped right in front of his window. She was carrying an apple-basket but appeared to have sold most of her wares, as it was almost empty. On one shoulder was a sack of wood-shavings which she had most probably collected at some place where they were building and was on her way home. The sack was clearly very heavy and was hurting her, so to shift it to her other shoulder she put it down on the pavement, placed the apple-basket on a post and gave the shavings a shake. Just as she was doing this a boy in a ragged cap suddenly ran up, grabbed an apple and tried to run off with it. But the old woman had spotted him, turned round and grabbed his sleeve. The boy tried to struggle free, but the woman seized him with both hands, knocked his cap off and caught hold of his hair. The boy screamed and the woman cursed. Martin did not wait to make fast his awl but threw it down, rushed through the door and stumbled up the stairs, dropping his spectacles on the way. Out in the street the woman was cursing away, and evidently intended hauling the boy off to the police station. He struggled and protested his innocence.

'I never took it!' he said. 'What are you hitting me for? Let me go!'

Martin separated them, took the boy by the hand and said, 'Let him go, Grandma. Forgive him, for Christ's sake!'

'I'll forgive him, but not before he's had a taste of some new birch twigs! I'm taking the little devil to the police station.'

Martin did his best to dissuade her. 'Please let him go, Grandma. He won't ever do it again. For Christ's sake, let him go.'

The old woman released the boy, who wanted to run off, but Martin stopped him.

'You should ask the old woman to forgive you,' he said. 'And don't you ever do it again – I saw you take it.'

The boy burst into tears and begged her to forgive him.

'That's the way! Now, here's an apple for you,' Martin said, taking an apple from the basket and handing it to the boy. 'I'll pay for it, Grandma,' he added.

'But you'll only spoil little devils like him that way,' she said. 'What he deserves is such a thrashing he won't be able to sit down for a week.'

'Oh, Grandma!' Martin retorted. 'That may be our way, but it's not God's way. If the punishment for stealing just one apple is a thorough thrashing, then what should we deserve for our mortal sins?'

The old woman did not reply.

And Martin told her the parable of the master who excused one of his servants a great debt and how that servant went out and seized his own debtor by the throat. The old woman listened and so did the boy.

'God has commanded us to forgive, otherwise He will not forgive us. We should forgive everyone – not least thoughtless little boys!'

The old woman shook her head and sighed. 'That's all very well, but children are terribly spoilt these days.'

'Then it's up to us, their elders, to teach them what's right,' Martin said.

'Yes, I agree,' the old woman replied. 'I had seven children once, but now I've only one daughter.'

And she told him how and where she and her daughter were living, and how many grandchildren she had.

'As you can see, I'm not very strong,' she said, 'but I still have to work myself to the bone. I feel so sorry for my grandchildren – such lovely boys, all of them! No one is as kind to me as they are. And my Aksyutka wouldn't leave me for anyone. "Dear Mummy," she says, "you're such a dear!"' And the old woman was quite overcome.

'Well, I suppose it's because he's so young,' she added, looking at the boy. 'May God be with him.'

She was about to lift her sack on to her shoulders when the boy immediately ran forward to help. 'Let me carry that for you, Grandma,' he said, 'I'm going your way.'

The old woman accepted and put the sack on the boy's back.

And off they went down the street. The old woman forgot to ask Martin to pay for the apple and Martin stood there, watching and listening to them talking as they went.

When they were out of sight Martin returned to his room. His spectacles lay unbroken on the steps and he took his awl and started work again. But before long he found that he could not see to pass the cord through the holes in the leather. Then he saw the lamplighter on his rounds.

'Yes, it's time I had some proper light in here,' he thought. So he trimmed his lamp, hung it up and got to work. After finishing off one boot he turned it over to inspect it: it was perfect. So he put his tools to one side, swept up the cuttings, cleared away all the cords, laces and pieces of leather, stood his lamp on the table and took the Gospels from the shelf. He meant to open them at the place he had marked with a strip of morocco the previous day, but the book fell open at a different page. And when Martin saw it he remembered last night's dream. And no sooner did he remember it than he heard footsteps, as if someone was there, moving around behind him. Martin turned round and saw what appeared to be people in the dark corner, but he could not make out who they were. A voice whispered in his ear, 'Martin, Martin! Don't you know me?'

'Who is it?' Martin asked.

'It is I,' the voice said. 'Behold, it is I!'

And out of the dark corner stepped Stepanych. He smiled and then he was gone, melting away like a small cloud.

'It is I,' repeated the voice. And out of the dark corner stepped the woman with the baby. She smiled, and so did the child, and then they too vanished.

'It is I!' said the voice. And out stepped the old woman and the boy with the apple. Both smiled, and then they too disappeared.

And Martin's heart was filled with joy. He crossed himself, put on his spectacles and looked at the page where the Bible had fallen open. At the top he read, 'For I was an hungred, and ye gave me meat: I was thirsty, and ye gave me drink: I was a stranger, and ye took me in . . .'

And, lower down, 'Inasmuch as ye have done it unto one of the least of these my brethren, ye have done it unto me.' (Matthew xxv)

And Martin understood that his dream had come true, that his Saviour had visited him that day and that he had welcomed Him into his house.

WHAT MEN LIVE BY

We know that we have passed from death unto life, because we love the brethren. He that loveth not his brother abideth in death. (I John iii, 14).

But whoso hath this world's good, and seeth his brother have need, and shutteth up his bowels of compassion from him, how dwelleth the love of God in him? (I John iii, 17)

My little children, let us not love in word, neither in tongue; but in deed and in truth. (I John iii, 18)

. . . for love is of God; and every one that loveth is born of God, and knoweth God. (I John iv, 7)

He that loveth not knoweth not God; for God is love. (I John iv, 8)

No man hath seen God at any time. If we love one another, God dwelleth in us . . . (I John iv, 12)

God is love; and he that dwelleth in love dwelleth in God, and God in him. (I John iv, 16)

If a man say, I love God, and hateth his brother, he is a liar: for he that loveth not his brother whom he hath seen, how can he love God whom he hath not seen? (I John iv, 20)

I

Once there was a shoemaker who had neither house nor land of his own and who lived in a peasant's cottage with his wife and children, supporting them by what work he could get. Bread was expensive but his work was cheap and the little he earned was spent on food for his family. He and his wife had only one winter coat between them and even that was in a sorry state. For the past two years he had been saving to buy sheepskins for a new one.

By autumn he had scraped together a small sum: there was the three-rouble note that his wife kept in a little wooden box, as well as the five roubles and twenty copecks that some of the villagers owed him.

One morning he decided to go to the village to buy the skins. He put his wife's wadded twill jacket over his shirt and over that his own cloth coat. After breakfast he put the three-rouble note in his pocket, cut himself a walking-stick and set off.

'With the five roubles that one of them owes me,' he thought, 'plus the three I already have, I should have enough to buy the sheepskins.'

When he reached the village he stopped at a cottage, but the owner was out. His wife did not have the money, but she promised to send her husband over with it by the end of the week. So he called on another peasant who swore he was short of cash and that all he could manage was twenty copecks that were owing for some boot repairs. And then, when the shoemaker tried to buy the skins on credit, the dealer would not trust him.

'Bring me the money first,' he said. 'Then you can pick whatever skins you like. We all know how hard it is to collect what's owing to us!'

And so the shoemaker did no business that day, apart from twenty copecks for the repairs and a pair of felt boots that needed soling.

All this depressed the shoemaker and after spending the twenty copecks on vodka he set off for home without any skins. Earlier that morning he had felt a sharp nip in the air, but after a few vodkas he warmed up – even though he had no proper winter coat. As he walked down the road, striking frozen clods of earth with his stick in one hand and swinging the felt boots in the other, he started talking to himself.

'I feel quite warm without a coat,' he said. 'I've only had a drop, yet I can feel it rushing through every vein in my body. I don't need any sheepskins! I'm going home, with all my troubles behind me. That's the sort of man I am! Why should I worry? I can survive without a new coat – I won't need one for ages. Only, the wife won't be too happy. But it's really rotten when you do a job and the customer tries to string you along and doesn't pay up. You just wait – if you don't bring me the money I'll have the shirt off your back, I swear it! It's a bit much, what with a measly twenty copecks at a time. What can I do with twenty copecks? Spend it on drink, that's all. You say you're hard up. Well, what about me? You've a house, cattle, everything, but all I have is on my back. You grow your own corn, while I have to go out and buy mine. Whatever happens I must spend three roubles a week on bread alone. By the time I get home there won't be any left and I'll have to fork out another rouble and a half. So, you'd better pay up!'

The shoemaker kept rambling on like this until he drew near the wayside chapel at the bend in the road where something whitish just behind it caught his eye. But by now it was growing dark and although he strained his eyes he could not make out what it was. 'There wasn't any stone there before,' he thought. 'Perhaps it's a cow? No, it doesn't look like one at all. From the head it looks like a man and it's all white. But what would a man be doing there?'

He went a few steps closer and could now make it out quite clearly. How amazing! It *was* a man sitting there, but he could not see if he were dead or alive, and he was naked and quite motionless, his back propped against the chapel wall. The shoemaker was terrified and thought, 'A man's been murdered, stripped naked and dumped. If I go any nearer I might get mixed up in all sorts of trouble.'

And so the shoemaker went on his way. He walked behind the chapel to avoid having to look at him again. After a short distance he turned round and saw that the man was no longer leaning against the wall, but was moving, as if trying to see who he was. The shoemaker felt even more frightened and thought, 'Shall I go back or simply carry on? If I go back something terrible might happen. Who knows what kind of man he might be? I bet he's up to no good. Besides, he might suddenly jump to his feet and start choking the life out of me – and there'd be nothing I could do about it. And if he doesn't throttle me I might get lumbered with looking after him. But how can I help a naked man? I couldn't let him have the last shirt off my back. Please God, help me!'

And the shoemaker quickened his stride. He had almost left the chapel behind when his conscience began to prick him. He stopped in the middle of the road.

'How could you do such a thing, Semyon?' he reproached himself. 'That man might be dying miserably and you're such a coward you'd leave him there to die. Or have you become so rich all of a sudden that you're scared stiff he might steal all your money? You should be ashamed, Semyon!'

And he turned round again and went right up to the man.

2

After a closer look Semyon could see that he was young and healthy. There were no bruises on his body: he was just chilled to the bone and terrified. There he sat, leaning forward without looking at Semyon and apparently too weak to raise his eyes. When Semyon was right next to him he suddenly seemed to wake as if from a trance. He turned his head, opened his eyes and looked straight at Semyon. That one look was enough to allay all Semyon's fears. He threw down the felt boots, undid his belt, laid it over the boots and took off his cloth coat.

'There's no time for talking,' he said. 'Put that on – and be quick about it!'

Then Semyon took the man under the arms and tried to lift him, but he got to his feet without any help. And then Semyon saw that his body was slender and clean, that his legs and arms bore no trace of any wounds; his face was mild and gentle. Semyon threw his coat over his shoulders, but the man could not find the sleeves, so Semyon guided his arms into them, pulled on the coat, wrapped it around him and fastened it with his belt.

Then Semyon took off his tattered cap, intending to put it on the naked man's head, but he felt the cold on his own head and thought, 'I'm completely bald, while he's got long, curly hair.' And he put it back on again. 'It would be better to give him the boots,' he thought.

So he made the man sit down again and put the felt boots on his feet, after which he said, 'There you are, my friend. Stretch your legs a bit and warm yourself. Don't worry, it will all be sorted out later. Now, can you walk?'

The man stood up, looked tenderly at Semyon, but was unable to say one word.

'Why don't you say something? Come on, we can't spend all winter here, we must be on our way. Here, you can lean on my stick if you feel weak. Right, come on!'

And the man started walking – and he walked effortlessly, without lagging behind.

As they went down the road Semyon asked, 'Where are you from?'

'Not from these parts.'

'I thought so – I know everyone round here. But how did you come to be there, by the chapel?'

'I cannot tell you that.'

'Did some men attack you?'

'No, no one harmed me. It was God who punished me.'

'Well, we are all in His hands. All the same, you must have somewhere to go. Where are you heading?'

'Nowhere in particular.'

Semyon was amazed. The man did not strike him as a ruffian, he was so softly spoken, yet he revealed nothing about himself. 'Anything can happen in this world,' Semyon reflected and he told the man, 'All right, come home with me, even if it is a bit out of your way.'

As Semyon walked down the road the stranger did not lag behind for one moment, but kept abreast. The wind got up and the cold air crept under Semyon's shirt. The drink was beginning to wear off and he felt chilled to the marrow.

Sniffling as he went, he wrapped his wife's jacket tighter around himself and thought, 'So much for sheepskins! I go off to buy some and all I do is come home without even the old coat on my back, and with a naked stranger into the bargain! Matryona won't be too pleased about that!' And the thought of his wife depressed him. But the moment he looked at the stranger he remembered the look he had given him at the chapel and his heart filled with joy.

3

Semyon's wife had finished her chores early that day. She had chopped the wood, fetched water, fed the children, had a bite to eat herself and had then sat for a long time wondering when she should bake the bread – that same day or the next. There was still one thick slice left.

'If Semyon has his dinner in the village,' she thought, 'then he won't want much for supper and there'll be enough bread for tomorrow.'

She turned the slice over. 'I shan't do any baking today,' she decided, 'there's only enough flour for one loaf. But we can make this last till Friday.'

So Matryona put the bread away and sat down at the table to patch her husband's shirt. As she worked she thought of him buying the sheepskins for the new winter coat.

'I hope the dealer won't swindle him. He's so simple, that husband of mine. He'd never cheat a soul himself and even a little child could trick him. Eight roubles is a lot of money, enough to buy very good sheepskins. Not the best quality tanned ones perhaps, but still good enough for a nice coat. Last winter was so hard without a proper one! I couldn't even go down to the river, couldn't go anywhere. And when he left this morning he took all the warm clothes we have, leaving me with nothing to wear. Now, he didn't leave all that early. All the same, it's time he was back. I hope my old man hasn't gone drinking!'

These thoughts had just crossed Matryona's mind when the front steps creaked and someone came in. Matryona stuck her needle into the shirt and went out into the hall. There she saw two men – Semyon and someone in felt boots and without a cap.

Matryona immediately smelt the vodka on her husband's breath. 'So, I was right, he's been on the drink,' she thought. And when she saw him standing there, empty-handed and with a guilty grin on his face, wearing nothing but the jacket she had lent him, her heart sank. 'He's gone and spent all that money drinking with some good-for-nothing. What's more, he's got the nerve to bring him home.'

Matryona ushered them in and followed them into the living-room. Now she could see that the stranger was a thin young man and that he was wearing her husband's coat. She could see no shirt under it and he had no cap. Once inside he stood quite still and kept looking down. Matryona concluded that he was a bad lot, as he seemed so nervous.

Frowning, she went over to the stove and waited to see what they would do next.

Semyon took off his cap and sat down on the bench as if he had done no wrong.

'Come on, Matryona, let's have some supper!' he said.

Matryona muttered something to herself and stayed quite still by the stove. She kept looking first at one, then the other, shaking her head. Semyon realized that his wife was annoyed, but there was nothing he could do about it. Pretending not to notice, he took the stranger by the arm.

'Sit down,' he said. 'Let's have something to eat.'

The stranger sat on the bench.

'Well, don't you have anything?'

Matryona lost her temper. 'Yes, I do, but not for you. It seems you've drunk your brains away. You went out to buy some sheepskins and back you come without even the coat you left in. What's more, you bring some half-naked tramp back with you. I don't have any supper for a pair of drunkards like you!'

'Now that's enough of your stupid tongue-wagging, Matryona! You might at least ask who he is.'

'And you can tell me what you did with the money.'

Semyon felt in his pocket, took out the three-rouble note and unfolded it.

'Here it is. Trifonov wouldn't give me any money, but he promised to pay up in a day or so.'

Matryona grew even more furious: in addition to not buying the sheepskins, her husband had lent their only coat to some naked stranger. What's more, he'd brought him back home.

She snatched the note from the table and went off to hide it somewhere.

'I've no supper for you,' she told them. 'You can't expect me to feed every naked drunkard.'

'And you mind your tongue, Matryona. First hear what he has to say . . .'

'What sense will I get from a drunken fool like him? I was right in not wanting to marry an old soak like you! You sold all Mother's linen for drink. And then, instead of buying sheepskins you spend the money on drink.'

Semyon tried hard to make his wife understand that all he had spent on drink was a mere twenty copecks and to explain where he had found the stranger. But she would not let him get a word in edgeways, rattling away nineteen to the dozen and even reminding him of things that had happened ten years ago. On and on she went, until finally she dashed over to Semyon and grabbed his sleeve.

'Give me my jacket back, it's the only one I have and you took it to wear yourself. Give it back, you flea-bitten dog. May you die of a fit!'

Semyon began taking the jacket off and turned a sleeve inside-out, but his wife tugged so hard that it came apart at the seams. Then she seized it, threw it over her head and made for the door. But then she stopped. Her heart seemed to melt and she felt that she wanted to banish all those spiteful feelings and to find out who that man really was.

4

As she stood there, quite still, Matryona said, 'If he were an honest man he wouldn't be going around without a shirt to his back. And if you'd been doing what you were supposed to you'd have told me where you picked up this fine young fellow!'

'All right, I'll tell you. I was on my way home when I saw this man sitting by the chapel, naked and frozen. Now, it's not the kind of weather to go about naked! God must have led me to him, or he'd have perished. What could I do? Who knows what may have happened to him? So, I made him stand up, clothed him and brought him back here. Please don't be angry, Matryona, it's sinful. Don't forget that we must all die one day.'

Matryona was about to give him a piece of her mind again, but then she looked at the stranger and became silent. There he sat, motionless, on the edge of the bench, his hands folded on his knees, his head drooping on his breast. His eyes were closed and he wrinkled his face as if something were choking him. Matryona still said nothing, but Semyon asked, 'Matryona, is there no love of God within you?'

At these words Matryona glanced at the stranger and her heart suddenly filled with pity. She came back from the door, went over to the stove, took out the supper, placed a cup on the table, poured out some kvass, brought out the last slice of bread and set out a knife and some spoons. 'Please eat,' she said.

Semyon nudged the stranger and told him, 'Come and sit at the table.'

Semyon divided the bread into small pieces and they started eating. Matryona sat at one corner of the table, her head on her hand, gazing at the stranger. And she was filled with pity and her heart went out to him. Suddenly, his face brightened, the wrinkles disappeared and he looked up at Matryona and smiled.

After supper Matryona cleared the table and began questioning him.

'Where are you from?'

'Not from these parts.'

'How did you come to be by the wayside?'

'I cannot tell you.'

'Who stole your clothes?'

'God punished me.'

'And you were lying there, all naked?'

'Yes, naked and freezing. And then Semyon saw me and took pity on me. He took off his coat, put it over me and insisted I came home with him. You have given me food and drink and shown compassion. God will reward you!'

Matryona got up, took from the window-sill the old shirt of Semyon's she had been patching and handed it to the stranger. Then she found him some trousers.

'Here, I see you've no shirt, so put this on and lie down where you like – up on the sleeping-bench or over the stove.'

The stranger took off the coat, put on the shirt and trousers and lay on the sleeping-bench. Matryona blew out the candle, took the coat and joined her husband over the stove.

Matryona drew the skirts of the coat over herself and lay down. But she did not fall asleep, for she could not get that stranger out of her mind.

When she remembered that he had eaten their last slice of bread and that they would have none for tomorrow, and that she had given him the shirt and trousers, she became terribly dejected. But then, when she recalled his smile her heart leapt up. For a long time she lay awake and she noticed that Semyon was awake too, as he kept pulling the coat up.

'Semyon!'

'What is it?'

'You two have eaten the last slice of bread and I haven't prepared any more. I don't know what we're going to do tomorrow. Perhaps I can borrow some from our neighbour Malanya.'

'Yes, we'll get by, we won't starve.'

Matryona lay silently for a while and then she said, 'He seems to be a good man, only he doesn't tell us anything about himself.'

'I suppose he can't.'

'Semyon!'

'What?'

'We're always giving, but why does nobody ever give *us* anything?'

Semyon didn't know what to reply. All he said was, 'Let's talk about that another time,' after which he turned over and went to sleep.

5

Next morning, when Semyon woke up, the children were still asleep and his wife had gone over to the neighbour's to borrow some bread. Only the stranger was sitting on the bench, wearing the old trousers and shirt and looking up. His face was brighter than the evening before. Semyon said, 'Well, my friend. The belly needs food and the body clothes. We all have to earn a living, so what sort of work can you do?'

'I can't do anything.'

Semyon was amazed and replied, 'If a man has the will he can learn anything.'

'Yes, men work for their living, so I'll work too.'

'What's your name?'

'Mikhail.'

'Well, Mikhail, if you don't want to tell us about yourself that's your affair. But we have to earn our living. If you do as I tell you I'll see you have enough to eat.'

'God bless you! I'll learn how to work, just tell me what to do.'

Semyon took a piece of yarn, wound it round his fingers and twisted it.

'It's not hard, just watch . . .'

Mikhail watched and right away he caught the knack, winding the yarn and twisting it just like Semyon.

Then Semyon showed him how to wax it and Mikhail understood at once. Then he showed him how to draw it through and how to stitch. Again Mikhail immediately understood.

Whatever Semyon showed him he mastered right away and within three days was working as if he had been making shoes all his life. He would work without any let-up and ate very little. Only when one job was finished would he stop for a moment and silently look up. He never went out, only spoke when he really had to, and he never joked or laughed.

And in fact the only time they had seen him smile was on that very first evening, when Matryona had given him supper.

6

The days passed, weeks passed, and a year ran its course. Mikhail was still living with Semyon and working for him. The word got round that Semyon's new workman could make boots better and stronger than anyone else. People from all over the district came to Semyon for new boots and he prospered.

One winter's day Semyon and Mikhail were sitting at their work when a three-horse carriage on sleigh runners drove up to the cottage, its bells gaily ringing. When they looked out of the window they saw it had stopped right outside. A boy jumped down from the box and opened the carriage door. A gentleman in a fur coat stepped out, walked up to the front door and climbed the steps. Matryona rushed to fling open the door.

As he came in, the gentleman had to lower his head and then straighten up. But still his head almost touched the ceiling and he filled a whole corner of the room.

Semyon stood up and marvelled at the gentleman: he had never seen anyone like him. Semyon himself was lean, Mikhail was skinny, while Matryona was as thin as a rake. But this visitor seemed like someone from another world: with his full red face and his bull's neck he seemed to be made of cast iron.

He puffed, took off his fur coat, sat on the bench and asked, 'Who is the master bootmaker here?'

Semyon stepped forward and said, 'I am, Your Honour.'

Then the gentleman shouted to his boy, 'Hey, Fedka, bring the leather!'

The boy ran in with a parcel, which the gentleman took and placed on the table.

'Untie it,' he said. The boy untied it.

Then the gentleman pointed at the leather and told Semyon, 'Now, listen to me, bootmaker. Do you see that leather?'

'Yes, I do, Your Honour.'

'Do you know what kind it is?'

Semyon felt it and said, 'It's very good quality.'

'I should say it's good quality! You fool, I bet you've never set eyes on leather like that. It's German and I paid twenty roubles for it.'

Semyon quailed and said, 'Now where would *I* see leather like that?'

'Yes, where indeed! Could you make me a pair of boots out of it?'

'It's possible, Your Honour.'

'I'll give you possible!' the gentleman shouted. 'Now, see you don't forget for whom you're making them and the quality of the leather you'll be using. I want a pair of boots that will last me a year without losing their shape or coming apart at the stitches. If you can do the job, take the leather and cut it up. But if you can't, you'd better tell me here and now. I'm warning you: if the boots split or lose their shape before the year's out I'll have you clapped in prison. But if they keep their shape and don't split for a year I'll pay you ten roubles.'

Semyon was quite afraid and did not know what to reply. He glanced at Mikhail, nudged him with his elbow and whispered, 'Well, shall I take it on?'

Mikhail nodded as if to say, 'Yes, take it on.'

So Semyon followed Mikhail's advice and undertook to make a pair of boots that would not lose their shape or split for a whole year.

Then the gentleman called the boy over to take off his left boot for him and stretched out his leg.

'Take my measurements!'

Semyon sewed together a strip of paper about seventeen inches long, smoothed it out, knelt down, wiped his hands thoroughly on his apron so as not to dirty the gentleman's sock and started measuring. He took the sole and instep measurements. But when he tried to measure the calf he found that the strip of paper was not long enough – the gentleman's calf was as thick as a log.

'Mind you don't make them too tight in the leg,' he said.

Semyon sewed another piece to the strip of paper, while the gentleman sat wriggling his toes in his sock and surveying the people in the room. And then he noticed Mikhail.

'Who's that over there?' he asked.

'He's my master craftsman, he'll be making the boots.'

'Now you watch out,' the gentleman said, 'remember they have to last a whole year.'

When Semyon turned towards Mikhail he saw that he was not even looking at the gentleman, but staring into the corner, as if someone was standing behind him. Mikhail kept staring until suddenly he smiled and his whole face lit up.

'What are you grinning at, idiot?' the gentleman asked. 'You'd better see to it that the boots are ready on time!'

'They'll be ready whenever you want them,' Mikhail replied.

'Good.'

The gentleman put on his boots again, then his fur coat, which he wrapped tightly around him and went to the door. But he forgot to lower his head and banged it against the lintel. He cursed and rubbed it. Then he climbed into the carriage and drove off.

As soon as he had gone Semyon remarked, 'He's as tough as nails! You couldn't kill him with a mallet. Why, he nearly knocked the lintel out and still he hardly felt a thing!'

'You'd expect him to be strong with the kind of life he leads,' Matryona said. 'Death itself couldn't touch that iron girder!'

7

'Well, we've taken on the work now,' Semyon told Mikhail, 'and I only hope it doesn't land us in trouble. The leather's very expensive and the gentleman's short-tempered, so we'd better not slip up. Your eyes are sharper than mine and your hands are more skilled, so take the measure and start cutting the leather. I'll sew the vamps later.'

Mikhail obediently took the leather, spread it on the table, folded it in two, took a knife and started cutting.

Matryona went over to watch Mikhail working and was amazed to see what he was doing. Naturally she knew all about boot-making and could see that instead of cutting the leather into the normal shape for boots Mikhail was cutting it into round pieces.

Matryona felt she should point it out, but then she thought, 'Maybe I don't understand how a *gentleman's* boots should be made. Maybe Mikhail knows best, so I won't interfere.'

When he had finished cutting Mikhail took some thread and started sewing the pieces together – not with two ends, as he should have done for boots, but with one end, as if for slippers.

Although Matryona was astonished by this as well, she did not interfere and Mikhail carried on sewing until midday.

When Semyon got up and saw that Mikhail had made a pair of slippers from the gentleman's leather he groaned.

'I don't understand,' he thought, 'how Mikhail, who's been with me for a whole year without making one mistake, should now go and make such a dreadful mess of things. The gentleman ordered welted high boots and he's made slippers without soles and ruined the leather. How can I face the gentleman now? I can't replace leather of that quality.'

And he told Mikhail, 'What on earth have you done, my friend? You've ruined me! The gentleman ordered high boots and just look what you've made!'

And he was just about to give Mikhail a stern lecture when someone knocked hard on the front door with the iron ring. They looked out of the window and saw that someone had ridden up and was tethering his horse. When the door was opened in came the same young boy who had accompanied the gentleman.

'Good afternoon to you!'

'Good afternoon. What can we do for you?'

'The mistress sent me about those boots.'

'What about them?'

'Just this: the master won't be needing them. He's dead.'

'What did you say?'

'He died in the carriage even before we got home. When we reached the house the others came to help him out, but there he lay, slumped like a sack of potatoes. He was already stiff, stone-dead, and we had a real struggle getting him out. So the mistress told me to come back here. "Tell that shoemaker," she said, "that the gentleman who called and ordered some boots and left the leather won't be needing them and that instead he must make a pair of soft corpse-slippers as soon as he can." She told me to wait until they're ready. So here I am.'

Mikhail collected the offcuts from the table and rolled them up. Then he took the soft slippers he had already made, slapped them together, wiped them with his apron and handed them to the boy, who took them.

'Goodbye, masters! Good luck to you!' he said as he left.

8

Another year passed, then another, until Mikhail was in his sixth year with Semyon. He lived just as before, never going out, speaking only when he had to. And all that time he smiled only twice – when the old woman had first given him supper and then when the rich gentleman called. Semyon thought the world of his workman and no longer inquired where he was from. His only fear was that Mikhail might leave him.

One day they were all at home and Matryona was putting iron pots into the oven, while the children were scampering along the benches and looking out of the windows. Semyon was stitching at one window, while Mikhail was heeling a boot at the other.

One of the little boys ran along the bench to Mikhail, leant on his shoulder and looked through the window.

'Look, Uncle Mikhail! There's a lady with two little girls. I think she's coming here. One of the girls is limping.'

When the boy said this, Mikhail put down his work, turned to the window and looked out into the street.

Semyon was amazed: Mikhail had never looked out into the street before, but now he was glued to the window and staring at something. Semyon, too, looked out and saw that a well-dressed woman with two little girls in fur coats and thick woollen shawls were in fact coming towards the cottage. The girls were so alike it would have been impossible to tell them apart were it not that one had a crippled left leg and walked with a limp.

The woman climbed the steps, fumbled for the latch and opened the door. She let the little girls in first and then followed them.

'Good day, everyone!' she said.

'Welcome! What can we do for you?'

The woman sat at the table while the girls, feeling shy with all those people in the room, snuggled against her knees.

'I'd like some leather shoes for the girls, for the spring,' she said.

'That's no problem. Although we've never made such small ones before we can do them – either welted or lined with linen. This is Mikhail, my master shoemaker.'

Semyon turned to Mikhail and saw that he had stopped working and was sitting there with his eyes fixed on the little girls.

Semyon was quite surprised. True, the girls were very pretty – plump, with black eyes and rosy little cheeks – and wore fine fur coats and shawls. Still, he could not understand why Mikhail should be staring like that, as if he knew them.

Semyon kept wondering and then started discussing the price with the woman. This was finally agreed and Semyon took his measure. The woman lifted the lame girl on to one knee and said, 'Measure her twice and make one shoe for her lame foot and three for the sound one: they take exactly the same size, because they're twins.'

Semyon took the measurements and inquired about the little lame girl.

'What happened? Such a pretty little girl. Was she born like that?'

'No, she was crushed by her mother.'

Just then Matryona joined in. She was wondering who the woman was and whose children they were.

'You're their mother, aren't you?'

'No, dear woman, I'm not their mother, nor am I a relative. They were complete strangers and I adopted them.'

'They're not your own and yet you seem so fond of them!'

'How can I help being fond of them? I breast-fed them both. I did have a child of my own once, but it pleased God to take him. I didn't love him as much as these little girls, though.'

'So whose are they?'

9

And the woman proceeded to tell them the whole story.

'It all started about six years ago, when these little girls lost their father and mother the same week – the father was buried on the Tuesday and the mother died on the Friday. So, for three days they had no father and on the fourth they lost their mother. At that time my husband and I were farm-workers and our yard was right next door. The father was a lone wolf and worked as a woodcutter. One day when they were cutting down some trees they let one fall right on him and it crushed his insides. They had hardly got him back to the village when his soul went up to heaven and the same week his widow gave birth to twins – these little girls. She was a poor woman, all on her own, with no other women, young or old, to help her. Alone she gave birth and alone she died.

'The next morning I went to see how she was, but the poor thing was already stiff and cold. When she died she'd rolled over on to this little girl and twisted her leg out of shape. Then the villagers came, washed the body and laid it out. Then they made a coffin and buried her. Good folk they were. So the two little girls were left alone in the world, and who was going to look after them? I happened to be the only woman in that village who'd had a baby at the time and I'd been breast-feeding my first-born for about eight weeks. So I took care of the girls for the time being. The men thought hard about what to do with the orphans and in the end they told me, "You'd better look after them for now, Marya, until we manage to sort something out." So I breast-fed the girl who hadn't been harmed, but not the one who'd been crippled, as I didn't expect her to live. And then I thought to myself, "Why should that little angel be left to fade away?" I took pity on her too and started feeding her, so that in the end I was feeding all three of them – my own first-born and these two, at my own breasts! I was young, strong and well-nourished and God gave me so much milk that it filled my breasts to overflowing. Sometimes I'd feed two at a time, with the third waiting, and when one had had its fill, I'd put the third to my breast. But it was God's will that I should nurse these little girls and bury my own child before he was two years old. And God never gave me another one. But after that I became quite well off. My second husband's working for a corn merchant and we live at the mill. He earns good money and we live well. But as we've no children of our own I'd be terribly lonely without these two little girls. How can I help loving them? They are the apple of my eye!'

The woman pressed the lame girl to her with one hand and wiped the tears from her cheeks with the other.

Matryona sighed. 'There's a lot of truth in the saying "You can live without mother or father, but you can't live without God."'

They chatted together for a while and then the woman got up to leave. Semyon and his wife saw them out and then they looked at

Mikhail: he was sitting there, his arms folded on his knees, and he was looking up and smiling.

10

Semyon went over to Mikhail and asked, 'What is it?'

Mikhail rose from the bench, put down his work, took off his apron, bowed to Semyon and Matryona and said, 'Please forgive me, you good people. God has forgiven me, so please forgive me too.'

And the shoemaker and his wife saw a light shining from Mikhail. And Semyon stood up, bowed in turn and said, 'I can see you are no ordinary mortal and I cannot detain you any longer or question you. But please tell me one thing: why were you so miserable when I first found you and brought you home? And why, when my wife gave you supper, did you smile and from that time onwards brighten up? And why, when that rich gentleman ordered those boots, did you smile again and become even more cheerful? And why, when that woman brought those little girls here just now, did you smile a third time and become the very picture of joy? Please tell me, Mikhail. What is that light coming from you and why did you smile three times?'

'The light is radiating from me,' Mikhail replied, 'because I had been punished, but now God has forgiven me. And I smiled three times because I was commanded to discover three truths and I have discovered them. I discovered the first truth when your wife took pity on me – that is why I smiled for the first time. The second truth I discovered when that rich gentleman ordered the boots – and then I smiled again. And just now, when I saw those two little girls, I discovered the last of the three truths – and I smiled for the third time.'

'Tell me, Mikhail,' Semyon asked, 'why did God punish you and what are those three truths, so that I too may know them?'

Mikhail replied, 'God punished me because I disobeyed Him. I was an angel of the Lord and I disobeyed Him. Yes, I was an angel in heaven and the Lord sent me down to earth to take a woman's soul. I flew down and saw the woman lying there. She was sick, all alone and had just given birth to twins, two little girls. There they were, crawling around their mother, but she was unable to put them to her breasts. When she saw me she understood that God had sent me to take her soul. She burst into tears and said, "Angel of the Lord! My husband has just been buried, killed by a falling tree. I have no sister, no aunt, no grandmother – no one to bring up my little orphans. So please don't take my soul, let me suckle my babies, bring them up and set them on their feet. Children cannot live without father or mother!" And I did what she asked, pressed one little girl to her breast, put the other in her arms and ascended to heaven. I flew to God and told Him, "I could not bring myself to take the soul of a woman who had just borne twins. The father was killed by a falling tree and the mother had just given birth and begged me not to take her soul. "Let me suckle my children, bring them up and set them on their feet. Children cannot live without a father or mother," she pleaded. So I did not take that woman's soul. And then God said, "If you go down to earth and take that woman's soul you will discover three truths: you will learn *what dwells in man, what is not given to man* and *what men live by*. When you have learnt these truths you shall return to heaven." So I flew down to earth again and took the mother's soul. The babies dropped from her breasts and her body rolled over on to one of them, crushing its leg. Then I rose above the village, wishing to return her soul to God, but I was seized by a strong wind and my wings drooped and fell off. And so the soul alone returned to God and I fell to earth, by the roadside.'

II

And now Semyon and Matryona realized whom they had been clothing and feeding and had taken in to live with them. And they both wept for joy and fear. And the angel said, 'I was alone and naked in that field. Never before had I known the needs of man, never had I known cold or hunger. But now I was an ordinary mortal, cold and hungry and not knowing what to do. And then I saw a chapel in the field, built for the glory of God. So I went to it to seek shelter. But it was locked and I could not enter. So I sat down behind it to shelter from the wind. Evening came and I was famished, freezing and in pain. Suddenly I heard a man coming down the road. He was carrying a pair of boots and talking to himself. For the first time since I became a man I saw the mortal face of man. It terrified me and I turned away. And I could hear this man wondering how to protect his body from the winter cold and feed his wife and children. And I thought, "I am perishing with cold and hunger, but here is someone whose only thought is how to find a warm coat for himself and his wife, and food for his family. I cannot expect any help from him." When the man saw me he frowned, looking even more terrifying and he passed me by. I was desperate. But suddenly I heard him coming back. As I looked he no longer seemed the same man. Before, his face had borne the stamp of death, but now he had suddenly become alive again and in that face I could see God. He came up to me, clothed me and took me to his home. When we arrived a woman came out to meet us and she spoke. This woman was even more terrifying than the man. Her breath seemed to come from the grave and I was almost choked by that deathly stench. She wished to cast me out into the cold and I knew that if she did that she would die. Then suddenly her husband told her to think of God and at once she was transformed. When she had given us supper I returned the look she gave me and saw that death no longer dwelt in her, but life. And in her too I could see God.

'And I recalled God's first lesson: *thou shalt learn what dwelleth in man.* And now I knew that it is Love that dwells in man. I was overjoyed that God had begun to reveal what He had promised to reveal, and I smiled for the first time. But I did not know the whole truth yet. I did not yet know what is not given to man and what men live by.

'And so I came to live with you and one year passed. One day a rich gentleman came to order a pair of boots that would last a year without splitting or losing their shape. When I looked at him I suddenly saw my comrade, the Angel of Death, standing behind him. No one but I could see that angel. And I knew that he would take the gentleman's soul before sunset. And I thought, "Here is a man who wants to provide for himself for a year from now but does not know that by evening he will be dead." And so I remembered God's second lesson: *thou shalt learn what is* not *given to man.*

'What dwells in man I already knew. Now I knew that which is not given to man: it is not given to him to know his bodily needs. And I smiled for the second time. I rejoiced that I had seen my fellow angel and that God had revealed His second truth.

'But still I did not know everything. I did not understand what it is that men live by. And so I lived on, waiting for God to reveal this last truth to me. In my sixth year that woman came here with the two little girls. I recognized the girls and learnt how they had stayed alive. After this discovery I thought, "The mother pleaded with me for her children's sake and I believed what she said, thinking that children cannot live without father or mother. But the other woman had nursed them and brought them up." And when I saw how much love this woman had for the children and how she wept over them I saw the living God in her and understood *what men live by*. And I realized that God had revealed His last lesson and had forgiven me. So I smiled for the third time.'

12

And the angel's body was bared and it was robed in light, so that the eye could not look upon it. And the angel's voice grew louder, as though it came not from him, but from heaven itself. And the angel said, 'I have learned that men live not by selfishness, but by love.

'It was not given to the mother to know what her children needed for their lives. Nor was it given to the rich man to know what his true needs were. Nor is it given to any man to know, before the sun has set, whether he will need boots for his living body or slippers for his corpse. When I became a mortal I survived not by thinking of myself, but through the love that dwelt in a passer-by and his wife, and the compassion and love they showed me. The two orphans' lives were preserved, not by what others may have intended for them, but by the love that dwelt in the heart of a woman, a complete stranger, and by the love and compassion she showed them. Indeed, all men live not by what they may intend for their own well-being, but by the love that dwells in others.

'Previously I had known that God gave life to men and desired that they should live. But then I came to know something else.

'I came to understand that God does not wish men to live apart and that is why He does not reveal to each man what he needs for himself *alone*. On the contrary, He wishes men to live in peace and harmony with each other and for this reason He has revealed to each and every one of them what *all* men need, as well as themselves.

'And I understood that men only think that they live by caring only about themselves: in reality they live by love alone. He who dwells in love dwells in God, and God in him, for God is love.'

And the angel sang the Lord's praises and the hut shook with the sound of his voice. And the roof parted and a pillar of fire rose from earth to heaven. Semyon and his wife and children prostrated themselves; the angel's wings unfurled and he soared into the sky.

When Semyon came to his senses the hut was just as it had always been and there was no one there but him and his family.

NEGLECT A SPARK
AND THE HOUSE BURNS DOWN

Then came Peter to him, and said, Lord, how oft shall my brother sin against me, and I forgive him? till seven times?

Jesus saith unto him, I say not unto thee, Until seven times: but, Until seventy times seven. Therefore is the kingdom of heaven likened unto a certain king, which would take account of his servants. And when he had begun to reckon, one was brought unto him, which owed him ten thousand talents. But forasmuch as he had not to pay, his lord commanded him to be sold, and his wife, and children, and all that he had, and payment to be made. The servant therefore fell down, and worshipped him, saying, Lord, have patience with me, and I will pay thee all. Then the lord of that servant was moved with compassion, and loosed him, and forgave him the debt. But the same servant went out, and found one of his fellowservants, which owed him an hundred pence: and he laid hands on him, and took him by the throat, saying, Pay me that thou owest. And his fellowservant fell down at his feet, and besought him, saying, Have patience with me, and I will pay thee all. And he would not: but went and cast him into prison, till he should pay the debt. So when his fellowservants saw what was done, they were very sorry, and came and told unto their lord all that was done. Then his lord, after that he had called him, said unto him, O thou wicked servant, I forgave thee all that debt, because thou desiredst me: Shouldest not thou also have had compassion on thy fellowservant, even as I had pity on thee? And his lord was wroth, and delivered him to the tormentors, till he should pay all that was due unto him. So likewise shall my heavenly Father do also unto you, if ye from your hearts forgive not everyone his brother their trespasses.

(Matthew xviii, 21–35)

In a certain village there once lived a peasant by the name of Ivan Shcherbakov. He was comfortably off, in the prime of life, the best worker in the village and had three sons who were all able to work.

One was married, the second engaged and the third was old enough to mind the horses and was just learning to plough. Ivan's wife was a sensible, thrifty woman, and his daughter-in-law quiet and hardworking. So Ivan and his family had everything to live for. The only person who did not work in that household and needed feeding was Ivan's ailing old father who suffered from asthma and had now been lying over the stove for seven years. Ivan had everything in abundance: three horses and a foal, a cow with calf and fifteen sheep. The women made all the men's boots and clothes and helped in the fields, while the men tilled the soil. They always had sufficient grain to see them through to the next harvest and they paid their taxes and met all their other needs by selling oats. Ivan and his sons, therefore, might have continued to live quite happily, but right next door there lived Lame Gavrilo, son of Gordey Ivanov. He and Ivan became deadly enemies.

In old Gordey's lifetime, when Ivan's father ran the house, the two peasants had been exemplary neighbours. If any of the women needed a sieve or a tub, or the men needed some sacking or a new wheel in an emergency, one household would send over to the other and they would help one another in true neighbourly fashion. If a calf happened to stray on to next door's threshing-floor, all they would do was shoo it away and remark, 'Please don't let it come in here, there's piles of grain that still haven't been stored away.' But as for taking and locking up in a shed or barn anything that was a neighbour's property, or casting aspersions on one another, that was quite unheard of.

This was the life they led when the old men were alive, but everything was different when the young ones took charge.

It all came about through some trifle.

Ivan's daughter-in-law's pullet began to lay early and she was able to collect the eggs the week before Easter. Every day she went to the cart in the shed to fetch an egg. But one day the pullet was frightened, probably by some children, and flew over the fence into the neighbour's yard and started laying there. The young woman could hear it clucking, but she thought, 'I've no time to collect it now, there's so much to do in the house before Easter. I'll collect it later.'

That evening she went to the shed, but no egg was there. So she asked her brother-in-law and his mother if they had taken it, but they told her they hadn't. Taska, her younger brother-in-law, said, 'Your hen's gone and laid her eggs in our neighbour's yard. I heard her clucking there and saw her fly back.' The young woman went to look, and there she was, roosting next to the cock, her eyes just closing for sleep. The young woman would have liked to ask the hen where she had laid the egg, but as she could expect no answer, she went over to the neighbour's.

The old woman came out and asked, 'What do you want, my dear?'

'Well, my hen's flown into your yard and I wonder if she's laid an egg somewhere?'

'Can't say I've seen one. Thank God our own hens started laying ages ago. We've collected all ours and we don't need anybody else's. We're not the kind of folk, dear, who go round stealing eggs from other people's yards.'

The young woman took great offence at this and said more than she intended. The old woman followed suit and a regular slanging-match followed. Ivan's wife happened to come past with some water and she joined the battle. Then Gavrilo's wife ran out and gave her neighbour a good talking-to, dragging in both fact and fiction. All hell broke loose. The women all shouted at once as they tried to shut each other up. And they were not too particular with their language, one shouting, 'You're a bitch; you're a thief; you're a filthy slut; you're starving your old father-in-law to death; you're a lousy sponger!' and the other, 'As for you, always begging and borrowing! You've worn that sieve I lent you to bits. And that's our yoke you've got there. Give it back!'

They grabbed the yoke, spilt the water, snatched each other's shawl off and let fly with their fists. Just then Gavrilo came back from the fields and took his wife's side. Out dashed Ivan and his son and they too joined in the fray. Ivan, a strong fellow, sent everyone flying and tore a handful of hair from Gavrilo's beard. The villagers ran up to see what was wrong and had great difficulty separating the combatants.

And that was how it all began.

Gavrilo wrapped the tuft of beard in a piece of paper and went off to the District Court to start proceedings.

'I didn't grow my beard,' he complained, 'for that pock-faced Ivan to pull it out!'

Then his wife went round bragging to the neighbours that Ivan was bound to be convicted and sent to Siberia. And so hostilities continued.

From where he lay over the stove the old man tried to make them see reason from the very start, but the young people would not listen.

'You're acting very stupidly, making a mountain out of a molehill!' he said. 'And all because of an egg! If some children took it – well, they can be forgiven. One little egg can't be worth very much. God provides for everyone. And even if your neighbour was too free with her tongue you can put matters right and show her what she should have said. So, you came to blows. Well, none of us is perfect, we are all human. These things do happen. Now, go and make it up and let that be the end of it. But if you let it rankle inside you it will only be worse.'

But the young people turned a deaf ear, so certain were they that none of what he said was to the point. After all, he was just an old man rambling on and on. And Ivan would not give in to his neighbour.

'I didn't pull his hair out!' he protested. 'He pulled it out himself. But his son ripped the front of my shirt off, buttons and all. Just look at that!'

And Ivan went off to start proceedings too. Both cases went before the justice of the peace and the District Court. While the cases were pending, the coupling-bolt from Gavrilo's cart disappeared, for which his womenfolk pinned the blame on Ivan's son.

'Last night,' they said, 'we saw him go past our window, towards the cart. And a neighbour says she saw him at the inn trying to get the landlord to buy it.'

So the two of them went to court again and not a day passed without swearing or fisticuffs. Even the children, in emulation of their elders, swore at each other and whenever the women happened to meet down by the river, where they did their washing, they would hurl insults – and quite nasty ones – at each other rather than rinse their clothes.

At the beginning of hostilities the men had restricted themselves to slandering each other, but then they began, in real earnest, to filch anything they could lay their hands on – and the women and children received tuition in stealing. And so things went from bad to worse. Ivan Shcherbakov and Lame Gavrilo were constantly locked in litigation, at the Parish Assembly, the District Court or before the justice of the peace, so that in the end all the magistrates became sick and tired of the whole thing. Gavrilo would have Ivan fined or clapped in gaol, and then Gavrilo would return the compliment. And the nastier they were to each other the more embittered they became, like two fighting dogs: the longer they fight the fiercer they become. If you hit one of them from behind it immediately thinks the other dog is biting it, so it grows even fiercer. This was the case with the two men. Off they would go to court and one would have the other fined or locked up, with the result that they became even deadlier enemies. 'You wait, I'll make you pay for this!' they would say. And this went on for six years. Only the old man over the stove kept trotting out the same old advice: 'What do you think you're doing, children? Let bygones be bygones, I say. Don't neglect your work, don't bear malice against a neighbour. Listen to me and all will be well. But the more you let things rankle the worse it will be.'

But no one took any notice of the old man.

In the seventh year matters came to a head when Ivan's daughter-in-law held Gavrilo up to shame at a wedding, accusing him of horse-stealing. Gavrilo was drunk, lost his temper and struck the woman, hurting her so badly she was laid up for a whole week. And she was pregnant at the time. Ivan was delighted and went straight to the investigating magistrate to lodge a complaint. 'Now I'll get rid of that neighbour of mine,' he thought. 'This time it'll be a long term in prison, or Siberia, that's for certain.' But once again he failed, as the magistrate dismissed the case. The woman was examined, but she was already up and about again and no bruises were found on her. So Ivan went to the justice of the peace, who referred the matter to the District Court, where Ivan soon got to work, treating the clerk and elder to two gallons of sweet cider, with the result that Gavrilo was sentenced to a flogging. The following sentence was read out to Gavrilo in court: 'This court decrees that the aforesaid Gavrilo Gordeyev shall receive twenty strokes of the birch at the District Court.'

When Ivan heard this he glanced at Gavrilo to see how he would take it. Gavrilo went as white as a sheet, turned round and walked out of the courtroom. Ivan followed him and was just on his way to his horse when he heard Gavrilo say, 'All right, he's arranged to have my back flogged and it'll burn terribly. But he'd better watch out that something of his doesn't burn even more painfully.'

When he heard this Ivan immediately returned to the courtroom and complained, 'Guardians of the law! Now he's threatening to burn my house down! That's what he said – and in front of witnesses!'

. Gavrilo was called back.

'Did you say that?' they asked.

'Didn't say anything. Flog me if you want. It seems I'm the only one to be punished, although I'm in the right. But he can go round doing what he likes.'

Gavrilo wanted to say something more, but his lips and cheeks began to tremble and he turned his face to the wall. Even the magistrates were alarmed when they looked at Gavrilo: they were convinced he might do himself or his neighbour an injury.

The senior (and very elderly) magistrate said, 'Now listen to me, my friends. Hadn't you better make it up? Was that right of you, Gavrilo, striking a pregnant woman as you did? Fortunately no harm was done, thank God, but supposing you had hurt her? Now, go and admit you're in the wrong and beg your neighbour's pardon. He'll forgive you, don't worry about that. Then we'll revoke the sentence.'

When the clerk heard this he said, 'That's not possible. Under Article 117 of the Penal Code no reconciliation has been reached by the two parties, and as sentence has been passed it must be carried out.'

The magistrate ignored the clerk.

'Stop wagging that tongue of yours, my friend,' he said. 'The law all of us must obey is God's law. Always think of God, who has commanded us to forgive our neighbour.'

And once again the magistrate tried to make peace between the two men, but he failed. Gavrilo just would not listen.

'Next year I'll be fifty,' he said. 'I've one married son and I've never been flogged in my life. And now that pock-faced Ivan's ordered me to be flogged you expect me to go crawling to him! No, go ahead and flog me. Don't worry, I'll give him something he won't forget in a hurry!'

Gavrilo's voice started trembling again and he was unable to say anything more. He turned round and left.

It was about seven miles from the court to the village and it was late when he got home. Ivan unharnessed his horse, stabled it, and went into the hut. No one was there. The women had already gone to bring the cattle in and his sons were still out in the fields. Ivan sat on a bench and thought hard. He remembered how they had sentenced Gavrilo, how white he had gone and how he had turned towards the wall. And his heart ached. He imagined how *he* would feel if he had been sentenced to a flogging and he felt sorry for Gavrilo. Then the old man over the stove coughed, sat up, lowered his legs, climbed down and managed to drag himself over to the bench and sit down. The effort exhausted him and brought on another fit of coughing. When he had cleared his throat he leant on the table and asked, 'Well? Have they passed sentence?'

Ivan replied, 'Yes – twenty strokes of the birch.'

The old man shook his head.

'What you are doing, Ivan, is terrible! Oh yes, really terrible. You're only harming yourself, not him. Will you feel better once he's been flogged? Eh?'

'He won't do it again.'

'What won't he do again? What has he done to you that's worse than you've done to him?'

'What has he done that's worse?!' Ivan said. 'He very nearly killed my daughter-in-law and now he's threatening to burn my place down! Do you expect me to go and say thank you?'

The old man sighed and said, 'You're free to go around the whole wide world, Ivan, while I have to lie all year round over the stove. And you think you can see everything and I can see nothing. No, dear boy, you can't see anything. You have been blinded by malice. You can see everyone else's sins, but not your own. "He's done me wrong," you say. But if he'd been the only one to blame we wouldn't have all this trouble now. Do you think a quarrel always starts with one side? No, it takes two to make a quarrel. You see only the wrong he's done, but you're blind to what *you've* done. If he'd been the only one at fault we'd never have had all this trouble. Who pulled the hair out of his beard? Who ruined his haystack? Who hauled him off to court? And yet you still say it's all his fault! It's you who's living wickedly, that's the cause of all the trouble. I never lived like you and it's not what I taught you. Do you think his father and I ever lived the way you do? How did we live? Well, like true neighbours. If he ran out of flour his wife would come over and ask, "Uncle Frol, we need some flour," and I'd reply, "Go to the barn, dear, and take as much as you want." And if they had no one to take their horses to pasture I'd say, "Off you go, little Ivan, give them a hand with the horses." And if I happened to be short of something myself I'd ask, "Uncle Gordey, I need such-and-such." And he'd reply, "Take whatever you want, Frol." That's how it was with us and everything went smoothly. But now . . . Only the other day a soldier was telling me about Plevna.* But the fighting between you and Gavrilo is far worse. Is this any way to carry on, eh? You're a working man, head of a family. You should be the responsible one – and what do you teach the women and children? To snarl like dogs! Why, only today that little sniveller Taras was rude to his Aunt Arina right in front of his mother, and all she did was laugh. Is that any way to behave? You're the one with responsibilities. Spare a thought for your soul. Is all this necessary? Do you always have to say two words to my one? Do I have to hit you twice if you hit me once? No, young man, when Christ walked this earth he did not teach us fools to behave like that. If someone insults you, keep a silent tongue in your head – sooner or later the other man's conscience will prick him. That's what Christ taught. If someone smites you on the cheek, turn the other and say, "Go on, hit me, if that's what I deserve." But the other man's conscience will catch up with him one day! Then he'll become humble and listen to you. That's what Christ taught us – not to be proud. Why don't you say something? Aren't I right?'

Ivan listened, and said nothing.

The old man coughed and after spitting out some phlegm continued. 'Do you think what Christ taught us was wrong? Surely it was for the common good. Just consider the life you're leading now. Are

---

* Bulgarian town, forty miles south of the Danube, scene of fierce fighting between the Russians and Turks in 1877.

you any better off since this "Plevna" started? Just think of what you've had to spend, taking him to court, all that travelling, food. You've raised such fine, strong sons and life should be wonderful for you. But you're going downhill and don't have so much money now. And why? Because of your pride. You ought to be out in the fields now, sowing with your sons, but because of that enemy of yours you keep rushing off to court to see the magistrate or some lousy little clerk. You're late with your ploughing and sowing, so the earth will not bring forth. Why aren't the oats sprouting, eh? When did you do your sowing? Only after you got back from town. And what did you gain from all those lawsuits? A millstone round your neck. Now, go and do what you should be doing. Go and plough with your sons and help the others in the house. If someone does you wrong, forgive him, like a Christian. Then you will have no more worries and there will always be peace in your soul.'

Ivan still did not reply.

'Now, go and do what your old father says, Ivan! Harness the roan, go straight to the District Court and withdraw all the charges. Then, in the morning, make it up with Gavrilo, like a good Christian. Invite him into the house, for tomorrow's a holiday (it was the eve of the Festival of the Birth of Our Lady), put the samovar on, get out a half-bottle of vodka and have done with this wickedness once and for all, so that it never happens again. And tell the women and children to do the same.'

Ivan sighed. 'What the old man says is true,' he thought, and a weight seemed to have dropped from him. Only, he did not know how to go about making peace with his neighbour.

As if he had guessed his son's thoughts the old man continued, 'Come on Ivan, don't delay. Put out the fire before it spreads – or it will be too late.'

The old man wanted to say more, but just then the women came back into the hut, chattering like magpies. They had already heard that Gavrilo had been sentenced to a flogging and that he had threatened to burn their place down. They knew all about it and even added some additional material of their own invention which they used to good effect in another quarrel with Gavrilo's womenfolk in the pasture. They told how Gavrilo's daughter-in-law had threatened them. Gavrilo was hand in glove with the magistrate, they said, and he would be bound to turn the whole thing upside-down. What was more, the village schoolmaster (so the women said) had sent a complaint about Ivan to the Tsar himself, in which everything was mentioned, including the coupling-bolt and the kitchen garden, etc. If the complaint were favourably received, half of Ivan's property would be made over to Gavrilo, as compensation. When Ivan heard this his heart hardened again and he abandoned all thought of reconciliation.

The head of a farmstead always has his hands full, so Ivan wasted no more time talking to the women, got up and left the hut and went on to the threshing-floor and from there into the barn. By the time he had cleared everything away and returned to the yard the sun had set and his sons had come back from the fields where they had been double-ploughing for the winter wheat crop. Ivan asked them about their work, helped them put the tools away, and set aside a broken horse-collar for repairing. He wanted to stow some poles under the shed, but it was too dark now. So Ivan left them until morning, fed the cattle, opened the gates for young Taras to take the horses to night pasture, locked them again and barred them. 'Now I can have my supper and get some sleep,' Ivan thought as he took the broken horse-collar and went towards the hut. By now he had forgotten all about Gavrilo and what his father had told him. Just as his hand was on the door handle and he was about to enter he heard his neighbour on the other side of the fence cursing someone in a hoarse voice. 'To hell with him, death is what *he* deserves!' When Ivan heard this all his hatred for his neighbour boiled up inside him. He stood there for some time listening to Gavrilo swearing. When he stopped he went into the hut, where the lamp had been lit. His daughter-in-law was spinning in one corner, while his wife was preparing supper. His eldest son was making trimmings for bast shoes and his second son was sitting at the table reading a book. Little Taras was about to take the horses to night pasture. Everything would have been so happy and cheerful were it not for that thorn in the flesh – an evil neighbour.

Ivan angrily threw the cat off the bench and told the women off for not having the wash-tub ready. He felt really miserable and sat there scowling as he repaired the horse-collar. He could not get those words of Gavrilo out of his mind – both the threats he had made in court and now that hoarse shout 'Death is what *he* deserves!'

Ivan's wife gave Taras his supper and when he had finished he put on his jacket and an old sheepskin coat, tightened his belt, took some bread and went out to see to the horses. The eldest son wanted to see the youngest off, but Ivan himself got up and went out on to the front steps. Outside it was quite dark, overcast and windy. Ivan went down the steps, helped his little son on to his horse, shooed the foal after him and stood watching and listening to them (Taras had been joined by some other boys in the village) riding down the street until they were all out of sight. He stood there for a long time by the gate and as he did so those words of Gavrilo's kept ringing in his ears: 'He'd better watch out that something of his doesn't burn even more painfully!'

'He'd stop at nothing,' Ivan thought. 'Everything's so dry now and it's windy too. He could break into the yard from the back, set something alight and off he'd go! Now, if only I could catch him in the act.'

Ivan was so taken by the idea that he did not go back up the steps, but out into the street and round the corner. 'I'll have a good look in the yard. Who knows, he might be there.' Stepping softly, he went past the gates.

The moment he turned the corner and glanced at the fence he thought he could see something move on the other side of the yard, as if someone had come out and then vanished. Ivan stopped, watched and listened in silence. All was quiet, only the wind rustled in the leaves of a young willow and a heap of straw.

At first everything seemed pitch-black, but when his eyes grew used to the dark he could see the far corner, a plough and the eaves. He stopped again, looked hard, but it seemed no one was there.

'I must have imagined it,' Ivan thought, 'but I'll take a look all the same.' And he crept stealthily along by the shed, moving so quietly in his felt shoes that he could not hear his own footsteps. But when he reached the far corner by the plough he saw something glimmer briefly and then disappear. Ivan's heart thumped. The moment he stopped he could see an even brighter light, in the same spot. Now everything was quite clear: a man was squatting with his back towards him. He was wearing a cap and he was setting light to a bundle of straw in his hand. Ivan's heart fluttered like a bird. He strained every muscle in his body as he strode out without hearing his own footsteps. 'Well,' he thought, 'he won't escape now. I'll catch him red-handed!'

He had barely gone more than a few yards when something suddenly flared up very brightly, in a different place now. It was no longer a small light – the straw beneath the eaves was blazing fiercely and the flames were spreading to the roof. And there was Gavrilo, as clear as daylight.

Ivan swooped on Gavrilo, like a hawk on a lark. 'He won't escape now. I'll wring his neck!' he thought. But Gavrilo must have heard him, as he turned round and scuttled off past the barn like a hare.

'You won't get away!' Ivan shouted as he flew after him. But just as he was about to grab him by the collar Gavrilo wriggled away from him. Ivan managed to catch hold of one of his coat-flaps, which tore right off and Ivan fell down. In a flash he was on his feet again, shouting, 'Help, help! Catch him!' and he gave chase again.

While he was struggling to his feet Gavrilo had managed to get back into his own yard, but Ivan caught up with him there and was just about to grab him again when suddenly something came crashing down on the crown of his head like a great stone. Gavrilo had picked up an oak stake that was lying in the yard and when Ivan ran up he brought it down on his head with all his might. Ivan was stunned and saw stars. Then all went dark and he slumped to the ground. When he came to his senses Gavrilo had gone. It was as light as day now and from the direction of his own yard came a crackling, roaring sound, like a machine at work. When Ivan turned round he could see that the whole of his back shed was on fire and that the side shed was burning too. Flames, clouds of smoke and bits of burning straw were pouring into his hut.

'Look at that, neighbours!' Ivan shouted, lifting his arms and then striking his thighs. 'All I had to do was pull the straw out of the eaves and stamp on it. Just look at that, neighbours!'

He wanted to shout even more, but he lost his breath and his voice had gone. He wanted to run, but his legs would not obey him and kept getting in the way of each other. Even when he tried to walk slowly he started reeling and he lost his breath again. So he stood still until he could recover his breath and then went on. By the time he had gone round the back shed and reached the fire, the side shed was blazing away. Flames leapt out of the hut, making it impossible to get into the yard. A large crowd of villagers had gathered, but there was nothing they could do. The neighbours dragged out their own belongings and drove their cattle out of the sheds. After Ivan's, Gavrilo's was the next hut to catch fire. The strengthening wind spread the flames right across the street, so that half the village was burnt down.

They barely managed to rescue Ivan's father and the rest of the family escaped in whatever they happened to be wearing. Everything else, except for the horses at night pasture, was lost – the cattle, roosting hens, carts, ploughs, harrows, women's chests, grain in the granaries – all was consumed in the fire.

Gavrilo's cattle was saved, however, together with a few things they managed to get out of his hut.

The fire raged all night. Ivan stood looking at his hut, continually muttering to himself, 'What is this, neighbours? All I had to do was pull the straw out and stamp on it!' But when the roof fell in he dashed into the heart of the fire, seized a charred beam and tried to drag it out. The women saw him and called him back, but he managed to get the beam out and was about to go in for another when he staggered and fell into the fire, whereupon his son came to the rescue and pulled him out. Although his beard and hair were singed, his clothes burnt and one arm scorched, Ivan felt nothing. 'The shock's numbed him,' the villagers said. When the fire began to die down Ivan still stood there muttering, 'Neighbours, what's all this? If only I'd pulled it out . . .'

In the morning the village elder sent his son for Ivan.

'Ivan, your father's dying and wants you to come and say goodbye,' the elder's son said.

'What father?' he asked. 'Who has he sent for?'

'He's sent for you, to say goodbye. He's dying and he's in our hut. Come on, Ivan,' the elder's son continued, pulling him by the arm. Ivan followed him.

When the old man was being carried out of the hut some blazing straw had fallen on him and badly burnt him. He had been taken to the elder's hut on the far side of the village that was untouched by the fire.

When Ivan arrived there was no one else in the hut beside the elder's wife and some children lying over the stove. All the others were still at the fire. The old man was lying on a bench with a candle in his hand and he kept looking towards the door out of the corner of his eye. When his son came in he stirred himself slightly. The old woman went over and told him that his son had come. The old man asked if he could be brought a little nearer. Ivan went closer and the old man started speaking.

'What did I tell you, Ivan? Who burnt the village down?'

'*He* did it, dear father!' Ivan replied. 'I caught him red-handed. I saw him put the burning straw under the eaves. All I had to do was pull it out and stamp on it and everything would have been all right.'

'Ivan,' the old man said, 'my time has come and you too will have to die sooner or later. Now, who is to blame?'

Ivan stared silently at his father, unable to utter a word.

'Now, tell me before God, who is to blame? What did I tell you?'

Only then did Ivan come to his senses, and he understood everything.

He sniffed heavily and said, 'It was my fault, father.' And he fell on his knees, burst into tears and begged, 'Forgive me, father, I'm guilty before you and before God.'

The old man moved the candle to his left hand and tried to put his right to his forehead, as if to cross himself. But he was too weak and his hand dropped back.

'Glory be to Thee, O Lord!' he said, looking at his son. 'Ivan, my dear Ivan!'

'What is it, Father?'

'Tell me, what should you do now?'

'I don't know, Father,' he finally said. 'I don't know how we're going to live after all this.'

The old man closed his eyes and bit his lips, as if to summon his last ounce of strength. Then he opened his eyes and said, 'You'll get by. If you obey God's commandments you'll get by.'

After a short pause the old man grinned.

'Now, Ivan, mind you don't breathe a word to anyone about who started the fire,' he said. 'If you hide another's sin, God will forgive two of your own.'

And the old man took the candle in both hands, folded them across his breast, sighed, stretched himself and died.

Ivan did not inform against Gavrilo and no one ever discovered the cause of the fire. And Ivan felt no malice towards Gavrilo, who was amazed that Ivan did not tell anyone of his terrible deed. At first Gavrilo was very wary of Ivan, but in time he became used to the new order of things. The men stopped quarrelling and so did their families. While new huts were being built, both families lived together. And after the village was rebuilt, with the huts further apart now, Ivan and Gavrilo lived like neighbours, with adjoining yards. In fact they were as good neighbours as their fathers had been. And Ivan did not forget the old man's instructions, nor God's command that we should put out a fire before it has time to spread.

And if anyone did Ivan harm, he would try to put matters right, instead of seeking revenge. And if anyone uttered a hurtful word against him he would try to teach the other not to speak wickedly, instead of giving something worse in return. And that was what he taught his womenfolk and his children. And so Ivan Shcherbakov mended his ways and from then on he prospered more than ever.

THE TWO OLD MEN

The woman saith unto him, Sir, I perceive that thou art a prophet.
Our fathers worshipped in this mountain; and ye say, that in Jerusalem
is the place where men ought to worship.

Jesus saith unto her, Woman, believe me, the hour cometh, when ye
shall neither in this mountain, nor yet at Jerusalem, worship the
Father. Ye worship ye know not what: we know what we worship:
for salvation is of the Jews. But the hour cometh, and now is, when
the true worshippers shall worship the Father in spirit and in truth: for
the Father seeketh such to worship him.

(John iv, 19–23)

I

Two old men once decided to make a pilgrimage to the ancient city
of Jerusalem. One was a prosperous peasant called Efim Tarasych
Shevelyev and the other, who was not well off, was called Elisha
Bodrov.

Efim was a steady, sober man: he never drank vodka, did not smoke
or take snuff and had never used bad language. He had twice served as
village elder and there had never been any discrepancy in the accounts.
His family was large – two sons and a married grandson – and they all
lived together. He was strong, healthy and erect, and his long beard
had only started to turn grey when he was in his sixties. Elisha was
neither rich nor poor, had once done odd jobs around the district as a
carpenter, but now he was old he never left the cottage and spent all his
time keeping bees. One son had gone away to earn his living, the other
lived at home. Although he liked the occasional drink, took snuff and
was fond of singing, he was a quiet man and was on good terms with
family and neighbours. He was short, with darkish skin and a curly
beard; like his patron saint, the prophet Elisha, he was completely bald.

The two old men had vowed a long time ago to make the
pilgrimage, but Efim could never find the time, as he had so much
on his hands: no sooner was one thing finished than he would start
another. First he would be arranging his grandson's marriage, then

he'd be waiting for his younger son to return from the army, then he would set about building a new cottage.

One holiday the two old men met and sat down on a pile of logs for a chat.

'Well,' Elisha said, 'when are we going on that pilgrimage?'

Efim frowned slightly. 'We'll have to wait,' he replied. 'I've had a hard year. When I started the new cottage I thought I could build it for about a hundred roubles, but already it's cost me three hundred – and it's not finished yet. I think we'll have to put it off until the summer. Yes, we'll go then without fail, God willing!'

'As I see it,' Elisha said, 'we shouldn't postpone it any more, but go right away. Spring is the best time.'

'The time of year's all right, but I've started on the new cottage. How can I leave that?'

'Surely there's someone you can leave in charge? What about your son, he can see to things.'

'See to things! I can't rely on my elder son, he drinks too much.'

'When we are dead, my friend, they will have to carry on without us. Your son must be taught what to do.'

'That's true, but I always like to be on the spot, to see a job's done properly.'

'Oh, my dear friend! There's *never* enough time to get everything done! A few days ago the women started washing and cleaning the house for Easter. But as soon as one thing's done, along comes something else, so it's impossible to finish everything. As my eldest daughter-in-law says – and she's a clever woman – "We can be grateful that Easter comes without waiting for us, because however hard we work we'd never manage to get it all done in time."'

Efim pondered for a moment and said, 'The new cottage has cost me a lot of money and you can't go on a long journey like this without anything in your pocket. We'll need quite a lot in fact – one hundred roubles each!'

Elisha laughed. 'I don't believe that, my friend. Why, you're worth ten times as much as me, yet all you talk about is money! Just tell me when you think we should start. Although I don't have the money now, I'll get hold of it in good time.'

Efim smiled. 'Well, you seem to be rich all of a sudden!' he said. 'Where will you get all that money from?'

'I'll scrape it together somehow from the family, and if that's still not enough I can sell a dozen hives or so to my neighbour. He's been after them for a long time now!'

'But if there's good swarms this summer you'll regret it.'

'Regret it? No, my friend, I've never regretted anything in my life, except my sins. There's nothing more precious than the *soul*.'

'That may well be, but it's wrong to neglect one's home.'

'But neglecting the soul is even worse. We made a solemn vow and we ought to go. Yes, I really mean it.'

2

Next morning Efim thought it over and went to see Elisha.

'All right, let's go,' he said. 'What you say is true. In life or in death we are in God's hands. We should go while we are still alive and strong.'

A week later the two old men began to make their arrangements. Efim had enough money at home. He took a hundred roubles for himself and gave his wife two hundred.

Elisha made his arrangements too. He sold his neighbour ten hives, plus whatever young swarms they might produce, taking seventy roubles for the lot. He managed to squeeze the remaining thirty from his family and fairly cleaned them out: his wife gave him all she had – including her funeral savings – and his daughter-in-law did the same.

Efim told his son exactly what to do: how much hay to make, where to cart the manure and how to finish the cottage and put the roof on. He thought of everything that needed doing, giving his son detailed instructions. Elisha, on the other hand, only told his wife to make sure to collect all the young bees from the hives that had been sold and not to try and cheat the neighbour out of them. But he did not say one word about household matters, saying that what had to be done would become obvious. 'You are the masters now,' he said, 'so you should be able to fend for yourselves.'

And so the two old men prepared to leave. Their families baked them cakes, made bags and cut new leggings for them. Then they put on their new shoes (taking some spare bast ones) and went out on to the road. Their families saw them to the end of the village where they said farewell and set off.

Elisha was in high spirits and he forgot all domestic worries the moment he left the village. His only concerns were helping his friend on the journey, not saying a rude word to anyone and making the round trip in peace and friendship. As he walked along he would either whisper a prayer to himself or recite the lives of the saints that he knew by heart. Whenever he met a stranger or stopped somewhere for the night, he would try to be as friendly as he could and speak the language of God, like a true Christian. And so he travelled on, his heart full of joy. However, there was just one thing that he could not bring himself to do. As he wanted to give up snuff, he had deliberately left his box at home. But now he felt a craving for it and a passer-by gave him some, so every now and then he would drop behind so that his companion wouldn't be tempted to take a pinch.

Efim made steady progress, did nothing for which he could reproach himself and never uttered one idle word. Yet his heart was heavy, for he could not stop thinking about what was happening at home. Was there something he had forgotten to tell his son and was he following his instructions? Whenever he saw potatoes being planted or manure carted he would wonder if his son was doing as he had been told. And he felt like turning back to show him or to do it himself.

3

The two old men had been walking for five weeks; their bast shoes were worn out and they had to buy new ones. They were now in the Ukraine and up to then food and lodging had to be paid for. But now the people vied with one another in their hospitality. They would invite them into their homes and feed them, for which they would take no money, even putting bread or cakes into their bags when they left.

And so the old men travelled about five hundred miles, without any expenses. They crossed another province and then reached a district where the crops had failed. The people there would not accept any money for putting them up, but had no food to give them. And in many places they were not even given bread; in others there was none to be bought. The people said that last year's harvest had been a disaster. Those who had been rich were ruined and had to sell up. Others who were not so well off were left with nothing and those who were poor either left for good, went begging, or stayed at home, living from hand to mouth. In winter their only food was corn husks or goosefoot.

One day the old men stopped in a hamlet, bought fifteen pounds of bread, stayed overnight and left before dawn so that they could be well on their way before it grew hot. After about seven miles they sat down by a stream, scooped up some water in a cup and steeped some bread in it. After eating, they changed their leggings and rested for a while. Then Elisha took out his snuffbox, which made Efim shake his head disapprovingly and ask, 'Why can't you give up that filthy habit?'

Elisha threw up his arms helplessly and said, 'It's stronger than me, so what can I do?'

Then they got up and moved on. After about eight miles they came to a large village and walked right through it. It was very hot now and Elisha was exhausted and wanted to rest and drink, but Efim did not want to stop. He was the stronger walker and Elisha was having great difficulty keeping up with him.

'I'm thirsty,' he said.

'Well, have something to drink, I'm not thirsty.'

Elisha stopped. 'You carry on,' he said, 'I'm going to that hut over there for some water. I'll catch you up in a moment.'

'All right,' the other replied and he walked on alone, while Elisha went to the hut, which was quite small and of daubed brick. The lower part was black and the upper white. The clay had crumbled and was falling off, and the hut had not been plastered for ages. There was a hole in one side of the roof. The entrance was on the other side of a yard. Elisha went in and saw a man lying near the earth bank★ around the hut. He was beardless, thin, wore his shirt tucked in his trousers, Ukrainian-style and had clearly lain down when there was some shade. But now the sun was high and was glaring straight down on him. Although he lay quite still, he was not asleep. Elisha called out and asked him for a drink, but the man did not reply. 'He's either ill or not very friendly,' Elisha thought as he

★ Small banks of earth around peasant huts served as protection from the weather.

went up to the door. Inside the hut he could hear a child crying. He knocked on the door with the iron ring that served as a handle.

'Is the master there?' he asked. No reply. He knocked again, this time with his staff. 'Good Christian folk!' Not a soul stirred. 'Servants of the Lord!' No reply. Elisha was about to go away when he heard what sounded like someone groaning on the other side of the door. 'They seem to be in some kind of trouble,' he thought. 'I must go and see what's wrong.'

4

Elisha turned the iron ring – the door was not locked, so he pushed it open and crossed the hall. The living-room door was open. To the left was a stove and directly opposite was an icon shelf with a table in front of it, behind which was a bench where an old, bareheaded, half-dressed woman was sitting, her head on the table. Beside her was a thin, waxen-faced boy with a distended belly. He howled dreadfully as he begged the old woman for something to eat and tugged her sleeve. Elisha stepped forward into the room, where the air was foul. He looked around and saw a young woman lying in bed behind the stove. She was face downwards, her eyes were closed and her throat whistled as she tossed from side to side, stretching first one leg out, then the other. The foul smell was coming from her. She was obviously in no state to look after herself, not was there anyone to help her.

The old woman looked up and saw the stranger.

'What do you want?' she asked. 'What is it? There's no one . . . there's nothing here.'

Elisha understood what she was saying* and went over to her.

'I've come for a drink of water, servant of God!'

'There's nothing here, nothing. And nothing to fetch any water in. Now go on your way.'

'Isn't there anyone here well enough to look after that woman?' Elisha asked.

'No one at all. That man out in the yard is dying – as we are in here.'

---

* The woman is speaking Ukrainian.

THE TWO OLD MEN

The little boy had stopped howling when he saw the stranger, but the moment the old woman spoke he started again, grabbing her sleeve and begging, 'Some bread, Granny, I want some bread.'

Just as Elisha was about to question the old woman further, the man staggered into the hut and clung to the wall. He wanted to reach the bench, but was too weak and slumped into the corner by the door. Without attempting to get up he tried to speak, but was so short of breath he could only produce one word at a time, 'We've ... been ... stricken ... by ... illness ... and ... hunger ... He's ... dying ... of ... hunger,' he said, bursting into tears and nodding towards the boy.

Elisha jerked up the bag behind his shoulders, freed his arms from the straps and threw it on to the floor. Then he lifted the bag on to the bench and began to untie it. When he'd opened it he took out the bread and a small knife, cut off a slice and offered it to the man, who refused it, motioning instead at the boy, and a little girl (who was also there, behind the stove) as if to say, 'Let them have it.' So Elisha offered the bread to the little boy, who sniffed at it, stretched out his arms, seized the slice in his little hands and went off with his nose buried in it. The little girl crept out from behind the stove and stared at the loaf. Elisha gave her some too. Then he cut off another slice and gave it to the woman, who took it and started chewing.

'Can you get us some water?' she asked. 'Their mouths are parched. I went to fetch some yesterday – or was it today, I really can't remember? – but before I could reach the well I fell down. The bucket's still there, unless someone's taken it.'

Elisha asked where the well was and the old woman told him. So he went off, found the bucket, brought the water and gave everyone a drink. The children ate some more of the bread with the water, and so did the old woman, but the man would eat nothing. 'I just can't take any food,' he said.

The sick woman was still delirious and lay tossing from side to side. Elisha went to the village and bought millet, salt, flour and butter. He managed to find an axe somewhere, chopped firewood and lit the stove. The little girl helped him. Then Elisha made some soup and porridge and fed the starving people.

5

The man ate a little, the old woman had a proper meal, while the little girl and boy licked the bowl clean and immediately fell fast asleep in each other's arms.

The man and the old woman then told Elisha how it had all come about.

'We were poor enough before,' they said, 'but when the crops failed we exhausted our stocks by the end of autumn. When everything was gone we started begging food off neighbours and other good Christian folk. At first they gave us some, but then they refused us. There were some who'd have been only too glad to help, but they didn't have anything for themselves. And then we became too ashamed to go out begging. We were up to our eyes in debt, owing people money, flour and bread.'

'I tried to find work,' the man continued, 'but there wasn't any. Everywhere people were crying out for work so that they could feed themselves. For every day you worked you'd have to spend two looking for it. So the old woman and the little girl had to go begging further afield. But they didn't get very much as no one had any bread. All the same, we somehow managed to find enough food and we thought we might get by until the next harvest. But in the spring people gave us nothing at all, and then we were struck down by this illness. It was terrible. One day we would eat and the next two we'd starve. We started eating grass. I'm not sure whether it was because of that, but my wife became very ill. She took to her bed. I had no more strength and we had no medicine to help us.'

'I struggled along on my own for a while,' the old woman said, 'but then I broke down from lack of food and became very weak. The little girl became weak too and frightened of everyone. We wanted to send her to stay with some neighbours, but she wouldn't go and huddled up in a corner. The day before yesterday the neighbour came and when she saw that we were hungry and sick she just turned round and left. Her own husband had just passed away and she could not feed her little ones. So there we were, waiting to die.'

When Elisha heard their story he changed his mind about catching his friend up that day and stayed the night. Next morning he got up and busied himself with the housework as if it was his own home. He helped the old woman knead the dough and lit the stove. Then he went off with the little girl to the neighbours to see if they could borrow some things they urgently needed. There was nothing left in the hut, no kitchen utensils or clothes – everything had been sold to buy food. So Elisha supplied them with what they desperately needed, making some things himself and buying others. He spent the whole day with them, then another, then a third. The little boy recovered and could crawl along the bench whenever Elisha was there and nestle against him. The little girl brightened up considerably and helped with all the work. She was always running after Elisha, calling out, 'Uncle! Uncle!' The old woman improved too and went out to visit a neighbour, while the husband was soon able to get about with the wall to lean against. Only the wife could not get up and even she came to her senses after three days and asked for food. 'Well now,' Elisha thought, 'I didn't expect to spend so much time here, I must be on my way now.'

6

The fourth day happened to be a feast-day after a fast and Elisha thought, 'I'll buy these people a few things for their feast, break my fast with them and then set off in the evening.' So he went to the village again and bought milk, white flour and lard, and helped the old woman with all the baking. Next day he went to Mass and celebrated the feast-day with the villagers. The same day the wife got out of bed and went about her business, and her husband shaved and put on a shirt which the old woman had washed for him. Then he went to plead with a rich peasant in the village to whom his meadows and ploughland were mortgaged, asking if he could farm them until after harvest-time. He returned that evening feeling very miserable and burst into tears. The rich merchant had shown no mercy, had insisted on payment and told him to bring the money.

So Elisha thought things over again. 'How will they survive now?' he wondered. 'These people will go out to do their hay-making, but there's no point in it, as their crops are mortgaged. The rye will ripen, they'll go reaping (the crop this year has been wonderful!) but they'll have nothing to look forward to as their land is all in the hands of that rich peasant. If I leave now they'll soon be back where they were before.' Elisha was torn this way and that, but finally he decided not to depart that evening, but to put it off until the morning. He went outside to sleep, said his prayers, lay down, but could not sleep. Although it really was time to go now, as he had spent so much time and money, he was sorry for these people. But then he thought, 'I can't go on helping them indefinitely. All I intended was giving them some water and a few slices of bread – and now look where that water's landed me! No doubt I'll have to redeem that meadow and field for them. And once that's done I'll have to buy them a cow so the children can have milk, and a horse so the father can cart his sheaves. A fine mess you've got yourself into, Elisha! You've slipped your cables, gone miles adrift!'

Elisha got up, picked up his coat which he had been using as a pillow, unfolded it and took a pinch of snuff from his box, thinking it might clear his head. Not a bit of it! However hard he tried he was unable to come to any decision. He should be going, but at the same time he felt so very sorry for these people. He was at a complete loss. He folded his coat and lay down again until cock-crow, when he dozed off. Suddenly it seemed someone had woken him. He saw himself fully dressed and ready to go, the bag on his back and staff in hand. He had to pass through some gates which were open just wide enough for one person to squeeze through. But first he caught his bag on one side of a fence and when he tried to free it he caught his leggings on the other side and they became undone. When he tried to unhook the bag he saw that it had not caught on the fence at all and that a little girl was holding it and calling out, 'Uncle, Uncle! Give me some bread!' He glanced at his leg and the little boy was holding on to his leggings, while the old woman and the peasant were looking out of the window. Elisha woke up and said out loud, 'Tomorrow I'll redeem their field. I'll buy them a horse, and flour to last them until the next harvest, and a cow for the children. If I don't do that, when I'm across the seas searching for Christ, I might lose Him within me. I *must* help these people.' And Elisha slept until morning. He awoke early and went off to see the rich peasant. He redeemed the rye field and paid the rent for the meadows. Then he bought a scythe (theirs had been sold) and brought it back to the hut.

He sent the peasant out to mow, while he himself went to see the men in the village. He discovered that the tavern-keeper had a horse and cart for sale, so he struck a bargain with him and bought it, together with a sack of flour which he loaded on to the cart. Then he went to buy the cow. On his way he passed two Ukrainian women who were chatting to each other. Although they were talking in their own language, Elisha understood that they were talking about him.

'When he first arrived no one could make out who he was and reckoned he was quite ordinary. He came to beg for water, but he's stayed ever since. You should see what he's bought for them! They say he bought them a horse and cart from the tavern-keeper this morning. You don't find many like him in this world. Let's go and have a look.'

When Elisha heard this he realized that they were singing his praises, but he did not go to buy the cow. Instead he went back to the tavern-keeper and paid for the horse. Then he harnessed it and returned to the hut with the flour. He drove up to the gate, stopped and climbed down. The people in the hut were amazed when they saw the horse: they thought that it was for them, but dared not say so. The husband came out to open the gate.

'Where did you get that horse, my friend?' he asked.

'I just bought it,' he replied. 'It was going cheaply. Now, cut some hay and put it in the manger for tonight. And get that sack down.'

The man unharnessed the horse, carried the sack into the barn and put it in the manger. They all lay down to sleep. Elisha went outside to lie down, taking his bag with him. When everyone was asleep Elisha got up, tied his bag, put on his shoes and coat and went off to catch up with Efim.

7

When Elisha had walked about three miles it began to grow light. He sat beneath a tree, opened his bag and started counting his money. When he had added it up he found he had seventeen roubles and twenty copecks left. 'Well,' he thought, 'that won't get me across the sea! But begging my way, in Christ's name, might be more sinful than not going at all. Yes, Old Efim will get to Jerusalem without me and light a candle for me there, and I'll never fulfil my vow in my lifetime. Thankfully, though, the Lord is merciful and suffers sinners.'

So Elisha got up, slung his bag over his shoulder and turned back. But he gave the village a wide berth, so that no one would see him, and was soon briskly making his way home. The outward journey had been very difficult and he had always had to struggle to keep up with Efim. But now that he was on his way back God seemed to have given him renewed strength and he hardly felt tired at all. He strode along in high spirits, swinging his staff and covering forty miles a day.

When he arrived home the harvest had been gathered in. The old man's family was overjoyed to see him and asked all kinds of questions: what had happened? why hadn't he kept up with his friend? why had he come back without reaching Jerusalem? But Elisha would not tell them.

'It was not God's will,' he replied, 'that I should reach Jerusalem. I lost my money on the way and couldn't keep up with my friend. That's why. Forgive me, for Christ's sake!'

And he gave his wife all that was left of the money and then questioned her about domestic matters. She told him that all was well, that all the work had been done, that nothing had been neglected and that everyone was living in peace and harmony.

That same day Efim's family heard that Elisha was back and they came to inquire about their old man. Elisha told them exactly what he had told the others.

'Your Efim walked at a cracking pace,' he said, 'and we parted three days before the Feast of St Peter. I meant to catch him up, but all kinds of things happened. I lost my money, so I could not go on and so I came home.'

The people were astonished that such an intelligent man could have been so stupid as to have set out without reaching his destination and had only wasted his money. However, after their initial surprise they forgot all about it, and so did Elisha. He got to work in the house, chopped firewood for the winter with his son and helped the women thresh the corn. Then he mended the barn roofs, saw to the bees and handed over the ten hives with their young that had been sold to his neighbour. His wife had tried to conceal the number of swarms but Elisha knew very well which hives had produced young bees and which had not. And instead of ten he handed over seventeen swarms to his neighbour. When he had seen to everything he sent his son to look for work, while he sat down to make bast shoes for the winter and fashioned clogs from the chunks of wood.

8

While Elisha was looking after the sick people in the hut Efim had waited the whole day for his friend. First he had gone on a short distance and then sat down. After waiting a long time he took a nap, woke up and sat down again to wait – but still there was no sign of his friend. He kept straining his eyes until they hurt. The sun sank behind a tree – but still no Elisha. 'I wonder if he's passed me,' he thought. 'Or perhaps someone gave him a lift and he drove by without noticing me as I slept. But he *must* have seen me. You can see for miles on the steppe. If I go back for him now he might have gone on ahead and we'll never meet up, which will be far worse. I'd better push on, I'm sure we'll meet at some place where they put travellers up for the night.' He came to a village and asked the local constable to make sure that any old man of Elisha's description was brought over to his hut if he happened to turn up. But Elisha did not turn up, so Efim moved on and kept asking everyone he met if they had seen a little old bald man. But no one had seen him. Efim was amazed and set off on his own. 'We'll bump into each other again at Odessa, or on board ship,' he decided and thought no more about it.

On the road he became friendly with a long-haired monk, with skull-cap and cassock. The monk had been to Mount Athos and was going to Jerusalem for the second time. They stayed the night at the same place, talked a great deal and set off together in the morning.

Having safely reached Odessa they stayed there three days waiting for a ship. Many pilgrims, from all over Russia, were waiting too. Efim made further inquiries about Elisha, but no one had seen him.

Efim obtained a passport, which cost him five roubles. He paid forty roubles for the return passage to Jerusalem and bought himself bread and herring for the journey. When the cargo was loaded, the other pilgrims embarked and Efim went on board with his new friend.

The ship weighed anchor, cast off and set sail. During the day the passage was smooth, but towards evening the wind got up, it started raining, the ship tossed and waves flooded over the sides. The passengers panicked – the women wailed, while some of the more faint-hearted men ran around looking for somewhere safe down below. Efim was terrified too, only he did not show it. All that night and all next day he did not budge from the place on deck where he had settled on first coming on board, near some old men from Tambov. There they sat, clutching their bags and not saying one word. On the third day it became calm and on the fifth they put into Constantinople.

Some of the pilgrims went ashore to see the Church of St Sophia (now a Turkish mosque). Efim stayed on board and only bought some white rolls. After a day they put to sea again, stopping at Smyrna and Alexandria and finally arriving safely at Jaffa, where all the pilgrims disembarked to walk the forty miles to Jerusalem. But the passengers were terrified when they had to leave the ship, as it stood high out of the water and they were dropped down into small boats that rocked so violently there was every chance that they might miss them and end up in the water. Two men did get a soaking, but finally everyone came safely ashore. Immediately they were on dry land the two men set off and reached Jerusalem around noon, after a three-day walk. They stayed outside the city, at the Russian hostel, where their passports were stamped, and after eating went off to see the holy places. That day the Holy Sepulchre was closed to the public, so they visited the Monastery of the Patriarch, where all the pilgrims assembled, the women being separated from the men, who were told to take off their shoes and sit in a circle. Then a monk entered with a towel and began to wash their feet. He went to each of them, washing, drying and kissing feet. Efim's feet were washed, dried and kissed, along with the others. Right through vespers and matins they stood. They lit votive candles and handed in pieces of paper with names of dead or sick relatives on them, so that prayers could be said. Then they were given food and wine. Next they went to the cell where Mary of Egypt did penance. They placed candles there and held a short service. Then they visited the Monastery of Abraham and the Garden of Saveki, where Abraham wished to sacrifice his son to God. From there they went to the place where Christ appeared to Mary Magdalene and then to the Church of

James, our Lord's brother. The monk showed Efim all the holy places, advising him at which ones it was customary to give money, and how much. Later, they returned to the hostel and had supper. Just as they were preparing for bed, the monk suddenly gave a loud groan and started turning his clothes inside out. 'My purse has gone!' he said. 'There were twenty-three roubles in it – two tens and three in small change.'

For a long time he sat there bemoaning his loss, but there was nothing that could be done and in the end everyone went to bed.

9

As Efim lay in bed he was tempted by the following thought: 'No one could have stolen money from that monk, as he didn't have any in the first place. He didn't give any money at the shrines, although he told me to do so. Yes, he even borrowed a rouble from me.'

But he immediately reproached himself for entertaining such a thought. 'Who am I to judge another?' he reflected. 'It's a sin. I'll forget all about it.' But the moment he let his mind wander he remembered once again how careful the monk had been with his money and how unlikely it was that the story of the stolen purse was true. 'He never had any money in the first place. He made it all up,' he thought.

Next morning they went to early Mass at the Great Church of the Resurrection, where Our Lord's Sepulchre is situated. The old monk never left Efim for one moment and accompanied him everywhere he went. When they entered the church they found a large congregation of pilgrims – Russians, Greeks, Armenians, Turks and Syrians. Efim went to the Holy Gates with the others and a monk took them past the Turkish guards to the place where the Saviour was taken from the Cross and anointed, and where candles were burning in nine great candlesticks. The old monk showed and explained everything to them. Then some monks took Efim up the steps on the right to Golgotha, where the Cross had stood. Efim said a prayer there. Then he was shown the deep cleft in the rock where the earth had opened up to its nether regions. After that he saw where Christ's hands and feet had been nailed to the Cross. Then he was shown the Chapel of Adam, where Christ's blood had trickled down on to

Adam's bones. Then they showed him the stone on which Christ had sat when he was crowned with thorns and the pillar to which Christ was bound when He was scourged. Finally Efim saw the stone with the two holes for Christ's feet. The monks wanted to show him more, but the others surged foward, impatient to see the actual cave of the Lord's Sepulchre. The Latin Mass had just finished and the Russian was just about to begin. Efim went to the tomb in the rock together with the crowd.

He wanted to get rid of the monk, as he found he was constantly sinning in his thoughts against him. But the monk would not leave him and went with him to the Sepulchre to say Mass. They tried to get to the front, but it was impossible: the crowd was so tightly packed that they could move neither backwards nor forwards. As Efim stood there, looking in front and praying, he couldn't help checking his pockets every now and then to see if his purse was safe. He did not know what to think. Firstly he was inclined to think that his companion had been lying all along, but then he reasoned that if the monk had *not* been lying and really had been robbed, then he himself might suffer the same fate.

10

While Efim stood gazing over the people's heads towards the chapel in which the Sepulchre itself was situated, with thirty-six lamps burning over it, he saw something quite amazing. Directly beneath the lamps, where the sacred flame is always kept burning, he saw an old man in a coarse serge coat and with a shiny bald head just like Elisha's right at the front of the congregation. 'He's the image of Elisha,' he thought, 'but it can't be him! He couldn't possibly have got here before me. The ship before ours left a week earlier, he could never have caught it. And he definitely wasn't on my ship, as I saw every single pilgrim on board.'

These thoughts had scarcely passed through Efim's mind when the old man started praying. He bowed three times – first forward, towards God, and then once to each side, to the whole Orthodox world. It was when the old man turned to the right that Efim recognized him. Yes, it *was* Elisha Bodrov in person, with that dark curly beard touched with grey, those same cheeks, eyebrows, nose –

every single feature was his. No doubt about it, it definitely was Elisha.

Efim was delighted at having found his friend again and was amazed that he had managed to arrive before him. 'Good old Bodrov!' he thought. 'He left me miles behind! He must have met someone who helped him. Anyway, I'll catch him as we go out and get rid of this monk in the skull-cap. Then I'll make sure I don't get separated from Elisha – perhaps he can show me how to get to the front!'

Efim kept a watchful eye on Elisha, so as not to let him out of his sight. The service finished and the crowd began to disperse. There was such a crush as everyone surged forward to kiss the tomb that Efim was pushed to one side. He was terrified that his purse might be stolen. Clutching it in one hand he forced his way through to get out of there as quickly as he could. Having escaped from the crowd, he ran up and down looking for Elisha inside and outside the church. In the monks' cells he saw people of all kinds eating, drinking wine, sleeping and reading. But Elisha was nowhere to be found. Efim returned to the hostel – his friend was not there. That evening the old monk did not return: he had left without repaying the rouble and Efim was all on his own again.

Next day Efim went to the Holy Sepulchre again with the old man from Tambov who had been on board ship with him. He wanted to push his way to the front but once again he was caught up in the crush. So he stood by one of the pillars and prayed. Then he looked in front – and there, beneath the lamps over the Sepulchre, stood Elisha. He was right at the front, arms outstretched like the priest's at the altar, and his bald head was shining all over. 'Right,' Efim told himself, 'this time I shan't lose him.' And he shoved his way to the front. But Elisha had disappeared. 'He must have got out some other way,' Efim thought. On the third day at the Holy Sepulchre he looked again and there was Elisha in the holiest place, quite conspicuous, arms outstretched and eyes uplifted as if he were watching something above him. 'This time,' Efim thought, 'I shan't lose him. I'll go and stand at the exit. I can't possibly miss him there.' Efim stood and waited until noon. Everyone had left – but there was no Elisha.

Efim stayed six weeks in Jerusalem and visited all the holy places:

Bethlehem, Bethany, the River Jordan. At the Holy Sepulchre he had a new shirt stamped with a seal, for use as his shroud when his time came; he bought a bottle of water from the River Jordan and some holy soil and some candles lit with the healing flame. He spent all his money, except what was needed for the return journey. And then he left for home. From Jaffa he sailed to Odessa and made the rest of the way back on foot.

11

So Efim travelled alone, along the same road. As he drew nearer home he began to worry again about how they had been coping in his absence. 'A lot of water flows under a bridge in one year,' he reflected. 'You can spend a lifetime building up a home, but it doesn't take long to destroy it.' He wondered how his son had been managing without him, if they'd had a good spring, how the cattle had come through the winter, whether the new cottage was finished. When Efim reached the place where he had left Elisha last summer he could hardly recognize the people there. The previous year they had been suffering terrible hardship and now they all seemed to be prospering: the harvest had been good, the people had recovered from illness and had forgotten all about the misery of the past.

It was evening when Efim approached the village where Elisha had stayed behind the previous year. The moment he entered it a little girl in a white smock came skipping from behind a small hut.

'Grandpa, Grandpa! Please come into the hut!'

Efim wanted to carry on, but she would not let him, caught hold of a fold of his coat and laughingly pulled him towards the hut.

Then a woman with a small boy came out on to the front steps and she beckoned to him. 'Please come in, Grandpa,' she said, 'and have supper with us. You can spend the night here.'

So Efim went in. 'It wouldn't do any harm asking about Elisha,' he thought. 'Perhaps it's the same hut where he came for a drink of water.'

Inside, the woman took his bag and gave him water to wash himself. Then she made him sit down and brought milk, curd cakes, and porridge, and put them before him. Efim thanked her and praised the villagers for being so hospitable to pilgrims. The woman shook her head.

'How can we refuse pilgrims hospitality?' she said. 'It was a pilgrim who showed us the true way to live. We had become forgetful of God and He punished us so severely we were all at death's door. Last summer it was so bad that we were all ill in bed, with nothing to eat. We surely would have died if God had not sent us an old man like yourself. It was around noon that he came, to beg for water, and when he saw us all lying here he took pity on us and stayed here. He saw that we had food and drink, and set us on our feet. And he redeemed our land, bought a horse and cart and gave them to us.'

Just then the old woman came in and interrupted the young one.

'We just don't know whether it was a man or an angel,' she said. 'He loved us all, took pity on us and then he left without telling us who he was. So we don't know whom to pray for. I can see it all as plain as anything: there I lay, waiting for death, when I looked up and in came an old man. He was bald, very insignificant-looking and he asked for water. So I thought to myself, sinner that I am, "What's this tramp doing in here?" And when I think what he did for us! The moment he saw us he put his bag down – just there – and untied it.'

The little girl broke in, 'No, Grandma. First he put his bag over there, in the middle of the hut, and then he put it on the bench.'

And they started arguing, trying to remember all that Elisha had said and done: where he had sat, where he had slept, what he had told each one of them.

At night the husband returned on horseback and he too took up the story.

'If he hadn't come in,' he said, 'we would all have died in sin. Yes, we were dying in despair, complaining about God and man. But he put us on our feet again and through him we came to know God and believe in the goodness of man. May Christ be with him! We were living like animals and he made human beings of us!'

After giving Efim food and drink they gave him a place to sleep and then lay down themselves.

But although he lay down. Efim could not sleep, for he could not get Elisha out of his mind and how he had seen him three times in Jerusalem, in front of the congregation.

'So that's how he got ahead of me! Whether my own pilgrimage has been accepted I cannot tell, but the Lord has accepted his!'

Next morning the villagers said farewell to Efim, loaded him with pies for the journey and went off to work, while Efim went his way.

12

Efim had been away exactly one year and it was spring when he returned.

It was in the evening. His son was not at home; he had gone to the tavern. When he returned he was tipsy and Efim questioned him. It was abundantly clear that the son had been living dissolutely while the father was away. He had wasted the money and had neglected things. When his father told him off, he received a very rude reply.

'Then you should have seen to it yourself,' he said, 'instead of wandering off like that – and with our money! And now you're asking me to give it back!'

The old man was furious and struck him.

Next morning Efim went to have a word with the village elder about his son and passed Elisha's hut. Elisha's wife greeted him from the front door. 'And how are you, my old friend?' she asked. 'So you've come back safe and sound, then?'

Efim stopped and said, 'Yes, I have, thank God. I got separated from your old man, but I gather he's back now.'

The old woman (a real chatterbox) told him the whole story.

'Yes, my dear neighbour,' she said, 'he came back ages ago – not long after Assumption, I think it was. We were so glad God brought him back safely, it was so miserable here without him. We can't expect him to do much work at his age, but he's still head of the house and we all feel much more cheerful now. You should have seen how glad our son was! "Without Dad," he said, "it was as if the sun had gone in." We were all so miserable while he was gone. We love him, my dear friend, and we'll take good care of him.'

'Is he at home now?'

'Yes, he's in the bee-garden, hiving the bees. He says they're swarming beautifully this year. God's given the bees such strength that he can't remember anything like it. "God doesn't reward us according to our sins," he says. Come on, he'll be so pleased to see you.'

Efim went through the hall and across the yard into the bee-garden. There he found Elisha standing without face-net or gloves, wearing only his grey jacket. There he stood, arms outstretched and his bald head shining all over, just as he had done at the Holy Sepulchre in Jerusalem. And above him the sun shone through the birches, burning fiercely as it had done in Jerusalem, while golden bees wound themselves in a garland and circled his head without stinging him. Efim stood stock-still.

Elisha's wife called out to her husband, 'Your friend's here!'

Elisha looked round. He was delighted and went to greet him, gently plucking bees out of his beard.

'I'm so pleased to see you again, my dear friend . . . so pleased . . . Did you have a good journey?'

'Yes, my legs carried me here safely and I've brought you some water from the River Jordan. You must come and collect it. But whether God has accepted my pilgrimage or not . . .'

'I'm sure He has, glory be to God!'

Efim fell silent.

'Well, I was there in body, but whether I was there in *spirit*, . . . or if it was someone else . . .'

'That's God's business, my dear friend.'

'On the way back I looked in at the hut where you stayed behind . . .'

Elisha appeared alarmed and hastily said, 'That's God's business, my friend. Now, come into the hut and I'll give you some honey.' And he quickly turned to domestic matters.

Efim sighed and did not talk to Elisha about the people in the hut, nor about having seen him in Jerusalem. And now he came to understand that God has charged every one of us to do His holy will, through love and good deeds, until his dying day.

THE RAID

A VOLUNTEER'S STORY

I

On July 12th Captain Khlopov came through the low door of my mud hut, complete with epaulettes and sabre. This was the first time I had seen him in full dress uniform since my arrival in the Caucasus.

'I've come straight from the colonel's,' he said in reply to my quizzical look. 'Our battalion is moving out tomorrow.'

'Where to?' I asked.

'To N——. All the forces are to assemble there.'

'And from there they'll make some sort of attack, will they?'

'I think so.'

'But in which direction? What do you think?'

'What should I think? I'm telling you what I know. Last night a Tartar galloped over from the general with orders for the battalion to move out with two days' biscuit rations. As to where, why and for how long – well, we don't ask such questions, my friend. Orders are orders and that's that.'

'But if you are taking rations for only two days, that means the troops won't be away longer than that, doesn't it?'

'No, it doesn't mean a thing . . .'

'Why not?' I asked, very surprised.

'Because that's how it is here. When we went to Dargo we took a week's rations, but we were there almost a month!'

'Can I go with you?' I asked, after a brief silence.

'Yes, you can, but I wouldn't advise it. Why run risks?'

'Well, please allow me to ignore your advice. I've been waiting here a whole month just for the chance of seeing some action and you want me to miss it!'

'You must do as you think fit, but in my opinion you should stay behind. You could do a spot of hunting while you're waiting for us, while we would go and do what we have to. That would be splendid for you!'

He spoke with such conviction that for a moment I really did think it would be splendid. But then I bluntly told him that nothing would induce me to stay behind.

'But what do you expect to see there?' the captain went on, still trying to dissuade me. 'If you really want to know what battles are like, read Mikhaylovsky-Danilevsky's *Description of War** – it's a fine book and you'll find all you want there, where each corps was positioned, how battles are fought.'

'But it's just that kind of thing that doesn't interest me!' I replied.

'What *does* interest you, then? Want to see how people are killed? In 1832 there was a civilian here, like you ... I think he was a Spaniard. He accompanied us on two expeditions and wore a kind of blue cloak ... well, the poor fellow got killed. But that's nothing new here, my friend.'

However humiliated I felt at the captain's misinterpretation of my motives I did not start arguing with him.

'Was he a brave man?' I asked.

'God knows! He was always riding out in front and where the fighting was, there he'd be!'

'So he must have been brave,' I said.

'No. Poking your nose in where you're not wanted isn't what I'd call brave.'

'Then what would you call brave?'

'Brave? Brave?' the captain repeated with the air of someone asking the question for the very first time.' 'The man who behaves as he ought to is brave,' he replied after some thought.

I remembered that Plato had defined bravery as *the knowledge of what should and what should not be feared* and, despite the looseness and vagueness of the captain's definition, I felt that in their basic ideas the two definitions were not so different as they might appear and that the captain's was even more accurate than the Greek philosopher's since, had he been able to express himself as well as Plato he would most probably have said that the brave man is the one who fears only what *ought* to be feared, and not what *should* not be feared.

I wanted to explain my idea to the captain. 'Yes,' I said, 'it seems

---

* More exactly, *Description of the Patriotic War of 1812*. Tolstoy used material from this well-known book for *War and Peace*.

to me that in every danger there is a choice, and the choice that springs from a sense of duty, for example, is courage, while a choice made under the influence of base feelings is cowardice. Therefore, the man who risks his life from vanity, curiosity or greed cannot be called brave. Conversely, the man who avoids danger from an honest sense of responsibility to his family, or simply out of conviction, cannot be called a coward.'

The captain looked at me with rather a strange expression as I spoke. 'Well, I'm not much good at arguing about such things,' he said, filling his pipe, 'but there's a cadet here who's fond of philosophizing. Go and have a chat with him. He writes poetry too.'

It was only when I was in the Caucasus that I got to know the captain, but I had heard about him before I left Russia. His mother, Marya, has a small estate less than two miles from mine. Before I left for the Caucasus I visited her. The old lady was absolutely delighted that I would be seeing her Pashenka (her pet name for the elderly, grey-haired captain) and that, like a 'talking letter', I could tell him all about her and deliver a small parcel. After treating me to some excellent pie and smoked duck, she went to her bedroom and returned with a rather large black leather pouch containing an amulet with a black silk ribbon attached to it.

'This is the icon of our Lady of the Burning Bush,' she said, crossing herself and kissing the icon as she handed it to me. 'Please give it to him. You see, when he left for the Caucasus I said prayers for him and vowed if he remained alive and unharmed I would have this icon of the Mother of God made for him. For eighteen years Our Lady and the saints have been merciful to him: not once has he been injured – and when I think of the battles he's taken part in! What Mikhailo, who was with him, told me, was enough to make one's hair stand on end! You understand – all I know about him is only through others. The dear boy never writes back about his campaigns for fear of frightening me.'

(Later in the Caucasus I found out – not through the captain, however – that he had been severely wounded four times but, needless to say, had not written one word to his mother either about wounds or campaigns.)

'So, let him wear this holy image now,' she contiued. 'My blessing goes with it. May the Holy Mother of God protect him! Especially in battles – that's when he must never forget to wear it. Please tell him, dear sir, that those are his mother's wishes.'

I promised to do exactly as she asked.

'I know you'll like my Pashenka,' the old lady went on, 'he's a wonderful man. Why, he never lets a year go by without sending me money. And he's a great help to my daughter Annushka too. And all he has is his army pay! I shall always be so thankful to God for giving me such a son,' she concluded with tears in her eyes.

'Does he write often?' I asked.

'Rarely. Perhaps a few words once a year, when he sends me money, but not otherwise. "If you don't hear from me," he writes, "that means I'm alive and well. But should anything happen to me, God forbid, they'll be sure to let you know!"'

When I gave the captain his mother's present (it was in my quarters) he asked me for some paper, carefully wrapped it and put it away. I told him a great deal about his mother's life, but he said nothing. When I had finished, he retired to one corner of the room and took what appeared to be ages to fill his pipe.

'Yes, she's a fine old lady,' he said from over there in a rather muffled voice. 'Will God ever let me see her again?'

In those simple words there was much affection and sadness.

'Why do you serve here?' I asked.

'One has to,' he replied with conviction. 'The double pay means a lot for poor devils like me.'

The captain lived frugally: he did not play cards, rarely went out drinking, and he smoked very cheap tobacco which, for some reason, he was too proud to call shag, giving it some obscure brand-name instead. I had taken to the captain from the start: he had one of those simple, calm Russian faces that are easy and pleasant to look straight in the eye. After this conversation I felt deep respect for him.

2

Next morning at four o'clock the captain came for me. He wore an old threadbare coat without epaulettes, wide Caucasian trousers, a sheepskin cap which once had been white but which was now yellow and tattered; a rather inferior Asiatic sabre was strapped around his shoulder. His small white horse ambled along, its head hung low and its thin tail swinging. Although the good captain's appearance had nothing particularly martial or handsome about it, it expressed such equanimity towards everything around that it could only inspire respect.

I did not keep him waiting, but immediately mounted my horse and together we rode out of the fortress gates.

The battalion was about five hundred yards ahead of us and resembled some dense swaying black mass. One could tell that it was the infantry only from the bayonets, which looked like a bunch of tightly packed needles, and from the snatches of songs, the beating of a drum and the delightful voice of the Sixth Company's second tenor (I had often admired it back in the fortress) which occasionally reached us. The road ran along a deep and wide ravine by the side of a small stream in full spate. Flocks of wild pigeons circled over it, settling on its rocky banks or turning, swiftly wheeling and disappearing from sight. The sun was not yet visible, but the top of the right slope of the ravine was just beginning to brighten. Grey and whitish pebbles, yellow-green moss, dew-covered Christ's Thorn bushes, dogwood and dwarf elm could all be seen with extraordinary clarity in the limpid, golden light of dawn. But the other side of the ravine and the valley, which was shrouded in drifting, smoky layers of dense mist, were damp and gloomy and presented an elusive medley of colours – pale lilac, shades of black, dark green and white. Directly in front of us rose the dazzling white masses of snowy mountains, strikingly clear against the deep azure of the horizon, their shadows and outlines fantastic but graceful in every detail. Crickets, dragonflies and myriads of other insects awoke in the tall grass and filled the air with their clear incessant sounds: it was as if countless numbers of tiny bells were ringing in our ears. The air smelled of water, grass, mist – all the scents of a beautiful early summer's morning. The captain struck a flint and lit his pipe. I found the smell of his cheap tobacco and tinder extremely pleasant.

We rode along the side of the road to catch up more quickly with the infantry. The captain seemed more pensive than usual, never took his Daghestan pipe from his mouth and at every step prodded his little horse with his heels. Swaying from side to side, the horse left barely perceptible, dark green tracks in the tall wet grass. A pheasant flew out from under its hoofs with that cry and whirr of wings that makes every huntsman involuntarily start, and then slowly rose into the sky. The captain didn't take the slightest notice of it.

We had almost caught up with the infantry when we heard the thud of hoofs behind us and a very handsome young man in officer's uniform and tall white sheepskin cap galloped past, nodding at the captain and flourishing his whip ... I only had time to notice the unique grace with which he sat in the saddle and held the reins, his beautiful black eyes, his fine nose and the first signs of a moustache. What I particularly liked about him was the way he could not stop smiling when he saw us admiring him. The smile alone showed that he was indeed very young.

'Where does he think he's dashing off to?' the captain muttered with a dissatisfied look, his pipe still in his mouth.

'Who is he?' I asked.

'Ensign Alanin, a subaltern from my company. He arrived from the Cadet Corps only last month.'

'So this is the first time he's seen action, is it?'

'Yes – that's why he's so pleased!' the captain replied, thoughtfully shaking his head. 'Youth!'

'But why shouldn't he be pleased? I can imagine how interesting it must be for a young officer.'

For a couple of minutes the captain did not reply.

'That's just what I mean by *youth*!' the captain continued in his deep voice. 'Why be pleased when you haven't even seen the real thing? When you've seen it a few times you're not so pleased! Now, I reckon there's about twenty officers going into action today and you can bet your life that someone or other will be killed or wounded. Today it might be me, and him the day after. So what's there to be pleased about?'

3

The moment the bright sun appeared above the hill and began to light up the valley through which we were passing, the rolling layers of mist lifted and it grew hot. The infantry, rifles and kitbags on their backs, slowly marched along the dusty road. Now and then laughter and the sound of Ukrainian could be heard in their ranks. A few old campaigners in white tunics – mostly non-commissioned officers –

were walking by the roadside smoking their pipes and in solemn conversation. Heavily laden wagons, each drawn by three horses, trundled along, raising clouds of dust that hung motionless in the air. The officers rode in front. Some of them were dhzigiting,* as they say in the Caucasus. That is, they kept whipping their horses to make them perform three or four leaps and then jerked their heads backwards to bring them to an abrupt halt. Others were busy with the singers who untiringly sang song after song, in spite of the stifling heat.

About two hundred yards ahead of the infantry a tall handsome officer in Caucasian costume rode with the mounted Tartars on a white stallion. Renowned in the regiment for his reckless daring, he was not afraid to tell anyone what he thought of them, no matter who that person was. He wore a black quilted jacket trimmed with gold lace, leggings to match, new tight-fitting soft Caucasian boots that were also trimmed with gold, a yellow Circassian coat and a tall sheepskin cap that was tilted backwards. Over his chest and back were silver straps, to which a powder-flask and pistol were fastened. Another pistol and a silver-mounted dagger hung from his belt. Above them was a sword in a red morocco sheath and a rifle in a black case was slung over his shoulder. From the way he dressed, his posture in the saddle, his general bearing and movements, it was obvious that he was trying to look like a Tartar. He even said something to the Tartars with whom he was riding in a language I did not understand and I gathered from the bewildered mocking looks the Tartars gave each other that they did not understand either. He was one of those young, daredevil officers who model themselves on Marlinsky's or Lermontov's heroes. These young men view the Caucasus only through the prism of these Mullah Nurs† and Heroes of our Time‡ and in everything they do are guided by the example of these models and not by their own inclinations.

* 'Dhzigit' means 'brave' in Kalmuck. Translated into Russian, 'to dhzigit' means 'to put on a brave show'. [*Tolstoy*]

† *Mullah Nur*, an exotic novel by A. Bestuzhev-Marlinsky, set in the Caucasus. Marlinsky was at one time exceedingly popular for his Byronic tales of adventure. He was killed at the age of forty in a skirmish with Circassians under mysterious circumstances.

‡ Lermontov's famous novel is set in the Caucasus.

The lieutenant, for example, may well have liked the company of well-bred women, of high-ranking men such as generals, colonels, aides-de-camp, and I do not doubt for one moment that he doted on such company, for he was extremely conceited. Nevertheless, he considered that it was his solemn duty to show all important people his rough side, although always in moderation. For example, whenever a lady appeared at the fortress he considered it his duty to parade beneath her window with his Tartar friends, wearing only a red shirt and slippers over his bare feet, shouting and swearing at the top of his voice. But his intention was not so much to cause offence as to show the lady what fine white legs he had and how easy it would be for her to fall in love with him, had he so wished. He would make frequent excursions into the hills with two or three of his Tartar friends to lie in ambush by the roadside and kill a few hostile passing Tartars. And although his heart told him more than once that there was nothing very daring in this, he felt that he must cause suffering to those who disappointed him for some reason, or whom he professed to hate or despise. There were two things he always carried – a large icon which hung round his neck and a dagger which he wore over his shirt, even in bed. He genuinely believed that he had enemies and convincing himself that he must take revenge on someone and wash away some insult with blood brought him the greatest pleasure. He was quite certain that hatred, vengeance and contempt for the human race were the noblest and most poetic of emotions. But his mistress (a Circassian girl, of course), whom I happened to meet later, maintained that he was the kindest and gentlest of men, and that every evening he would enter his melancholy thoughts in a diary, draw up his accounts on ruled paper, and then go down on his knees to pray. And how that man suffered, just to appear in his own eyes the way he wanted to appear, for his fellow officers and the soldiers could never see him the way he wanted to be seen.

Once, during one of those nocturnal expeditions on the road with his Tartar friends, he happened to wound a hostile Chechen in the leg with a bullet and took him prisoner. For seven weeks after that incident the Chechen lived with the lieutenant, who nursed and looked after him as though he were a bosom friend and then, when he had recovered, loaded him with presents and let him go. Not long afterwards, during an engagement, when the lieutenant was retreating

with his men, firing as he went, he heard an enemy soldier call out
his name and the Chechen he had wounded rode out and motioned
to him to do the same. The lieutenant rode out to his Chechen friend
and shook hands. The other Chechens kept their distance and did not
shoot, but the moment the lieutenant turned his horse several of them
fired at him and one bullet grazed the small of his back. Another
time, at night, when a fire broke out in the fortress and two
companies of soldiers tried to put it out, I suddenly saw the tall figure
of a man on a black horse, lit up by the red glow, appear in the
crowd. Forcing his way through, he rode right up to the fire, leapt
from his horse and ran into a house, one side of which was burning.
Five minutes later he emerged with singed hair and his arm badly
burnt around the elbow, carrying in his bosom two pigeons he had
rescued from the flames.

His name was Rosenkrantz, but he would often speak of his
ancestry, somehow tracing his origins back to the Varangians,* thus
clearly proving that he and his ancestors were pure Russians.

4

The sun had run half its course and cast its fiery rays through the
glowing air on to the dry earth. The dark blue sky was perfectly
clear; only the foot of the snowy mountains was beginning to be
cloaked by pale, lilac clouds. The motionless air seemed filled with a
kind of transparent dust and the heat was becoming unbearable.
When the troops reached a small stream – the half-way stage – they
halted. The soldiers stacked rifles and rushed to the water. The
battalion commander sat down on a drum in the shade. Demonstrat-
ing the importance of his rank by the expression on his face, he
prepared to have a snack with his fellow officers. The captain lay
down on the grass under his company's wagon. The intrepid Lieutenant Rosenkrantz and some other young officers sat on their outspread

* Varangians were Norsemen who in the ninth century raided the eastern
shores of the Baltic, penetrated into the interior and established the great trade
route to Byzantium along the River Dnieper. According to legend the East Slavs
invited them to rule Russia, and thus the dynasty of the Ruriks began. It would
appear that Tolstoy is poking fun at Rosenkrantz here.

cloaks, intending to make merry, judging from all the bottles and flasks around them and from the peculiar animation of the singers who stood before them in a semicircle, whistling and singing a Caucasian dance-song:

> Shamil thought he would rebel,
> In bygone years . . .
> Tra-ra, ra-ta-tai . . .
> In bygone years.

Among these young officers was the young ensign who had overtaken us that morning. He was extremely amusing – his eyes sparkled, his speech was rather muddled and he wanted to kiss and declare his love for everyone . . . Poor young man! As yet he had no idea that he might look ridiculous or that the frankness and affection which he lavished on everyone might arouse only ridicule, and not the affection he greatly yearned for. Nor did he realize how exceptionally appealing he looked when, with flushed face, he threw himself at last on to his cloak, rested on one elbow and tossed back his thick black hair.

Filled with curiosity, I listened to the soldiers' and officers' conversations and closely studied their expressions. But I could find absolutely no trace in any of them of the nervousness I was feeling: their jokes and laughter, the stories they told – all this was indicative of their high spirits and their indifference to impending danger. It was as though it was unthinkable that some of them were fated never to return by that road.

5

After six o'clock that evening, dusty and tired, we passed through the wide fortified gates of the fortress at N–. The sun was setting and cast slanting rosy rays on the picturesque batteries, on the gardens surrounding the fortress, with their tall poplars, on yellow wheat fields and on the white clouds that hung low over the snow-covered mountains: as if imitating them, they formed a range that was no less fantastic and beautiful. On the horizon the new moon was like a tiny translucent cloud. A Tartar was calling the faithful to prayer from the roof of a hut in the village just by the fortress gates. Our singers burst into song again with renewed vigour and energy.

When I had rested and tidied myself up I went to see an aide-de-camp I knew to ask if he would convey my intentions to the general. On the way from the suburb where I was billeted I saw things in the fortress of N— that I had not at all been expecting to see. I was over taken by a handsome two-seater carriage in which I caught sight of a fashionable bonnet and from which I could hear the sound of French. The strains of some 'Liza' or 'Katenka' polka played on an out-of-tune piano came from the open window of the commandant's house. I passed a tavern where some clerks with cigarettes in their hands were sitting over glasses of wine and I could hear one saying to the other, 'Look here, old chap, when it comes to politics, Marya Grigorevna is first and foremost amongst the ladies here.' A hunch-backed sickly-faced Jew in a threadbare coat was dragging a wheezy old barrel-organ and the whole suburb echoed to the finale from *Lucia.* Two women in rustling dresses with silk kerchiefs on their heads and brightly coloured parasols in their hands glided past me on the wooden pavement. Two young girls, one in a pink dress, the other in a blue, stood bareheaded outside a low-roofed cottage and broke into shrill, forced laughter, evidently to attract the attention of passing officers. As for the officers, they swaggered up and down the street in new uniforms, with white gloves and glittering epaulettes.

I found my acquaintance on the ground floor of the general's house. I scarcely had time to explain my wish and to hear that there was no problem in carrying it out when the same handsome carriage I had seen earlier rattled past the window where we were sitting and stopped at the entrance. A tall, well-built man in an infantry major's uniform climbed out and went into the house.

'Please excuse me,' said the aide, getting up. 'I must go and announce them to the general immediately.'

'Who is it?' I asked.

'The countess,' he replied, buttoning his uniform as he rushed upstairs. A few minutes later a short but extremely good-looking man in a frock-coat without epaulettes and with a white cross in his buttonhole went out on to the front steps, accompanied by two other officers. The general's gait, his voice, his every movement, showed that here was a man fully conscious of his own worth.

'*Bonsoir, Madame la Comtesse,*' he said, offering his hand through the carriage window.

A small hand in a kid glove pressed his and a pretty, smiling face in a yellow bonnet appeared at the window. All I could hear of their conversation, which lasted several minutes, was the smiling general saying as I passed, '*Vous savez que j'ai fait voeu de combattre les infidèles; prenez donc garde de le devenir.*'

Laughter came from the carriage.

'*Adieu donc, cher Général.*'

'*Non, au revoir,*' said the general as he went up the steps, '*n'oubliez pas, que je m'invite pour la soirée de demain.*'

The carriage clattered off down the street.

'Now there's a man,' I thought as I walked home, 'who possesses all that Russians strive after: rank, wealth, family. And the day before a battle that could finish God knows how, he can joke with a pretty woman and promise to have tea with her the next day, just as if they had met at a ball!'

Later, at the aide-de-camp's house, I met someone who surprised me even more. He was a young lieutenant from K— Regiment, a man of almost feminine gentleness and timidity, who had called on the aide to give vent to his bitterness and annoyance towards certain people who had apparently intrigued against him to stop him taking part in the forthcoming action. He maintained that it was very caddish of them, not the decent thing at all, that he would not forget it, and so on. The more I scrutinized his face and listened to his voice, the more convinced I became that he was not play-acting, that he was deeply resentful and distressed at not being allowed to go and shoot Circassians and expose himself to their fire. He was as upset as an unfairly beaten child . . . I was completely mystified by it all.

6

The troops were to move out at ten that night. At half past eight I mounted my horse and rode to the general's house, but on the assumption that the general and his aide would be busy I stopped in the street, tied my horse to a fence and waited for him to come out.

The heat and glare of the sun had already given way to the coolness of night and the soft light of the new moon which was just setting – a pale, shimmering crescent against the dark, starry sky. Lights appeared in the windows of the houses and shone through chinks in the shutters of the mud huts. Beyond those whitewashed moonlit huts with their rush-thatched roofs, the graceful poplars seemed even taller and darker on the horizon.

The long shadows of houses, trees and fences formed pretty patterns on the bright, dusty road ... From the river came the incessant, resonant call of frogs.* In the streets I could hear hurried footsteps and voices, a galloping horse. Now and then the sound of the barrel-organ playing the song 'The Winds are Gently Blowing' or some 'Aurora' waltz drifted over from the suburb.

I shall not say what I was thinking about then, firstly because I am too ashamed to admit to the succession of gloomy thoughts that kept nagging at me, while all around there was only joy and gaiety; and secondly because they would be quite irrelevant to my narrative. I was so deep in thought that I did not even notice when the bell struck eleven and the general rode past me with his suite. I hurriedly mounted my horse and raced off to catch up with the detachment.

The rearguard was still inside the fortress and I had great difficulty crossing the bridge, with all those guns, ammunition wagons, supply carts, and officers shouting out orders. Once through the gates I trotted past the line of soldiers which stretched in a line almost a mile long and who were silently moving through the darkness, and finally I caught up with the general. As I passed the guns drawn out in single file and the officers riding between them I suddenly heard a voice call in a German accent, 'A linshtock, you *schwein!*', which struck a jarring, discordant note amid the quiet solemn harmony, followed by a soldier hurriedly shouting, 'Shevchenko! The lieutenant wants a light!'

Most of the sky was overcast with long, dark-grey clouds, with only a few dim stars twinkling here and there. The moon had disappeared behind the black mountains on the near horizon to the right and shed a faint, trembling light on their peaks, in sharp contrast to the impenetrable gloom enveloping their foothills. The air was so warm and still that not one blade of grass, not one cloud moved. It was so dark that it was impossible to make out even the closest objects: by the side of the road I thought I could see rocks,

---

* Frogs in the Caucasus make a noise quite different from the croaking of Russian frogs. [*Tolstoy*]

animals, strange people and it was only when I heard them rustle and smelled the fresh dew that lay on them that I realized they were only bushes.

Before me I could see a dense, heaving black wall, followed by several dark spots: this was the cavalry vanguard, and the general and his suite. Behind us was a similar dark mass, lower than the first: this was the infantry.

The whole detachment was so quiet that I could distinctly hear all the mingling sounds of night, so full of enchanting mystery: the mournful howling of distant jackals, now like a despairing lament, now like laughter; the sonorous, monotonous song of crickets, frogs, quails; a rumbling noise whose cause baffled me and which seemed to be coming ever nearer; and all of Nature's barely audible nocturnal sounds that defy explanation or definition and merge into one rich, beautiful harmony that we call the stillness of night. And now that stillness was broken by – or rather, blended with – the dull thud of hoofs and the rustle of the tall grass as the detachment slowly advanced.

Only occasionally did I hear the clang of a heavy gun, the clatter of clashing bayonets, hushed voices, or a horse snorting. Nature seemed to breathe with pacifying beauty and power.

Can it be that there is not enough space for man in this beautiful world, under those immeasurable, starry heavens? Is it possible that man's heart can harbour, amid such ravishing natural beauty, feelings of hatred, vengeance, or the desire to destroy his fellows? All the evil in man, one would think, should disappear on contact with Nature, the most spontaneous expression of beauty and goodness.

7

We had been on the move for more than two hours. I began to feel shivery and drowsy. In the darkness I could still catch glimpses of vague shapes: not far ahead was that same black wall and those same little moving dots. Close by I could make out the rump of a white horse swishing its tail, with its hind legs wide apart; the back of a white Circassian coat with a rifle in a black case swinging against it and a white pistol butt in an embroidered holster; the glow of a cigarette lighting up a fair moustache, a beaver collar and a hand in a kid glove. Every now and then I leant forward over my horse's neck, closed my eyes and forgot myself for a few minutes. But then the familiar tramping of hoofs and rustling would suddenly bring me to my senses and I would glance round, feeling that I was standing still and that the black wall in front was moving towards me, or had stopped and I was about to ride straight into it. At one such moment I was even more conscious of the unbroken rumbling that I had been unable to explain and which was drawing nearer. What I had heard was in fact the sound of water. We were entering a deep gorge and approaching a mountain torrent that was in full spate at this time of year.*

The roar grew louder, the damp grass became thicker and taller; there were more bushes and the horizon gradually closed in. Now and then bright lights flared up here and there in the dark mountains and immediately vanished.

'Please tell me what those lights are?' I whispered to a Tartar riding beside me.

'Don't you know?' he replied.

'No.'

'It's the mountain tribesmen. They tie bundles of straw to poles, light them and wave them around.'

'Why are they doing that?'

'To warn everyone the Russians are coming. They must be running around like mad in the villages now,' he added, laughing. 'Everyone will be dragging his belongings down into the gorge.'

'Surely they can't already know from right up there, in the mountains, that a detachment is coming?' I asked.

'Oh yes, they know all right! They always know. We Tartars are like that!'

'So Shamil† too is preparing for action?' I asked.

'No,' he replied, shaking his head. 'Shamil himself won't be taking part – he'll send his henchmen while he watches from up there through a telescope.'

---

* In the Caucasus rivers tend to overflow in July. [*Tolstoy*]

† Shamil (1797–1871), religious and political leader of the North Caucasian Muslim tribes in their resistance to Russian expansion. In 1859 he surrendered at Gunib and was taken to central Russia. He died in Mecca.

'Does he live far away?'

'No, not very far. About eight miles away, over to the left.'

'How do you know?' I asked. 'Have you been there?'

'Yes. All our people have been there.'

'And did you see Shamil?'

'No! It's not for the likes of us to see Shamil! He's always surrounded by his bodyguard – a hundred, three hundred, perhaps a thousand of them, with Shamil himself somewhere in the middle!' he added with an expression of servile respect.

When I looked up I saw that the sky had cleared and it was growing brighter in the east, while the Pleiades were sinking towards the horizon. But it was damp and gloomy in the gorge through which we were advancing.

Suddenly, not far ahead, several lights flashed in the darkness and almost instantaneously some bullets whistled past. The shots rang out in the silence, together with a loud shrill cry from the enemy's advance picket, made up of Tartars, who whooped, fired at random and scattered.

When all was quiet again, the general summoned his interpreter. The Tartar in the white Circassian coat rode up and had a long talk with him, gesticulating and whispering.

'Colonel Khasanov! Tell the men to advance in open order,' the general drawled, softly but audibly.

The detachment advanced towards the river, leaving the towering dark sides of the gorge behind. It began to grow light. The sky immediately above the horizon, where a few pale stars could just be seen, seemed higher. The dawn glowed brightly in the east, while from the west blew a fresh, piercing breeze; shimmering mist rose like steam over the rushing river.

8

Our scout showed us the ford and the cavalry vanguard, followed by the general and his suite, started crossing the river. The water, which came up to the horses' chests, rushed with tremendous force between the white boulders which appeared here and there above the surface, and foamed and eddied around the animals' legs. Startled by the noise, the horses lifted their heads and pricked up their ears, but they stepped carefully and steadily against the current, over the uneven river-bed. The riders lifted their feet and weapons; the infantry, in literally nothing but their shirts, and holding above the water their rifles, to which their clothes were tied in bundles, linked arms in groups of twenty and struggled bravely against the current, the enormous strain clearly showing in their faces. The mounted artillerymen gave a loud shout and drove their horses into the water at a trot. Now and then the water splashed over the guns and green ammunition-wagons whose wheels rang against the bottom. But the sturdy little horses all pulled together, churning the water, until finally they clambered up on to the opposite bank with dripping manes and tails.

Immediately the crossing was completed, the general's face suddenly became thoughtful and serious. He turned his horse and trotted off with his cavalry down the broad glade which opened out in the middle of the forest before us; a cordon of Cossacks spread out around the edges.

In the forest we spotted a man on foot dressed in a Circassian coat and a tall sheepskin cap . . . then a second . . . and a third . . . One of the officers said, 'They're Tartars,' and at that moment a puff of smoke appeared from behind a tree, followed by the report, then another. Our rapid fire drowned the enemy's and only occasionally did a bullet come flying past with a sound like the slow buzz of a bee, as if to show us that not all the shots were ours. First the infantry, at the double, followed by the field guns at a trot, joined the cordon. I could hear the guns booming, then the metallic sound of flying grapeshot, the hiss of rockets, the crackle of rifles. All over the broad glade could be seen cavalry, infantry and artillery. Puffs of smoke from the guns, rockets and rifles mingled with the dewy verdure and the mist. Colonel Khasanov galloped over to the general and sharply reined in his horse.

'Your Excellency,' he said, touching his cap, 'shall I order the cavalry to charge? The enemy's colours are in sight.' And he pointed with his whip at some mounted Tartars headed by two men on white horses bearing poles decorated with bits of red and blue cloth.

'Carry on – and good luck!' the general replied.

The colonel turned his horse on the spot, drew his sabre and shouted, 'Hurrah!'

'Hurrah! Hurrah! Hurrah!' echoed from the troops and the cavalry flew after him.

Everyone watched with great enthusiasm as one colour appeared, then a second, a third, fourth, fifth . . .

Without waiting for us to attack, the enemy hid in the forest from where they opened fire with their rifles. The bullets flew thicker.

'*Quel charmant coup d'oeil!*' the general remarked, rising slightly, English-style, in the saddle of his slim-legged black horse.

'*Charmant,*' replied the major, rolling his r's and striking his horse as he rode over to the general. '*C'est un vrrai plaisirr que la guerre dans un aussi beau pays,*' he said.

'*Et surtout en bonne compagnie,*' the general added, pleasantly smiling. The major bowed.

Just then, an enemy cannon-ball flew past with a nasty hiss and struck something. Behind us we heard the moan of a wounded soldier. This moan had such a peculiar effect on me that the spectacle immediately lost all its charm. However, I seemed to be the only one to notice it – the major was laughing with great gusto; another officer was repeating with the utmost composure what he had just been saying; and the general was looking the other way and saying something in French with the most tranquil of smiles.

'Shall we return their fire?' the artillery commander asked, galloping up.

'Yes, let's give them a fright!' the general replied nonchalantly, lighting a cigar.

The battery took up position and the firing began. The earth groaned under the shots, lights continually flashed and my eyes were blinded by the clouds of smoke through which it was almost impossible to make out the gun crews at work.

The village was bombarded and Colonel Khasanov galloped up once more and then rode off to it at the general's command. The war cry rang out again and the cavalry disappeared in clouds of dust. It was a truly magnificent scene. But the one thing that spoilt the general impression for me, an inexperienced onlooker, who had not taken part, was all that movement, animation and shouting, which seemed quite superfluous. I could not help comparing it to a man swinging an axe to cut only thin air.

9

Our troops had occupied the village, in which not one of the enemy was left by the time the general arrived with his suite, to which I had attached myself. The long clean huts with their flat earthen roofs and pretty chimneys were scattered over small stony hillocks, through which flowed a stream. On one side were green sunlit gardens with enormous pear and plum trees, while on the other were the strange shadows cast by the tall, erect headstones in the cemetery and the long poles with balls and multicoloured flags fixed to their ends which marked the graves of the dhzigits, the bravest warriors.

The troops were drawn up outside the gates.

A few moments later dragoons, Cossacks and infantrymen poured down the crooked lanes with evident delight and the deserted village immediately sprang to life. Somewhere a roof came crashing down, an axe rang out against a strong wooden door. Somewhere else a haystack, a fence and a hut were set on fire and a thick column of smoke rose into the clear air. A Cossack dragged a sack of flour and a carpet along; a soldier emerged from a hut, gleefully carrying a tin basin and some bits of old cloth. Another, with outstretched arms, was trying to catch two hens that were cackling and beating their wings by a fence. A third soldier, who had found a huge pot of milk, drank some and then threw it down with loud guffaws.

The battalion with which I had left N— fortress was also in the village. The captain sat on the roof of a hut smoking his cheap tobacco and sending streams of smoke from his short pipe with such a casual air that when I saw him I forgot that I was in an enemy village and felt quite at home.

'Ah, so you're here too,' he said when he saw me.

The tall figure of Lieutenant Rosenkrantz flitted around the village. He gave one order after the other and seemed to have a lot to do. I saw him emerge from one hut with a triumphant expression, followed by two soldiers leading an old Tartar whose hands were tied. This old man, whose only clothing was a gaily coloured but ragged coat and much-patched trousers, looked so frail that his bony arms, tightly bound behind his hunched back, seemed about to part company with his shoulders, and he could hardly drag his bare crooked feet along.

His face, and even part of his shaven head, was deeply furrowed; his misshapen, toothless mouth with a close-cut grey moustache and beard around it, was always moving, as if he were chewing. But there was still a gleam in those red, lashless eyes which quite clearly expressed an old man's indifference to life.

Rosenkrantz asked him, through the interpreter, why he had not gone with the others.

'Where could I have gone?' he replied, quietly looking away.

'Where the others have gone,' someone suggested.

'The dhzigits have gone off to fight the Russians, but I'm an old man.'

'Aren't you afraid of the Russians?'

'What can they do to me? I'm an old man,' he repeated, nonchalantly surveying the circle that had formed around him.

Later, when I was returning, I saw that same old man bumping along behind a Cossack's saddle, bound and bareheaded, still looking around with the same indifferent expression. They needed him for an exchange with Russian prisoners.

I climbed up on to the roof and sat beside the captain.

'It seems there weren't very many of the enemy,' I told him, wishing to find out his opinion of the raid.

'The enemy?' he repeated in surprise. 'But there wasn't any enemy! Do you call that the enemy? Just you wait until this evening when we leave – they'll be simply pouring out from over there to speed us on our way!'

He pointed with his pipe at the small wood through which we had passed that morning.

'What's that?' I asked anxiously, interrupting the captain and pointing to a group of Don Cossacks who had gathered around something not far from us.

Something like a baby's cry came from there and the words, 'Hey, stop . . . don't cut it . . . they'll see. Got a knife, Yevstigneich? Give it me . . .'

'They're up to something, the devils,' the captain calmly remarked. But just then the handsome ensign, his face flushed and frightened, ran out. Waving his arms he dashed over to the Cossacks.

'Don't touch it! Don't hurt it!' he cried in a childlike voice. The moment they saw the officer, the Cossacks stepped aside and released a little white kid. The young ensign seemed quite confused, kept muttering something and stood before them with an embarrassed look. When he saw the captain and myself on the roof he blushed even deeper and skipped over to us. 'I thought they were killing a child,' he said with a timid smile.

IO

The general and the cavalry left the village, while the battalion with which I had come from the fortress formed the rearguard. Captain Khlopov's and Lieutenant Rosenkrantz's companies withdrew together.

The captain's prediction proved perfectly correct: the moment we entered the narrow strip of woodland he had mentioned, hostile hillsmen suddenly appeared everywhere, on both sides of us, mounted and on foot, and they were so close that I could quite plainly see some of them running from tree to tree, stooping and with rifles in their hands. The captain took off his cap, piously crossed himself and some of the older soldiers followed suit. From the woods we could hear them whooping and calling, 'Watch out, Russkies!' Short, dry rifle shots rang out in quick succession and bullets whizzed past on both sides. Our men silently volleyed back at them – only occasionally did I hear shouts from their ranks such as, 'It's all right for *him*⋆ in the trees. We ought to use a gun . . .'

Finally the guns were brought out and after a few salvoes of grapeshot the enemy seemed to weaken. But a moment later, with every step our men advanced, the firing and whooping intensified.

We had withdrawn barely six hundred yards from the village when enemy cannon-balls began to whistle overhead. I saw a soldier killed by one. But why go into detail over a terrible scene I would give anything to forget?

Lieutenant Rosenkrantz kept firing incessantly, shouting hoarsely at his men and galloping at top speed from one end of the line to the other. He looked rather pale, which perfectly suited his belligerent face. 'We'll beat them back,' he said convincingly. 'Oh yes, no doubt about it!'

⋆ *him* – the collective noun by which soldiers in the Caucasus indicate the enemy. [*Tolstoy*]

'It's not necessary,' the captain replied softly. 'What we must do is retreat.'

The captain's company was holding the edge of the forest and his men were firing at the enemy in lying position. The captain, in his shabby coat and crumpled cap, sat on his white horse, the reins held loosely, his knees bent in the short stirrups. He stayed silent and still: the soldiers knew their job too well to need any orders. Only now and then did he raise his voice to shout at anyone who exposed his head.

There was nothing very martial about the captain's appearance, but it had much in it that was sincere and natural, which greatly impressed me. 'Now, there's a truly brave man,' I couldn't help thinking.

He was exactly the same as I had always seen him: those calm movements, the same even voice, that same ingenuous expression on his plain but honest face. Only his eyes which were brighter than usual showed the concentration of a man quietly doing his job. It is easy enough to write that he was 'the same as always', but how many different shades of character had I observed in the others – one trying to appear calmer than usual, another sterner, a third more cheerful. But the captain's face showed that he did not see why he should appear other than his normal self.

The Frenchman who said at Waterloo, '*La garde meurt, mais ne se rend pas*', along with other – particularly French – heroes who uttered such memorable sayings, were brave and did in fact produce unforgettable phrases. But there was this difference between their courage and the captain's: even if a memorable phrase had stirred in my hero's heart, whatever the circumstances, I am quite convinced that he would never have uttered it. Firstly, because by uttering some memorable phrase he would have been afraid of spoiling some great deed; and secondly, because when a man feels he has the strength to perform a great deed, there is no need for words. In my opinion, this is the distinctive and noble characteristic of Russian valour. If this is so, then how can a Russian heart help aching when our young warriors utter trite phrases that claim to imitate antiquated French chivalry?

Suddenly a rather disjointed and weak 'Hurrah!' came from the side where our handsome young ensign was standing with his platoon. When I looked round I saw about thirty soldiers with kitbags over their shoulders and rifles in their hands running over a ploughed field with very great difficulty. They kept stumbling, but still they ran on, shouting as they went. In front galloped the young ensign, sabre in hand. They all disappeared into the forest . . .

After a few minutes' whooping and crackling, a frightened horse ran out of the forest and some soldiers appeared bearing the dead and wounded. Among the latter was the young ensign. Two soldiers supported him under the arms. He was as white as a sheet and his handsome face now showed only a faint shadow of that eagerness for the fray which had enlivened it a minute earlier. His head had sunk horribly between the shoulders and dropped on his chest. There was a small bloodstain on the white shirt beneath his unbuttoned coat.

'Oh, what a pity!' I could not help saying as I turned away from that sad sight.

'Of course it's a pity,' said an old soldier who was standing near me, mournfully leaning on his rifle. 'He's not afraid of anything – how can anyone go on like that?' he added, staring at the wounded officer. 'He's stupid too – and now he's paid for it.'

'Aren't you afraid?'

'What do you think?'

I I

Four soldiers bore the ensign on a stretcher. Behind them a medical orderly led a thin, broken-down horse with two green cases of medical equipment on its back. As they waited for the doctor, a few officers rode over to the stretcher and tried to comfort and cheer up their wounded comrade.

'Well, Alanin old man, it'll be some time before you go dancing again!' Lieutenant Rosenkrantz said with a smile.

He probably thought that these words would help to raise the ensign's spirits, but they did not have the desired effect, judging from the latter's cold sad look.

Then the captain rode up. He took a close look at the wounded man and his normally icily indifferent face took on an expression of genuine sympathy.

'Well, dear Anatoly,' he said in a voice of tender concern that I never expected from him, 'it seems it was God's will.'

The wounded man looked round and a sad smile passed over his pale face. 'Yes, I disobeyed you.'

'Let's say it was God's will,' the captain repeated.

The doctor, who had now arrived, took some bandages, a probe and another instrument from the orderly. Then he rolled up his sleeves and went over to the ensign with an encouraging smile.

'Well, it seems they've given you a hole where you didn't have one before!' he said in a light-hearted, jocular tone. 'Let's have a look.'

The ensign let the doctor examine him, but the look he gave that cheery man was of surprise and reproach, which the latter did not notice. The doctor probed and examined the wound from every angle, but then the wounded man could stand no more and he pushed the doctor's hand away with a deep groan.

'Leave me,' he said, barely audibly. 'I'm going to die anyway.'

With these words, he fell back and five minutes later, when I went over to the group standing around him and asked one of them, 'How's the ensign?' the reply was, 'Passing away.'

12

It was late when the detachment, drawn up in a wide column and singing as it went, approached the fortress.

The sun was hidden behind the snowy mountain ridge and cast its dying pink rays on a long thin cloud that hung motionless over the clear horizon. The snow-covered mountains were becoming enveloped in a lilac mist and only the highest peaks stood out, amazingly distinct against the crimson glow of sunset. A transparent moon, long risen, was growing pale against the deep azure of the sky. The green of the grass and the trees darkened and became covered with dew. Dark masses of troops marched with measured tread over the lush meadow. The sound of tambourines, drums and cheerful songs came from various directions. The second tenor of the Sixth Company was singing vigorously, and the sound of his pure, sonorous voice, full of power and feeling, carried far and wide in the limpid air of evening.

A PRISONER OF THE CAUCASUS

A TRUE STORY

I

An officer called Zhilin was serving in the Caucasus. One day he received a letter from home. It was from his elderly mother who wrote, 'I'm getting old now and should like to see my beloved son before I die. Please come and say farewell. Bury me and then go back to the army, and God be with you. I've found you a fiancée, who is both intelligent and pretty and who has some property. If you like her, perhaps you'll marry her and settle down here for good.'

Zhilin thought it over. 'Yes, the old lady is really quite poorly and I may never see her again. Yes, I'd better go. And if the girl is pretty I could marry her.'

So he went to see the colonel, was granted leave, said goodbye to his fellow officers, treated his men to four pailfuls of vodka as a parting gift and prepared for the journey.

At that time there was war in the Caucasus. Travelling along the road on one's own, either by day or night, was far too dangerous: any Russians who ventured any distance from the fortress, on horseback or on foot, would either be killed by the Tartars or carried off into the mountains. Therefore arrangements had been made for civilians to be escorted twice weekly from one fortress to the next, with the soldiers in front and at the rear.

It was summer. At dawn the baggage-train gathered just outside the fortress and was joined by the escort and moved off. Zhilin was on horseback and his luggage was in one of the carts. They had about sixteen miles to go and the baggage-train made slow progress.

Every now and then the soldiers would stop for a rest, or a wheel would come off, or a horse would refuse to go on, and then the whole convoy would have to stop and wait.

By the time the sun was past its highest point they had covered only about half the distance. It was hot and dusty, the sun beat down and there was no shade anywhere: all around was the bare steppe, without a tree or bush in sight.

Zhilin rode on ahead and then he stopped to wait for the baggage-train to catch him up. Yet again he heard the bugle give the signal to stop. Zhilin wondered, 'Why don't I go on ahead without the soldiers? I have a fine horse and if I come across any Tartars I can gallop away. Or perhaps I should be patient . . .?'

As he stopped to reflect, another officer, Kostylin, armed with a rifle, rode up and said, 'Let's go on alone, Zhilin. I can't stand it – I'm starving, it's simply sweltering and my shirt's wringing wet.' Kostylin was a heavily built, stout man and the sweat poured down his red face.

After a pause for thought, Zhilin asked, 'Is your rifle loaded?'

'Yes.'

'Let's go then – but only on condition we stick together.'

And they rode on ahead over the plain, keeping a look-out on both sides and chatting away. They could see for miles.

Soon the steppe ended and the road ran along a narrow defile between two hills.

'We'd better ride up and have a look round. You never know – the Tartars might leap out on us before we know it,' Zhilin said.

Kostylin objected, 'What's the point? Let's carry straight on.'

Zhilin would not agree. 'No,' he said. 'You wait here while I go up and have a quick look.'

And he rode up the slope to the left. Zhilin's horse was a hunter which he had bought as a colt for one hundred roubles and had broken in himself. It simply flew up the steep slope with him. He had barely reached the top when he saw some thirty mounted Tartars a stone's throw away. He immediately turned back, but the Tartars had seen him and chased after him, drawing their rifles as they rode at full tilt. Zhilin tore down the slope as fast as his horse's legs would go, shouting to Kostylin, 'Get your rifle ready!' at the same time telling his horse in his thoughts, 'Get me out of this mess, old girl! If you stumble I'm finished. They won't get me once I have my gun!'

But as soon as Kostylin saw the Tartars, instead of waiting he rode hell for leather back towards the fortress, whipping his horse first on one side, then the other. All that could be seen in the clouds of dust was the horse's waving tail.

Zhilin saw that the situation was hopeless. His rifle was gone and he could not offer much resistance with a sabre. So he headed back towards the escort, thinking that he might escape that way. But there were six of them rushing to cut him off. His horse was a good one, but theirs were even better and they were already across his path. He tried to rein in his horse to change direction, but it was going too fast and made straight for the Tartars. Zhilin saw a red-bearded Tartar coming at him on a grey horse, baring his teeth, yelling and ready to shoot. 'Well,' Zhilin thought, 'I know all about you devils. If you capture me alive you'll put me in a pit and flog me. Well, I won't let you take me alive.'

Although a small man, Zhilin had courage. He drew his sabre and rode straight at the red-bearded Tartar. 'Either I'll ride him down or hack him to pieces with my sabre,' he thought.

Zhilin was still a horse's length away when his horse was struck by some bullets from behind. It crashed to the ground, falling across his leg.

He tried to get up, but already two evil-smelling Tartars were sitting on him, tying his arms behind his back. He struggled free, but then three more leapt from their horses and began beating him on the head with their rifle butts. His head swam and he staggered. The Tartars grabbed him, took the spare girths from their saddles, twisted his arms behind his back, bound them with a Tartar knot and dragged him off. They knocked his cap off, pulled off his boots, searched him all over, took his money and watch and tore his clothes to shreds. Zhilin glanced round at his horse and saw that the poor beast was lying where it had fallen, kicking its legs as it vainly struggled to plant them on the ground. There was a hole in its head and black blood poured out, soaking the dust for about two feet around.

One of the Tartars went over and began to remove the saddle. The horse was still kicking, so he took his dagger and cut its throat. There was a whistling sound, a final convulsion – and the animal breathed its last.

The Tartars took away the saddle and harness. Then the red-bearded one mounted his horse while the others lifted Zhilin into the saddle behind him, strapped him to the horseman's waist to stop him falling off and took him away into the mountains.

There Zhilin sat, rocking from side to side, his face pushed up against the Tartar's evil-smelling back. All he could see was that powerful back and a sinewy neck, blue and clean-shaven at the nape. Zhilin had a nasty head wound and the blood had dried over his eyes, but he could neither sit upright nor wipe the blood away. His arms were so tightly bound that his collar-bone ached.

For a long time they rode up and down the hills, forded a river and followed a hard track through a valley. Zhilin wanted to see where they were taking him, but his eyes were caked with blood and it was impossible to turn.

Twilight began to fall. They forded another river and rode up a rocky hillside. Here there was a smell of smoke and dogs barked: they had reached the aul, or village. The Tartars dismounted and Zhilin was surrounded by Tartar children, who showered him with stones, shrieking with delight.

His captor drove the children away, took Zhilin off the horse and summoned his servant. A Nogay* tribesman with high cheek-bones came over. He wore a shirt that was so ragged the whole of his chest was visible. The Tartar gave him an order and the servant went to fetch a shackle, which consisted of two blocks of oak with iron rings attached to them, one of them punched through and with a lock fixed to it. They untied Zhilin's arms, put the shackle around his ankle, led him to a barn, pushed him inside and locked the door. Zhilin fell into a heap of manure. After lying quite still for a few moments he groped about in the dark for somewhere soft and lay down.

2

That night Zhilin did not sleep a wink. At that time of year the nights were short and soon Zhilin was able to see daylight through a chink in the wall. He got up, scratched at it to widen it and peeped out. Now he could see a road leading downhill, with the Tartar hut to the right and two trees near it. A black dog was lying on the threshold, a goat and her kids were running about, jerking their tails. Then he saw a young Tartar girl coming up the hill, wearing a brightly coloured loose blouse, trousers and boots. On her head,

* Turkic-speaking people in the north of Daghestan and North Caucasus.

which was covered with a shawl, she carried a large tin jug. Her back quivered as she led by the hand a Tartar boy whose head was shaven and who was dressed in only a shirt. She carried the water into a hut and the red-bearded Tartar whom Zhilin had seen the previous day appeared in a quilted silk tunic, shoes over his bare feet and with a silver dagger hanging from his belt. He wore a tall black sheepskin cap that was tilted backwards. He came out, stretched himself, smoothed his red beard, stood there a while, gave his servant an order and went off somewhere.

Then two village lads rode up from what must have been a watering place as the horses' noses were wet. Then some more lads with close-cropped heads, in shirts but no trousers, ran over to the barn in a crowd, picked up a long twig and poked it through the chink. When Zhilin shouted they screamed and took to their heels. He could see their bare, shiny knees as they ran away.

Now he felt thirsty, and his throat was parched. 'If only someone would come,' he thought. Then he heard someone opening the door and in came the red-bearded Tartar, and with him was another man, smaller and dark-haired. He had black, bright eyes, red cheeks and a small trimmed beard. His face was cheerful and he laughed all the time. This man was even better dressed than the other: his blue quilted silk tunic was trimmed with silver braid, he had a silver dagger in his belt and his red morocco leather slippers, which he wore over his thick boots, were also embroidered with silver. His tall hat was of white lambskin.

The red-bearded Tartar entered and seemed to utter something like a curse as he leant against the doorpost, playing with his dagger and eyeing Zhilin suspiciously, like a wolf. But the dark-haired one, so quick and nimble he seemed to be walking on springs, went straight up to Zhilin, squatted, slapped him on the shoulder and revealed his teeth as he muttered in his own language, winking, clicking his tongue and repeating, 'Good Russky! Good Russky!'

Zhilin understood nothing and asked, 'Drink! Give me some water!'

The dark-haired Tartar laughed and kept rattling away, 'Good Russky!'

Zhilin motioned with his lips and hands that he wanted a drink. The dark-haired one finally understood, laughed, looked through the doorway and called, 'Dina!'

A thin, slight girl of about thirteen with a face like the dark-haired Tartar's came running up. She was obviously his daughter, with the same black, bright eyes and handsome face. She wore a long blue shirt without any belt and with broad sleeves trimmed in red, trousers, and over her slippers a pair of high-heeled shoes. Around her neck was a necklace made entirely of Russian fifty-copeck pieces. She was bareheaded and her black hair was plaited with a ribbon hung with brass pendants and a silver rouble.

At her father's command she ran off and returned with a tin jug. She handed it to Zhilin and squatted so low that her knees came up to her head. There she sat, staring wide-eyed at Zhilin drinking as if he were some wild animal.

Zhilin gave her back the jug and she suddenly jumped back like a wild goat. Even her father laughed and he sent her on another errand. She took the jug, ran out and returned with some unleavened bread on a wooden plate. Then she squatted again, drew her knees up and did not take her eyes off Zhilin for one second.

Then the Tartars left, locking the door again. Soon afterwards the Nogay tribesman went up to Zhilin and said, 'Aidá! Aidá!'* He too did not speak Russian. All Zhilin understood was that he was telling him to follow him somewhere.

Zhilin limped after the Nogay – with those shackles he could only drag himself along. Once outside the barn he saw he was in a Tartar village of about ten huts and a mosque with a small tower. Three saddled horses were standing by one of the huts and some village boys were holding the reins. The dark-haired Tartar sprang out of the hut and beckoned to Zhilin to follow. Laughing and talking in his own language, he went inside again. Zhilin followed. The room was very pleasant, with smoothly plastered clay walls. By the front wall lay a pile of brightly coloured feather-beds and the side walls were covered with rich carpets. Guns, pistols, swords – all of silver – were hung over the carpets. Close to one wall was a small stove on a level with the earthen floor, which was as clean as a threshing-floor. One entire corner was covered with felt, on top of which were feather cushions and rugs. On these rugs some Tartars were sitting in their slippers – the dark-haired one, the red-bearded one and three

---

* 'Come on! Come on!'

guests, each of them with a feather cushion in place behind his back. Before them, on a round tray, were millet pancakes, a large cup of melted butter and a jug of Tartar beer or bouza.* They ate with their hands, which were smeared with butter. The dark Tartar leapt to his feet and ordered Zhilin to sit on the bare floor, not on a rug. Then he sat on his own rug again and helped his guests to pancakes and bouza. The servant made Zhilin sit down where the dark Tartar had indicated, took off his over-shoes, put them with the others by the door and sat on a felt mat closer to his masters. He watched them eating, slavering and wiping his mouth.

When the Tartars had eaten their fill of pancakes, a Tartar woman came in, wearing the same kind of shirt as the girl's, trousers, and with a kerchief over her head. She took away the butter and pancakes that were left and brought a handsome tub and a jug with a narrow neck. The Tartars washed their hands, folded their arms, knelt, breathed out towards the four corners and said their prayers. They chatted for a while in their own language and then one of the guests turned towards Zhilin and spoke to him in Russian.

'You were captured by Kazi-Muhammed,' he said, pointing to the red-bearded Tartar, 'and he handed you over to Abdul-Murat' – and he pointed at the dark-haired one. 'So Abdul-Murat is your master now.' Zhilin was silent.

Then Abdul-Murat spoke to the others, pointing at Zhilin the whole time, laughing and repeating, 'Russky soldier. Good Russky!' along with some words in Tartar.

The interpreter said, 'He's ordering you to write home to tell them to send a ransom. As soon as the money is here, he will set you free.'

Zhilin pondered and asked, 'How much does he want?'

The Tartars conferred and then the interpreter said, 'Three thousand roubles.'

'No,' Zhilin said, 'I can't possibly pay that.'

Abdul leapt to his feet, waving his arms and speaking to Zhilin as if the latter understood. The interpreter translated, 'How much can you pay?'

Zhilin thought for a moment and replied, 'Five hundred.'

At this all the Tartars started speaking rapidly and at once.

* A beverage made from millet, buckwheat or barley.

Abdul jabbered away at the red-faced Tartar so much that he sprayed him with saliva. But the other merely screwed up his eyes and clicked his tongue.

Now they all quietened down and the interpreter said, 'The master thinks five hundred isn't enough. He paid two hundred for you himself. Kazi-Muhammed owed him money, so he took you as payment. Three thousand roubles! We won't take anything less! If you refuse to write, we'll throw you into the pit and you'll be whipped.'

'Oh, God!' Zhilin thought. 'The more I show this lot I'm afraid, the worse it will be for me.'

So he sprang to his feet and said, 'You can tell that dog – if he's trying to scare me – that he won't get one copeck and I won't write either. I'm not afraid of you dogs and I never will be!'

The interpreter translated again and they all started talking at once. They muttered to themselves for a long time and then the dark Tartar jumped up, went over to Zhilin and said, 'Russky! Dhzigit, Russky! Dhzigit!' (In Tartar, dhzigit means 'brave man'.) The Tartar laughed and said something to the interpreter who translated, 'One thousand roubles will do.'

But Zhilin stood firm. 'I won't pay more than five hundred. And if you kill me you won't get anything.'

The Tartars conferred again, sent the servant away and kept glancing now at Zhilin, then at the door. The servant returned, followed by a stout barefooted man in rags: he was also shackled.

Zhilin groaned – it was Kostylin. So they'd caught him too.

The Tartars put them side by side and the two men started talking, while the Tartars looked on in silence. Zhilin told Kostylin what had happened to him and Kostylin told how his horse had pulled up, his gun had misfired and how this same Kazi-Muhammed had caught up with him and taken him prisoner.

Abdul leapt up and said something as he pointed at Kostylin. The interpreter explained that the two of them now belonged to the same master and that the first to pay the ransom would be the first to be freed. 'You see, you fly off the handle,' he told Zhilin, 'but your comrade is co-operating. He's written home and they will be sending the five thousand roubles. So he'll be well fed and well treated.'

Zhilin retorted, 'He can do what he likes. Perhaps he's rich, but

I'm not. I'm sticking to what I said. If you kill me you will get nothing. I refuse to write for more than five hundred.'

The Tartars were silent. Then Abdul suddenly sprang up, brought a small box and took out a pen, ink, a scrap of paper, pushed them in front of Zhilin, slapped him on the shoulder and motioned to him to write. He had agreed to five hundred.

'Wait a moment,' Zhilin told the interpreter. 'Tell him he must feed us properly, give us decent clothes and boots and let us stay together – that will cheer us up a bit. And he must take these shackles off.'

And he looked at the master and laughed – so did the master and when Zhilin had finished he told the interpreter, 'I'll give them the very finest clothes, a cloak and boots fit to be married in. I'll feed them like princes. And if they want to be together they can both stay in the barn. But I can't take those shackles off, they'd only run away! They can have them off at night.' And he leapt up and slapped Zhilin on the shoulder. 'You good, me good!' he said.

Zhilin wrote the letter, but he addressed it wrongly, so that it would never arrive. 'I shall escape!' he thought.

Zhilin and Kostylin were led away to the barn and the Tartars brought them maize straw, a jug of water, some bread, two old coats and some worn-out army boots evidently taken from dead Russian soldiers. At night their shackles were removed and they were locked in the barn.

3

And this was how Zhilin and his comrade lived for a whole month. The master was always laughing and saying, 'You Ivan – good. Me Abdul – good.' But he fed them badly, giving them nothing but unleavened millet bread of flat cakes made of unbaked dough.

Kostylin wrote home again and felt thoroughly dejected as he waited for the money to come. For days on end he would sit in the barn counting the days, or sleeping. But Zhilin knew very well that his letter would never arrive and he did not write another one.

'Where could my mother get enough money for the ransom?' he wondered. 'As it is, she has to live on what I've sent her. If she had to raise another five hundred it would ruin her completely. With God's help I'll get myself out of this mess.'

And he would walk through the village, whistling and looking around for a way to escape. Or he would sit and model a clay doll or weave a basket from twigs: Zhilin was very clever with his hands.

One day he made a doll, with nose, arms, legs and a Tartar shirt, and put it on the barn roof.

When the Tartar girls went to fetch water, Dina, Abdul's daughter, spotted the doll and called the others, who put down their jugs and stood there laughing. Then Zhilin brought it down and offered it to them, but they kept laughing and dared not take it. So he left it and went to the barn to see what would happen.

Dina came running up, looked round, grabbed the doll and ran away. Next morning, at dawn, he saw Dina sit down at the door of the hut with the doll. She had dressed it with bits of red cloth and was rocking it like a baby and singing a Tartar lullaby. An old woman came out, scolded her, snatched the doll, smashed it and sent Dina off to do some work.

Then Zhilin made another doll, even better than the first, and gave it to Dina.

Later on Dina brought him a jug, put it down and sat on the ground gazing at him and pointing to the jug.

'What's she so pleased about?' Zhilin wondered. He took the jug and drank from it: instead of water, it was milk. When he had finished drinking, he said to himself, 'Very good!' How pleased Dina was!

'Good, Ivan, very good!' she said. And she jumped up, clapped her hands and ran off with the jug.

After that she stealthily brought him milk every day. And she also managed to smuggle some of the rich flat cakes that Tartars make from goat's cheese and leave on the roof to dry. Once, when Abdul slaughtered a sheep, she brought a piece of mutton in her sleeves, threw it down and scampered off.

One day there was a violent storm and the rain bucketed down for a whole hour. All the rivers became turbid and at the ford the water rose several feet above its banks, rolling the stones about. Everywhere there were rushing streams and the hills were filled with the roar of water. The storm passed, leaving the village flooded. Zhilin managed to borrow a knife from Abdul, made a wooden spindle and wheel and tied two dolls to the wheel. The girls brought him some rags and he dressed the dolls up, one as a man, the other as a woman. After fixing them in place he put the wheel in a stream and it started turning, so that the dolls danced up and down.

The whole village turned out to watch – boys, girls and women. And even the men appeared, clicking their tongues, saying, 'Ay, Russky! Ay, Russky!'

Abdul had a Russian watch which was broken. He summoned Zhilin and showed it to him, clicking his tongue. Zhilin said, 'Give it to me, I'll mend it.'

He took it to pieces with the knife, sorted out the parts, put them together again and handed it back. The watch worked.

Abdul was overjoyed and presented him with an old quilted coat. It was in tatters, but he was glad of it – it would come in handy for covering himself at night.

From then on, Zhilin's fame as a master craftsman spread. Tartars started coming from distant villages, bringing rifles, locks, pistols or watches for him to repair. The master supplied him with tools – tweezers, gimlets and files.

One day a Tartar fell ill and they went to Zhilin and asked, 'Please come and cure him.' Zhilin had no idea about medicine, but he went and examined the sick man, thinking, 'Perhaps he'll recover anyway.'

He returned to the barn and mixed some water and sand. In the presence of the others he whispered some words over it and gave it to the Tartar to drink. Fortunately for him, the sick man got better. Zhilin had by now begun to pick up a little of the Tartar language and some of the villagers became used to him. Whenever they needed him they would shout, 'Ivan, Ivan!' whilst others would look at him askance, as if he were a wild animal.

The red-faced Tartar disliked Zhilin. Whenever he saw him, he would frown, turn away or swear at him. There was also an old tribesman who did not live in the village, but who would come up the hill now and again. Zhilin only saw him when he went to the mosque to pray. He was short and had a white cloth wrapped round his cap. His beard and moustache were clipped and as white as down, but his face was wrinkled and brick-red. He had a hooked nose, like a hawk's beak, and his eyes were grey and evil. He was toothless, except for two stumps. He would pass by in his turban, leaning on his crutch and scowling like a wolf. Whenever he saw Zhilin he would angrily snort and turn his back.

One day Zhilin went down the hill to see where the old man lived. At the bottom of the path he saw a small garden with a stone wall, on the other side of which were cherry and peach trees, and a small flat-roofed cottage. He went closer and saw some beehives made of plaited straw, with swarms of bees buzzing around them. The old man was kneeling and busying himself at one of the hives. Zhilin walked a little higher to see better and his shackles rattled. The old man turned with a wild screech, pulled a pistol from his belt and fired at Zhilin who only just managed to take cover in time behind a rock.

Later the old man went and complained to Zhilin's captor, who summoned him and laughed as he asked, 'Why did you go to the old man's cottage?'

'I did him no harm,' Zhilin replied. 'I only wanted to see how he lived.'

When his master translated what Zhilin had said, the old man was furious, hissed, muttered something, stuck out his two stumps and waved his arms at Zhilin. Although Zhilin could not understand a word, he could tell that the old man was ordering Abdul to kill the Russians and not to keep them prisoner in the village. Then he went away.

Zhilin asked Abdul who he was and he replied, 'He's a great man! He used to be our best fighter. He killed many Russians and once was very rich. He had three wives and eight sons, and all of them lived in the same village. Then the Russians came and destroyed the village and killed seven of his sons. The son who survived went over to the Russians, so the old man joined them too. He lived for three months with them, then he found his son, killed him and escaped. After that he gave up fighting and went to Mecca to pray. That's why he wears a turban – anyone who's been there is called *Khadji* and wears a turban. He doesn't like your people and he's ordered me to kill you. But I can't do that – I've paid money for you. Besides, I've become fond of you, Ivan. Far from having you killed, I wouldn't even set you free if I hadn't given my word.' Then he laughed and added, 'You Ivan – good! Me Abdul – good!'

4

Zhilin lived this way for a month. During the day he would wander around the village, or busy himself making things, but at night he would dig a hole in the floor of the barn. It was hard work, with all the stones, but he filed them down and managed to tunnel a hole under the wall large enough to crawl through. 'Now, if I could only get to know the lie of the land! But none of the Tartars will ever tell me anything.'

So he chose a day when his captor was away and after supper he set off up the hill beyond the village to have a good look round. But before Abdul had left, he told his little son to follow Zhilin and not to let him out of his sight. The boy ran after Zhilin shouting, 'Don't go! My father said you mustn't – I'll call the villagers if you do!'

Zhilin tried to win him over. 'I won't go far,' he said. 'I only want to climb that hill over there. I need some herbs to make your people better. Come with me. I can't escape with these shackles. Tomorrow I'll make you a bow and arrows.'

He managed to induce the boy to let him go and off they went. The hill did not seem very far away, but with the shackles it was hard going. Still, he struggled to the top. He sat down and noted the lie of the land. To the south, on the other side of the hill, was a valley, with another village and some horses grazing there. Beyond the village was another, even steeper hill and beyond that, another. Between the hills was the blue haze of a forest and further off were mountains, rising higher and higher. The loftiest mountains were covered with snow, as white as sugar. One snowy peak towered above all the others. In the east and west was the same mountain range. Here and there smoke rose from Tartar villages in narrow gorges. 'Well,' thought Zhilin, 'that's all Tartar country.' And he looked towards the Russian side. Far below was the stream and his Tartar village, surrounded by its small gardens. Women like tiny dolls were washing clothes in the stream. Beyond the village was a hill, with two more beyond it, covered with trees. Between them, in the far distance, he could make out a stretch of level ground that was bluish, as if smoke were spreading over it. Zhilin tried to remember where the sun rose and set when he had been living in the fortress.

Yes, there was no doubt about it: the fortress must be over there, in that valley, and his escape route lay between those two hills.

The sun was setting. The snow-covered mountains turned crimson and the dark hills became even darker. Mist rose from the hollows and that same valley where he assumed the fortress to be seemed ablaze in the sunset glow. Zhilin looked harder and he thought he could see something rather indistinct in the valley, like chimney smoke rising, and he felt sure that this must be the Russian fortress.

It was late now. He could hear the mullah calling and the lowing of cattle being brought back from pasture. The boy kept urging him, 'Let's go back!' but Zhilin did not want to.

Eventually they returned. 'Well,' thought Zhilin, 'now I know the way, I *must* escape.' He wanted to try that same night – the nights were dark then, as the moon was new. Unfortunately for Zhilin, the Tartars came back that evening. They usually returned in high spirits, driving cattle they had captured before them, but this time they had no cattle: all they brought back, stretched across a saddle, was a dead Tartar, the red-bearded one's brother. They were terribly angry as they prepared to bury him. Zhilin went out to watch. They wrapped the body in a piece of linen, bore it out of the village and laid it, without any coffin, on the grass under the plane-trees. The mullah came, the old men assembled, wound cloths around their caps for turbans, took their shoes off and squatted on their heels in a row by the corpse.

The mullah led the procession, with three old men in turbans following him and with more Tartars following them. All of them sat there, eyes downcast, and they sat in silence for some time, until the mullah raised his head and said, 'Allah!' When he had uttered this one word, the others looked down again and remained still and silent for a long time. Then the mullah raised his head again and repeated, 'Allah!' whereupon they all repeated, 'Allah!' and then fell silent again. All of them were as still as the corpse that lay on the grass. No one moved an inch. All that could be heard was the rustle of the plane-trees in the breeze. Then the mullah said a prayer, and everyone stood up, lifted the corpse in their arms and bore it away to a hole in the ground. This was no ordinary hole, but had been hollowed out like a vault. They took the corpse under the arms, lowered it gently, placing it in a sitting position in the hole and crossing the arms over the stomach.

A Nogay tribesman brought some green reeds to the hole and they filled it in. Then they briskly filled it with earth and levelled it off, placing a stone to mark the spot where the dead man's head was. After treading the earth down they sat in a row by the grave. For a long while they remained silent. Then, after repeating, 'Allah! Allah! Allah!' they sighed and got up.

The red-bearded Tartar distributed money among the old men, after which he got up, took a whip, struck himself three times on the forehead and went home.

Next morning Zhilin saw the red-faced Tartar leading a mare out of the village, followed by the others. The red-bearded Tartar took off his cloak, rolled up his sleeves – he had very strong hands – took out his dagger and sharpened it on a whetstone. The Tartars held the mare's head back and he came and cut its throat. The mare slumped to the ground and he started skinning it, ripping off its hide with his strong hands. Women and girls came to wash the entrails. The carcass was cut up and the pieces dragged to the red-bearded Tartar's hut, where the whole village gathered to say prayers for the dead brother.

For three days they ate mare's flesh, drank bouza and prayed for the dead man. All of them stayed home, but on the fourth day around dinner-time Zhilin saw them all preparing to leave. When the horses were brought round, about ten of them rode off, including the red-bearded Tartar. Only Abdul stayed behind. The nights were still dark, as the moon had only just started to wax.

'Well,' thought Zhilin, 'we must escape tonight.' He told Kostylin. But Kostylin became frightened. 'How can we?' he asked. 'We don't even know the way.'

'I know the way,' Zhilin replied.

'But we can't possibly make it in one night.'

'In that case we can shelter in the forest. I've saved some of those cakes. What's the point of staying here? Well and good if they send the money, but what if they don't manage to collect it all? What's more, the Tartars are furious that the Russians have killed one of them. They're talking about killing us.'

After a long pause, Kostylin finally agreed. 'All right, let's go,' he said.

5

Zhilin crawled into the hole and widened it so that Kostylin could get through as well. They waited until all was quiet in the village and then Zhilin crawled under the wall and came out the other side. 'Come on!' he whispered to Kostylin. Kostylin crawled through too, but caught his foot on a rock, making a clattering sound. Now their captor had a very vicious spotted guard-dog called Ulyashin. But Zhilin had been prudent enough to feed it for some time before with millet cakes. When it heard the noise, Ulyashin started barking and ran out, followed by some other dogs. Zhilin whistled very softly and threw it a piece of cake. Ulyashin recognized him, wagged its tail and stopped barking.

The master had heard the dog and shouted to it from his hut. But Zhilin stroked Ulyashin behind the ears so that it quietened down, rubbed against his legs and wagged its tail.

The two men sat just round the corner for a while. All was quiet, except for a sheep coughing in its fold and water rippling over pebbles in the stream below. It was dark, the stars were high in the sky. The new red moon was setting over the mountains, its horns upwards. A milky-white mist drifted along the valleys.

Zhilin stood up and told his comrade, 'Well old man, let's go!' But they had hardly set off when they heard the mullah crying from the roof, 'Alla! Besmillah. Ilrahman!' That meant the people would be going to the mosque. So they hid behind a wall and squatted there for a long time, until everyone had passed. Then all was quiet again.

'Well, God be with us!' they said to each other as they crossed themselves and set off. They went down the hill to the stream, crossed it and walked along the valley. Down below the mist was thick but the stars were bright enough overhead for Zhilin to tell which direction to take. It was cool in the mist and walking was easy. But their boots were uncomfortable and almost worn out, so Zhilin took his off, threw them away and carried on barefoot, skipping from rock to rock and observing the stars. Kostylin began to fall behind.

'Not so fast!' he said. 'These damned boots are giving me blisters!'
'Then take them off, you'll find it's easier without them.'

Kostylin struggled on, barefoot, but this was even worse: he cut his feet on the stones and lagged behind even more.

Zhilin told him, 'If you rub all the skin off your feet they'll heal again. But if the Tartars catch you they'll kill you. So which is worse?'

Kostylin said nothing and kept on, groaning as he went. For quite a while they followed the low ground. Then they heard some dogs barking to the right. Zhilin stopped and looked around. He groped his way up the hill.

'Oh!' he exclaimed, 'we've gone too far to the right. There's the other village, the one I saw from the hill. We must go back and then up the hill on the left. That's where the forest should be.'

But Kostylin objected, 'Wait a moment. I must rest a bit, my feet are all cut and bleeding.'

'Never mind, old man, they'll heal. Just try and step more lightly – like this!'

And Zhilin ran back up the wooded hillside to the left. Kostylin lagged behind, still groaning. Zhilin hissed at him and went on.

They climbed the hill – and there was the forest. They fought their way through the brambles, tearing their clothes on the thorns. At last they stumbled on to a forest path and followed it.

'Wait!' Zhilin called out: they could suddenly hear what sounded like the stamping of horses' hoofs on the path. They stopped and listened. Again they heard the noise and then it stopped. When they moved on it started again, and whenever they stopped so did the stamping. Zhilin crawled nearer and it was light enough for him to see something on the path. It looked like a horse, but it had something very odd on top of it, not at all like a man. It snorted when it heard Zhilin. 'How extraordinary!' thought Zhilin. He whistled softly and the creature dashed from the path into the forest with a great crashing sound, as if a hurricane was tearing through the trees and breaking the branches.

Kostylin nearly died of fright, but Zhilin laughed and said, 'It's only a stag. Can't you hear him breaking the branches with his antlers? We're afraid of him, but he's afraid of us!'

They moved on. Now the stars were sinking in the west and it was not long till morning.

They had no idea whether they were going in the right direction.

Zhilin thought that this was the same road along which he had been brought to the village and that it was another six miles to the fortress. But there were no landmarks to go by and it was impossible to see much in the dark. They came to a clearing. Kostylin sat down and said, 'You do as you like. I'll never make it – I can't walk any more.'

Zhilin tried to encourage him.

'No,' Kostylin said, 'I won't make it . . . I can't.'

Zhilin lost his temper, spat and swore at him.

'All right, I'll go on alone. Goodbye!'

Kostylin jumped up and followed him. They walked another three miles. The mist in the forest had closed in even more densely and they could see nothing in front of them. Even the stars were barely visible.

Suddenly they heard a horse ahead of them, its shoes clattering over the stones. Zhilin flattened himself and put his ear to the ground. 'As I thought – someone's coming this way.'

They dashed off the path, crouched in the bushes and waited. Zhilin crawled back to the path and saw a Tartar on horseback driving a cow along and softly humming. When he had ridden past, Zhilin turned to Kostylin and said, 'Well, thank God for that! Get up now and let's be off.'

Kostylin tried to stand up but fell back again. 'I can't go on, honestly! I've no more strength.'

He was a heavily built, stout man and the sweat was pouring off him. He was chilled by the cold fresh mist, his feet were badly cut and he was completely exhausted. When Zhilin struggled to lift him he cried out, 'Oh, that hurts!'

Zhilin's heart sank. 'Why are you shouting? Don't you know there's a Tartar close by and he'll hear.' But then he thought, 'He's really very weak. What shall I do with him? I can't desert a comrade.'

'Well,' he said, 'get up now and sit on my back. I'll carry you if you really can't walk any more.'

He lifted Kostylin up on to his shoulders, gripping him under the thighs and struggled up on to the path.

'Mind you don't choke me with your legs!' Zhilin said. 'For Christ's sake hold on to my shoulders!'

It was a heavy load for Zhilin, his feet were bleeding too and he was exhausted. Every now and then he had to stop and jerk Kostylin up so that he sat higher on his back.

The Tartar must have heard Kostylin shout, for Zhilin could now hear someone riding behind them and calling out in Tartar. Zhilin dived into some bushes. The horseman seized his gun and fired, but he missed, screeched something in Tartar and galloped off down the path.

'Well, old man,' Zhilin said, 'now we're done for. That swine's gone to fetch the others to hunt us down. If we can't put two miles between us, we're finished.' Then his thoughts turned to Kostylin. 'What the hell did I saddle myself with this fat lump for? If it weren't for him I'd have escaped ages ago.'

Then Kostylin told him, 'You go on alone. Why should you die because of me?'

'No, I can't desert a comrade.'

So he took him on his shoulders again and pressed on for about a mile. But that forest was never-ending. The mist had started to lift, but the clouds seemed to have come down as they could no longer see the stars. Zhilin was absolutely exhausted.

They came to a small spring by the path with a low stone wall around it. Zhilin stopped and put Kostylin down.

'Let me have a little rest. We can have a drink and eat some of those cakes. It can't be much further.'

But as soon as he lay down to drink, he heard horses' hoofs which seemed to be coming from behind. Once again they plunged into the bushes down on the right and lay quite still.

They heard Tartar voices – the Tartars had stopped at the very spot where they had turned off the path. They had a brief discussion and then it seemed they were setting their dogs on their scent. The two men heard a crackling in the bushes and a dog came straight towards them, stopped and barked. Some Tartars whom Zhilin had not seen before came after it. Zhilin and Kostylin were seized, bound, put on horseback and taken away.

After about two miles they were met by Abdul and two other Tartars from the village. Abdul spoke to the Tartars who had captured them, transferred the Russians to their own horses and rode back with them to the village. Abdul was in no laughing mood and did not say one word to them.

It was dark when they reached the village and they were set down in the main street. Screaming children ran up, threw stones and whipped them. Then the Tartars gathered in a circle and were joined by the old man who lived down the hill. Zhilin could understand that they were deciding what to do with them. Some said that they should be taken further into the mountains, while the old man said they must kill them. Abdul started arguing, saying, 'I paid good money for them and I want the ransom.'

But the old man retorted, 'You won't get anything out of them and they'll only cause trouble. It's a sin to feed Russians. Kill them and have done with it!'

They dispersed and Abdul went up to Zhilin. 'If they don't send the money within two weeks,' he said, 'I'll flog you to death. And if you try to escape again I shall kill you like dogs. Now write that letter – and mind you do it properly!'

They were brought paper and they wrote the letters. Then they were shackled again and taken behind the mosque. Here there was a pit about twelve feet deep – and into this pit they were lowered.

6

Life was sheer hell now. The shackles were never taken off and they were not allowed out of the pit for a breath of fresh air. They were thrown unbaked dough, as if they were dogs, and water was lowered in a pitcher. There was a terrible stench in that damp, stuffy pit. Kostylin became quite ill and his body was bloated and ached all over. He either slept or just lay there moaning. Zhilin's spirits fell too – he could see that the outlook was bleak, but he had no idea how they could escape.

He started to dig a tunnel, but there was nowhere to hide the earth, and his captor spotted it and threatened to kill him.

One day he was squatting on his haunches on the floor of the pit; he felt wretched and yearned for freedom. Suddenly a millet cake dropped into his lap, then another, and then a shower of cherries. He looked up and there was Dina. She glanced down, laughed and ran off. Zhilin wondered, 'Perhaps Dina can help me?'

He cleared a small space in the pit, scraped up some clay and started making models. He made men, horses, dogs. 'When Dina comes I'll throw them up to her,' he thought. But Dina did not come next day. Zhilin heard horses rushing past and the Tartars gathered at the mosque, where they started arguing, shouting and kept mentioning Russians. He could hear the old man's voice and although he could not quite make out all that was said, he gathered that the Russians were not far off, that the Tartars were afraid they might attack the village and that they did not know what to do with their prisoners.

After their talk, they all went away. Suddenly Zhilin heard a rustling noise up above. He looked up and saw Dina squatting there, her knees higher than her head. She leaned over the edge, her necklace of coins dangling. Her eyes sparkled like tiny stars. She took two cheese cakes out of her sleeves and threw them down. Zhilin took them and asked, 'Where did you get to? I've made you some toys. Here, catch!'

And he started throwing them up, one at a time. But Dina shook her head and would not look at them.

'I don't need them,' she said. After sitting silently for a few minutes, she continued, 'Ivan, they want to kill you!' – and she pointed to her throat.

'Who wants to kill me?'

'My father. The old men have ordered it. I feel so sorry for you.'

Zhilin said, 'Well, if you feel so sorry, you can bring me a long pole.'

She shook her head as if to say that this was impossible. Zhilin clasped his hands and pleaded with her, 'Please, Dina! *Please* bring me one!'

'I can't!' she replied. 'Everyone's home now and they'd see me.' And she left.

That evening Zhilin sat wondering what would happen. He kept looking up – there were stars in the sky, but the moon had not risen yet. The mullah called and then all was quiet. Zhilin thought as he began to doze off, 'The little girl must be too frightened.' Suddenly some bits of clay fell on his head. He looked up and saw a long pole poking into the far side of the pit. It kept poking about for a while and started coming down. Zhilin was overjoyed, grabbed it with one hand and lowered it. It was a strong pole – he had seen it before on the roof of Abdul's hut.

He looked up again and saw the stars shining high in the sky. And just above the pit Dina's eyes were glinting in the dark, like a cat's. She put her face close to the edge and whispered, 'Ivan, Ivan!', waving her arms in front of her face to tell him to keep quiet.

'What is it?' Zhilin asked.

'They've all gone away. There's only two at home.'

Zhilin said, 'Well, Kostylin, let's go. We'll have one more try. I'll help you up.'

But Kostylin would not hear of it. 'No,' he replied 'I'm obviously stuck here for good. And where could I go when I haven't even the strength to turn round?'

'Well, goodbye. Don't think ill of me.' The two men kissed each other's cheeks.

Zhilin grabbed the pole and told Dina to hold it firmly as he climbed up. Twice he slipped back as his shackles got in the way. But then Kostylin supported him from below and somehow he managed to clamber out. Dina laughed and tugged as hard as she could at his shirt with her little hands. Zhilin pulled the pole out and said, 'Now, put it back where you got it from, Dina, or they'll see it's missing and give you a good hiding.'

She dragged the pole away and Zhilin went down the hill. At the bottom of the slope he picked up a sharp stone and tried to wrench the lock off his shackle. But it was strong and the shackle hampered his attempt to force it. Then he heard someone running down the hill, skipping lightly. 'That must be Dina,' he thought. She ran up to him, took the stone and said, 'Let me try.' She knelt and tried to break the lock, but her hands were as thin as twigs and she just did not have the strength. So she threw the stone away and burst into tears. Zhilin set to work again on the lock, while Dina squatted by his side, her hand on his shoulder.

Zhilin looked around and saw a red glow behind the mountain to the left: the moon was rising. 'Well,' he thought, 'I must go along the valley and try to reach the forest before the moon is up.' He stood up and threw the stone away: shackle or no shackle he had to be on the move now.

'Goodbye, dear Dina,' he said. 'I shall never forget you.'

Dina grasped him and felt for somewhere to put the cakes. He took them from her. 'Thank you – you clever little girl! Who's going to make dolls for you when I'm gone?' And he stroked her head.

Dina burst into tears and buried her face in her hands. And then, like a young goat, she bounded up the hill. All Zhilin could hear in the dark was the coins in her hair jingling.

He crossed himself, held the lock in his hand to stop it clattering and set off down the road, dragging his shackled leg and constantly watching that red glow where the moon was rising. He recognized the road – he had to keep straight on for about six miles. If only he could reach the forest before the moon was high! When he crossed the stream the light behind the mountain was turning white. He followed the valley and looked round – the moon was not yet visible.

The red glow was white now and one side of the valley was growing lighter and lighter. Shadows were creeping down the slope towards him, getting ever nearer.

Zhilin carried on, keeping in the shadow. He started hurrying, but the moon was rising even faster. The peaks to the right were bathed in light now. Before he could reach the forest the moon came out from behind the mountains and everything was as bright as day. Every leaf on the trees was clearly visible. In the mountains all was bright – and as quiet as the grave. All that could be heard was the murmuring stream down below.

Finally, Zhilin reached the forest – not a soul was there. He chose a dark spot and sat down to rest. After a rest he ate some cakes. Then he found a stone and tried to force the lock again. He badly bruised his hands but still he could not break that lock. So he got up and carried on. After about half a mile he felt worn out and his feet ached: he had to stop every few paces. 'There's nothing else for it,' he thought, 'somehow I must drag myself along while I have the strength. If I sit down I'll never get up again. I'll never reach the fortress tonight, but when dawn breaks I'll lie low in the forest all day and then start again at night.'

All night he kept going. Two Tartars rode past, but Zhilin had heard them in the distance and hid behind a tree.

The moon was growing paler, dew was falling and dawn was not far away. Zhilin still had not reached the end of the forest. 'Well,' he thought, 'another thirty steps and I'll turn back into the trees and sit down.' But when he had walked the thirty steps he saw that he was near the end of the forest. At the edge he saw the open steppe and the fortress quite clearly. Not far off, at the foot of the hill to the left, fires were dying out and smoke drifted upwards. And around those fires were men. He strained his eyes and saw the glint of guns, and that those men there were Cossacks, Russian soldiers! Zhilin was overjoyed. Summoning his last ounce of strength, he set off downhill. 'God forbid any Tartar horseman spots me here, out in the open,' he prayed. 'It may not be far, but I wouldn't stand a chance.'

Hardly had this thought crossed his mind when he saw three mounted Tartars on a hillock about three hundred yards to the left. They had seen him and were galloping towards him. His heart felt as if it were about to break. He waved his hands and shouted at the top of his voice, 'Help me, comrades! Help me!'

The Cossacks heard him and rode out to cut off the Tartars. The Cossacks were a long way away, the Tartars were near. With what strength he had left, Zhilin lifted his shackle and ran towards the Cossacks, hardly knowing what he was doing; he crossed himself and shouted, 'Comrades! Help me!'

There were fifteen Cossacks. The Tartars took fright and stopped before they reached Zhilin. He ran to the Cossacks who surrounded him and asked who he was and where he had come from. But Zhilin was too excited to answer and could only weep and mutter, 'Comrades! Comrades!'

Some soldiers ran out and crowded around Zhilin. Some of them offered him bread, others gruel, others vodka. One of them wrapped his greatcoat around him, another started breaking the shackle.

The officers recognized him and rode with him into the fortress. The soldiers were delighted and Zhilin's old comrades crowded round him. Zhilin told them everything that had happened to him and said, 'So, that's how I went home and got married! No, it seems I wasn't destined for matrimony!'

And he continued to serve in the Caucasus. It was a month before Kostylin's five-thousand-rouble ransom was paid and he was barely alive when they brought him back.

READ MORE IN PENGUIN

In every corner of the world, on every subject under the sun, Penguin represents quality and variety – the very best in publishing today.

For complete information about books available from Penguin – including Puffins, Penguin Classics and Arkana – and how to order them, write to us at the appropriate address below. Please note that for copyright reasons the selection of books varies from country to country.

In the United Kingdom: Please write to *Dept. EP, Penguin Books Ltd, Bath Road, Harmondsworth, West Drayton, Middlesex UB7 ODA*

In the United States: Please write to *Consumer Sales, Penguin Putnam Inc., P.O. Box 12289 Dept. B, Newark, New Jersey 07101-5289*. VISA and MasterCard holders call 1-800-788-6262 to order Penguin titles

In Canada: Please write to *Penguin Books Canada Ltd, 10 Alcorn Avenue, Suite 300, Toronto, Ontario M4V 3B2*

In Australia: Please write to *Penguin Books Australia Ltd, P.O. Box 257, Ringwood, Victoria 3134*

In New Zealand: Please write to *Penguin Books (NZ) Ltd, Private Bag 102902, North Shore Mail Centre, Auckland 10*

In India: Please write to *Penguin Books India Pvt Ltd, 11 Community Centre, Panchsheel Park, New Delhi 110017*

In the Netherlands: Please write to *Penguin Books Netherlands bv, Postbus 3507, NL-1001 AH Amsterdam*

In Germany: Please write to *Penguin Books Deutschland GmbH, Metzlerstrasse 26, 60594 Frankfurt am Main*

In Spain: Please write to *Penguin Books S. A., Bravo Murillo 19, 1° B, 28015 Madrid* ·

In Italy: Please write to *Penguin Italia s.r.l., Via Benedetto Croce 2, 20094 Corsico, Milano*

In France: Please write to *Penguin France, Le Carré Wilson, 62 rue Benjamin Baillaud, 31500 Toulouse*

In Japan: Please write to *Penguin Books Japan Ltd, Kaneko Building, 2-3-25 Koraku, Bunkyo-Ku, Tokyo 112*

In South Africa: Please write to *Penguin Books South Africa (Pty) Ltd, Private Bag X14, Parkview, 2122 Johannesburg*

A CHOICE OF CLASSICS

Francis Bacon	**The Essays**
Aphra Behn	**Love-Letters between a Nobleman and His Sister**
	Oroonoko, The Rover and Other Works
George Berkeley	**Principles of Human Knowledge/Three Dialogues between Hylas and Philonous**
James Boswell	**The Life of Samuel Johnson**
Sir Thomas Browne	**The Major Works**
John Bunyan	**Grace Abounding to The Chief of Sinners**
	The Pilgrim's Progress
Edmund Burke	**A Philosophical Enquiry into the Origin of our Ideas of the Sublime and Beautiful**
	Reflections on the Revolution in France
Frances Burney	**Evelina**
Margaret Cavendish	**The Blazing World and Other Writings**
William Cobbett	**Rural Rides**
William Congreve	**Comedies**
Cowley/Waller/Oldham	**Selected Poems**
Thomas de Quincey	**Confessions of an English Opium Eater**
	Recollections of the Lakes
Daniel Defoe	**A Journal of the Plague Year**
	Moll Flanders
	Robinson Crusoe
	Roxana
	A Tour Through the Whole Island of Great Britain
	The True-Born Englishman
John Donne	**Complete English Poems**
	Selected Prose
Henry Fielding	**Amelia**
	Jonathan Wild
	Joseph Andrews
	The Journal of a Voyage to Lisbon
	Tom Jones
George Fox	**The Journal**
John Gay	**The Beggar's Opera**

READ MORE IN PENGUIN

A CHOICE OF CLASSICS

Oliver Goldsmith	**The Vicar of Wakefield**
Gray/Churchill/Cowper	**Selected Poems**
William Hazlitt	**Selected Writings**
George Herbert	**The Complete English Poems**
Thomas Hobbes	**Leviathan**
Samuel Johnson	**Gabriel's Ladder**
	History of Rasselas, Prince of Abissinia
	Selected Writings
Samuel Johnson/	**A Journey to the Western Islands of**
James Boswell	**Scotland and The Journal of a Tour of the Hebrides**
Matthew Lewis	**The Monk**
John Locke	**An Essay Concerning Human Understanding**
Andrew Marvell	**Complete Poems**
Thomas Middleton	**Five Plays**
John Milton	**Complete Poems**
	Paradise Lost
Samuel Richardson	**Clarissa**
	Pamela
Earl of Rochester	**Complete Works**
Richard Brinsley Sheridan	**The School for Scandal and Other Plays**
Sir Philip Sidney	**Arcadia**
Christopher Smart	**Selected Poems**
Adam Smith	**The Wealth of Nations (Books I–III)**
Tobias Smollett	**Humphrey Clinker**
	Roderick Random
Edmund Spenser	**The Faerie Queene**
Laurence Sterne	**The Life and Opinions of Tristram Shandy**
	A Sentimental Journey Through France and Italy
Jonathan Swift	**Complete Poems**
	Gulliver's Travels
Thomas Traherne	**Selected Poems and Prose**
Henry Vaughan	**Complete Poems**

A CHOICE OF CLASSICS

Louisa May Alcott	**The Inheritance**
Kate Chopin	**The Awakening and Selected Stories**
James Fenimore Cooper	**The Deerslayer**
	The Last of the Mohicans
	The Pathfinder
	The Pioneers
	The Prairie
	The Spy
Stephen Crane	**The Red Badge of Courage**
Frederick Douglass	**Narrative of the Life of Frederick Douglass, An American Slave**
Nathaniel Hawthorne	**The Blithedale Romance**
	The House of the Seven Gables
	The Marble Faun
	The Scarlet Letter and Selected Tales
	Selected Tales and Sketches
Henry James	**The Ambassadors**
	The American Scene
	The Aspern Papers/The Turn of the Screw
	The Awkward Age
	The Bostonians
	The Critical Muse
	Daisy Miller
	The Europeans
	The Figure in the Carpet
	The Golden Bowl
	The Jolly Corner and Other Tales
	The Portrait of a Lady
	The Princess Casamassima
	Roderick Hudson
	The Sacred Fount
	The Spoils of Poynton
	The Tragic Muse
	Washington Square
	What Maisie Knew
	The Wings of the Dove

READ MORE IN PENGUIN

A CHOICE OF CLASSICS

Thomas Wentworth Higginson	**Army Life in a Black Regiment**
William Dean Howells	**The Rise of Silas Lapham**
Gilbert Imlay	**The Emigrants**
Sarah Orne Jewett	**The Country of the Pointed Firs**
Herman Melville	**Billy Budd, Sailor and Other Stories**
	The Confidence-Man
	Moby-Dick
	Pierre
	Redburn
	Typee
Thomas Paine	**Common Sense**
	The Rights of Man
	The Thomas Paine Reader
Edgar Allan Poe	**Comedies and Satires**
	The Fall of the House of Usher
	The Narrative of Arthur Gordon Pym of Nantucket
	The Science Fiction of Edgar Allan Poe
Jacob A. Riis	**How the Other Half Lives**
Elizabeth Stoddard	**The Morgesons**
Harriet Beecher Stowe	**Uncle Tom's Cabin**
Henry David Thoreau	**Walden/Civil Disobedience**
	Week on the Concord and Merrimack
Mark Twain	**The Adventures of Huckleberry Finn**
	The Adventures of Tom Sawyer
	A Connecticut Yankee at King Arthur's Court
	Life on the Mississippi
	The Prince and the Pauper
	Pudd'nhead Wilson
	Roughing It
	Short Stories
	A Tramp Abroad
	Tales, Speeches, Essays and Sketches
Walt Whitman	**The Complete Poems**
	Leaves of Grass

READ MORE IN PENGUIN

A CHOICE OF CLASSICS

Honoré de Balzac	**The Black Sheep**
	César Birotteau
	The Chouans
	Cousin Bette
	Cousin Pons
	Eugénie Grandet
	A Harlot High and Low
	History of the Thirteen
	Lost Illusions
	A Murky Business
	Old Goriot
	Selected Short Stories
	Ursule Mirouët
	The Wild Ass's Skin
J. A. Brillat-Savarin	**The Physiology of Taste**
Charles Baudelaire	**Baudelaire in English**
	Selected Poems
	Selected Writings on Art and Literature
Pierre Corneille	**The Cid/Cinna/The Theatrical Illusion**
Alphonse Daudet	**Letters from My Windmill**
Denis Diderot	**Jacques the Fatalist**
	The Nun
	Rameau's Nephew/D'Alembert's Dream
	Selected Writings on Art and Literature
Alexandre Dumas	**The Count of Monte Cristo**
	The Three Musketeers
Gustave Flaubert	**Bouvard and Pécuchet**
	Flaubert in Egypt
	Madame Bovary
	Salammbo
	Selected Letters
	Sentimental Education
	The Temptation of St Antony
	Three Tales
Victor Hugo	**Les Misérables**
	Notre-Dame of Paris
Laclos	**Les Liaisons Dangereuses**

READ MORE IN PENGUIN

A CHOICE OF CLASSICS

La Fontaine	**Selected Fables**
Madame de Lafayette	**The Princesse de Clèves**
Lautréamont	**Maldoror and Poems**
Molière	**The Misanthrope/The Sicilian/Tartuffe/A Doctor in Spite of Himself/The Imaginary Invalid**
	The Miser/The Would-be Gentleman/That Scoundrel Scapin/Love's the Best Doctor/Don Juan
Michel de Montaigne	**An Apology for Raymond Sebond**
	Complete Essays
Blaise Pascal	**Pensées**
Abbé Prevost	**Manon Lescaut**
Rabelais	**The Histories of Gargantua and Pantagruel**
Racine	**Andromache/Britannicus/Berenice**
	Iphigenia/Phaedra/Athaliah
Arthur Rimbaud	**Collected Poems**
Jean-Jacques Rousseau	**The Confessions**
	A Discourse on Inequality
	Emile
	The Social Contract
Madame de Sevigné	**Selected Letters**
Stendhal	**The Life of Henry Brulard**
	Love
	Scarlet and Black
	The Charterhouse of Parma
Voltaire	**Candide**
	Letters on England
	Philosophical Dictionary
	Zadig/L'Ingénu
Emile Zola	**L'Assomoir**
	La Bête humaine
	The Debacle
	The Earth
	Germinal
	Nana
	Thérèse Raquin

READ MORE IN PENGUIN

A CHOICE OF CLASSICS

Leopoldo Alas	**La Regenta**
Leon B. Alberti	**On Painting**
Ludovico Ariosto	**Orlando Furioso** (in two volumes)
Giovanni Boccaccio	**The Decameron**
Baldassar Castiglione	**The Book of the Courtier**
Benvenuto Cellini	**Autobiography**
Miguel de Cervantes	**Don Quixote**
	Exemplary Stories
Dante	**The Divine Comedy** (in three volumes)
	La Vita Nuova
Machado de Assis	**Dom Casmurro**
Bernal Díaz	**The Conquest of New Spain**
Niccolò Machiavelli	**The Discourses**
	The Prince
Alessandro Manzoni	**The Betrothed**
Emilia Pardo Bazán	**The House of Ulloa**
Benito Pérez Galdós	**Fortunata and Jacinta**
Eça de Quierós	**The Maias**
Sor Juana Inés de la Cruz	**Poems, Protest and a Dream**
Giorgio Vasari	**Lives of the Artists** (in two volumes)

and

Five Italian Renaissance Comedies
(Machiavelli/**The Mandragola**; Ariosto/**Lena**; Aretino/**The Stablemaster**; Gl'Intronati/**The Deceived**; Guarini/**The Faithful Shepherd**)
The 'Poem of the Cid
Two Spanish Picaresque Novels
(Anon/**Lazarillo de Tormes**; de Quevedo/**The Swindler**)

READ MORE IN PENGUIN

A CHOICE OF CLASSICS

Jacob Burckhardt	**The Civilization of the Renaissance in Italy**
Carl von Clausewitz	**On War**
Meister Eckhart	**Selected Writings**
Friedrich Engels	**The Origin of the Family**
	The Condition of the Working Class in England
Goethe	**Elective Affinities**
	Faust Parts One and Two (in two volumes)
	Italian Journey
	Maxims and Reflections
	Selected Verse
	The Sorrows of Young Werther
Jacob and Wilhelm Grimm	**Selected Tales**
E. T. A. Hoffmann	**Tales of Hoffmann**
Friedrich Hölderlin	**Selected Poems and Fragments**
Henrik Ibsen	**Brand**
	A Doll's House and Other Plays
	Ghosts and Other Plays
	Hedda Gabler and Other Plays
	The Master Builder and Other Plays
	Peer Gynt
Søren Kierkegaard	**Fear and Trembling**
	Papers and Journals
	The Sickness Unto Death
Georg Christoph Lichtenberg	**Aphorisms**
Karl Marx	**Capital** (in three volumes)
Karl Marx/Friedrich Engels	**The Communist Manifesto**
Friedrich Nietzsche	**The Birth of Tragedy**
	Beyond Good and Evil
	Ecce Homo
	Human, All Too Human
	Thus Spoke Zarathustra
Friedrich Schiller	**Mary Stuart**
	The Robbers/Wallenstein

READ MORE IN PENGUIN

A CHOICE OF CLASSICS

Anton Chekhov	**The Duel and Other Stories**
	The Kiss and Other Stories
	The Fiancée and Other Stories
	Lady with Lapdog and Other Stories
	The Party and Other Stories
	Plays (The Cherry Orchard/Ivanov/The Seagull/Uncle Vania/The Bear/The Proposal/A Jubilee/Three Sisters)
Fyodor Dostoyevsky	**The Brothers Karamazov**
	Crime and Punishment
	The Devils
	The Gambler/Bobok/A Nasty Story
	The House of the Dead
	The Idiot
	Netochka Nezvanova
	The Village of Stepanchikovo
	Notes from Underground/The Double
Nikolai Gogol	**Dead Souls**
	Diary of a Madman and Other Stories
Alexander Pushkin	**Eugene Onegin**
	The Queen of Spades and Other Stories
	Tales of Belkin
Leo Tolstoy	**Anna Karenin**
	Childhood, Boyhood, Youth
	A Confession
	How Much Land Does a Man Need?
	Master and Man and Other Stories
	Resurrection
	The Sebastopol Sketches
	What is Art?
	War and Peace
Ivan Turgenev	**Fathers and Sons**
	First Love
	A Month in the Country
	On the Eve
	Rudin
	Sketches from a Hunter's Album